The
Invitation

Also published in Large Print
from G.K. Hall by Jude Deveraux:

Twin of Ice
Twin of Fire
The Princess
The Awakening
The Maiden
The Taming
The Conquest
A Knight in Shining Armor
Wishes
Mountain Laurel
The Duchess
Eternity
Sweet Liar

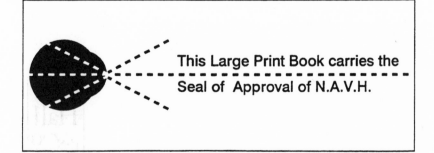

This Large Print Book carries the
Seal of Approval of N.A.V.H.

The Invitation

Jude Deveraux

G.K. Hall & Co.
Thorndike, Maine

Published in 1994 by arrangement with Pocket Books, a division of Simon & Schuster, Inc.

G.K. Hall Large Print Romance Collection.

The text of this Large Print edition is unabridged.
Other aspects of the book may vary from the original edition.

Set in 16 pt. News Plantin by Minnie B. Raven.

Printed in the United States on acid-free, high opacity paper. ∞

Library of Congress Cataloging in Publication Data

Deveraux, Jude.
The invitation / Jude Deveraux.
p.   cm.
ISBN 0-8161-5662-X (alk. paper : lg. print)
ISBN 0-8161-5663-8 (alk. paper : lg. print : pbk.)
1. Large type books. I. Title.
[PS3554.E9273I5   1994]
813'.54—dc20   93-49508

Book I

The Invitation

Chapter One
1934

Jackie was flying a plane, so Jackie was happy.

Soaring high, catching the breezes, winking at the setting sun, Jackie stretched and the plane stretched. Jackie moved and the plane moved. As though the body of the plane were a second skin to her, she could move the airplane as easily as she moved her arm or her leg. Smiling, she dipped one wing downward to look at the beautiful high mountain desert of Colorado.

At first she didn't believe what she saw. Sitting in the middle of nowhere, miles from the nearest road, was a car. Thinking that the vehicle had been abandoned, she turned her plane, dipping the wings, turning on a dime, to backtrack to have a second look. The car hadn't been there yesterday, so perhaps someone needed help.

She swooped down as low as she dared, not that the piñon trees, rarely over twenty feet tall, were going to interfere with the height she needed to stay aloft. As she came back for a second pass she saw a man stand up from the shade of the car and raise his arm in greeting. Smiling, she turned her plane back toward her home base. He was all right, then, and as soon as she landed at her airstrip in Eternity, she'd call the sheriff to send the stranded traveler some help.

She was chuckling to herself. Travelers often were stranded in Colorado. They looked at the flat landscape off the side of the road and decided to see nature up close. But they didn't take into consideration the thorns as large as a man's little finger and rocks whose sharpness had not been worn away by heavy yearly rainfall.

Maybe it was because she was laughing and not watching what she was doing that she didn't see the bird, as big as a lamb, that flew straight into her propeller. She doubted that she could have avoided hitting it, but she would have tried. As it was, everything happened very quickly. One minute she was flying toward home and the next minute there were feathers and blood all over her goggles and the plane was going down.

Jackie was a good pilot, one of the best in America. She'd certainly had a great deal of training, having received her license at eighteen years of age, and now, at thirty-eight, she was an old hand. But coping with this bird took all of her knowledge and skill. As the engine began to sputter, she knew she was going to have to do a dead-stick landing, a landing without power. Quickly, tearing off her goggles so she could see, she looked about for a place to set it down. She needed a wide, long clearing, someplace free of trees and rocks that could tear the wings off the plane.

The old road to the ghost town of Eternity offered the only possibility. She didn't know what had grown or rolled across the road in the many

8

years that it hadn't been used, but she had no other choice. Within the flash of an eye, she lined up the nose to the "runway" and started down. There was a boulder blocking the road — it had probably rolled down during the spring thaw — and she was praying to stop the plane before she hit the enormous rock.

Luck wasn't with her, for she plowed into the rock. As she crashed, she could hear the sickening crunch of her propeller being destroyed. She didn't think anymore. Her head flew forward, hitting the stick; she was out cold.

The next thing Jackie knew, she was being held in a pair of very strong, masculine arms and carried away from the plane. "Are you my rescuing knight?" she asked dreamily. She could feel something warm running down her face. When she put up her hand to wipe it away, she thought she saw blood, but her eyes weren't functioning properly and the daylight was fading fast.

"Am I badly hurt?" she asked, knowing the man wouldn't tell her the truth. She'd seen a couple of men mangled in airplane wrecks, and as they lay dying everyone had reassured them that tomorrow they'd be fine.

"I don't think so," the man said. "I think you just bumped your head, cracked it a bit."

"Oh, well, then, I'll be okay. Nobody's head is harder than mine." He was still carrying her, but her weight didn't seem to bother him at all. As best she could, considering how dizzy she felt, she pulled her head back to look at him. In the fading light he looked great, but then, Jackie reminded herself, she'd just cracked her skull in a plane wreck. For all she knew, he had three heads and six eyes. No one could be so lucky as to crash in the middle of acres of nothing and find a handsome man to rescue her.

"Who are you?" she asked thickly, because all of a sudden she felt very sleepy.

"William Montgomery," he answered.

"A Montgomery from Chandler?" When he said yes, Jackie snuggled against his wide, broad chest and sighed happily. At least she didn't have to worry about his intentions. If he was a Chandler Montgomery then he was honorable and fair and would never take advantage of the situation; Montgomerys were as honest and trustworthy as the day was long.

More's the pity, she thought.

When they were some distance from the plane, near his car, which she could just make out in the dim light, he gently set her on the ground. Cupping her chin in his hand, he looked into her eyes. "I want you to stay here and wait for me. I'm going to get some blankets from the car, then build a fire. When you don't show up at the airfield, will anyone come looking for you?"

"No," she whispered. She liked his voice, liked the air of authority in it. He made her feel as though he'd take care of everything, including her.

"I was planning to spend the night out here, so no one will look for me either," he said. "While I'm gone, I want you to stay awake, do you hear me? If your head is concussed and you go to sleep, you might not wake up again. Understand?"

Dreamily, Jackie nodded and watched him walk away. Very good looking man, she thought as she lay down on the ground and promptly went to sleep.

Mere seconds later he was shaking her. "Jackie! Jacqueline!" he said over and over until she reluctantly opened her eyes and looked up at him.

"How do you know my name?" she asked. "Have we met before? I've met so many Montgomerys that I can't keep them straight. Bill, did you say your name was?"

"William," he said firmly, "and, yes, we've met before, but I'm sure you wouldn't remember. It wasn't a significant meeting."

" 'Significant meeting,' " she said, closing her eyes again, but William sat her up, draped a blanket around her shoulders, then rubbed her hands.

"Stay awake, Jackie," he said, and she recognized it for the order it was. "Stay awake and talk to me. Tell me about Charley."

At the mention of her late husband, she stopped smiling. "Charley died two years ago."

William was trying to collect wood and watch her at the same time. The light was fading quickly, and he had difficulty seeing the pieces of cholla on the ground, as well as the deadfall. He had met her husband many times, and he'd liked him very much: a big, robust gray-haired man who laughed a lot, talked a lot, drank a lot, and could fly anything that could be flown.

11

Now, looking at her, drowsy, he knew he needed to warm her up, get some food inside her, and make her stay awake. Right now she was in a state of shock, and that, combined with her injury, might keep her from seeing another dawn.

"Jackie!" he said sharply. "What's the biggest lie you ever told?"

"I don't lie," she said dreamily. "Can't keep them straight. Always get caught."

"Sure you lie. Everybody lies. You tell a woman her hat is nice when it's hideous. I didn't ask you if you had lied or not; I just want to know what your biggest lie was." He was stacking up what wood he could find as he questioned her, his voice loud; he couldn't let her sleep.

"I used to lie to my mother about where I was."

"You can do better than that."

When she spoke, her voice was so soft he could barely hear her. "I told Charley I loved him."

"And you didn't love him?" William encouraged her to talk as he dropped a pile of wood near her feet.

"Not at first. He was older than me, twenty-one years older, and at first I thought of him as a father. I used to skip school and spend the afternoons with him and the airplanes. I loved planes from the first moment I saw them."

"So you married Charley to get near the planes."

"Yes," she said, her voice heavy with guilt. She sat upright and put her hand to her bloody head, but William brushed her hand away and turned her face up toward his as he used his handkerchief

12

to wipe away the blood.

After he'd reassured himself and her that the cut on the side of her head was minor, he said, "Go on. When did you realize that you loved him?"

"I didn't think about it one way or another until after we'd been married about five years. Charley's plane was lost in a snowstorm, and when I thought I might never see him again, I found out how much I loved him."

After a moment of silence she looked at him as he bent over the wood he was trying to coax into a fire. "What about you?"

"I didn't once tell Charley I loved him."

Jackie smiled. "No, what's the biggest lie *you* ever told?"

"I told my father it wasn't *me* who dented the fender of the car."

"Mmm," said Jackie, becoming a little more alert. "That's not a very horrible lie. Can't you come up with something better?"

"I told my mother I wasn't the one who'd eaten the whole strawberry pie. I told my brother that my sister had broken his slingshot. I told —"

"Okay, okay," Jackie said, laughing. "I get the picture. You're a consummate liar. All right, I have one for you. What's the worst thing a woman can say to a man?"

William didn't hesitate. " 'Which silver pattern do you like best?' "

Jackie grinned. She was beginning to like this man, and her overwhelming sleepiness was starting to subside.

"What's the worst thing a man can say to a woman?" he asked.

Jackie was as quick to answer as he had been. "When you're shopping and the man says, 'Just exactly what is it you're looking for?' "

Chuckling, he walked the few feet to his car to open the door and remove camping gear. "What's the *nicest* thing a man can say to a woman?"

"I love you. That is, if he means it. If he doesn't mean it, then he should be horsewhipped for saying it. And you? What's the nicest thing for you?"

"Yes," he said.

"Yes what?"

"Yes is the very best thing a woman can say to a man."

Jackie laughed. "To any question? No matter what she's asked, it's what you most want to hear?"

"It would be rather nice to hear yes from a woman's lips, at least now and then."

"Oh, come on, a man who looks like you has never heard a woman say yes to whatever you asked her?"

His arms full of blankets and canteens and a basket of food, he grinned at her. "One or two, but no more."

"Okay, it's my turn. What's the kindest thing you ever did for someone and didn't tell anyone about?"

"I guess that would have to be adding a wing to the hospital in Denver. I sent the money anonymously."

"Oh, my," she said, remembering how rich the Montgomerys were.

"And you?"

Jackie began to laugh. "Charley and I had been married for about four years, and with Charley you never stayed in one place long enough to learn your neighbors' names, much less put down roots. But that year we had rented a small house that had a very nice kitchen in it, and I decided to cook him a marvelous Thanksgiving dinner. I talked about nothing else but that dinner for two weeks. I planned and shopped, and on Thanksgiving Day I got up at four A.M. and got the turkey ready. Charley left the house about noon, but he promised he'd be back by five when everything would be ready to serve. He was going to bring some of the other pilots from the airfield, and it was going to be a party. Five o'clock came and there was no Charley. Six came and went, then seven. At midnight I fell asleep, but I was so angry that I slept in a rigid knot. The next morning there was Charley, snoring away on the sofa, and there was my beautiful Thanksgiving dinner in ruins. You know what I did?"

"I'm surprised Charley lived after that."

"I shouldn't have let him live, but I figured the worst thing I could do was not let him have any of my dinner. I bundled everything up in burlap bags, went to the airfield, took up Charley's plane and flew into the mountains — we were in West Virginia then, so it was the Smokies — where I saw a dilapidated old shack perched on the side

15

of a hill, a measly little trickle of smoke coming out of the chimney. I dropped the bags practically on the front porch."

She pulled her knees up to her chest and sighed. "Until now I never told anyone about that. Later I heard that the family said an angel had dropped food from heaven."

He had the fire going now, and he smiled at her over it. "I like that story. What did Charley say when he got no turkey?"

She shrugged. "Charley was happy if he had turkey and happy if he had beans. When it came to food, Charley was into quantity, not quality." She looked up at him. "What's the worst thing that's happened to you?"

William answered without thinking. "Being born rich."

Jackie gave a low whistle. "You'd think that was the *best* thing that had happened to you."

"It is. It's the best and the worst."

"I think I can see that." She was thinking about this as William poured water from a canteen onto a handkerchief and, with his hand cupping her chin, began to clean the wound on the side of her head.

"What's your deepest, darkest secret, something that you've never told anyone?" he asked.

"It wouldn't be a secret if I told."

"Do you think I'd tell anyone?"

She turned her head and looked up at him, at the shadows the firelight cast across his handsome face: dark hair, dark eyes, dark skin, that long

16

Montgomery nose. Maybe it was the unusual circumstances, the dark night surrounding them, the fire at the center, but she felt close to him. "I kissed another man while I was married to Charley," she whispered.

"That's all?"

"That's pretty bad in my book. What about you?"

"I backed out on a contract."

"Was that really bad? If you changed your mind . . ."

"It was a breach of promise, and *she* thought it was *very* bad."

"Ah, I see," Jackie said, smiling as she wrapped her arms around her knees. "What's your favorite food?"

"Ice cream."

She laughed. "Mine too. Favorite color."

"Blue. Yours?"

She looked up at him. "Blue."

He came to sit by her, dusting off his hands. When Jackie shivered in the cool mountain air, he put his arm around her shoulders, as naturally as breathing, and pulled her head to his chest. "Do you mind?"

Jackie couldn't even speak. It felt so good to touch another human being. Charley had always been cuddly and affectionate, and she had often sat on his lap, snuggling in his arms, while he read some airplane magazine aloud to her.

She didn't realize she was drifting off to sleep until his voice jolted her awake.

"What's the biggest regret in your life?" he asked sharply.

"That I wasn't born with a few Mae West curves," she answered quickly. She used to whine to Charley that the guys treated her like one of them because she *looked* like them: an angular face, with a square jaw, broad shoulders, straight hips, and long legs.

"You are joking, aren't you?" William said, his voice full of disbelief. "You're one of the most beautiful women I've ever seen. I can't tell you how many times I've stopped dead in my tracks as I watched you walk down the streets of Chandler."

"Really?" she said, now wide awake. "Are you *sure* you know who I am?"

"You are the great Jacqueline O'Neill. You've won nearly every flying award that is given. You've been everywhere in the world. You once were lost for three days in the snow of Montana, but you managed to walk out."

"Actually, I rolled down a mountain. It was only by luck that I landed at some cowboys' camp."

He knew she was lying, for he'd read everything written about her at that time. After crashing in a snowstorm, she had made her way out, climbing down the side of a steep mountain by using dead reckoning, by navigating with the faint sunlight during the day and the stars at night. She'd kept her head, often leaving huge arrows made from tree branches in the snow so airplanes looking for her could find her. Smiling, he tightened his arm

18

around her shoulders and was pleased when she moved closer to him.

"Ah, how do I walk?" She asked tentatively, not wanting to sound as though she were asking for a compliment, which was just what she was doing.

"With long strides that eat up the earth. Grown men stop what they're doing just to watch you walk, your shoulders back, your head held high, your beautiful thick hair catching the breeze, your —"

Jackie started to laugh. "Where have you been all my life?"

"Right here in Chandler, waiting for the day you would come back."

"You might have had to wait forever, because I never thought I would return. I was so restless back then. All I wanted was to get out of this tiny, isolated town. I wanted to move, to go places and see things."

"And you got to do that. Was it as good as you thought it would be?"

"At first it was, but after seven or eight years I began wanting things, like a flower box. I wanted to plant seeds and watch them grow. I wanted to know for sure that where I went to sleep was going to be the place where I woke up."

"So after Charley died, you came back to dreary old Chandler."

"Yes," she said, smiling against his chest. "Boring old Chandler where nothing changes and everyone knows everyone else's business."

19

"Are you happy now?"

"I — Hey! why am I doing all the answering? What about you? Why haven't I met you before? But that's right, it was not a 'significant meeting.' I don't think we have met before, because I would have remembered you."

"Thank you. I take that as a compliment." He moved away from her to throw more wood on the fire. "How about something to eat? A sandwich? Pickles?"

"Sounds delicious." She could tell that he didn't want to discuss their original meeting, and she figured it was because she'd probably snubbed him. She used to do that to men; it saved her pride. She'd tell a boy she wouldn't be caught dead at a dance with a bullfrog like him rather than tell the truth — that she couldn't afford a new dress.

She'd grown up in Chandler. After her father died when she was twelve, her mother, who considered herself a southern belle, had prostrated herself on a fainting couch and spent the next six years there. They had insurance money, and her mother's brother sent them money, but it was barely enough. It had been left up to Jackie to see that the decaying old house at the edge of town didn't fall down on top of their heads. While other girls were learning to wear lipstick, Jackie was spending her weekends hammering the roof back on. She chopped wood, built a fence, repaired the porch, built new steps when the first set wore out. She knew how to use a hand saw, but had no idea how to use a nail file.

One day when Jackie was eighteen an airplane flew overhead, a long banner tied to its tail announcing an air show the next day. Jackie's mother, who was as healthy as a dandelion in a manicured lawn, decided to have a fainting fit on that day because she didn't want Jackie to leave her. But Jackie did go, and that was where she met Charley. When he pulled out of town three days later, Jackie was with him. They were married the next week.

Her mother had gone back to Georgia where her brother refused to put up with her hypochondria and put her to work helping with his six children. Judging from the letters Jackie received until her mother's death a few years ago, that had been the best thing for her. She had been very happy after she'd left Chandler and gone back to her own people.

"Twenty years," Jackie whispered.

"What?"

"It was twenty years ago when I left with Charley. Sometimes it seems like yesterday and sometimes it seems like three lifetimes ago." She looked up at him. "Did we meet back then, before I left with Charley?"

"Yes," he said, smiling. "We met then. I adored you, but you never even looked at me."

She laughed. "I can believe that. I was so full of youthful pride."

"You still are."

"Pride maybe, but no longer am I youthful."

At that, William looked at her across the fire,

and for a moment Jackie thought he was angry at her. She was about to ask him what was wrong when he briskly stepped around the fire, pulled her up into his arms and kissed her firmly on the mouth.

Jackie had kissed only two men in her life: her husband, Charley, and a pilot who was just taking off and might not come back. Neither of those kisses had been like this one. This kiss said, I'd like to make love to you, like to spend nights with you, like to touch you and hold you.

When he released her, Jackie fell back against the ground with a thud.

"I think there's still a little youth left in you," William said sarcastically as he pushed a stick back into the fire.

Jackie was speechless, but her eyes never left him. How in the world could she not remember him? There were at least half a dozen Montgomerys in her high school class, but she couldn't remember one named William. Of course the Montgomerys all seemed to have five or six last names on the front of their family name. Maybe he'd been called something else, like Flash or Rex, or maybe the girls just called him Wonderful.

After William kissed her, there was an awkward silence between them, which he broke. "Okay," he said enthusiastically, "you get three wishes, what are they?"

She opened her mouth to speak but closed it again, looking up at him sheepishly.

22

"Come on," he said, "it couldn't be that bad. What is it?"

"It isn't really a bad wish at all. It's just that it's so . . . so boring."

"Jackie O'Neill, the greatest female pilot who ever lived, has a thought that's *boring?* Not possible."

Right away she realized that she didn't want to tell him her wish because she didn't want to disappoint him. He seemed to know all about her — if one can know anything about another from records broken and set, from inflated newspaper accounts that dramatized happenings that were in truth actually rather ordinary.

"I want to put down roots, stay somewhere, and Chandler is familiar to me," she said. "Now that I've seen the rest of the world, I know Chandler is a nice place. But I can't live anywhere if I don't have a way to make money." She put up her hand when he started to speak. "I know, I know, your family and the Taggerts pay me well when they want me to fly somewhere, but I'll never make any money in a one-man operation. I want to hire a few young pilots, run a little business. I'd like to delegate some of the work. I'd like to run passengers and freight, maybe some mail, between here and Denver, but I'll need a healthy nest egg to be able to set up an operation like that."

"But . . ." He couldn't think how to word his thoughts so he wouldn't be offensive.

But Jackie knew what he was thinking. "Jackie O'Neill, the greatest female pilot of this century reduced to flying mail from Colorado to the East Coast. Queen of the snap roll reduced to hauling picture post cards. Oh, the horror of it. Oh, the great tragedy of it. Is that what you're thinking?"

William ducked his head, but she could see that his face was as red as the fire. A man who blushes, she thought.

"All that daredevil stuff is for kids. I've had my fill of it."

He came to sit by her again and looked at her earnestly. "I'm sure you could get your business established if you wanted it. There are ways to make that kind of thing happen."

If you have as much money as the Montgomerys do, she thought, but of course she didn't say that. "Even the very, very best pilot has to have an airplane, and the last time I saw mine, its nose was pressed against a three-ton boulder." There was a patronizing tone to her voice.

"I see your point." As he put his arm around her, he kept his eyes lowered. "Wish number two."

"Nope. I want your wish number one."

"I have only one wish. I wish I could accomplish something on my own, something that Montgomery money couldn't buy for me." He looked at her. "Your turn. Second wish."

"Curly hair?" she asked, making him smile.

"Tell me the truth. There must be things in life you want besides a business." He made it sound as though she had disappointed him by not wishing for a magic carpet or perhaps world peace. "What

24

about another husband?"

There was so much hope in his voice that she laughed. "Are you volunteering?"

"Think you'd accept my offer?"

At the eager, almost-serious tone in his voice, she tried to pull away from him, but he held her fast. "All right, I'll behave."

"What's *your* second wish?" she asked.

"Probably to be as good a man as my dad."

"With your lying you're not as good as the Beasley girls."

He laughed, and the tension between them was gone. "So you won't tell me your other wishes, your other wants out of life?"

"If I told you, you'd think I was ridiculous."

"Try me."

There was something earnest about him that made her want to tell the truth. If she'd been with some of Charley's friends, she'd have made up something entertaining, like winning the Taggie, but now she just wanted to say what she really wanted. "All right, what I want most is normalcy. For the first twelve years of my life I had an ailing father and a hypochondriac mother. After my father's death, I had an invalid mother. I longed to go to school dances and such, but I didn't get to. One of my parents always needed me. For the last twenty years I have traveled and flown and had an enormously exciting life. Sometimes it seemed that every day brought some new and thrilling event. Charley was as unsettled, as fidgety, as my mother was unmovable. I've had lunch

25

at the White House, been to about half the countries of the world, met an enormous number of famous people. After the . . ." She barely glanced at him. A few years ago she had performed a service that had to be done at the time, and afterward America had made a fuss about it. "I've had my photo in the newspapers," she finished.

"An American heroine," he said, his eyes glowing.

"Perhaps. Whatever I was, I loved it all."

"But then Charley died and you changed," he said, sounding almost jealous.

"No, it was before that. Somewhere in there I realized that people wanted my autograph for themselves, not for me. Don't get me wrong, I loved it all. But one day after Charley and I, in separate planes, had spent three days with no sleep, on harrowing flights through a raging forest fire, I was told the president was calling to congratulate me. I sat there on a stiff chair in some dingy little office and thought, Not again."

She smiled. "I think that when you get to the point where a call from the president of the United States elicits nothing but boredom, it's time to do something else."

William was silent for a moment. "Normal. You said you wanted normal. What is normal?"

She grinned at him. "How would I know? I've never even seen it, much less lived it. But I don't think calls from the president, champagne in hot air balloons, living in hotels, and being rich one day and poor the next is normal. It's exciting, but it's also very tiring."

He chuckled. "It's true that we all want what we don't have. *I* have had the most normal life in the world. I went to the right schools, studied business administration, and after college I came back to Chandler to help run the family businesses. The most exciting thing I ever did was spend three days in Mexico with one of my brothers."

"Yes?"

"Yes what?"

"And what did you do in Mexico during those three days?"

"Ate. Saw the sights. Fished a little." He stopped. "Why are you laughing?"

"Two handsome young men alone in a place as decadent as Mexico and you went to see the sights! Didn't you even get drunk?"

"No." William was smiling. "What is the most exciting thing you've done?"

"It would be difficult to choose from the list. Dippy twist loops are rather exciting." Her head came up. "Once I had a Venetian count try to tear my clothes off."

"You found that exciting?" William asked coldly.

"It was, when you consider that we were flying at about ten thousand feet and he was crawling across the plane toward me. A few sideslips and he got back in his seat. But he was crying that an airplane was the *only* place where he hadn't yet made love to a woman."

William laughed. "Tell me more. I like hearing

27

about your life. It beats mine."

"I'm not sure that's true. I once made a dead-stick landing — that's with a dead engine — in a plane with no wheels and only one and a half wings. That was more excitement than I wanted."

"Which countries did you like best?"

"All of them. No, I'm serious. Each country has something to recommend it, and I try to over-look the bad parts."

William was silent for a few minutes, staring into the fire. "Charley was a very lucky man to share so many years with you. I envy him."

She turned her head up to look at him, frowning in concentration. "You sound as though you've been carrying a torch."

"For you? Yes, I have. I used to adore you from afar."

"How flattering. But back then you could have told me you loved me and offered me a few Mont-gomery millions and I still wouldn't have stayed in Chandler."

They sat together, his arm slipping about her shoulders as they watched the fire. "What do you need to open your freight business?" he asked.

"Seriously?"

"Very seriously."

She took a moment before she answered. She may have just had a bump on the head, but her brains were still intact. Charley had drummed into her that a pilot without any money must always be on the lookout for an airplane-lover who did have money. "Now, that's a marriage made in

28

heaven," he used to say. She wouldn't want to take advantage of this man, but if he was bored and had pots of money, maybe they could find something that would help him occupy his time.

She took a deep breath, trying to banish her feelings of guilt. If he wanted to do something for her, it was because he believed her to be an American heroine. But if Jackie took money from him, it would have to do with something much less altruistic, something much more primitive, such as putting bread on the table and maybe a few really nice dresses on her back. "A couple of good, light planes. A full-time mechanic, hangars, a few old planes I can cannibalize for parts, money for salaries until I can pay the pilots."

"Anything else you need? A partner perhaps?"

Right away she knew that he was suggesting himself. Now was not the time to make such a decision. Her head was still seeping blood, and her thinking was fuzzy. However, it was delicious to think of this man as her partner. Smiling, she looked up at him, trying to place him. "Who are your parents?"

"Jace and Nellie."

"Ah, that explains it. Half the town is parented by those two."

William smiled. All his life he'd heard jokes about the number of children in his family. "Twelve in all." He was emptying the big picnic basket that seemed to hold enough food for half a dozen loggers. Without saying a word, he began making her a sandwich. Jackie watched in astonishment as he made it just the way she would have made it for herself: chipped beef piled high, lots and lots of mustard, tomatoes; then he sliced a sweet pickle and placed the slices on top of the tomato, using two leaves of lettuce to protect the bread so it wouldn't get soggy. Watching his face, she could see that he wasn't paying any attention to what he was doing, that he was concentrating totally on whatever was running through his mind. But it was odd that he would make her a sandwich that was just what she would have made, especially since her sandwiches were, well, unique.

"Look what I've done," William said. "I was going to make you a sandwich first and now I . . ." He looked at her. "What do you want?"

"Just like the one you made for yourself."

His handsome face showed a moment's consternation before he smiled. "Honest? Everyone hates my sandwiches."

"Mine too," she said, reaching out her hand. "How about halves and I'll make the second one? I cut up olives instead of pickles."

"And then everyone complains that the olives fall off."

"The idiots don't know how to hold the bread."

They looked at each other across the sandwich and smiled. "Do you think we'll be able to sandwich this friendship together?" Jackie asked and they both laughed. "What do you think of ketchup?"

"Hate the stuff."

"Onions?"

"Overpowering. All you can taste is onions. Popcorn?"

"I could eat my weight in it. You?"

"Same here." Leaning back on his elbows, he looked into the fire, and she could tell that he was getting ready to say something important. "If I came up with the money for a few planes and the other things, would you consider me as your partner?"

"Ever flown before?" It didn't matter if he had, but the question gave her time to think. Even if he weren't a Montgomery and endowed with all that that name meant, she was good at judging people and this man was salt of the earth, rock solid. Sometimes things around an airport could get hectic, maybe even frightening when there was a crash, but she doubted if this man would panic if caught in a volcano. The problem was that she knew she was ripe for involvement with a man. It had been two years since Charley's death and over a year since she'd returned to Chandler, and she was lonely. She was tired of eating alone, sleeping alone, tired of sitting alone in the evenings with no one to talk to. And this man was very, very attractive, both in looks and in disposition.

"I have been taking lessons for two years," he said softly, looking at her with eyes that were almost pleading.

"All right," she said just as softly, and when she did, she could feel little chills on her body. She liked this man, liked him very much. She liked the way he took responsibility, liked what he talked about, liked the way he moved, the way he ate, what he ate. She liked the way he kissed her, the way he made her feel when he kissed her. In all her life she didn't remember ever just plain old-fashioned *liking* a man as much as she did him. She'd been attracted to men before — she'd be a liar if she didn't admit that — but there was a difference between being sexually attracted to a man and wanting to cuddle up with him and eat popcorn and tell each other secrets.

Years ago there had been a gorgeous pilot whom Charley had hired to work with them. He was so divinely handsome that she could hardly speak to him; the first time she saw him she dropped a wrench straight through the engine and almost hit Charley on the head. For days she had been tongue-tied when she was near him. But after a few weeks she'd began to grow used to his looks and soon found out that he liked his own looks even better than she did. After spending six months near him she couldn't remember that she'd ever thought he was handsome. She'd learned in her long, happy marriage with Charley that what was important between a man and a woman was friendship.

"All right," she said, holding out her hand to shake his. "But on one condition."

He took her hand and held it firmly. "Anything. Anything at all."

"You have to tell me what *your* deepest darkest secret is. And I want the truth, no telling me about contracts that are a matter of public record."

William groaned. "You are a fierce bargainer, Jackie O'Neill."

She wouldn't release his hand. "Tell me or we don't work together."

"All right," he said, with a slow grin. "You make me an olive sandwich sometime and I'll tell you the truth about Mexico."

"Oh?" she said, raising an eyebrow.

There are times in a person's life that are magic, and that night was one of them. Later, Jackie thought the night was perfect, perfect in every way, from the storybook rescue, to a romantic cut on her forehead, to a handsome man taking care of her. And take care of her he did. He made sure she was fed and warm and comfortable. More than that, he made her feel good. He flattered her by knowing every aerobatic stunt she'd performed, every record she'd set, every accident she'd had. It was almost as though he'd been in love with her for years.

They talked as though they were old friends — friends, not lovers. Jackie often got tired of men whose only interest was in trying to get a woman into bed, who directed their every word, every gesture toward that end. They bragged about themselves, told how much money they had, how much land they owned, how they were better than other men. But William was as comfortable as a woman friend.

Somewhere during the evening, he had her stretch out on his pallet of blankets and put her head on his firm thigh. Leaning back against a tree, he stroked her hair and encouraged her to talk about herself. Within seconds she found herself telling him about Charley, about her years with him, of the frustrations and hardships, of the triumphs and the failures.

In return he told her about his life of perfection — or at least that was how he described what to Jackie seemed like an ideal situation. He had never had anyone be cruel to him, never had anyone take an instant dislike to him, never had to struggle for anything.

"My life makes me wonder about myself. If I were tested, would I hold up?" he asked, frowning into the fire. "Would I be able to do something without my father's money and the support of the Montgomery name?"

"Sure you would," Jackie answered. "You'd be surprised at what you can do when you have to."

"Like land a plane that's just had the propeller knocked off by an eagle?"

"Is that what that was?"

"You brought that plane down as easily as someone stepping off a chair. Were you frightened?"

"I had too much to do to be frightened. Hey!" She looked up at him in the soft light. "Why haven't you married? Why hasn't some woman snatched you up already?"

"I haven't met a woman I wanted. I like a woman to have a head on her shoulders."

"A beautiful head, no doubt," Jackie said sarcastically.

"That's of less importance than what's inside the head."

"You know, I *like* you. I really do."

"And I have always liked you."

She was silent for a moment. "I wish I could remember you."

"Time enough. Are you cold? Hungry? Thirsty?"

"No, nothing. I'm perfect."

"That you are."

Jackie was embarrassed by his compliment but pleased by it, too. "When do you want to start . . . ah, our partnership?" When do you want to start spending enormous amounts of time together? was what she wanted to ask him.

"Tomorrow I have to go to Denver for a few days, and I'll get money from the bank there. I'll return on Saturday. How about if I come to your place in the afternoon? Can you give me a list of what you need so I can pick it up in Denver?"

She laughed at that. "How about some new planes for a start?"

"What type would you like?"

He was as serious as she was being lighthearted, and Jackie was suddenly serious too. "How about a couple of Wacos for a start?" And, she thought, maybe later something heavy that can carry a dozen rich passengers in style.

"All right, I'll see what I can do."

"Just like that?" she said. "I snap my fingers and two new planes show up?"

"They're not free. *I* come with them. You have

to take me with the planes."

That didn't seem like much of a punishment. "I guess beggars can't be choosers." Stretching, she yawned, snuggling her head on his leg.

"I think it would be all right if you went to sleep now," he said, tucking the blanket around her.

"What about you?" she asked dreamily. "You need to sleep too."

"No, I'll stay awake and watch the fire."

"And protect me," she murmured as she closed her eyes. No, she didn't think there was going to be any problem with this man's reliability. Smiling, she dozed off, feeling as safe as though she were home in her own bed, not in the open with coyotes howling in the distance.

Chapter Two

Good morning."

Wearily, Jackie sat up on the hard ground, and for a moment she didn't know where she was. Blinking against the bright light of day, she squinted at the woman sitting on the rock across from her.

"Would you like some coffee?"

Rubbing her eyes, covering a yawn, Jackie took the tin mug that was held out to her. "Who are you?"

"William's sister."

"Oh," she said, still too groggy to ask any questions, but she looked around. William's car was gone, and in its place was a pickup truck.

The woman — pretty, dark haired, about thirty — smiled. "You must be confused. Here's what happened. last night my mother had one of her spells, as the family calls them. She often gets the idea that one of her children is hurt, is going to be hurt, or is in some danger. Since most of these hunches of hers are correct, my father listened when she said that her son William was lost. That was at about three this morning. I happened to be up, so I said I'd go. It wasn't difficult to find William; he'd left a map showing where he'd be." She raised her eyebrows in sisterly mockery. "William is a very responsible person." She said this last in a sarcastic voice, accompanied by some eye-rolling, as though she also thought William was a bit of a stick-in-the-mud.

Jackie opened her mouth to defend him, but she closed it. "So you found us."

"Yes. I guess my mother sensed the danger you'd been in." She nodded toward Jackie's airplane, still smashed against the boulder.

"Where is he?"

"William? Oh, he had to leave. He said he had to get to Denver as soon as possible, that he had to buy something very important. He wouldn't tell Dad or me what it was." She looked down at her coffee cup. "Do *you* have any idea what he's after?"

Jackie pulled her knees into her chest and didn't answer. William was very responsible, she thought, feeling a little bit of a thrill run through her. A man who knew what responsibility was would be nice to be around. Charley had been a lot of fun; people loved Charley — but they didn't have to live with him. Charley never remembered where he put anything; Jackie used to say that she'd spent half of her life looking for whatever Charley had lost that hour. When Charley agreed to go to two different houses for dinner on the same evening, it was Jackie who had to play the villain and get him out of one engagement. There was never a question of how much money Charley brought home; he never got that far with whatever money he received. One time they had spent a grueling week with an air show, flying through a burning barn for the edification and delight of a few hundred farmers and their families. The owner of the show made the mistake of giving Charley their pay while he was in a bar. Charley was brought home the next day, too drunk to stand up, and he hadn't a penny left; he'd bought everyone round after round of drinks. No, responsibility in a man was not something Jackie was used to.

"Whenever you're ready, Dad and I will take you back to Chandler, and we'll send someone for the plane."

"Thanks, that would be great." Drinking the last of her coffee, she stood and stretched. Looking about her, she couldn't help smiling. Last night William had said he would take care of everything and he'd already started. He was not only a man of responsibility but a man of his word as well.

Many years ago Eternity was a thriving little town, close to the big city of Denver, on the way to San Francisco. The discovery of silver was the reason for the town's existence, and for years the inhabitants thrived. They built rather quickly, but thanks to a Rumanian carpenter, who had grown wealthy, the buildings were sturdy and well constructed. They weren't the usual flimsy fire traps that were the mainstay of so many towns that sprang up and died within a decade.

After the silver was played out, most of the residents left the town to die a slow death, but in the 1880s there was a short-lived revival. A rich young woman from an extremely wealthy eastern family named Montgomery moved to town and opened a dress shop that was patronized by other wealthy people from hundreds of miles away. But the young woman fell in love, began to produce babies, and lost interest in the dress shop. And when her interest slackened, so did the quality of the shop. Gradually the town of Eternity renewed its downhill slide, and more people left. The ones who stayed produced children, who left as soon as they were able. Each person who left sold his home and land to the relatives of the young woman who'd once tried to revive the town, until at last every house, every piece of land, was owned by the Montgomery family.

By the beginning of the twentieth century there

was no one living in the town, and the buildings, which had weathered the years well, thanks to the expert carpenter and his harassed crew, were vacant.

Nearly two years ago, only days after Charley's death, Jackie had received a letter from the scion of the Montgomery family telling her that his family, now living in the nearby town of Chandler, Colorado, needed a freight service from Chandler to Denver to Los Angeles, and if she was interested in the job, he would build to suit. She accepted his offer right away, but it was six months before she could meet all of her commitments and free herself to move to Chandler. When Charley died, she'd been too grief-stricken to consider her future, but after he was gone, she found that a lot of her ambition had gone with him. Maybe Charley's praise when she accomplished some great aerobatic feat had pushed her to higher and more difficult deeds. Whatever it was, she no longer wanted to spend her life traveling around the world flying upside down in an airplane before audiences that were holding their breath in fear.

She sent Mr. Montgomery a detailed list of what she'd need: a landing field, a hangar big enough for four planes — she had great hopes for the future — and a comfortable house that she could eventually buy, since it was her dream to own her own home, a place that no one could take from her.

After her decision, she had to figure out what to do with Pete, Charley's mechanic. She had known Pete since she was a girl; she'd met him the day she met Charley, and he had always been there. But that didn't mean she knew anything about him. Pete didn't talk, rarely said a word. At first she'd found his constant silent presence almost eerie, for he was wherever Charley was and he was absolutely loyal to him.

"Doesn't he ever say anything?" Jackie had demanded of Charley when they were alone in bed. Sometimes she thought she should look under the bed to make sure Pete wasn't there.

Charley'd just laughed at her. "Don't ever underestimate Pete. He may not talk, but he sees and hears everything. And he's a brilliant mechanic."

"He gives me the willies," she'd said, but Charley laughed at her again, pulled her on top of him, and began kissing her. They'd rarely mentioned Pete after that; he was just something that was *there,* rather like the planes themselves.

Over the years she began to understand how valuable Pete was, and when the thin little man saw that Jackie was also loyal to Charley, that she didn't run around with other men, didn't give Charley too hard a time, he began to take care of her, too. Pete made sure that her planes were ready and that nothing that a mechanic could foresee was wrong with them.

Gradually, over the years, Jackie grew used to him and talked to him at times, and somehow his silent presence was comforting. He never offered any advice, never even made a comment when

41

she talked to him. He just listened to her and let her sort out her own problems.

After Charley's death it was natural that Pete should stay on the circuit with her, but when she decided to move to Chandler, she had no idea what he would do. She told him what she had planned and fully expected him to say that he'd start working for one of Charley's thousands of male friends. But Pete listened to her, his weather-beaten old face showing nothing; then he said, "When do we leave?" Those few words told Jackie that he had transferred his loyalty to her, and she knew it was high tribute. Charley had said that Pete was a snob; he'd only work for the best. No amount of money could make him work for someone he thought was less than the best. So when Pete said he was going with her, she knew he was complimenting her on her talents and on the decision she had made. On impulse she kissed his leathery old cheek and then had the great pleasure of seeing him blush.

So she had flown to Chandler, and Pete had driven her car, pulling a trailer full of all the necessities of their life — that is, mechanics' tools and engine parts. Neither she nor Pete owned any furniture or much clothing to speak of.

She had no idea what she'd find in the renovated ghost town of Eternity. She was prepared for run-down houses with the wind whipping through the boards — she and Charley, when they were down on their luck, had certainly lived in such places — but what she'd found was beautiful. Mr. Montgomery had renovated the town's hotel for her and it was, quite simply, lovely. The lobby had been freshly covered with cream-colored wallpaper splashed with pink roses. All of the oak woodwork had recently been varnished. Brandnew telephone wires had been strung from Chandler into Eternity so she'd have a telephone. A beautiful bathroom of pink marble had been installed on the first floor. Everything was clean and welcoming.

The town livery stables had been turned into an enormous hangar with overhead doors so they could work on the planes in bad weather. The parsonage — Charley would have laughed at that — had been made over for Pete. The blacksmith's shop had been converted into a machine shop with tools so new and fine they almost brought tears to Pete's rheumy eyes.

Outside, Mr. Montgomery had built Jackie the best runway she'd ever seen; no expense had been spared. And in the fields behind the town were three wrecked planes that could be cannibalized for repair parts.

Never in her life had Jackie felt so welcome as she did in this town. She was close enough to Chandler so as not to feel isolated but far enough away to have privacy. She knew that she had come home.

She also knew there had to be a catch, so when she went to Mr. Montgomery to negotiate a salary, she was prepared for a fight. She could almost hear Charley telling her, "Stick to your guns, kid. Don't let him cheat you. Set the highest price you can think of and bargain from there." By the time

43

she saw Mr. Montgomery, whom she'd known all her life, her hands were sweating. She wanted the pretty little ghost town so badly that she thought she'd pay him to let her live there.

Thirty minutes later she walked out in a daze. Mr. Montgomery had offered her three times what she had been planning to ask him for, and he'd given her a bonus for signing a two-year contract. She'd be able to buy furniture. She'd be able to buy things that would belong to *her!*

Now, a year later, she was serving tea in the living room of her pretty house.

"What in the world is wrong with you?" Terri Pelman asked her friend as Jackie entered her living room, a tray of tea things in her hands. Over the last year she'd spent every cent she'd earned on making her house beautiful: fat upholstered chairs, a deep couch covered in mossy green and rose, a needlepoint rug, a mahogany desk, antiques everywhere.

"Nothing is wrong with me," Jackie said, setting the tray containing a lovely teapot and cups down on the table in front of the sofa. No one who'd ever known Jackie would have guessed how she hungered for pretty things. With Charley she'd always lived from hand to mouth; Charley believed that possessions weighed a person down. "Absolutely nothing."

"You can't lie to me, Jacqueline O'Neill. I'm not the press whom you can bamboozle. I've known you all your life, and something is definitely going on."

Smiling, Jackie sat down on a chair slipcovered in a cotton print of flowers and paisley ferns. As she sipped her tea, she looked at her friend. They were the same age, both thirty-eight, but no one would have guessed it from looking at them. After they'd graduated from high school, Jackie had taken off to spend her life in every corner of the world, but Terri had married her boyfriend the day after graduation. She had produced three children within as many years, kids who were now big, hulking boys of nineteen, eighteen, and seventeen. With each child Terri had gained weight and had never lost it, and somewhere along the way she had decided she was old. When Jackie chided her for not taking care of herself Terri would say, "The kids and Ralph only care what I put on the table, not what I'm wearing when I do it. I could look like Harlow and they wouldn't notice."

"Come on, tell me," Terri urged; then, her eyes widening, she gasped. "You've met a man! That's it, isn't it? We women are such fools. Even marriage can't cure us of falling in love, and if marriage can't cure a person, nothing can. So what's he like? Where did you meet him?"

Jackie wanted to tell Terri about William, but she didn't want to look like a fool. What if William hadn't been as affected by their night together as she had? What if he thought it was an ordinary encounter? Maybe he'd forgotten about her by now, forgotten about their partnership. Charley would have. Charley often got drunk and met people and made them feel he was their best friend.

45

He made plans to do things together, got them enthusiastic, but twenty-four hours later, when the people sought him out, ready to act on the plans, he could hardly remember them. Of course it was left to Jackie to smooth ruffled feathers and get Charley off the hook once again.

"Actually, it isn't a man," Jackie lied as smoothly as she could. "Well, it is, but not in the way you mean. You remember when my plane went down a couple of nights ago?"

Terri shook her head in disbelief. After being in an airplane crash, anyone else would have been in a hospital getting medical care and flowers, but Jackie was absolutely nonchalant about the mishap. She spoke of her plane crashing the way one might speak of going to the beauty parlor. "Yes, I remember," Terri said, marveling at her friend's bravery.

"There was a man there and —"

"What? You met a man in the middle of nowhere? What's his name? Where does he come from? Did he try anything?"

Jackie laughed. When they were in high school, she and Terri had barely known each other. Terri had had a normal family while Jackie's had been strange and eccentric. It was after Jackie left Chandler that they got to know each other. When they were both twenty yeas old, Terri had sent Jackie a letter of congratulations on winning her first race, saying that she understood Jackie's life because her own life was quite exciting as well. On the day Jackie had won the race, Terri's son had caught a wasp in his mouth, where it managed to sting his tongue before he swallowed it, her husband had dropped a crate on his foot and would be out of work for a month, and she had found out she was pregnant with her third child. "Now all I need is a plague of locusts and my life will be complete," she'd written. "Please tell me about your boring life; I need something to counteract the thrill and exhilaration of mine."

The letter had appealed to Jackie. She had received a lot of letters from people who had known her in the past, but many of those letters made her feel guilty, since the writers usually said that they doubted if she remembered them now that she was so famous. It was as though they thought that winning a race that was reported in the newspapers had instantly wiped out her memory. Or that every celebrity she met replaced an "insignificant" person from her past.

Happily, Jackie had written Terri all about the race, about the people she had met, about what it was like to soar high above the crowd at air shows. At first, she wrote of the applause, but as the years passed, she began to write of the defeats and the heartaches. She wrote of people whom she'd seen die in fiery crashes, of men and women who passed in and out of her life. She wrote of Charley and how sometimes his irresponsibility nearly drove her mad. She told Terri that she envied her her quiet, peaceful life, envied her her husband, who was always there for her, who was interested in their home and the kids.

47

Terri tried never to let on to Jackie how much their correspondence meant to her. The letters they exchanged were, at times, the best part of Terri's life. She used all her creativity to make her letters to Jackie interesting and fun and, above all, light. It was wonderful to have a glamorous and exciting woman like Jackie write to her with such intimacy and such trust. Jackie began to see Terri as wise beyond her years, someone who had had a chance to go off and see the world, but who had wisely decided to stay at home and settle down and raise children.

Terri never wrote anything to disabuse her friend of this notion. Oh, she was sarcastic at times, always making wisecracks about Ralph and the boys, but somehow Terri presented a picture of a life that was so good, so splendid, that she had to make jokes about it. If she told the truth she'd be able to do nothing but brag.

The real truth was that Terri had married the first man who asked her because she was terrified of ending up an old maid. Although he wanted to wait to have children, she was so afraid Ralph would leave her that she got pregnant on their wedding night — or maybe a week or so before, she was never sure. She never wrote Jackie the truth about her life — that her husband spent most of his time with his men friends drinking beer and that when he was home he held a newspaper in front of his face and slept. Instead she wrote Jackie of a life that sounded as though it had come out of a book written by Betty Crocker. She told of the garden she and her husband planted so they would have fresh vegetables and herbs for the boys. The truth was that her husband had lost his fourth job in as many years and her father had planted a small garden in her back yard to help feed her family. Of course the boys were just like their father and wouldn't touch a vegetable, so Terri had spent long hours canning produce to trade to a bachelor hog farmer for the meat the men loved. Terri wrote Jackie that Ralph always spent Sundays with his family; actually, he was sleeping off Saturday night. She told Jackie how quietly rewarding it was having a family. She painted a glorious picture of tiny loving hands bringing her flowers, of little mouths eating her delicious food. Terri poured every bit of her imagination into her narrations of an ideal existence.

It was writing those letters, and planning what she was going to write, that got Terri through some of the roughest times of her life. While one big, sturdy boy was terrorizing the little girl next door and the second one was throwing his food against the kitchen wall, while Terri was in the bathroom throwing up because she was carrying the third one, she thought of how she'd present her life in letters to Jackie.

When the boys grew older and as big as their father, she couldn't control them, and the letters she exchanged with Jackie became even more important in her life. Her husband's attitude toward child rearing was that the meaner the boys were, the more masculine they were. The more often they got into trouble in school, the prouder he was of them. Terri tried to talk to him, to tell him that he was encouraging their delinquent behavior, but his reasoning was that this was the way he had been raised and he'd turned out all right. Terri knew better than to point out that he'd never been able to keep a job for longer than eight months because he got into fights with his bosses. His sons were turning out just like him, arguing with teachers and principals and store owners and anyone who happened to get in their way.

Terri's real life and the life she wrote Jackie about bore little relation to each other. Now that her big, awkward sons were nearly grown and were rarely at home, the brightest point in her life was these visits to the old ghost town to spend time with Jackie. She had no idea if Jackie knew the truth about her life. It wouldn't have been too difficult for her to find out, as everyone in Chandler knew everyone else's business, but somehow Terri doubted Jackie did. To the folks of Chandler, Jackie was a celebrity, and she didn't think people would be rushing to tell her about Nobody Terri Pelman's boring life.

So, as often as possible, Terri visited Jackie, and the two of them kept up the façade of Terri's splendid golden life in which she had everything: the steady love of a good man, three beautiful children who had turned into fine, upstanding young men, and a lovely, gracious home.

"It wasn't like that," Jackie said, laughing. "It

wasn't a romantic encounter. I mean, he did kiss me but —"

"You crash a plane, a gorgeous man comes out of the night, rescues you" — she raised her eyebrows — "and kisses you, and you say, 'It wasn't like that.' So, Jackie, what was it like?"

"Terri, you are incorrigible. I don't think you'll be happy until you get me married and pregnant."

"And why shouldn't you be as miserable as the rest of us?"

"Sometimes I almost think you mean what you say. If I didn't know the truth about how much you love that family of yours I'd —"

"*Tell* me!"

"Really, there isn't much to tell." Actually, Jackie thought, that was the truth. What had passed between her and William could have been one-sided. She didn't want to tell Terri what she was feeling and then end up looking as though she'd made a fool of herself over some man. And most definitely she did not want to tell Terri that this man was one of Jace and Nellie Montgomery's sons. For some odd reason, Terri seemed to believe that every man in Chandler was worthless. Maybe she thought she'd gotten the only good one, or maybe it was just that familiarity breeds contempt. She'd known all the men of Chandler for so long that she considered them incapable of inspiring passion or even love. Terri had her own idea of a perfect man: the more exotic the better. She once asked Jackie how she could have been to France and not fallen in love with a Frenchman.

51

"Or an Egyptian," Jackie had said, laughing. "They're the best-looking men on earth."

"This is really a business arrangement. I mentioned my wanting to start a freight business, and he said he was looking for something to do, so it just happened. He's gone to Denver to buy a couple of planes."

"And that's it?"

"That's all there is to it."

Terri didn't say anything, but put her teacup down, leaned back in her chair, and stared at her friend. "I'm not leaving here until you tell me everything. I can call Ralph and have him send my clothes here. If the boys get lonely for their mother I hope you won't mind if they come to stay with us. They'll be no bother at all."

At that threat Jackie almost shuddered but caught herself in time. Terri was a perfect example of the saying that love is blind, for those huge, semiliterate, lecherous sons of hers were no pleasure to anyone except her. The last time one of them had driven to Eternity to pick Terri up, he had cornered Jackie in the kitchen and started telling her how a woman like her must be "dyin' for a man" and he'd be "willin' to scratch her itch." Jackie had brought her foot down hard on his instep while "accidentally" dropping a skillet on his left hand. Since then Jackie had volunteered to drive Terri home whenever her friend was unable to borrow a car.

"I . . . I liked him," Jackie said, wanting to talk to someone about William but at the same time not wanting to talk. Her reaction to William didn't make any sense, since Jackie had been married for most of her life, but the truth was, she had never been "in love." She had married Charley so she could get out of Chandler. Charley had known that and hadn't cared that he was being used. He was quite willing to trade a few marriage vows for the company of a long-legged colt of a girl with an insatiable curiosity and a willingness to work such as Charley had never seen before. Within twenty hours of meeting her, Charley had a feeling that she would take care of him. He hadn't misjudged her. In all their years together, she had made sure the bills were paid, that they had a roof over their heads, and she had smoothed out all his problems, making Charley's once tumultuous life as peaceful as it could be. He had repaid her by showing her the world.

"I liked him," Jackie repeated. "That's all there was to it. He was there when I crashed, he took care of me, and we talked. Very simple." Talked as though we'd known each other forever, she thought. Talked as though we would never stop; talked as though we were friends, old friends, new friends, best friends.

"Who is he?"

"Ah, uh, William something, I don't remember."

"He lives in Chandler?"

"I'm not really sure." She talked quickly so Terri wouldn't ask her why she'd agreed to be partners with a man whose last name she didn't know.

"Terri, really, you're making too much of this. It was nothing. I've met a thousand men in my life, given flying lessons to hundreds of them, and this one is no different."

"You can lie to yourself, but you can't lie to me. You are blushing like a schoolgirl. So when do I get to meet him?"

"I don't know. I think his sister said he might be back on Saturday." The day was emblazoned in her mind. Saturday, late afternoon, she'd been told. At three P.M. Jackie planned to be wearing a pretty little yellow and white pinafore, something with ruffles around the wide straps and a white blouse underneath. She might just dab some perfume in a few strategic places and have bread baking in the oven. He had seen her in a leather flying suit, hair plastered to her head by a cotton-lined leather helmet, so next time she thought it might be nice to show him another side of her — say, the side that could take care of a house, maybe even be somebody's wife.

Jackie's head came up at the sound of Terri's laughter. "Oh, honey, you have it bad, very bad. You remind me of myself when I was eighteen years old." Terri's tone said clearly that the way Jackie was acting was understandable in an eighteen-year-old but rather silly at thirty-eight.

At the sound of a horn, Jackie jumped, her head swiveling toward the window, again causing Terri to laugh. "That's my eldest," Terri said.

"You must invite him in for milk and cookies," Jackie said, but she hoped she wouldn't have to

54

endure the smutty leers of the "boy."

"No, I must return," Terri said, bravely trying to keep the misery out of her voice. Her three sons and husband always felt betrayed when she dared take an afternoon off and not stay in the house at their beck and call, so they punished her by doing what they could to destroy the house while she was away. She knew that now she would return to food spilled on the floor, screen doors left open to admit thousands of flies, and angry men complaining that they hadn't been fed in hours. "I'll call you on Sunday, and I want to hear everything," Terri said as she left Jackie's house, running because her son was lying on the horn so it made a constant stream of deafening noise.

Chapter Three

Jackie tried to be sensible during the following days, but it wasn't any use. She tried to talk to herself, telling herself that she was an adult woman, not a frivolous, starry-eyed girl, but she didn't listen to her own advice. She cursed herself for having been born a woman. What in the world was wrong with women anyway? They met a man who was nice to them, and within minutes they began planning the wedding. She told herself that it had been an ordinary encounter, that what had made it seem extraordinary was that she had just been hit hard on the head. Otherwise she would have had her wits about her and she wouldn't have given another thought to the incident.

She made herself remember all the many men she'd met over the years. There was the time she'd been on a boat with Charley and a very nice man who . . . well, the truth was, he was more than nice. He was absolutely gorgeous, tall, with dark blond hair, crystal-clear blue eyes, and he had spent eighteen years or so in various universities studying a number of subjects, so he'd been fascinating to talk to. He was brilliant, educated, terribly handsome, everything a woman could want, but although they had spent the whole four days of the trip together while Charley was prostrate with seasickness, Jackie had not fallen in love with the man. Of course, she argued with herself, she had been married, and maybe that had something to do with it. Maybe William was the first interesting, handsome man she'd had any contact with since she'd become a single woman.

She had to smile when she thought that. After Charley's death she had been amazed at the number of men who came to "pay their respects." At the time she had been grieving, wondering what she was going to do with herself without Charley to take care of, and suddenly there were many men offering her anything she wanted. It was flattering and annoying at the same time.

She didn't so much as go out with a man for six months after Charley died, but the combination of loneliness and the constant invitations she received broke her. After months, she began to go out to dinner and movies, to auto races, to picnics. You name it and she went to it. And at each one it was the same thing: "How many brothers and sisters do you have?" "Where did you grow up?" "Where did you go to school?" "How many races have you won?" "Who are the celebrities you've met?" "What was it like having dinner at the White House?"

After six months of these dates, she began to consider having cards printed with vital information on them, so she could avoid having the same boring conversation over and over. Didn't anyone ever have anything interesting to say? Like "What's the biggest lie you ever told?" she couldn't help thinking. That was what William had asked her. And he had made her a sandwich she liked, not a conventional sandwich of grilled cheese or beef with mustard, but a real sandwich.

A year after Charley died she had moved to Chandler, for she was tired of the circuit, tired of people who had seen so much and done so much that they were dying of ennui by the time they were thirty. Jackie was afraid that if she stayed with them she would become one of them. She wanted to be with people who had wonder in their voices when they talked of airplanes. "I don't know how those things stay up," they'd say. Words that once bored her to tears, words that made her angry with their very stupidity, now pleased her with their simplicity. She liked Chandler, liked the people in it, people who had done little in their lives — little except keep the world going, that is.

And now, here in this sleepy little town, she had met a man who had done what no other man since Charley had been able to do: he had interested her.

On Thursday she cleaned house. On Friday she went shopping and spent twice her three-month clothing budget, and when she got home she decided she hated everything she'd bought. She went through all the clothes in her closet, pulling out things she'd kept for years. She couldn't decide whether to try to look like a sweet-tempered housewife or a sexy woman of the world. Or maybe she should aim for the movie-star-at-home-look of tailored trousers and a silk shirt.

By Saturday morning she was sure that her whole life depended on this afternoon, and she knew that whatever she chose would be wrong. When she awoke that morning she was angry, angry at herself for acting like a love-starved girl, for making something out of nothing. Maybe this man wouldn't show up. Even if he did show up, it could be very embarrassing to be dolled up as though she were going to the school dance. What if he came wearing work clothes, ready to get started overhauling a plane engine or whatever he wanted to do? What if he didn't show up at all?

She went to the stable that had been converted into a hangar, climbed a ladder and began trying to take the ruined propeller off her wrecked plane. The first thing she did was drop the wrench, tear one fingernail half off, then cut the bright red polish off another nail. Holding her hands up to the light, she grimaced. So much for having beautiful hands, she thought, but then she shrugged. Maybe it was better that she didn't try to impress him.

Standing on a ladder, wearing greasy coveralls that once had been a rather pleasant gray but were now stained into a non-color, Jackie was pulling on the bent propeller with a wrench. Wiping her hair out of her eyes, she left a smear of grease on her cheek as she looked around the shaft and saw a pair of feet. Expensively shod feet. After wiping her face on the sleeve of her coveralls and smearing more grease on herself, she looked down to see a good-looking young man staring up at her. He was a tall man, with dark hair and eyes, and he was staring at her in a very serious way, as though he expected something from her.

"You need some help?" she asked. Most people who came to Eternity, if they weren't friends, were tourists wanting to see the ghost town, or they were lost.

"Remember me?" he asked in a very nice voice.

She stopped trying to loosen a nut and looked down at him. Now that he mentioned it, there was something familiar about him. But she couldn't place him. No doubt he lived in Chandler and she had gone to school with him.

"Sorry," she said, "can't seem to place you."

Without so much as a smile, he said, "Do you remember this?" Holding out his hand, he had something in his palm, but she couldn't tell what it was.

Curious, she climbed down the ladder to stand in front of him. She was considered a tall woman, but this man topped her by several inches, and now that she was closer to him, he seemed quite familiar. Taking the trinket from his hand, she saw that it was a school pin. CHS was embossed in gold on an enameled background of the school colors, blue and gold. At first the pin meant nothing to her, but then, looking into the tall man's dark, serious eyes, she began to laugh. "You're little Billy Montgomery, aren't you? I wouldn't have recognized you. You've grown up." Stepping back, she looked at him. "Why, you've become quite handsome. Do you have hundreds of girl-friends? How are your parents? What are you doing now? Oh, I have a thousand questions to ask you. Why haven't you come to see me before now?"

There was only the smallest smile on his face that betrayed that he was pleased by her enthusiastic greeting. "I have no girlfriends. You were always the only girl I ever loved."

She laughed again. "You haven't changed much. You're still too serious, still an old man." Easily she slipped her arm into his. "Why don't you come in and have a cup of tea and tell me all about yourself? I remember how awful I used to be to you." As they started walking, she looked up at him. "It's hard to believe that I used to change your diapers."

Still smiling, arm in arm, they walked toward her house. Billy had never talked much when he was a child, and now his silence gave Jackie time to remember. He and his brothers and sisters were her first baby-sitting job. He had given her her first experience in child care and her first experience with dirty diapers. After that first day, she had gone home to tell her mother that she would never, never have any children, that children should be kept in a barn with lots of straw until they were housebroken.

She'd always liked Billy. He was so quiet and always ready to listen or to do whatever Jackie wanted to do. If she suggested reading a book aloud to the other kids, they'd invariably want to play monkeys-in-the-grape-arbor. If Jackie wanted to play rolling-down-the-hill, then the kids would want to sit quietly in the house and play with their dolls or trains.

But Billy was different. He always wanted to do what Jackie wanted to do when she wanted to do it. At first she thought he was just being agreeable, but too many times over the years Billy's mother had asked Jackie what she was going to do with the children that day. When Jackie told her, his mother would laugh and say, "That's just what Billy was saying he wanted to do."

Jackie was pleased with the quiet little boy, but she wasn't so pleased when she wasn't baby-sitting and he'd show up wherever she was. If he was downtown with his family and he saw Jackie, he'd leave his family and follow her. Never mind that sometimes he had to cross a wide street in front of rearing horses and motorists frantically slamming on their brakes. He just wanted to be with Jackie wherever she was. Jackie's mother started to tease her daughter, saying that Billy had fallen in love with her. Jackie thought it was kind of cute until Billy began showing up on her doorstep in the evenings. Then he became a pest. He became the pesky little brother she never had — and had never wanted.

Her mother made an agreement with Billy's mother that Jackie would look after Billy three afternoons a week. When Jackie heard, she was furious, but her mother wouldn't listen, so Jackie decided to get rid of the kid. She planned to do that by scaring him to death. At fifteen she was a complete tomboy, and Billy, at five, was big for his age and quite sturdy. Jackie would climb a tree, leaving Billy alone at the bottom for hours. She hoped he'd complain to his mother, but he never did. His patience was endless, and he seemed to have a sixth sense about what he could and could not do. When he was five, he wouldn't swing on the rope tied to the tree branch that overhung the river, nor would he when he was six, but when he was seven, he grabbed the rope and swung. Jackie could see that he was terrified, but he set his little mouth and did it, then dog-paddled over to her in the water. She was tempted to not say one word of congratulations, but then she grinned at him and winked. She was rewarded with one of Billy's rare smiles.

They were better friends after that. Jackie taught him to swim and allowed him to help her around her house. Billy, who spoke only when he had something to say, said that Jackie's house was more fun than his. In his house the servants got to do everything, but at hers the people got to do the good stuff themselves.

"That's one way of looking at it," she'd said.

Billy's mother was the one who suggested that he ask Jackie to go to the movies with him. Jackie, who had no money for such frivolities, was thrilled — until she saw the most handsome boy in her class outside the theater. She stopped to say hello to him, but Billy put his little body between them and told the six-foot-tall teenager that Jackie was *his* date and he should get lost — if he knew what was good for him. It was six months before the ribbing at school stopped. The other kids were merciless in teasing her about her three-foot-tall bodyguard who was going to bruise their kneecaps with his fists. "Do you pick him up to kiss him good night, Jackie?" they taunted.

By the time Billy was seven the townspeople referred to him as Jackie's Shadow. He was with her whenever possible, and no matter what she did she couldn't make him stop following her. She yelled at him, told him what she thought of him, even tried telling him she hated him, but he was still always there.

One day when she was seventeen, a boy walked her home from school. They stopped by the mailbox for a moment, and as the boy reached out to remove a leaf from Jackie's hair, out of the bushes sprang little seven-year-old Billy, as wild as a wet cat, launching himself at the unsuspecting boy. Jackie, of course, wanted to die. She pulled Billy off the boy and tried to apologize, but the boy was embarrassed because Billy had knocked him flat into the dirt road. The next day at school everyone gleefully renewed taunting Jackie about her midget lover whom she kept hidden in the bushes.

Billy's mother, a sweet woman, heard of the fracas and came to apologize to Jackie, justifying her youngest son's actions by saying, "He loves you so much, Jackie." That was not what she wanted to hear at seventeen. She wanted to hear that the captain of the football team loved her, not some kid half her size.

She wouldn't speak to Billy for three weeks after that episode, but she relented when she woke up one morning and found him asleep on the porch swing. He'd climbed out of his bedroom window sometime during the night and waited for the milk truck to arrive. After hiding himself among the milk cans, he got out when the driver stopped at Jackie's house, where he curled up into a ball on the hard slats of the swing and fell asleep. When Jackie saw him, she said that he was a curse of the magnitude of the plagues of Egypt, but her mother thought Billy was cute.

Billy had been tagging along behind her the day she met Charley and fell in love with the airplanes.

Billy had said, "Do you love airplanes more than you love me?"

"I love mosquito bites better than I love you," she'd answered.

Billy, as usual, said nothing, which always made her feel worse than if he'd yelled or screamed or cried like other kids. But Billy was an odd little boy, more like an old man in a kid's body than an actual child.

When she ran away from home with Charley, she was too cowardly to face her mother, so she left her a note. But she was halfway to the airfield when, impulsively, she ran back. She caught a ride with a man she knew, and he dropped her off at Billy's house, where a birthday party was going on. Most of Billy's eleven brothers and sisters, along with most of the children of Chandler, were terrorizing each other and making enough noise to cause an earthquake, but there was no sign of Billy. His mother, calm in the midst of chaos, saw Jackie and pointed to the side of the porch.

She found Billy there, sitting alone, reading a book about airplanes, and as Jackie looked at him she thought that maybe she did love him just a little bit. When solemn little Billy, who rarely smiled, saw her coming toward him, his face lit up with joy. "You never come to see me," he said, and the way he said it made her feel guilty. Maybe she'd been too hard on him. After all, they'd had some laughs together.

He looked at her suitcase. "You're going away

65

with them, aren't you?" There were tears in his voice.

"Yes, I am. And you're the only one I'm telling. I left my mother a note."

Billy nodded in an adult way. "She wouldn't want you to go."

"She might make me stay."

"Yes, she might."

She was used to his old man ways, but she could see his sadness. Reaching out her hand, she ruffled his dark hair. "I'll see you around, kid," she said and started to turn away, but Billy flung his arms around her waist and held her tight.

"I love you, Jackie. I will love you forever and ever."

Dropping down on her knees, she hugged him back. Then, holding him away from her, she smoothed back his hair. "Well, maybe I love you a little bit, too."

"Will you marry me?"

Jackie laughed. "I'm going to marry some fat old man and go see the world."

"You can't," he whispered. "I saw you first."

Standing up, Jackie looked down at him, at the tear streaks down his cherub cheeks. "I've got to go now. I'll see you again someday, kid. I'm sure of it." Even Jackie didn't believe those words; she planned to leave this one-horse town and never return. She was going to see the *world!* On impulse, the way she did most things, she pulled her blue and gold school pin from her blouse and handed it to him. What did she need with a pin from a nowhere school in a nowhere town?

Billy was staring so hard at the pin in his palm that he didn't realize Jackie had started to walk away, walk at her normal pace, which was closer to a run. "Will you write to me?" he called, racing after her, trying to keep up but failing.

"Sure, kid," she called over her shoulder. "Sure I'll write."

But of course she never did. In fact, she hadn't thought of Billy more than half a dozen times over the following years, and then only when she was with a group that was laughing and comparing small towns. To the accompaniment of raucous laughter, she'd tell the story of little Billy Montgomery who had plagued her from the time she was twelve until she'd escaped at eighteen. A couple of times she'd wondered what had happened to him, but she knew he had the Montgomery money and connections, so he could do anything he liked.

"Probably married now and has half a dozen kids," some guy said once.

"Not possible," Jackie said. "Billy's just a kid. I used to change his diapers."

"Jackie, I think you ought to do a little arithmetic."

To her horror she had realized that "little" Billy Montgomery was about twenty-five years old. "You're making me feel old," she'd laughed. "It couldn't have been more than three years since I left Chandler." She groaned when Charley reminded her that they had been married for seventeen years.

So now, many years after she'd left Chandler,

she was standing face to face with the little boy who had flung himself on her and sworn that he'd love her forever. Only he didn't look too much like the little boy she remembered. Six feet one if he was an inch, broad-shouldered, slim-hipped, very handsome. "You must come in and have some hot chocolate," she said, "and some cookies." She wanted to remind herself that, compared to her, Billy was just a child. Looking at him, it wasn't easy to remember that he was a boy.

"I'd prefer coffee," he said, motioning to her to lead the way.

Once inside the house she felt awkward and had to force herself to move. "How is your family?"

"All of them are well. And your mother?"

"Died a couple of years ago," she said over her shoulder as she moved into the kitchen.

Billy was right behind her. "I'm sorry. Here, let me help you," he said, reaching above her head for a canister of fresh coffee beans.

Jackie started to turn around and found herself looking straight into Billy's sun-browned throat, then, as her eyes lifted, at his chin, a chin so square it could have been sculpted with a carpenter's hand plane. For a moment she found her breath catching in her throat. Then she stopped herself and stepped from under his encircling stance. "My goodness, but you do look like your father. How is he, by the way?"

"The same as he was when you saw him four days ago."

"Yes, of course. I . . . ."

68

Billy smiled at her, at some joke that only he knew, then pulled out a chair at the table in the corner of the pretty kitchen and motioned for her to sit down. "I will make the coffee," he said.

"You can do that?" Jackie was of the school that believed that men could do nothing except what they were paid for or received awards for. They could fight wars, run huge businesses, but they couldn't feed themselves or choose their own clothes without a woman beside them.

Billy poured the right number of beans into the grinder, then began to turn the crank, all the while watching her with a slight smile.

"So tell me all about your life," she said, smiling up at him, trying her best to remember that she had once changed this man's diapers.

"I went to school, graduated, and now I help my father do whatever needs to be done."

"Managing the Montgomery millions, right?"

"More or less."

"No wife or children?" It seemed impossible to think that a kid she used to baby-sit could possibly be old enough to have a wife, let alone children.

"I told you that you were the only woman I would ever love. I told you that on the day you left."

At that Jackie laughed. "On the day I left, you were eight years old and your nose came to my belt buckle."

"I've grown up since then." As he said this he turned around and poured the ground beans into the coffee pot, and Jackie couldn't help noticing that he had grown up very, very well. "So how's your family?" she asked for at least the third time.

Billy turned, removed his wallet from his back pocket, took out a stack of photographs, and handed them to her. "My nieces and nephews," he said, "or at least some of them."

While the coffee was brewing he bent over her and showed her the photos, some of them of groups, some of individual children. She liked the fact that this man was sentimental enough to carry photos of children with him, that he knew their ages and something about the personality of each child. But for Jackie the experience wasn't all that pleasant. She remembered the parents of these children as children themselves. There was one little dark-haired girl who was the same age as her mother had been when Jackie had last seen her.

"I think I'm getting old," Jackie murmured. In her own heart she hadn't aged a day since she'd left Chandler. She still felt eighteen, still felt that there were lots of things she had to do before she became a grown-up and started acting like an adult. She wasn't yet sure what she wanted to do with her life. She'd had a long adolescence flying airplanes in shows and races, doing stunts and tricks to dazzle the world, but now she was nearly ready to settle down and become an adult. She thought she might be ready to marry a "real" man, a guy who had a nine-to-five job, a man who came home at night and read the newspaper. She was even thinking that maybe now she was about ready to start a family. Terri thought this was hilarious since two girls from their high school class were grandmothers already.

"You'll never be old, Jackie," Billy said softly, from just beside her ear.

His breath on her skin made her jump, and Jackie had to mentally shake herself. What was wrong with her that she could allow the nearness of a child like Billy to affect her? "What —" she began but stopped as she heard a plane. It sounded as if it was coming in to land.

Putting down her coffee cup, she went through the living room and out the front door toward the landing field, Billy just behind her. As she shaded her eyes against the sun, she could see the plane heading toward the airstrip. Immediately Jackie knew that the pilot wasn't very experienced: the plane was too low too soon.

The pilot managed to land the plane but only by the skin of his teeth, and Jackie planned to give him a piece of her mind. He could have taken the chimney off the old house on the hill, and the impact could have caused the plane to crash.

As she briskly walked across the field, Billy passed her to get to the plane first, and he held up his arms when the pilot stepped out. Jackie realized belatedly that the pilot was a woman. Only a female could be that slender, that delicately curvaceous, and only a beautiful woman could so easily accept a man's uplifted arms to help her down. She removed her goggles and leather helmet to release a torrent of midnight black hair before

71

turning to Jackie with a look of chagrin on her lovely face. "I was so hoping to impress you," she said, "but instead I nearly killed myself, a few trees, and . . ." She looked at Billy. "Was that a chimney I nearly hit?"

"None other," he answered.

The words of scolding died on Jackie's lips. She remembered the time she had wanted to impress Charley with her flying skills only to fly her worst when he was around. Instead of lecturing, she smiled at the girl.

"You remember my cousin Reynata, don't you?"

At first Jackie didn't, but then she looked at the girl in horror. "Rey? You're little Rey?" When she had known this girl Reynata had been a plump five-year-old with perpetually dirty clothes and skinned knees. She was always trying to run after the older children, always falling and hurting herself. Now she was tall and beautiful and nubile. "Of course I remember you," Jackie said, trying to sound gracious, but wondering if her hair was turning gray with every one of these "adults" she met. After shaking hands with the young woman, Jackie invited her in for coffee.

"I'd love to, but I saw the truck just down the road and — Ah! Here it is now."

Jackie stood where she was as Rey, all energy and movement, ran toward the road leading into Eternity where a large truck was just now coming into view.

"I think I'd better help," Billy said, then moved

forward to follow his cousin.

Puzzled, Jackie followed them slowly. Just what was going on? The plane Rey had flown was a Waco, so shiny-new that it must have left the factory yesterday. It was the type of plane that she had told her rescuer, William, that she most wanted. Was this a coincidence or was the plane from William?

By the time she reached the truck, it was being unloaded and things were being carried into the old hotel that she rented from Billy's father — a bed and linens, a chair, a couple of small tables, lamps, clothes, and a rack to hold the hangers. The whole situation was so confusing that it was several moments before Jackie could speak. "Would you mind telling me what is going on?" she asked Billy after pulling him aside. "And would you mind telling those men to stop putting furniture inside *my* house? I already have enough furniture."

Billy looked surprised. "The top floor is empty, isn't it? You didn't rent that floor, did you?"

"No, I didn't. Your father —"

"Oh, I bought the hotel from Dad. He charged me five dollars for it. I tried to get him down to one dollar, but he wouldn't hear of it. At first the scoundrel wanted ten, but I don't have a degree in business for the fun of it. I won't be cheated, even by my own father."

Jackie was sure the story was very amusing, but at the moment she wasn't ready to be amused. "What is going on?"

"I guess I should have asked your permission first. I mean, it is your house, or at least the bottom three floors are, but I really didn't have time to ask. I had to make arrangements as fast as possible to give us as much time as possible to get ready for the Invitational. I thought it would be much more convenient if I lived nearby instead of driving from Chandler every day, so I bought the hotel from Dad and hired people to clean the top floor. My mother found the furniture in the attic for me and —"

"Wait a minute!" she half shouted. "What do *you* have to do with the Invitational? What do *I* have to do with a race like that? Why do you keep talking about 'we'?" The instant she said the words, she knew the answer. Standing in front of her, shading her from the sun, was not little Billy Montgomery but William, her rescuing knight, the man who had pulled her from a wrecked plane, the man who had intrigued her with his talk, had made her interested in life, and had even made her think about love once again. He was the man she had been fantasizing about, dreaming about, conjuring up a future with. The man she was beginning to fancy that she was in love with was actually a very tall little boy.

Embarrassment was Jackie's first emotion. "I think there's been a mistake. You'll have to remove your furniture and go back to Chandler."

With her head down so he wouldn't see her reddened face, she started toward the hotel where the men were carrying a small table through the front door. But William caught her arm.

"Jackie —" he began.

"Didn't your family teach you to call your elders by their proper title? I'm Miss O'Neill to you."

He didn't release her arm. "I think we should talk about this."

"I don't think we should talk at all. Hey!" she yelled to a man leaving the hotel to go back to the truck. "Don't take anything else inside. Little Billy won't be staying."

The men chuckled as they looked from Jackie to William, hovering over her. He was several inches taller than she, a good deal heavier, and he didn't look like anyone's idea of "little Billy."

William gave the men a curt nod. "Take a break," he ordered. Then, still holding Jackie's arm firmly, he pulled her down the street, a tumbleweed blowing across their path. He didn't say a word as he pulled her into a building that had once been one of Eternity's saloons. Inside were half a dozen broken chairs and a few dirty tables. Firmly he ushered her to the only chair that had all four legs and sat her on it. "Now, Jackie —"

Like a jack-in-the-box, she came out of the seat immediately. "Don't try explaining anything to me. This has been one huge mistake, that's all. Now I want you to get your things out of my house —" She hesitated. "Or, if the place now belongs to you, I shall be the one to move." At that statement her heart wrenched. She had taken a ninety-nine-year lease on the first two floors of the hotel, planning to lease a floor a year until it was all hers. When she'd first approached Jace Montgomery about renting the hotel, he'd asked for more than she had to spend, so she asked him how much per floor. Trying to keep from smiling, he had divided the rent into five equal parts. Then Jackie had asked for a discount for renting two floors. With a ten percent discount, she was able to afford both floors, and after six months she'd added the third floor, at a twelve and one-half percent reduction. The ninety-nine-year lease made her feel secure enough to spend all the money she had in decorating it, and now she was going to have to leave her pretty house.

"I'll start moving now."

"What is wrong with you?" William asked, putting himself between her and the door. "You'd think I'd jilted you in a love affair. I thought we agreed that we were going to run a business together. Was there any more between us? Something I didn't know about?"

Jackie sat back down, praying that she would be able to live through this day. Of course he was right. She was acting like an idiot. There had been nothing between them except what was in her head. He had known all along that night who she was, had known that she was old enough to be his . . . well, his older sister. He had known that she was his former baby-sitter.

So that meant that everything, absolutely everything that she had imagined herself feeling, was all on her side. He had kissed her, but she had to be honest with herself: it wasn't a kiss to set the world on fire. Well, maybe at the time she'd thought it was a great kiss, but in hindsight it was more of a friendship kiss. And what about all their talk? That had been normal too. If he wanted her awake he couldn't very well have asked her boring questions about her second grade teacher.

"Why are you looking at me like that?" he asked.

She was looking at him and thinking that this could not possibly work with both of them living under the same roof in the isolated ghost town. She would have liked to think that the town gossips would be up in arms, but the truth was that they would no doubt think of her and William as teacher and pupil, with no possibility of scandal. Jackie was sure this was the way William saw it, too. Jackie was his mentor, his hero, his teacher, the one who had shown him how to catch bugs, how to swing on ropes, how to hold his breath for a full minute. No, she was sure she would have no problem with William.

The problem would be with Jackie herself. For the life of her she could not look at this gorgeous young man and remember that he was just a boy and that she was, by comparison, an old woman. When you feel that you are eighteen, it's difficult to remember that you aren't. Sometimes it's a shock to look in the mirror and see the aging face looking back. Never again was a man going to say to her, "When you wake up, you look like a kid." Now she didn't look like a kid even after an hour spent putting on makeup. Oh, she looked good, and she well knew it, but she no longer looked eighteen and she never would again.

"I think it would be better if you lived in Chandler," she said in her best adult voice. "It would be better for . . . It would just be better, that's all." She did her best to keep her voice neutral. If you lusted after a man ten years younger than you, a man you used to baby-sit, was that incest?

"In order to start a business we must spend a great deal of time together, and I think it would be ridiculous to have to drive the forty miles back and forth to Chandler every day. What if we wanted to discuss something at night?"

"Telephone."

"What if you needed help with the planes?"

"I've gotten along rather well without you until now. I think I can continue to manage."

"What if *I* suddenly had a question?"

"Wait until morning. You know, like you have to wait until morning to open your Christmas presents."

He walked away from her, put his foot on the rail of the bar, his elbow on the counter, and his head on his hand. Now all he needed was a shot of red-eye and a six-gun at his hip and he'd look like a gunslinger, Jackie thought. Out, she thought. She definitely had to get him *out* of Eternity and as far away from her as possible.

After a while he turned back to her, his face serious, and she remembered the solemn little boy he had been. "No," he said, then held out his hand to her as though to help her up.

Jackie didn't feel quite old enough yet to need

help getting out of a chair. "What does that mean? No?"

"It means that I will live in Eternity for as long as it takes. I have decided."

"You have —" she said, nearly sputtering. For a moment she felt as though she were again his baby-sitter and he were disobeying her, but when she stood in front of him, she had to look up, and she was looking into the eyes of a man, not the eyes of a child. Turning on her heel, she left the saloon, her anger evident with every step she took.

She walked for some time, walked far out into the desert that surrounded Eternity and tried to think about what she was doing. It embarrassed her greatly that she had felt such . . . such strong feelings for this young man that first night. Why hadn't some sixth sense told her that she knew more about life than he did? Why hadn't she picked up on the clues that she was dealing not with a grown-up but with a large child? And of course there must have been clues. There was . . . And, well, there was . . . Think as hard as she might, she couldn't remember anything that would have been a clue that he was a great deal younger than she was.

Except maybe that he was a lot of fun that night. Why was it that the older people got, the less they wanted to laugh? It would seem that the opposite would be true. Age *needed* laughter to help it along. Where once you bounced out of bed in the morning, as a person got older there wasn't much bouncing. Laughter might help a person through all the aches and pains, the muscles that no longer stretched but seemed to catch in place. But the older people got, the less they laughed. Maybe that was a way to guess their age. If they laugh fifty times a day, they're kids. Twenty times a day means they're in their twenties. Ten times a day and they're mid-thirties. By the time they reach their forties nothing seems to make them laugh.

About a year ago Jackie had gone out with a very nice man to dinner where they had met three other couples. Throughout the dinner there had not been one scrap of laughter. It had been all talk of money and mortgages and where the best steak bargains could be had. Later, her date had asked Jackie if she'd had a good time, and she had replied that the people seemed . . . well, a little old. To this the man had stiffly replied that his friends were younger than she was. "In years only," she had snapped, and that was the last time she'd heard from him.

So now her problem was one young man, one very young man by the name of William Montgomery. She needed to get rid of him, needed to get him away from her. She didn't trust herself around him. She had felt a pull toward him the night he had taken her from the plane, and she'd felt it again this morning. Maybe it was just the absence of male company for so many months, especially when she had spent so many years almost exclusively with men, but she didn't think so.

There was something about Billy's solemnity, something about the way he did what he said he was going to do, that appealed to her. Hell, she thought, after years of Charley, she might fall in love with a blue-faced monkey if the creature followed through on his ideas, if he did what he said he was going to do.

Chapter Four

As Jackie drove into the ghost town that had become home to her, she couldn't seem to keep her heart from leaping a bit. The light on the porch glowed warmly, and more lights shone from inside the house. Someone was waiting inside for her. It wasn't an empty house but one warm with the life of another person.

Mentally she shook herself, forcing herself to stop fantasizing. The man inside was just a boy, and he was her *business* partner and nothing more. Quietly, so as not to alert him, she closed the car door and entered the house. It was redolent of cooking, alive with warmth and light. Never had the pretty house felt more welcoming.

He was standing in the kitchen, facing the sink, his back to her. His sleeves were rolled up, his strong brown forearms damp with soapy water as he washed a sink full of dirty dishes. For a moment she stood silently in the doorway watching him. She knew that he was a banker, a student of numbers, a man who had spent most of his life with his nose pointed toward a book, but he had the body of an athlete. Having grown up in Chandler, she knew that the Montgomerys loved any form of exercise; they rowed and swam, rode horses, climbed up rock faces to the tops of mountains, walked when they could have ridden.

William's body was evidence of all that exercise. Under his thin cotton shirt, his brown back was one hillock of muscle after another, hills and valleys of a landscape of great beauty. Strong thighs strained against his trousers, tight buttocks curved against the fabric. Jackie had to put her hands to her sides, her fingers curled into a taut ball, to try to still the ache she felt at wanting to touch him. She wanted to slip her arms about his waist, press her face against his back, then feel him turn to kiss her upturned face.

"Would you like some coffee?" he asked softly, his back still turned toward her. His words made her jump. How long had he known she was there? Had he been watching her face in the reflection of the dark kitchen window in front of him?

"No," she managed to whisper as she turned to leave the room. She should, of course, have accepted his offer of coffee, then sat down with him and had a bit of conversation. She had sat with hundreds of men in the evenings, talking of planes or of people they both knew, of politics, of anything that came to her mind. Rarely had she been attracted to any of them. And certainly she'd never felt like this before. What caused attraction anyway? she wondered. What made you able to sit and talk comfortably with one man and not with another? Often she'd seen women fall hard for some guy or another, men who didn't seem in any way special to her. Now she was the one who was falling, the one whose palms got sweaty whenever a certain man was near. She was the one who was unable to talk or even to think coherently when he was close to her.

But whatever she felt for him, she reminded herself, *this* man was taboo.

Her head came up, and she gave her best adult smile to William. "Isn't it past your bedtime?"

She meant to insult him, to put him in his place, which was in the nursery, but he didn't look insulted. Instead, he gave her a slow smile that made her feel quite warm. "I wouldn't mind going to bed. How about you?"

To her consternation, Jackie felt herself blushing like an eighteen-year-old virgin. Worse than her confusion was the fact that she could think of no lighthearted put-down that would let him know that he was a boy while she was a mature, sophisticated woman.

Looking at her confusion, he gave a little laugh, then said, "Come outside. I want to show you something."

Companionably he slipped her hand through his strong bent arm and led her outside. "I missed you tonight," he said softly, holding on to her hand when she tried to pull away. "All right," he said cheerfully. "I'll behave. I have been thinking about expansion."

That got her attention. "Expansion? How can we expand something that hasn't even been born yet? When you're as young as you are, you think that everything is possible, but when you get older, you learn that there are limits to what a person can do." There, she thought, that should do it. That should put him in his place. Her body might lust after him, but her mind was a great deal wiser than his.

William didn't even seem to notice the little bit of wisdom she was offering him. "When you're as rich as I am, a great many things are possible."

So much for wisdom, she thought. When it came to a toss-up between wisdom and money, unfortunately money usually won. She told herself that she should be offended by his blatant reference to his wealth, but on the other hand, she rather liked it. She'd always had contempt for people who pretended that they had a difficult life in spite of the fact that they had servants lounging about, waiting for the opportunity to serve.

However, like what he said or not, she wasn't going to miss an opportunity to remind him of the age difference. "I think that as you grow older, you'll find that there are some things in this world that carry more weight than money."

"And what are they?"

"Intelligence. Wisdom. Happiness. Ah . . . ah

. . ." She thought for a moment, then looked up into his smiling eyes, the moonlight on his hair. He was firmly holding on to her hand. With a sigh of defeat, she said, "What's your idea?" She was a woman who liked to *do,* and this talk of philosophical ideals was wearing on her.

William laughed — that patronizing little laugh that was beginning to annoy her — kissed her on the forehead as though she were a child, and pointed to the empty fields that lay to the south of Eternity. "We could build another airstrip there, a place where a couple of big planes could take off. A Bellanca maybe. Is that the right name?"

"Yes," she said softly, "that's the right name."

"We could start a carrier service from Denver to Los Angeles."

"This is Chandler, not Denver."

"We open an airstrip outside Denver, but we run the business from here, carrying goods from my family to Denver, delivering there, picking up people and cargo in Denver, then flying to Los Angeles."

He didn't seem to notice how quiet Jackie had become. "Who's going to fly these planes?"

"You can train people. I have a few cousins who'd love to learn how to fly. And if you become the first woman to win the Taggie, you'll attract many women who want to learn to fly. Maybe you could have all women pilots. You'd like that, wouldn't you?"

She was sure he was trying to be nice to her, saying he'd fund a company of all women pilots, and in other circumstances she'd have been grateful, but now all she heard was the word "Taggie." Instantly she pulled away from him. "Win the Taggie? Are you out of your mind? I have no intention of entering that race, much less trying to win it."

"Why?" he asked simply. "You're the best pilot in the world, better than any man, certainly better than any other woman. You can fly rings around anyone. Last year the man who won the Taggie didn't have half your experience or skill. He was nothing compared to you."

Heaven, but it felt nice to be confronted with such blatant hero worship. Especially since she knew that what he'd said was true. She'd once flown with the winner of last year's Taggie, and at the time she'd thought he shouldn't have a license to fly a child's string toy, much less his own plane. He'd won on luck, not skill.

"I'm not going to enter that race or any other," she said, turning on her heel and starting to walk away.

He caught her arm. "But why, Jackie? You're the best pilot in America, maybe in the world, but you never enter any of the big races. You used to set records for endurance and speed, but a few years ago you stopped entering races. It was as though everyone else kept moving forward but you stopped. I used to think you'd lost your nerve, but that's not true; I've *seen* that you haven't lost your nerve. So why won't you enter the race and win it?"

"Because I'm too old," she said quickly, wanting to say anything to make him stop talking about this. "My reflexes aren't as fast as those of these youngsters flying today. I've been in this business a long, long time and —"

William said a very vulgar word that perfectly and quite correctly described what she was trying to make him believe. "You are lying to me. Why?"

She hated it when people didn't believe what they were told. Why couldn't people just accept what others told them? Why couldn't William accept that she was too old to fly in that blasted race and leave it at that? "I don't like races," she said. "They are a useless waste of gasoline in a time of need in our country. While other people are hungry, pilots are engaging in senseless waste. When you're older, you'll realize that money can be better spent in more intelligent ways than on races and other folderol."

At that little speech, William snorted in derision. "What's wrong with the American economy right now is the absence of money in circulation. People are hoarding what funds they have, too terrified to spend. What this country needs is more spending, not less. And races like the Taggie give depressed people pleasure."

He stopped talking and looked at her hard, as though he wanted to see inside her soul. When she turned her head away so he couldn't see into her eyes, he put his fingertips under her chin and raised her face to meet his eyes. "There's more to this than you're saying. Why won't you tell me the truth?"

Angrily she jerked away from him, moving into the darkness of the night, into the black shade of the old dress shop so he couldn't see into her eyes. Stupid, she thought, it was really stupid of her to feel so bad because she was disappointing him. Many, many people had thought she should enter races and competitions, and she'd laughed their suggestions off. But she had an irrational desire to please William.

In spite of what she meant to say, the words that came out of her mouth startled her. "Why? What does it matter whether I win some race or not?" There was an almost plaintive tone to her voice, she thought in disgust. Why don't you like me as I *am?* she seemed to be saying.

"I want you to be remembered," he answered simply, and it didn't take a genius to know what he meant. The history books always remembered the people who did the most, the best, who flew the highest, the fastest, the longest, whatever. If Jackie stopped setting records, winning races, the things that she had done would die with her. Never in her life would she say so aloud, but she had thought of this many times. Sometimes she felt anger and quite a bit of envy to read that some whippersnapper of a pilot who didn't have as much knowledge in his head as Jackie had in her little finger, had won a place in the history books by setting some aviation record.

"You've thought of it," he said, as much to himself as to her. When she turned away from him again, he took a deep breath. "All right, I'll stop. For tonight, anyway, but not forever. You're going to tell me the truth if I have to . . ."

"To what?" she asked, meaning to challenge him in a tough sort of way, but her voice came out instead in a tone of teasing.

"I'll have to challenge you to a duel." Even in the dark she could see that his eyes were sparkling.

"Do I get to choose the weapons?"

"Sure," he answered in the same tone. "Anything you want. Swords, pistols." He wiggled his eyebrows. "A wrestling match."

"Airplanes," she said. "We will duel with planes." She started laughing when William groaned as though in great agony.

As they laughed, their eyes locked. What was more dangerous than shared laughter? Laughter was more powerful than all the kisses in the world. You could keep from falling in love with a man whose only attraction was a feeling of sexual interest, but how could you not fall in love with a man who made you laugh? Laughing with a man made you dream of a life with a man who could see the bright side of life, a man who would smile when the going got worse.

"Don't," she said softly and turned away from him, starting back to the house.

He didn't move from where he was but instead watched her walk away from him.

Chapter Five

Two days later, after yet another restless night, Jackie knew she had to do something. Each night she seemed to turn over many times, and each time she awoke and listened for a sound from William. Of course she knew that he was two floors above her and she couldn't possibly hear him, but that didn't make any difference. She knew he was there; she could feel his presence.

On the morning of the third day, at about three A.M., she awoke and had a mature, intelligent talk with herself. Her conclusion was that either he had to leave or she would go crazy. When she was younger, she always liked to know why she did something, and if she found that her behavior was based on something childish, like jealousy or envy, she tried to overcome the feeling. But with age came the wisdom to know that everyone was human. For whatever reason, she knew that she *had* to get rid of him. Suppose Terri came to visit and found her and William occupying the same house? She could hear all the snide hometown things that would be said about "robbing the cradle" and "wet behind the ears." If this were Paris she might get away with what seemed to be occupying her every waking and sleeping thought, but this was backwoods, unsophisticated Chandler, Colorado, and a thirty-eight-year-old woman did not take up with a man ten years younger than herself.

And if the age difference wasn't enough, there was William's talk of the Taggie. She needed to stop that right now. William had the eyes of a zealot, of a do-gooder. He meant for her to win that race so she could enter the history books. With that sparkle in his eyes, he was likely to do something absurd, such as announce to the town that she was going to enter, hoping to force her to change her mind.

As she began to dress, Jackie couldn't help feeling sad, for she knew that what she was doing was possibly the stupidest thing she'd ever done in her life, but even that knowledge didn't keep her from doing it. Having a man with the money and business acumen of William Montgomery was something that every underpaid glory hound of a pilot dreamed of. William wasn't trying to steal the spotlight from Jackie, nor was he trying to take over the directorship of the business. He just wanted to stay in the background and do all the boring work of managing the money. He deferred to Jackie at every turn, saying things like "I'm sure you know best."

It was infuriating. But what was *really* infuriating about him was that she loved being around his slow, deliberate ways. She didn't know how else to explain it: William made her feel safe.

The first day he had asked her where she kept

91

her books, and they then had gone through an annoying hassle while Jackie figured out that he wasn't trying to get into her bedroom where she had her one and only bookcase. He had wanted ledgers telling who owed what and how much to her. "Oh, that," she'd said, then began to rattle off to him how much various people in town owed her for the use of the airfield, for carrying a package to Denver, for begging a ride with her to Trinidad. She could remember who had paid her and how much was still owed. She remembered dates of flights and how long they took. She remembered who had paid her in chickens and who in cash.

After sitting spellbound while listening to this rendition of her monetary life, William blinked a few times and said he'd buy ledgers and draw up a proper set of books. Trying to be as flippant as possible, Jackie had swept from the room, tossing over her shoulder, "I hope you don't expect me to record every penny I make in some book."

Jackie's plan was to make William say he was leaving; also she wanted to make it quite clear to him and to anyone visiting them that there was nothing whatsoever between them except business. So maybe in trying to reach this end she hadn't exactly been the most gracious of business partners. And it was indeed stupid to try to sabotage herself, but with every passing day she liked William more.

Nothing she said seemed to bother him. He was the soul of calmness. When three people had called in one day to cancel planned flights to Denver, she could have pulled the hair out of the nearest person, which of course was William. All day long she'd picked on him. "Of course, what would a kid like you know about disappointment?" she said. "You haven't been alive long enough to understand how difficult life can sometimes be." William hadn't said a word to her, just raised one eyebrow in a way that made her want to crawl under a table. It would have been easier to believe he was a kid if he had acted like one.

With each passing minute Jackie could see the possibility of danger in being too near this young man. So she strengthened her resolve to stay away from him. The first night he had used her kitchen when she wasn't there, but the second night he'd asked if he could come down from the top floor and use her kitchen, since all he had was a hot plate. She didn't feel she could refuse him this request, and for one long, delicious moment, she thought of sitting at the table in the kitchen with a man and laughing across a bottle of wine. She had to shake herself to make the image go away. At dinnertime she had found that she had to make an emergency drive into Chandler to pick up a box of tissues.

While she was in the local diner having a plate of something the cook called the day's special, Reynata had come to sit by her.

"Do you mind?" the young, beautiful girl asked.

"Not at all," Jackie replied.

After the girl was seated and had ordered a Coke, she looked at Jackie. "Are you going to be the first woman to win the Taggie?"

That had brought Jackie out of her melancholy. "Where did you hear something like that?"

"One guess."

Jackie smiled. "I seem to remember that William did mention that. He has a bad case of hero worship. You know, a lot of young men feel that way about older women."

"I'm not sure that's how William feels about you." Rey was smiling and fiddling with her straw.

At that Jackie jumped up from the table. "Look, there is nothing between Billy Montgomery and me except a business arrangement, and anyone who says there is, is a damned liar! He's a kid to me and nothing more. I used to change his diapers. I can't even look at him without seeing him with a milk mustache on his fat little-boy face. I'm always wanting to pat his head and sing lullabies to him. I want to —" She broke off because every person in the diner had stopped talking and was looking at her.

Great, Jackie thought, where there had been no suspicion, now there was. "I have to go," she had mumbled to Rey before practically running out the door.

So now, after three days of William's calm, of William's organization, of William's eyes, which sometimes made Jackie shiver, she knew that she had to get rid of him. But how? Insults didn't seem to affect him — they never had. When he was a kid, Jackie had said lots of rude things to him to try to get him to go away, but nothing had worked. And oddly enough, she had begun to enjoy his silent company. He was so rock solid, something dependable in her life that seemed to have no stability.

So, now, how did she make him go away? Make him go away before the whole town started talking about the two of them?

Chapter Six

W ould you like to go flying with me, Billy?" Jackie asked in her sweetest voice. "I'd like to see what you can do with a plane." The smile she gave him made honey look poisonous. It had taken some thought, but she had remembered William's caution, his great love of safety. As a child, the only time she'd ever been able to get rid of him was one day when she'd pulled him onto a log stretched high across a cold, rock-filled, rushing stream. He'd walked the log, but later he'd said, "I don't like you anymore," and Jackie hadn't seen him for over a week. Of course she wouldn't admit it back then, but she'd found herself missing him. In the end, she'd "stopped by" his house for a visit. His mother had pointed Billy out and Jackie had found herself walking toward him. They didn't say anything — nothing so ridiculous as apologies — but when she left, William was tagging along behind her, and it was four whole days before Jackie had told him he was a nuisance.

Today, she thought, this airplane was going to be another log across a stream. Only this time she wouldn't go after him and bring him back.

One of the Wacos William had purchased was equipped with pilot and student gear so the plane could be flown from both seats. William was in front, Jackie in the back. Pete, her mechanic, gave the propeller a turn, and Jackie gave a thumbs-up sign to William as he started down the runway.

Again she smiled at him. He looked so sweet, so innocent, sitting there, and his every gesture told her that he wanted to impress her with his flying skills. William was so methodical that she wondered if he'd taken lessons just because his heroine, Jackie, knew how to fly.

But Jackie knew that flying, like anything else in life, was a talent and talent could not be taught. You could teach a skill and a person could learn to fly by the book, but there were some who had the talent and some who didn't.

A few years ago a manufacturer had produced a beautiful little single-wing plane. He thought it was going to revolutionize aviation, and with great hope, he sent the first test pilot up. The plane performed better than anyone had expected, but a few hours later the pilot, for no apparent reason, crashed into a mountain.

The designer tried to tell people that the crash was the result of pilot error, but pilots, a superstitious lot, said the plane was jinxed. Another prototype rolled off the line and a second pilot took it up. Exactly the same thing happened. After the second crash, no one in the flying world could get near the plane without crossing himself or laughing, or both.

Desperate, the designer went to Jackie and offered her a large sum of money to take his plane up. Jackie felt that if your time came, it didn't matter if you were on the ground or in the air and she would much rather be in the air, so she accepted the man's offer. Many people asked her not to go, but she didn't listen to them.

In the air, the little plane was a dream. It handled beautifully, the stick so easy that she felt she could almost go to sleep while flying, and she wanted to stay up forever. Unexpectedly, the first tank ran out of gas about thirty minutes before it should have. The engine sputtered and died in the air. Without much concern, Jackie flipped the switch to the second tank and restarted the engine. Nothing happened. Either the second tank was empty or there was a blockage in the line and the gas couldn't get to the engine.

"This is it," Jackie said to herself and for a moment she wondered how she could tell the people on the ground that what had killed the other pilots was a faulty fuel line. Oddly enough, considering she was facing certain death, her head was completely clear as she looked at the switch to the gas tank. On and off, the little printed label said. Or did it read, Off and On? She flipped it the other way, tried the engine, and it started.

Laughing, she brought the plane to the ground and had the great pleasure of informing the designer that the only thing wrong with his plane was that someone had labeled the fuel switch wrong. The other pilots had inadvertently switched it off. No one but Jackie had thought of flipping the switch the other way. Talent. Instinct. Whatever. Jackie had lived because she *didn't* fly by the book.

After ten minutes in the plane with William, Jackie knew that he would never have thought to flip the switch the other way. William was an utterly perfect flyer. There was a rule behind every movement he made. He took no chances, was absolutely safe.

After thirty minutes, Jackie was bored to tears. Couldn't he understand that flying was creative? Airplanes had nothing to do with books. Airplanes moved through the air. What could be more creative than that? Yet William flew as though there were road signs stuck in the clouds. She fully expected to see him extend his hand and signal a right turn.

After forty-five minutes, she could stand no more. Mentioning to him that she wanted to take over, she took the controls.

There were two ways to fly: with passengers and without. Usually Jackie tried to behave herself when she had a passenger, but now she wanted to make William say that he didn't want to be partners with her and maybe, too, she wanted to show off a bit.

First off: clean out the cockpit. Daredevil pilots loved to brag that they had very clean cockpits. All they had to do was turn the plane upside down and give a little wiggle to the wings. Simple. Of course you had to make sure the seat belt was fastened. It had happened that people had fallen out.

Jackie turned the plane upside down and wiggled, then did it again. Quickly she came out of the position to move forward and swoop upside down again. She didn't want to miss a smidgen of debris. Dust and dirt, a few chewing gum wrappers, flew past her face. In front of her, William's strong hands were gripping the sides of the cockpit as he held himself in.

Jackie had made a good living and a name for herself with barnstorming and thrilling crowds. The more chances she took, the more she got paid — and she was paid very well.

Twists came next. She flipped wing over wing over wing. Quickly she went into a loop, turning in a complete vertical circle. This was followed by her own special creation that someone had called a dippy twist loop, in which she did a twist and a loop at the same time.

When she came out of the dippy, she went into a stall and the world suddenly seemed unnaturally silent until she started the engine again.

Years before, when she was learning to fly, Charley had made sure that she knew how to handle herself in every emergency. He'd made her take off from beaches, roadways, ball parks, racetracks.

She'd had to fly right-side up, upside down, in crosswinds, tailwinds, no wind. He'd taught her how to handle a fire on board and ice on the wings. When there was thick fog between her and the ground, he'd shown her how to orient herself by burning a hole in the fog with her engine heat. He'd taught her how to land on water and what to do if she was swept out to sea.

She decided to show William nearly everything she'd learned. She raced around tall trees, calculating the distance between them by inches. One miscalculation and the wings would have been torn off. The moment she was through the trees, she did a couple of snap rolls. Nailing the nose to the horizon, she did several three hundred and sixty degree lateral turns, one after another, coming out about a quarter of an inch before she would have flown smack into a mountain.

About a week after she ran off with Charley, during which time he'd rarely let her out of a plane, he'd said, "Kid, you got a gyroscope in your head. If you're upside down and backwards it's all the same to you. You know where you're going." Now Jackie flew upside down for a while, maneuvering through the trees with her head pointed toward the ground.

She knew she was getting low on gas so she headed back to Eternity, writing her name in the sky as she went. Skywriting lost something with no flares attached to the tail of the plane, but the motion was the same.

As she hit the hard-packed runway in Eternity,

the engine died from lack of gas. Perfect, she thought. She had calculated perfectly. Charley would have been proud of her.

After Jackie landed the plane, William stayed in his seat, not moving, his head back, his eyes closed, and she could see that he was fighting hard not to be ill. There weren't many people who could go through what William had just experienced and not lose a meal. But somehow he was managing to control his stomach.

Standing up, Jackie reached her hand out to him, and briefly — *very* briefly — he opened his eyes to glance at her, then gave a faint shake of his head. He was not going to accept her offer of a steadying hand when he disembarked.

On the ground, Jackie politely looked away as he somehow climbed down from the plane without anyone's help. When she turned to look at him his face was white, his skin clammy-looking, and he wasn't too steady on his feet.

"All right, Jackie," he said solemnly, as he took a deep breath, working hard to control his nausea. "You win. I'll pack my bags and leave. I'll be out of here in a matter of hours."

Now that she'd done what she planned, she couldn't help feeling bad. She didn't want to discontinue their friendship; she just wanted him out of her house and out of her life on a daily basis. "William, I . . ."

When he turned to look at her, his eyes blazed, and his white skin was tinged with the deep glow of anger. No, there was more in his eyes than anger; there was rage. Old-fashioned life-endangering rage.

When he spoke, his voice was very soft and very quiet. "So now I guess you'll tell me you want to be friends. That you've always had a high regard for me and you'll always treasure my friendship." He took a step toward her, looming over her. "I don't want your friendship, Jackie. I never wanted your friendship. Since I was a little boy I've wanted your love."

At that statement she made the mistake of giving the slightest smile, and that smile seemed to make something in William break. Even as a child he had been mild-mannered and sweet-tempered, but now he seemed to turn into something fierce, something dangerous. When he took a step toward her, she stepped back.

"Does my wanting your love amuse you? Is it something to make you laugh? Stupid little Billy Montgomery following tall, eccentric Jackie O'Neill around. Oh, yes, you've always been eccentric. Even as a child you were different from everyone else. The other kids were trying their best to be carbon copies of each other, but not you. Oh, I know you thought that what you wanted was to wear the latest fashions and be part of the group, but the truth was, you loved climbing on your mother's roof and hammering the tiles in place. You loved having an excuse to get away from the other kids in your class so you could do exactly what you wanted to do. When you were sixteen and no girl would be caught dead climbing trees and swinging on ropes, *you* were doing those things. You have always done what you wanted and the rest of the world be damned."

He wasn't presenting a very pretty picture of her. He made her sound odd and selfish. She opened her mouth to speak, but he leaned over her until her back was bent.

"And I loved you for having the courage to be who you were. You didn't try to conform. In this town where everyone knows everyone else, you found a way, an excuse, to be who you wanted to be. You found a way to do what you wanted to do. And when an opportunity came for you to get out of here, you didn't hesitate, you took that opening. No fear, no second thoughts, not even a backward glance. You saw what you wanted and you went after it.

"I loved that in you, Jackie. I may have been a little boy, but I saw quite clearly what you were and what you were going to do, and I loved you for it. I'm a man now and I know that what I felt then wasn't puppy love. I don't have any way to explain it. I loved you as a man then, and that's the way I love you now."

"Now?" she whispered, looking into his eyes. It certainly was difficult to think of him as a child at this moment.

"Yes, now! Maybe we're alike but in opposite ways. Since the first time I saw you I have loved you. I was just five years old when my mother opened the door to you. You stood there, fifteen years old, too tall, too thin, your hair hanging in your eyes because you'd been in too much of a hurry to tie it back. You were pretty in an obscure way, but you weren't going to make any man's heart stop beating. You very nearly made mine stop, though. I looked up at you and I fell in love with you, and I've never stopped loving you since."

He seemed to grow taller as he leaned over her even farther. "I was the one who got my father to establish the Taggie, hoping to entice you back to Chandler. I was the one who had my father write to you after Charley died and ask you to start a flying service for our family. I anonymously sponsored six air shows for you and Charley at times when I knew that Charley had drunk your funds away. It was my uncle who pointed out to the president your good deed in saving the burn victims."

She was blinking at him. "You?" was all that she could whisper.

"Yes, me. I have loved you always. Always. Without hesitation. Just as you took one look at an airplane and knew that flying was what you were supposed to do in life, I took one look at you and knew that you and I were meant to be together. I've dated very few women. I've never been to bed with a woman because I felt I would have been betraying you. I waited for you, and while I was waiting, I took care of you to the best of my ability."

Suddenly he straightened and glared at her. "And now this. You."

104

The way he said "you" made her skin crawl.

"I misjudged you. I thought you had a spine. I thought you had the courage of your convictions. You could run away with a man twice your age and thumb your nose at an entire town. You learned to fly an airplane better than any man alive, and you can laugh at the idea that a man is equal to *you*. You swung on tree branches when other girls were afraid to get their hair wet. You can do whatever you want in life. You live life exactly how *you* want, without thought for what the rest of the world thinks, but when it comes to loving, you're a coward. You're ready to throw me away merely because our drivers' licenses say we're different ages."

She started to defend herself, but he wouldn't allow it.

"Don't you dare try to lie to me or to yourself. The only thing standing between us is your ridiculous notion that we *shouldn't* be together because of our ages. You won't let yourself get to know me. You're afraid to have a conversation with me for fear you might find out that I have a head — a *man's* head — on my shoulders. I'm no more a boy than you are an adult. I was born an old man, and you, Jackie, were born a child, and you'll always be a child. You will never grow up, or at least you'll never grow old. Do you know one of the reasons I love you so much?"

"No," she whispered.

"Because you keep me young. No matter how old you get, you will always have the freshness of a child. You have no idea how other people's minds work. We who are ordinary think about mortgages and our aching backs, but you don't. You never have and you never will. You think in terms of doing whatever you want at any time you want. If you want to fly an airplane, you do so. Never mind that other people tell you not to. I was eaten with jealousy of Charley. He knew exactly what you were and he had sense enough to reach out and grab you. You were grateful to him, but he knew that he should have been on his knees kissing the ground in thanks that he'd had the privilege of meeting you. He knew that you'd take care of him and make him laugh while you were doing it. He knew your value very well."

William gave a little snort. "Before you left, Charley ruffled my hair and said, 'Better luck next time, kid.' You were a prize for him then, and you're a prize now."

William's handsome face distorted into the barest of sneers, and the way he looked her up and down made her feel ashamed of herself. "At least you *were* a prize. I never thought it would happen, but you got old, Jackie. You became an old woman."

He stood in front of her for a moment as though waiting for something. Maybe he expected her to throw her arms around him and tell him that she hadn't grown old, and her proof was that she was willing to live with a man ten years younger than she was. But she couldn't do it. She just couldn't do it. No matter what he said, when she looked

106

at him, she saw little Billy Montgomery, and until she got that image out of her head she'd never be able to think of him as anything except a child.

After a long moment of silence, at last he said, "All right, Jackie, you win. Or do we both lose?" He gave a sigh that came from deep within him. "I'll pack and be out of here immediately."

She didn't move as he walked away. Part of her was sad, but a big part of her was relieved. Now she'd have no more indecision, no more agony. No more watching his strong young body move about the house; no more lying awake to listen for the sound of him.

As she turned away from the house, she wanted to walk, walk for hours and miles. She didn't want to see him leave; she wanted to put off entering the empty house for as long as possible.

She wasn't crying, so she should have been able to see where she was going, but for some reason she wasn't looking. Maybe her mind was too pre-occupied, but whatever the reason, she didn't re-alize that there was no ground in front of her, just a steep drop down into a rocky arroyo filled with rusting debris from generations of litterers. Usually agile, she tried to catch herself, but her foot landed on loose rock and she went tumbling.

She didn't fall very far, but she landed in the middle of a rusty heap of metal that had once been a Ford. Dazed for a moment, she shook her head, mentally feeling if she'd broken any bones. She hadn't. Everything was all right, and she couldn't help smiling in relief. Still smiling, she wiped her hand across her forehead and felt the hot, thick, dampness that could only be blood. Pulling her hand away, she saw that it was covered with blood and there was more flowing out of what looked to be a deep cut in the palm of her right hand. All around her were sharp edges of rust-covered metal, and she knew that she'd cut herself on one of them. Thoughts of lockjaw immediately went through her head.

"Jackie!"

She wasn't surprised to hear William's voice, shouting for her with some urgency. As a child he'd been able to sense when she needed help. And no matter where she was, he could always find her.

"Here," she shouted up toward the ridge of the arroyo, but her voice didn't come out as a shout. It sounded weak and helpless, as though she were a shadow instead of a real person. But William obviously heard her, for he appeared at the top of the arroyo, high above her head, stopping for a moment, his back to the setting sun, as he looked down at her.

She had no idea how bad she looked until she saw William's face. He was as pale as she felt. Glancing down, she saw blood all over her — on her shirtfront, on her trousers, and no doubt on her face — and her hand didn't seem to be in any hurry to stop bleeding. An unending supply of fresh red blood seemed to be slowly making its way out of her palm.

Jackie closed her eyes for just a moment, but it was long enough for William to make his way down the arroyo. As though he were far away, she heard him tearing down the hillside, rocks flying. Dreamily she smiled and wondered if the rocks were moving out of William's way.

"Jackie," he said softly, "wake up. Do you hear me? Wake up."

"I'm not asleep," she answered, but she felt odd, as though she were in her body yet not in it. "Haven't we done this before?" she said, smiling. "Are you going to rescue me again?"

"Yeah, kid. Hang on and I'll get you out of here."

She smiled at his calling her kid. Charley used to call her kid. In fact most all men she came to know very well called her that at one point or another. She was vaguely aware of William moving about her. When she heard the sound of ripping cloth, she opened her eyes as wide as they would go, which didn't seem to be very far. William was bare-chested, his broad chest covered with nothing but clean, smooth muscle, no hair on his chest to speak of, just that lovely warm-looking skin.

"Listen to me, Jackie," he said. "You've lost quite a bit of blood and you seem to be going into shock. I want you to concentrate and do what I tell you. You understand?"

She nodded, smiling a bit, but she came alert when he quickly tied a tourniquet about her wrist, using strips of his torn shirt. There hadn't been any pain before, but that thing hurt.

"Does it hurt?" he asked.

"Yes," she answered, trying to be brave.

"Good. The pain will keep you awake. Now I'm going to get you up and out of here so a doctor can stitch you up."

"It doesn't need stitches. Really. It's hardly a scratch. Just a little cut. A bit of tape will fix it."

"Coward," he said, as he hoisted her over his bare shoulder and began the climb up the hill.

Jackie thought that her entire body was the same width as one of his shoulders. She was coming out of her initial shock, and her hand was beginning to hurt. "If your father fires you, you can get a job rescuing damsels in distress. Of course, it will be hard on your wardrobe. William, aren't I awfully heavy?" She practically purred the last remark, hoping he'd say that she weighed nothing at all.

"Yes, you are. You look rather thin, so one would think you'd be light, but you're not. You're quite substantial."

What had she expected from a man who organized everything inside her kitchen cabinets by size? Whimsy?

"You know, I can walk. I cut my hand, not my foot, and I'm feeling better now. If I'm too heavy for you, I should walk."

"No" was all William said.

When he reached the top of the steep arroyo, she thought he would put her down, but he didn't. Instead, he held on to her and walked back toward the house. She really was all right now, except that pain was shooting up her arm and beginning to fill her entire body. Her arms were hanging down William's back, and there was so much blood on her hand that she couldn't see the cut very well, but she told herself it wasn't very deep. Surely it wasn't deep enough to need stitches. She had always bled a great deal, hadn't she? That was just a sign of her good health. In fact, she didn't see any need to call a doctor. A little soap, a good tight bandage, and she'd be fine.

As though he were reading her mind, William said, "Stitches and no argument."

With a grimace, she put her hand back down and stopped looking at it.

Three hours later, stitched up, as she said, like a Hong Kong suit, and ensconced in bed, Jackie felt like an idiot. How could she have been so stupid as to fall down the side of a canyon?

While she was contemplating her lack of intelligence, her bedroom door opened and William entered carrying a tray of food, which he placed over her knees.

"Chicken soup, crackers, salad, lemonade, and chocolate pudding for dessert. Now eat and get well."

"Really, Billy, I am perfectly capable of feeding myself. Anyone would think I'd just had a bout of typhoid fever from the way you're acting. I'm going to get up and —" While William watched with a knowing expression on his face, she pushed the tray away and started to stand up. Immediately she felt light-headed and dizzy. The back of her hand to her forehead like the Victorian dainty she felt like, she lay back down on the bed.

"What were you saying? You're not feeling bad are you, Jackie? It's just a little cut, a mere twenty-six stitches, and the loss of enough blood to keep three vampires healthy for a month. So why are you in bed? Why don't you take a plane up? Do a few stunts?"

She was sure she deserved his sarcasm. After all, she had acted like a baby during the stitching. Young Blair had raced to her house, driving his father's car as though it were a grounded airplane, and the moment Jackie saw him, she had started trying to talk him out of sticking needles in her skin. Young Blair — called that to distinguish him from his mother, also a doctor and also named Blair — had blinked at her a few times, but then he had looked at William as though for permission.

"Stitch. I'll hold her."

And that was what was done. Young Blair stitched while William held Jackie in his strong arms and soothed her as though she were an infant. He stroked her hair and asked her really dumb questions about airplanes. He seemed to be trying to make her angry or to make her laugh, or maybe he just wanted to distract her. To some extent he succeeded, for after the twentieth stitch, William's constant questions, added to the pain, annoyed her to the point that she said, "William Montgomery, you don't know anything about air-planes. You might as well have stayed with paper airplanes for all you know about flying. You have no talent, no feel for the machines or the air."

"Why won't you enter the Taggie?" he shot back, taking advantage of what she was going through to find out what she refused to tell him.

"Because — Oh! What are you using? A needle for stitching saddles? That happens to be my flesh you're gouging."

Young Blair didn't pay any attention to her as he continued stitching her hand. "Almost finished. This is a very bad cut, Jackie, and I want you to use your hand as little as possible for the next few days. I want you to give this time to heal. And that means no flying."

"But —"

William cut her off. "I'll take care of her."

"And who is going to take care of a youngster like you?" Jackie shot back, in so much pain that she didn't care what she said or whose feelings she hurt.

William didn't seem in the least bothered by her nasty remark. "I've hired an eighteen-year-old virgin to change my diapers. Do you mind?"

Jackie could feel her face turning red as she looked at Young Blair's head bowed over her palm. He didn't look up, but she could feel him smile. William had implied that she was jealous and that they were lovers — which of course was far from true. She wanted to explain to the doctor, but she couldn't think of what to say.

After the stitching was done and Jackie was at last free to rest her head against the pillows, she couldn't help feeling annoyed that Young Blair had taken William aside and talked to him as though he were Jackie's husband or even her father. "Keep her quiet," she heard Young Blair saying softly. "She'll be okay in a day or two, but she's going to need looking after until then."

"Of course," she'd heard William say, as though it was understood that this young — very young — man would take care of her.

So now William had prepared her a meal and was insisting that she eat it. "I'm not hungry," she said, and even to her own ears she sounded like a whining child.

William stood over her, looking down at her from his great height. "All right," he said softly, "have it your way. I'll call a nurse and pay her to take care of you for the next few days. I won't impose myself on you further."

"I can take care of myself," she said defiantly.

"Can you?" He arched an eyebrow. "How are you going to wash your hair with one hand? I guess you could leave it full of dried blood. Of course you might attract flies, but what does that matter? You're tough. You can take it. How are you going to feed yourself with one hand? There isn't enough food in this house now to feed a goldfish much less a hungry female. I think I'd better call a nurse. I believe I heard that Miss Norton is free."

At that name Jackie paled. Miss Norton was every child's nightmare of a nurse: big, strong, utterly unsympathetic. She had been born full-grown, with steel gray hair, wearing a starched white uniform and looking about fifty years old, and she'd never aged a day since her birth, which had to have been over a century before Jackie was born.

"I . . . Uh . . . Couldn't someone else come? Whatever happened to dear, sweet Mrs. Patterson?"

"Some of the mothers in town figured out that that cough syrup she was giving the kids was straight whiskey. We suggested she might be happier in a town other than Chandler. You can put up with me, I can call Miss Norton, or you can find your own nurse. But one thing I won't do is leave you here alone to take care of yourself. Not that you deserve my assistance after what you did to me today, but I cannot leave you here alone."

He cocked his head to one side. "What is your problem with me anyway, Jackie? Have I made an improper gesture toward you? Have I said anything to make you think that I have depraved intentions toward you?"

"Nooooo," she said, using what willpower she had to keep from blushing. Considering how much blood she had lost today, it was a wonder she could blush.

"Then what is wrong? Do you think that I might make advances toward you? After all, as you constantly remind me, I am just a boy. How could a mere child like me do any of the things you seem to think me capable of. Besides, you're an old woman, remember?"

"Yes," she said hesitantly. "I guess so. I mean, yes, of course."

"All right, Jackie, I'll be honest with you. I'm a Montgomery, remember? Have you been away from town so long that you've forgotten the pride of my family? Do you think I'd try anything with a woman who has made it crystal clear that she can hardly bear the sight of me? Today you went to a great deal of trouble to show me that you wanted nothing to do with me. You showed me that you'd rather end a lifelong friendship than be around me. Do you know how you made me feel this afternoon?"

"You were rather explicit on that point," she said, trying hard not to remember all the things he had said to her. She had never felt so small as he had made her feel today.

"Okay, so you made me feel bad, and I gave you some of your own back. You've made it clear that you don't want me, that you never have, that I am and always will be a boy to you. So be it."

She was trying to read the expression on his face but couldn't. Even as a boy, Billy had been unreadable. He'd followed her around, but she'd never understood whether he liked her or just thought of her as an oddity.

"Right now you need help and it's easy for me to give it. Young Blair said you could move your hand in about a week. I'll do whatever you want. I'll stay, or I'll leave and hire someone else to take care of you, whatever you want. If I stay, it will

116

be on terms of . . . ."

He smiled. "Remember all the times you baby-sat me? Maybe now I can return the favor. I'll baby-sit you. Doesn't that seem like a fair trade?"

"I . . . I don't know," she managed to say. The entire right side of her body hurt, her hair itched, and she was extraordinarily tired. She didn't want to make decisions now. She just wanted to be clean and to sleep.

"Come on," he said, reaching out for her un-injured hand and pulling her out of bed. "You can't think now. You're going to take a bath, I'm going to wash your hair, and then you're going to sleep."

"I don't think —"

"You rarely do. You act first and think later." When she was standing in front of him, he looked into her eyes. "Jackie, do you really think I'm the kind of boy who'd take advantage of a woman when she's hurt and in pain?"

Something about what he said made her frown. Maybe it was the use of "boy" and "woman" to-gether. But no matter what bothered her, she knew that he would not take advantage of her. He wasn't the type of *man* a woman had to be afraid of. It was more likely that William should fear women.

"You can't wash my hair," she said at last. "I can do it."

"Not with one hand you can't."

What he was saying and what he was doing con-fused her. Maybe she shouldn't have compared him to Charley, but Charley was the only man

117

she'd ever really known. Charley had been a great father figure, he'd given orders and made decrees, said no more often than yes, but as a mother he was the worst. Thank heaven Jackie had almost always been as healthy as a pilot after the first solo, because during the few times she was ill, Charley had been annoyed and had stayed out of the house until she was well. She remembered running a fever, being horribly weak and in the kitchen trying to open a can of soup.

Maybe the men you knew well in your life shaped your ideas of what men should and should not be, because now she wondered if it was really a masculine thing for a man to wash a woman's hair. Which of course was absurd. If a man did "women's things," did his male body parts fall off? Or shrivel up until they were useless? Of course not. It was just that the two men in her life, her father and her husband, had spent their lives sitting on chairs asking her to bring them things. And maybe that was what she'd come to expect of men, that the woman was to give and the man to receive and when a man gave, it was somehow . . . not right, or not wholly masculine.

William had his arm around her shoulders in a companionable way, a nonsexual way, and she found his touch very confusing. This morning he had been yelling that he loved her, *had* loved her, but now he didn't even like her very much. Yet he was leading her into the bathroom to . . . what?

"Stop thinking so much," William said as he opened the bathroom door. He left her for a moment as he got a glass of water then took a pill from a little jar on the side of the sink. "Here, take this."

"What is it?"

"It could be a drug made from an ancient herb found in a tomb in South America, guaranteed to make a woman do anything a man wants her to do. Or it could be a painkiller that will make you feel the pain in your hand less. What do you think?"

She didn't even smile as she took the pill from his hand and swallowed it with the water.

"Okay, now off with that bloody shirt."

Jackie opened her mouth to say something, but what could she say? She had on a brassiere, and that certainly covered what little she had on top. And hadn't she often appeared in halter tops in public in the summer? What was the difference?

Abruptly, William grabbed her shoulders and turned her to face him, his nose to her nose. "Jackie, I am not a rapist. I am not a man who would take advantage of a woman who has lost a lot of blood. I am not so . . . so needy of female companionship that I have to resort to trickery to get a woman's clothes off. All I want to do is to wash a couple of quarts of blood off of you. You are a disgusting sight and you stink. Now will you be sensible and take your shirt off? You can wrap a towel around yourself so I won't see anything, but whatever you do, let's get you clean."

The pill had begun to take effect: the pain was

lessening and she was starting to feel woozy. With a little smile she started to unbutton her blouse, but it was difficult to do with only one hand. Pain shot through her when she tried to use her bandaged hand. In the end, William efficiently unbuttoned her blouse and slipped it off her shoulders. After that, she didn't give him any difficulty. One minute she was a thirty-eight-year-old woman and the next she was a child in pigtails leaning over a basin having her hair washed.

Jackie was startled to find that the most sensual thing in the world was having a man wash her hair. When she went to the beauty shop and a woman washed her hair, she did a good job, but she was always in a hurry because she had six other women lined up waiting to use the sink. But as every woman knew, men knew that the world would wait for them, so they took their time.

William's strong hands massaged her scalp. No fingernails to hurt her skin, no rushing, no feeling that he wanted to get this over with. The pain pill made her feel dreamy, as though she'd had a couple of drinks after a hard day's work. She wasn't drunk, but she wasn't quite sober. She just felt relaxed, and her body grew warm and soft with the pleasure of the massage that William was giving her. His fingers caressed her scalp, then her neck muscles; he seemed to know exactly which muscles were tight and where to rub to make her relax.

All too soon he rinsed her hair for the second time, wrapped a towel about her head, making her feel like a movie star, and stood her upright.

"I'm going to fill the tub while you undress and put on your robe."

With that, he turned his back to her and turned on the tub taps. After only seconds of hesitation, Jackie stripped off her filthy, stiff clothes, took her robe from the hook on the back of the door, and put it on. When William looked back at her, he had the tub full of steamy hot water with a five-inch-thick layer of foamy bubbles on top. If she plunged under that thick, opaque layer, she'd be completely hidden from sight.

"I'm going to get some more towels; you climb into the tub. And be careful you don't get your bandage wet." Before he left, he turned out the light so the only illumination in the room was through the glass transom into the bedroom.

After he left the room, she removed her robe and stepped into the hot, hot water. There was nothing more luxurious than a tub full to the brim of steamy water, topped by soft, fragrant bubbles. Rarely in her life had she allowed herself the pleasure of a long soak in a tub. Rarely did she have the time, but, more important, she seldom did things of such a decadent, purely sensual nature for herself. One could get clean in a shower, so why bother with all the time and waste of water and soap?

Closing her eyes, she let the water soak through her skin, all the way into her bones The bubble bath had been a gift from Terri two Christmases ago. Terri had the idea that a single woman did such delicious things as lounge about in a tub of hot water, but Jackie had never opened the jar. It smelled like a basket of freshly picked apricots warming in the sun, sweet and rich and luscious.

She was two-thirds asleep when William quietly opened the door to check on her. Turning her head as it rested on the back of the tub, she smiled at him. He smiled back and closed the door.

She must have been asleep when he reentered the room half an hour later and began to wash her face. When she opened her mouth to object, he said, "Don't even think of protesting," so she leaned back and closed her eyes. She was too sleepy, too relaxed, to think of anything. He washed her blood-encrusted face and neck, then her unbandaged left arm and hand. When he moved to the end of the tub, seated himself on the rim, pulled one of her feet out of the water and began a soapy massage of her foot, the feeling was too heavenly to consider resisting.

It was nearly dark in the bathroom and the gentle foot massage along with the hot water, the smell of the bubble bath, combined with the pill, made Jackie feel quite wonderful. It sometimes seemed that she had been working all her life and she'd never taken time to enjoy anything. There had always been goals to achieve and, if nothing else, the responsibility of putting bread on the table.

When William stopped massaging, she smiled at him, so handsome in the golden light that floated in from the bedroom.

122

"Thank you," she whispered as he moved toward the towel rack to take a fluffy white towel and hold it out for her.

"Get out and I'll dry you off."

As he said this, he turned his head to one side and closed his eyes. Reluctantly leaving the tub, Jackie stepped out, soap still clinging to her skin, and allowed him to wrap her in the towel. Her arms were pinned to her sides inside the towel and it was perfectly natural that his arms should go around her as he rubbed the ends of the towel up and down her back. In spite of her relaxed state, she shivered.

"Cold?"

"No," she whispered and found herself putting her head on his shoulder.

Pulling away from her, he lifted her chin with his fingertips. "You are exhausted." At that he swept her into his arms and carried her into the bedroom where he stood her beside the bed and handed her a pair of pink pajamas. "Put them on. I'd help you, but you'd remember it in the morning and hate me."

That made her laugh, and while he busied himself with putting all her cosmetics on top of the mirrored bureau in precise military order, she slipped into the pajamas, then gratefully got into the bed.

"Better," he said as he tucked the covers about her chin.

"Did you learn how to bathe people and tuck them in from your baby-sitter?" she teased.

William stopped tucking and gave her a very stern look. "My baby-sitter's idea of bathing children was to yell 'Fire' and have the fire department hose them down."

Jackie giggled. "That's not true."

"Word of honor. And she never tucked us into bed. All she did was say 'Bed!' and by golly, we *went*. If one of us dared to disobey her, she'd tie our feet together and dangle us over the balcony until we reconsidered our stand on going to bed."

"That's not true either."

"It is! I swear it."

"There must have been something good about your baby-sitter. She couldn't have been a complete monster."

"Mmmm, yes. She was unique. She had no idea what a schedule was, so when we were with her we could eat cereal for dinner and steak for breakfast. And she never tried to force us to be what we weren't."

"Oh?" Jackie said encouragingly.

"Sometimes parents have very odd ideas about their children. They think they should all be alike. They seem to think there is an ideal child, and they try to make them all like that ideal. If a child doesn't like sports, parents say, 'You should get out and play football.' If the kid likes to play games outside, parents say, 'Why don't you ever sit down and read a book?' It seems that whatever kind of a child you are, someone wants you to be different."

"But your baby-sitter wasn't like that?"

"No, she wasn't. She liked or disliked people for what they were. She didn't try to change them."

Jackie found this conversation extraordinarily interesting and very much wanted to continue it, but she was falling asleep. "She didn't try to change you?" she whispered, her eyes closed.

"No. She didn't complain that I was too . . . whatever. She didn't complain that I wasn't like the other kids, because she was like no one else, either, and she understood what it was like to be different."

"A misfit. You were both misfits." Her voice was barely audible.

"No, we were both unique." Leaning forward, he kissed her forehead. "Now go to sleep and maybe the Good Fairy will bring you what you most want during the night."

She smiled at that and was still smiling when he turned out the light and left the room.

Chapter Seven

When Jackie awoke the next morning she was immediately aware of a throbbing in her right hand and a spectacularly empty stomach. Too weak and too lethargic at first to get out of bed, she slowly became aware of a dull thudding noise coming from the direction of the kitchen. Curiosity won over her lethargy, and, too, there was a smell she couldn't identify coming from the kitchen: chicken? herbs? freshly baked bread? and something tangy, like hot apple cider. She got up and followed where her nose led.

William was just outside the kitchen, standing on the little flagstone pavement, straddling her unhinged screen door, which he was shaving with a small hand plane. The sun came in through the bright white lace curtains of the kitchen, and the round pine table was loaded with bowls of food covered with weighted cloths.

For a while she watched him, his strong back straining against a pale blue cotton shirt that was frayed at the cuffs. His strong, lean hands moved the plane along the edge of the door in what was almost a caressing motion.

Smoothing her hair with her hands, Jackie resisted the temptation to go back to the bathroom and spend an hour or so on her face and hair, maybe do her nails too. She forced herself to stay where she was. She wasn't going to give in to silly female ploys. "What are you doing?" she asked.

Turning, he smiled at her, a smile as bright as the sunshine. "Fixing a few things." He leaned the door against the side of the house and came toward her. "Let me look at my patient." Tenderly he put both his hands on her head and turned her face toward the light.

"My hand was hurt, not my face."

"You can tell a great deal from looking into a person's eyes."

"Nearsightedness? How much the person had to drink the night before? That sort of thing?"

"In your case, no. The whites of your eyes are clear this morning, whereas last night they were gray with pain and fatigue. Are you hungry?"

"Famished."

"I thought so. Have a seat and I'll get you a plate."

She allowed him to wait on her. It was so pleasant being waited on by a man that she didn't protest, didn't say that he was her guest and that she should be waiting on him. This morning she didn't feel as though he were her guest. This morning she felt . . . She didn't want to look too deep into how she felt.

Maybe it was the aftereffects of the pain pill or of the pain itself, but this morning she wasn't as nervous as she usually was around him. Usually she felt as though she had to run away from William, that her life depended upon getting away from him, but this morning the world seemed kind of fuzzy and pretty, as though she were seeing it through foggy glasses.

She sat quietly while he poured steaming coffee for her and didn't complain when he loaded it with both sugar and milk — coffee for a child, she thought, but she knew that today it would taste good.

"Breakfast or lunch?" he asked.

A quick glance at the clock told her that it was nearly one o'clock in the afternoon and that she had slept nearly fourteen hours. She doubted if she'd ever before in her life slept that long.

"Lunch," she answered, then watched as he piled her plate high with a generous scoop from an enormous chicken pot pie. Creamy gravy oozed over chicken, carrots, and peas. There was coleslaw flavored with fennel, and bread still warm from the oven. Hot apple cider filled a stoneware mug.

"Did you cook this?" she asked in disbelief.

He laughed. "Not quite. Compliments of my family's cook. One of my brothers drove it out here just an hour ago."

She was too busy eating to comment, ignoring the fact that William was staring at her, watching her with a dreamy smile on his face.

"Jackie, how long has it been since you took a vacation? A real vacation? No planes, nothing that even resembles planes."

"I've never wanted such a time." She smiled at him over her half-empty plate of food. "What about you? When was your last vacation?"

"Exactly the same time as yours."

They laughed together.

"Okay," he said, "I am the Red King and —"

"Who?"

"The Red King, as opposed to Alice's Red Queen."

"I see."

"Whatever. I declare this a holiday. No setting up books, no planning the future, no —"

"No talk of the Taggie?" she prompted.

"No talk of the Taggie. Now, what exactly do

people do on a holiday?" He looked genuinely puzzled.

"Let's see. . . . Spend more money than they can afford. Sleep in unfamiliar, uncomfortable places. Eat strange food that makes them sick. Get up at four A.M. and spend sixteen hours wandering around looking at things too big, too ancient, or too something-or-other to comprehend, all the while wanting nothing more than a good night's sleep at home in their own bed."

"Sounds great, doesn't it?"

"Divine."

"Anyplace you want to go?"

"You mean a place far away and exotic?"

"Sure."

She grinned. "How about if we walk up to one of the old mining towns and see if we can find anything interesting? Maybe we'll find silver nuggets."

"Sounds exotic enough for me. Do you think you're up to it?"

"Yes," she answered. "I'd like to get outside into the sunshine." In spite of her hurt hand, she felt good. She felt lazy and peaceful, not anxious or restless as she usually did. Maybe it was the loss of blood from yesterday; maybe that was why she didn't feel like avoiding William's company today. Or maybe it was that she felt a bit sorry for herself, like when you're on a diet and you make excuses for giving yourself a treat. You tell yourself that you deserve this because you sneezed and you might be coming down with the

129

flu and it's not good to starve yourself if you're ill. So you eat a five-scoop ice cream sundae.

Now she felt as though there were special circumstances between her and William. Yesterday he had rescued her, maybe even saved her life by keeping her from bleeding to death. So how could she continue her demand that he leave her house today? She'd have to be polite and nice to him, and tomorrow she'd resume her vigilance and make him leave. But for today, she'd be nice to him. And maybe in being nice to William, she would also be nice to herself.

"If you've finished eating everything on the table, let's get you dressed and go."

"I can dress myself," she said sarcastically.

At that he reached across the table and unbuttoned the top two buttons on her pajama top. "Now you button them back up," he said.

Jackie made an attempt with the buttons, but pain shot through her hand when she tried to move it. William just sat still, a smug look on his face as she tried to show him that she could fasten the buttons with her left hand. After several frustrating minutes, she looked up and stuck her tongue out at him. He could be such a brat at times. "I'll bet that you've made yourself completely at home while I was asleep," she said, trying to save her dignity. "What else have you taken liberties with besides my kitchen door?"

He kept smiling. "I tidied a few things."

At that Jackie got up from the table and opened kitchen drawers. She had been so proud of moving into her pretty house, and she had even a great deal of thought to where she wanted to put things. She had put cooking utensils in a drawer near the stove. Things that she used near the sink were placed near the sink. She'd put the equipment she used most often near the front of the drawers and the things like an egg slicer way to the back.

William had rearranged everything in her drawers. Where there had once been a pleasant, creative jumble, now every utensil was in military order. All of the spoons from every place in the kitchen were now in one drawer, lined up perfectly by size and material. Wooden spoons were together, then enameled, then stainless steel. Never mind that she cooked with some of the spoons, dyed socks with one, and used one to clean hair out of the drains. They were all together now. The same with the knives: her roofing knife was next to her bread knife. The pots of plants on her windowsill were arranged by size so they looked like a set of Russian dolls. He had placed a scented geranium next to the herbs so she'd have to read the labels rather than just reach for a stalk of basil.

His presumption was annoying at the least, and it would take hours to re-sort her kitchen drawers. But for now she'd do the best she could to let him know what she thought of his arrogant male assumption that he knew more about organization than she did — and that he had a right to rearrange her personal property.

She gave him a beautiful smile. Then, one by one, she opened the drawers and ran her uninjured hand through the too-orderly contents, jumbling them thoroughly.

At the third drawer, William jumped up from the table, frowning. "You're doing this out of defiance, but it makes much more sense to have an organized kitchen, an organized life, for that matter. The way I have everything, you could find things if you were blind."

"But I'm not blind, am I?"

She opened drawer number four, but William caught her hand. "Stop that." When she tried to pull her hand away he held it and pulled her against him.

"There is no excuse for disorganization!" William snapped and Jackie began to laugh, and her laughter made him smile. "I'm not going to let you do that," he said. "Do you have any idea how long it took me to sort everything in those drawers?"

"Less time than it took me to put them in order in the first place." Within seconds their disagreement turned into a playful tug-of-war, with William pulling her hand back every time she reached for a drawer knob.

"You're an idiot, you know that?" she said, laughing, pulling against him. "This is a stupid idea of organization. I put things where I *use* them."

"Ha! You may have started out that way, but now you just put things wherever you happen to be standing. Ninety-nine percent of this stuff was in one drawer, the drawer closest to the sink where you take them out of the dish rack. Laziness is your organizer."

So what if there was more than a little truth to his words? It was dreadful when people got to know you well enough to see your faults. It was so much better before they knew you well and thought you were perfect.

"Let me go," she said, wriggling against him. Then somehow she was fully in his arms, facing him, her arms pinned between them.

"I like this," he said, beginning to nuzzle her neck. "You smell good, like sleepy perfume."

"Like what?"

William was kissing her neck. His hands were firmly on her back, pressing against the thin fabric of her robe and pajamas.

"I . . . I don't think you should do that." Her head was back and her eyes closed. She should stop him, she thought. But it was the ol' ice cream subterfuge. How could she stop a fully grown man when she was so weak from loss of blood? She'd stop him when she felt better.

"Jackie, you are so beautiful. Do you have any idea what you look like in the morning?"

"Like I slept in the barn?"

"Yes." His lips were on her earlobe now. "You look warm and soft and sweet, so very sweet. Your voice is a little husky, and your eyes are only half open." His hands slid down her back to the curve of her buttocks, moving no farther, just resting firmly on that curvaceous area, as his lips crept to the center of her throat.

"William, I, ah, I think I'd better get, ah, dressed."

"Sure," he said, and stepped away from her so quickly she staggered back against the sink, where she caught herself with her good hand. He walked toward the doorway of the kitchen and stood there a moment, his back to her. She could see his shoulders moving as he took one deep breath after another as though to calm himself.

"I don't think we should do that again," she said softly.

"Me neither." His voice was firm, as though he was telling himself that he *could not* again do what he had just done. When he turned back to her, he was smiling once again. The only difference she could see was that the skin around his neck seemed to be a little pinker than usual.

With a detached air, William took a step forward and deftly, swiftly, unbuttoned her pajama top all the way down. "Now go get dressed. I'll do the buttoning and tie your shoelaces." His head came up and there was a look of pleading in his eyes. "But, Jackie, please try to close your own zippers."

She started to laugh, but the look in his eyes was too serious. "I'll do my best," she said solemnly, but she was bubbling with joy inside. It was lovely to feel desirable, she thought as she practically skipped to the bedroom. When you're seventeen and men desire you, it's frightening. You have no idea what to do with them. At that age you want to be thought of as an intelligent woman, no longer a child. At seventeen you

134

want to prove to your mother that you are an adult, that you can get a man, just as she did, and that you are adult enough to be able to run a house and take care of that man — just as she did. It annoys you that all a man can think of is putting his hands inside your clothes. Why weren't seventeen-year-old boys serious about life and the future? Didn't they know what lay ahead for them? There were few things in life more serious, more earnest, more confused, than a seventeen-year-old girl.

But at thirty-eight, you no longer had to prove yourself to your mother. By thirty-eight you knew that running a house and taking care of a man wasn't some great challenge; it was just repetition. Over and over again, washing his socks, figuring out what to feed him, doing the same things again and again. At thirty-eight you wanted to feel desirable — and you wondered what had happened to all the seventeen-year-old boys who couldn't keep their hands off girls. Just as a woman began to relax and want to have a little fun, she found herself married to a man whose only desire in life was to sleep until dinner, then sleep until bedtime. What had happened to all that energy? All that lust?

Sometimes it seemed to Jackie that men and women were mismatched. When she had first married Charley, she wanted to prove to him that she was worth his having married her. To her this meant cooking and keeping his clothes clean and, of course, flying. She so wanted to impress him with her flying. But Charley liked to spend afternoons in bed; Jackie wanted to spend afternoons in a plane.

Now, many years later, Jackie felt that she was where Charley had been years ago. She'd proved herself to herself — to the world, actually — and now she wouldn't mind . . . She wouldn't mind spending an afternoon or so in bed with a man.

Of course, she reminded herself, not *this* man. This man, this very young man, William Montgomery, was off limits. If she missed the company of a man she should look for someone more . . . appropriate. Yes, that was the right word. Appropriate meant the right age, the right social background, the right everything. It meant a man who could help her along life's pathways. Yes, that was right. An older man would have the wisdom to help a woman. At that thought Jackie snorted. She'd had one man in her life who was as much a father as a husband. She didn't need a third father in her life.

Jackie shook her head to clear it. Just enjoy this, she thought. As an elementary school teacher's students might fall in love with her, so William thought he was in love with an older woman. And she was mature enough to enjoy his attention, wasn't she? Enjoy it and handle it.

Smiling, feeling that she was being a mature adult, she did the best she could at getting out of her pajamas and into a pair of loose gabardine trousers, a rayon shirt with patch pockets, and a big white cardigan tied about her shoulders. She managed the zipper on her trousers, but the buttons were impossible. She took just a bit longer with her hair and face than she would have on an ordinary day, but she excused herself for that. Every woman wanted to look nice when she went out, didn't she? Never mind that many times in the past Jackie had laughed at women who fixed their hair just so before flying an airplane. An hour in a dust storm and you were lucky to have any hair left, much less have it arranged.

Holding her shirt together, she walked into the living room where William was occupying himself by rearranging the drawers of her desk. When she let out an exclamation, he turned and told her she looked beautiful, and there was honesty in his eyes.

"Would you mind staying out of my drawers?" she snapped angrily.

He was buttoning her shirt. "Is that drawers as in knickers?"

"Most certainly not!" she said, sounding like a shocked schoolmarm in a bad novel. "Would you behave yourself?"

"That depends on what one defines as correct behavior. From my point of view I am behaving myself."

"Then behave yourself from *my* point of view."

Bending over, he picked up a picnic basket, slipped the handle over his arm, then took her arm with his other hand. "Just as soon as you decide what your point of view is." He didn't give her a chance to reply to that nonsense. "Are you sure you're up to this?"

She knew that he was referring to her injury, but for some reason the question annoyed her. Did he think she was too *old* to go hiking? Was he hinting that she'd be better off in a rocking chair by the fire? "I can outclimb you, city boy, any day of the week. While you've been pushing a pencil, I've been crawling all over airplanes, pulling engines from —" She stopped because William was laughing at her. She narrowed her eyes threateningly, which just made him laugh harder.

"Come on, Tarzan, let's go," he said as he slipped his arm through hers and led her toward the door.

Who would have believed, she wondered, that little Billy Montgomery would turn out to be so much fun? Just plain old-fashioned fun. So maybe he didn't like to ride upside down in an airplane, but there were lots of people who wouldn't consider that activity fun. But William did enjoy other things.

For one thing, his sense of humor was childlike and physical. Jackie enjoyed the kind of humor where people sat in a bar and exchanged bons mots, but she also enjoyed the slip-on-a-banana-peel type of humor. William all too clearly understood her outburst when he'd asked her if she felt well enough to go hiking, so he pretended to be old and tired and ill, thereby forcing her to help pull him up the hills. The pulling, then William's collapsing against her in mock fatigue, made for a great deal of physical contact. Every few minutes he seemed to have his arms around her, his head on her shoulder, his face pressed into her neck. She told him to stop what he was doing, but there was about as much strength in her words and her gestures as there was in wet seaweed.

When Jackie allowed herself to be honest, she enjoyed this play with William. She'd missed play as a child and as a young woman. For all that William was right when he said she did what she wanted when she was growing up, what she had really wanted was to be an adult, to be independent. When she was ten years old she wanted to be an old woman. One time her mother had said in exasperation, "Jackie, are you *ever* going to be a child?"

Could a person age in reverse? Could a person get younger as she got older? When she was in high school all the kids wanted to do was play and have a good time. Jackie had been completely disdainful of them; all she thought of was her future and what she was going to do, how she was going to get out of this one-horse town and *do* something with her life. Other girls her age were saying they wanted to "Marry Bobby and be the best wife in the world." Jackie's arrogant laugh was now an embarrassment to her.

She had missed play. She had missed a time of courtship with Charley. What honeymoon they'd had was spent inside an airplane. He was her teacher as well as her husband. She had loved it then and she was glad for it, but now she wanted to relax, to . . . to smell the roses.

William made her laugh. He teased her and chased her around a tree, and in the late afternoon he spread a cloth in the sunlight, on sun-warmed rocks near the edge of a cliff, so they could sit and look out at a spectacular view. From the basket he removed a banquet: wine, cheese, bread, olives, mustard, cold fried chicken, tiny portions of pâté in the shape of flowers, sliced tomatoes, cold lemonade — a feast.

Jackie leaned against a warm rock and again allowed William to wait on her.

"You've been thinking very hard all day," he said as he poured her a glass of red wine.

"I hate it when you know what's going on in my head."

After waiting a moment in silence, he said, "You want to tell me what's been occupying your thoughts?"

She didn't want to tell him anything. Always in her head was the knowledge that soon what was between them would have to end and that it wasn't a good idea to get any closer than they were. But the truth was that she did feel close to him. "I was thinking about all the things you said yesterday."

"Jackie," he began, and she sensed that he was going to follow with an apology, but she waved her hand to stop him.

"No, don't say anything. I deserved everything you said. When I was a kid, I felt that I had to be the best, that I had to succeed. What no one

140

ever seemed to understand was that I *wished* I could be like the other kids. I tried. I wanted to be part of the groups that went to the drugstore after school and sipped sodas and flirted with boys. But for some reason I couldn't seem to do the right things."

She drank her wine and looked off into the glow of the sun, low in the sky. "You know my friend Terri Pelman? Well, back then I only knew her slightly, but I used to envy her so much. In school she was so popular, always surrounded by boys. She always knew what the latest fashion was and always wore it correctly. No mistakes, nothing out of place or wrong, as I always seemed to get things. I wanted a life like hers, wanted the captain of the football team to be crazy about me, but it just didn't happen. Can you imagine how that was?"

"Yes," he answered simply, and she knew that he understood. She remembered how many times she'd heard the other children teasing William because he followed Jackie around. She remembered that one of his older brothers had beaten up a couple of boys because of something they'd said to William. Although William had not reported what was said, his sister had heard it and repeated it, so his brother fought for him.

Jackie doubted if she would have found out what was said except that she didn't see Billy for a few days, so she wandered over to his house — not to see him, of course, but maybe to run an errand for her mother.

William, using a rake nearly twice as tall as he was, was tackling the leaves on the entire vast lawn of the Montgomery house while his older brother, sporting a remarkable black eye, slept under a tree. Billy wouldn't tell her what was going on, so she woke his brother and made him tell. No one, no matter what size or age, could intimidate Billy, but her age and size quickly intimidated his brother, so he told her. It seemed that some kids who were about four years older than Billy had been hanging around near the bridge with absolutely nothing to do, when one of them said, "We could always have a rock race. William against that boulder over there. My money's on the rock."

When Jackie heard this, it was all she could do not to laugh; she had to wait until that afternoon when she was alone, and then she howled. Billy's brother's punishment for beating up the boys had been the job of raking all the leaves off the front lawn. Billy had taken on his brother's punishment.

Now, many years later, she looked at Billy the man and said, "Participate in any rock races lately?"

She could almost see his mind working as he tried to understand what she was talking about. When he remembered, his face lit up, and he smiled before he turned toward her, his eyes twinkling. "You know, my brother took offense at that remark, but I never did. I thought the other kids were stupid for jumping from one thing to another. They couldn't understand that life needs planning. Half the fun is in the planning. Maybe I didn't say much and maybe because of that they thought I was a dullard, but I was always planning tomorrow and the next day and the next."

He paused a moment. "Something I've discovered in life that others don't seem to know is that if you plan hard enough you can make things happen."

"Yes," she said, but didn't ask what he wanted to make happen. She didn't want to hear. "You do understand. Just as you were different without meaning to be, so was I. I was strange and when I couldn't fit in, I began to thumb my nose at the other kids, telling them and myself that I didn't need them."

"And then you fell in love," he said softly.

"With Charley?" There was disbelief in her voice.

"Something a little larger than Charley."

She smiled. "Ah, yes, airplanes. You know, I used to think that airplanes were male, but the older I get, the more I think that planes are female. They're no longer something I'm trying to conquer, but they're my very, very good friends. Someone I've shared a great deal with."

"And what about men?"

She looked off into the horizon and didn't answer him.

He persisted. "What do you want to do with your life now, Jackie?"

She didn't look at him, but when she spoke, there was passion in her voice. "Something in me has changed. I don't know what it is. For so

143

many years I wanted to conquer the world. I had such a clear view of what I wanted and how I was going to get it, but I accomplished everything I set out to win, and now I don't know where I'm going to go next. Part of me is angry that the world seems to be moving while I'm standing still, but part of me just wants to sit still and let it go by. Part of me wants to grow roses and —"

Abruptly, she broke off and took a deep drink of her wine.

"And have kids," he filled in for her with amazing — and annoying — accuracy.

"Ridiculous! Do you realize that two girls from my high school class are now grandmothers? What would I do with kids, anyway? Besides that, what man my age wants to start a family?" She stopped because she was protesting too much. A family of her own was not something she had thought too much about in her life. She'd been too busy with planes and taking care of Charley to think about a bunch of kids. Now the urge to see the world was no longer pulling at her, and yet she still wanted to participate in the world.

"I guess what I really want is everything. Everything the world has to offer is what I want. I don't want to give up anything, yet I want to add everything that I don't have."

William was smiling and the sun on his face made him especially handsome. "I can't give you everything, but I'd love to marry you and give you as many kids as you want."

Jackie knew he was serious and for a moment

her mouth was dry. There was an almost overwhelming urge within her to say yes. The feeling was every bit as intense as what she'd felt the first time she saw an airplane. Then she'd known nothing about the world. She'd had no idea of the cruelty of people, how they were going to judge her and her abilities before they met her. Now she was older and she'd experienced a great deal of pain as well as joy and she knew what people were going to say. If she married William they would see nothing except the age difference.

"Don't answer," he said, forcing a smile. "It was just a thought."

"Yes, just a thought." She tried to compose her face so that when she turned to him he wouldn't see what was in her eyes. "We are too serious. What we *should* be thinking of is who is going to clean up the kitchen. And you are going to put my kitchen back the way it was, the way *I* want it. And my desk, too."

"Ha! Do you know that you have a packet of needles and thread in your desk and a stapler in your sewing basket?"

She didn't know any such thing, but didn't doubt it. Sometimes a person got busy and put things where it was handy, but that wasn't any of his business. "It doesn't matter where I put things. It's *my* house."

"Only temporarily. Did I mention that I own all the houses in Eternity, as well as the land?"

At that Jackie laughed. Only a Montgomery could say he owned a town in that offhand tone of voice. "So, did you get the buildings for your twenty-first birthday?"

She meant it as a joke, but from the way William's face turned red, she knew she had guessed right, and she gave a whoop of laughter. "Every other person on earth would ask for a trip around the world or a mansion or even a diamond necklace, but what does my rock-solid, always-thinking-ahead William ask for? A ghost town! A run-down, worthless old town that people didn't want even when it was alive. What in the world made you ask for this place?"

When he looked at her, his eyes were intense. "I could build a landing field here." His answer was simple, but it said so much. He'd said that he was always planning, and the town and the airfield had been a lure to her. Even though she had been married to another man and had had no intention of returning to her hometown, William had been planning to bring her back. What was it he had said? That if you plan hard enough you can make things happen. Was she here today because he had wanted her so much, planned so hard, that she had returned?

She smiled at him. Whether things worked out between them or not, she couldn't help being flattered. Charley had never courted her; he'd always made her feel that he was doing her a favor by taking her away from two-bit Chandler. He had let Jackie court him with work and more work and more work. But now here was a man who had spent years planning to win her.

146

"You make me feel valuable," she said softly. "You make me feel as though I am the most precious object in the world."

"You are."

There was such sincerity in his voice that Jackie didn't know whether to be pleased or embarrassed. She was some of both. In the end, all she could say was "Thank you."

Chapter Eight

This is heaven, Jackie thought. Next to fifteen snap rolls one after another, this was as good as life got. She was on her pretty couch, doing the best she could to keep her mind on the radio program that William had on, but the truth was, she was watching him as he polished a foot-high stack of shoes, both his and hers. She complained and she hated his presumption, but maybe it was rather nice to open a sewing basket and take out a pair of scissors instead of a stapler. And it would be nice to put on shiny shoes.

It was raining outside, so William had built a fire to take the chill off the cool mountain night. He'd insisted that Jackie stretch out on the couch, a thick blanket draped over her, and she was to do nothing but be quiet and listen to the radio. And watch him, she thought. Who would have thought that seeing a man do something as domestic as polish shoes could have such an effect on her? In a way this simple action made her think more of love than all his kisses did. As Jackie well knew, it wasn't passion that made for a good marriage, it was the little things. If something needed to be assembled, could one of you read the directions while the other constructed? In Jackie's experience, a man didn't like to take orders from a woman for anything at all. Did the two of you bicker? That petty arguing could ruin evenings and afternoons.

Jackie had learned that it wasn't enough for two people to fall in love; they had to get along on a day-to-day basis, had to be able to live in peace and harmony.

And that was her problem with William. He was *very* easy to live with. Forget that he had really stupid ideas about organization and was obsessed with putting things into what he thought of as the proper order. Day by day he was very easy to be with. When he was hungry, he didn't look to the nearest woman to produce hot, delicious food as though it were a gland secretion. Nor did he expect her to do everything on earth for him. Right now he was polishing Jackie's shoes, something she'd done only a couple of times in her life. After all, who was going to notice whether her shoes were polished or not? The other pilots? Charley? The airplanes?

His voice made her head come up. "Jackie," he said, and the innocence of his tone immediately put her on guard. He sounded as though he had done something he shouldn't or was about to do something he shouldn't.

"Yes?" she said with what she hoped was just as much innocence.

"While I was straightening your desk, I came across something rather interesting."

"Oh? And what was that? A pair of scissors half an inch out of line?"

He ignored her sarcasm, so she knew he was after bigger fish. "I found a letter from a national magazine asking you to please write something for them about flying."

"Oh," she said and tried to think of some way to get him onto another topic. But she knew that his main goal was to put her into the history books, and if he couldn't do that by making her win races, maybe he could do it by turning her into a writer.

"I think that's a splendid idea," he continued innocently. "What you know about airplanes is invaluable. You could help a new generation of young women learn about flying, make them want to fly. You could share your skills and inspire a whole nation."

"True, but if I were *that* good, I wouldn't ever need to get inside a plane again. I could just sprout wings and fly myself straight to heaven."

Again he ignored her. "Look at this. The magazine has sent a sample article: 'Nita Stinson, the Flying Typist, talks about her first flight.' " Looking at the article, William gave a snort of derision.

"Flying Typist, indeed. *You* are a real pilot."

"For your information, Nita happens to be a friend of mine, and she's an excellent pilot." There was some hostility in her voice, as though she were ready to fight for her friend.

"I apologize. I meant no offense. Forgive me if I happen to think that you are the best pilot, male or female, in the world. Your flying could make the Angel Gabriel sick."

When she glanced at him, he gave her a smile that let her know he was paying her back.

"So," he said, "why don't you try writing?"

With a helpless look on her face, she held up her bandaged hand, showing him that she was incapable of such a task.

Instantly William grabbed pen and paper. "Tell me what you want to say and I'll write it."

"Flying is fun. I like it. You should try it."

"Come on, Jackie, be serious. You must have something you'd like to say to the millions of young women out there who wonder what it's like to be a pilot."

She thought for a moment, then smiled. "Yes, there *is* something I'd like to say to the world. Got your pen ready?"

With a smile of satisfaction, William began to write as Jackie spoke.

"Whatever is the lowest occupation a woman ever has, that's what she is for the rest of her life. Even if she becomes president of the world, people will say, 'Miss Jones, a former receptionist, is now president of the world.' The implication is that she is getting above herself, because we all know that deep down inside, Miss Jones is really only a receptionist. On the other hand, if a man becomes president of the world, people say, 'Mr. Jones, who used to work in a mail room, is now running the world.' The implication is that Mr. Jones is magnificent for having pulled himself up from his lowly position. The difference between the two is that Miss Jones is a receptionist pretending to be a world leader while Mr. Jones was a world leader in the making even when he was sorting the mail."

Before she had completed the first sentence, William put down his pen and stopped writing. When she'd finished the whole statement, she smiled at him in a smug way. She wasn't about to write a bunch of sugar-coated, violet-scented articles to try to make young women enter aviation. A woman needed to have all the conviction in the world to fly an airplane, because the flying world was tough. It was tough facing men who felt certain that you were going to fail merely because you were female and therefore, in their opinion, not intelligent or competent.

"Is that what you had in mind?" she asked sweetly.

"It's what *I* had in mind, but I don't think it's what the magazine wants. Come on, I'm hungry. Let's go argue about who cuts up your food. I love the way I get to win."

Laughing, she allowed him to help her into the kitchen.

151

When Jackie awoke the next morning, it was to a delightful sense of well-being. She was still sick, wasn't she? Well, not really sick, but incapacitated enough to feel that she did not have to make a decision about William leaving. When she was well, he would, of course, have to leave, but for now she could put off that decision with a clear conscience. He was a friend and he was helping her. That's all there was between them.

What a glorious Sunday morning it was! William made blueberry pancakes and served them smothered in butter and syrup, and they laughed together like children. It was odd how childish two adults could be when they were alone. Everything either of them said seemed to be brilliant or funny or both to the other one. She didn't remember their laughing this much when they were children. Jackie had always considered life a challenge, something that had to be conquered, and William had seemed to think that Jackie was his challenge. Whatever had been in the past was now different, for they fit together easily and happily.

After breakfast William washed the dishes while Jackie, with a great show of pain that she didn't really feel, dried them. When the dishes were clean they went into the living room where William offered to read her the comics from the newspaper. It was the most natural thing in the world that she should sit in the circle of his arm so she could see the pictures. And she was eating an apple, so she'd take a bite, then give him a bite, then take one herself. It was a scene from paradise.

The sound of a horn and the crunching of gravel at the approach of a car sent a look of horror across Jackie's face.

"It's Terri," she said in fear, as though the worst possible thing had happened. The next second she had thrown William's arm off her shoulders and she was standing upright, frantically trying to straighten the room. It seemed that everywhere were signs of William's cohabitation. She *had* to remove all trace of him.

"What's wrong with you?" he asked, not having moved from the couch.

"That's Terri," she said, as though those words explained everything, William's house slippers were on the floor by the big chair. His shirt with a torn pocket was draped across her sewing basket; she'd promised to repair it for him when her hand healed. There were three magazines with his name on the subscription labels on the coffee table. His coat hung on the peg by the door.

Frantically she tried to gather up every trace of him, and when her arms were full, she looked about for some place to hide everything. What if Terri had some reason to look inside the coat closet? What if she wanted to look in the pantry? Jackie headed toward the bedroom, then stopped. That was the *last* place she should hide William's things.

Calmly William came forward and took the things from her arms. "I'll take care of them," he said softly.

There was something in his tone that she didn't want to hear. No doubt she had hurt his feelings, but she couldn't think of that now. She'd have to worry about soothing him later. "Terri can't see that I have a man living here with me," she said, trying to cover her actions with a lie. But one quick glance at William's eyes told her that he didn't believe her. He knew that she was embarrassed because the male things in her living room belonged to an "inappropriate" man, a younger man, and therefore not a man she wanted to introduce to her friends with pride.

As Jackie scurried about, looking for any other evidence of William's presence, she tried not to think about what she was doing. Later she'd make William — and herself — believe that she was only trying to protect their reputations.

She looked up at him, standing there with an armload of things that were clearly his. "Maybe you . . ." she began.

"Sure," he said, then turned on his heel and went toward the stairs.

She started to call after him but caught herself just as there was an urgent knock on the door. She turned and went to answer it.

"What in the world were you doing?" Terri asked. "I must have knocked four times. I just heard about your accident this morning. Why didn't you call me? Maybe I could have come out here and taken care of you."

"How kind of you to offer, but I was fine. Really."

"That's not what I heard." Terri walked past Jackie and looked around the room. There weren't many clues to the presence of another person but, even to Jackie's eyes, the room was different: less messy, more perfectly ordered, too tidy.

"Something is going on," Terri said as she turned and looked hard at her friend. "What's going on?"

"Nothing," Jackie answered, but she had to clear her throat in the middle of the word. Even to herself she sounded as though she were lying.

"Mmmm," Terri said, obviously not satisfied. "So what have you been doing with yourself this week?" As though she felt extremely tired, which she did, Terri plopped down on a big down-cushioned chair. Her husband had lost another job this week, and they'd had a blazing fight. "A job isn't like a set of keys," she'd yelled at him. "You can't just lose it for no reason. What did you do?" It was better not to remember what had happened after that. Only because Jackie had been injured was Terri allowed out of the house today.

But she didn't want to talk about her life. She didn't want to talk about it or think about it. Jackie had the exciting life; Jackie had everything that was good in life, everything a person could have.

Easing her weight off her bruised hip, Terri put her hand behind the cushion of the chair, and like Little Jack Horner, she pulled out a plum in the form of a man's sock.

Holding it up, at first she looked puzzled. Then, when she saw the redness of Jackie's face and when

Jackie snatched the sock from her hand, Terri began to laugh. "You have a man," she said, smiling. "That's why it took you so long to answer the door. Oh, do tell me who he is." It seemed that even a bad marriage could not cure a woman of hopefulness about romance. Even though her own man was no good, Terri honestly believed that somewhere out there was a knight in shining armor who was made for her.

At the look of embarrassment on Jackie's face, Terri began to push. "Who is he? I can't believe that something is going on and you told me nothing. I haven't heard a whisper of anything in town, so you're doing a great job of hiding it. You must tell me who he is."

"No one," Jackie said tightly. "You want some tea?"

"Sure, but I want information more."

It was all Jackie could do to keep from snapping that what was going on in her life was none of Terri's business. But Terri was an innocent, and so Jackie tried hard not to lose her patience no matter how many awkward, probing, embarrassing questions Terri asked.

"What kind of tea do you want?" Jackie asked finally, her hand gripping the tea canister so hard her knuckles were white.

"Whatever he drinks," Terri said smugly, making Jackie grimace.

"Looking for something?" William asked Terri's son. At first glance, the "boy" didn't seem to be doing anything wrong, just walking around the airplane parked in the hangar, but William knew everyone in Chandler. The Pelman men were worthless, lazy, stupid, and hostile. William didn't trust this overgrown lout even to go to church without an ulterior motive.

"What are you doin' here?" the big kid asked, his thick black brows pulled into a scowl. He was handsome in a brutish way, with thick lips and deep-set eyes, but he had that air of defensiveness that stupidity and arrogance often gave people. Whether he meant to or not, he seemed to be daring anyone to contradict him, daring anyone to hint that he wasn't as smart as the rest of the world.

Abruptly his face brightened and he looked pleased with himself — rather the way a monkey might look when it figured out the problem some scientist had set for it. "You're after her, ain't ya?"

"I beg your pardon?" William asked stiffly. He wasn't sure, but he thought this Pelman was about eighteen years old and named Larry.

"This here Jackie. You're after her, ain't ya?" To William's horror, Larry nudged him with his elbow as though they were fellow conspirators, the best of friends. "I've had my eye on her since she came to town. Mom says — not that she knows anything — that this lady flyer's been all over the world, so I figure she's done some things. You know what I mean?" He winked at William. "Done some things that the ladies of Chandler ain't even heard of. So now this Jackie is here in this one-horse town, and I ain't heard nothin' about her doin' nothin' with nobody, you know what I mean? So I figure she's dyin' for it. And I figure I'll just help myself to what she's got. She's kinda old, but I figure she'll be grateful to have a real man in her bed. She's probably beggin' for it after all this time and after havin' to put up with them fancy foreign fellas. 'Course I can see that you was here first, so I'll let you have her all you want, what with you bein' a Montgomery and all. Hey! Maybe later you can pay me back, since I saw her first. You can give me and my dad jobs. Nothing too hard or anything, just somethin' kinda friendly like, with maybe a bonus now and then. What'd'ya say?"

"Have you seen my shoes?"

In speechless horror, Jackie turned toward the kitchen door to see William standing there, a little-boy-lost expression on his face. She had just spent thirty minutes trying to make Terri believe that there was no man in her life, certainly not any man in Chandler, and now here was William. Asking about his shoes, no less!

She wanted to scream at him, but she knew that whatever she said would only make things worse. Within one hour after Terri saw William Montgomery in her house the town of Chandler was going to be alive with the gossip that old Jackie was having an affair with very young William.

"If it isn't Billy Montgomery," Terri said. "I

158

haven't seen you in ages. What have you been doing?"

Jackie braced herself. What was William going to say to that? Was he going to tell the truth? That he was spending his days trailing Jackie about, just as he'd done when he was a child?

"Jackie and I are going into business together."

"How nice. How is your mother? And your father?"

While William was answering these questions, Jackie looked at him. Usually William was very tidy, every hair in place, his shirt tucked in just so. But now he was slightly disheveled, and there seemed to be a place on his cheek that was darkening, as though it might be a bruise. Glancing down at his hands, she saw that the knuckles on his right hand were bleeding slightly. When he saw where her eyes were going, he put his hand behind his back and kept on talking to Terri, answering her questions about his family.

"And how did you do in school?" Terri was asking.

It took Jackie a long moment to grasp the fact that it had not entered Terri's head that William could be the man who was staying with Jackie, the man Terri had been asking about with all the gusto of an interrogator during the Spanish Inquisition.

The truth was, Terri was talking to William in that tone of voice that adults used with children. An aren't-you-cute voice. Any minute Jackie expected to hear her ask if William had washed behind his ears.

"So you've been taking care of Jackie," Terri was saying. "That's very kind of you, especially when you have your own life to lead. A handsome young man like you must have a hundred pretty little girlfriends."

"A few," William said with a soft smile.

It was a smile that enraged Jackie. It was the smile a boy would give to an older woman when he was trying to be on his best behavior.

Outside, a horn began to blow insistently — Terri's horrible son demanding that his mother leave and leave *now*.

"If you need any help with Jackie, let me know," Terri was saying as she started to put on her coat. Graciously, William held it for her. "You always were a gentleman. Wasn't he, Jackie? You remember how he was. Even as a little boy he was so polite."

Jackie could say nothing. She didn't want to remember that she'd known William as a little boy.

"But of course you remember," Terri said when Jackie didn't answer. "You were his baby-sitter, and he used to follow you everywhere. Oh, the escapades you two had! And now, Billy, how nice it is of you to help Jackie when she needs it. Well, please remember me to your parents, and maybe you can get together with my children."

"Yes," Jackie said in a very nasty tone. "Maybe we can arrange play dates for them. In a sandbox. Or maybe we can take them to the circus. They could ride the elephants and eat cotton candy."

At her hateful tone, Terri looked surprised and confused. "Well, yes, maybe."

"Jackie's hand hurts her," William said placidly, and his calmness made Jackie even angrier. "It puts her a bit on edge."

"Walk me out to the car, will you?" Terri said to Jackie.

Her hands clenched at her side, Jackie walked with her friend to the car where her big son sat glowering behind the steering wheel. As they approached, he turned his head away, but not before Jackie saw a smear of dried blood leading from his nose across his cheek.

"Don't think you can put me off," Terri said cheerfully as they reached the car. "I mean to find out who the man in your life is."

Jackie's teeth were locked together. "William is not a child, you know. In case you haven't noticed, he is a man." She had not meant to say that.

Terri looked puzzled, as though what Jackie had said had nothing whatever to do with what was going on in the world. "Of course he's a young man. I didn't mean to imply that he wasn't. Do you think I hurt his feelings by asking him about his parents? Children that age can be *so* sensitive."

"William is *not* a child!" Her words sounded more forceful than she meant them to. Why couldn't she be sophisticated and cool-tempered? She might as well tell Terri the truth about how she was beginning to feel about William.

"No," Terri said calmly, "Billy is not a child, but once you've seen a person in diapers you tend to always see that person in diapers." She cocked her head to one side. "What is wrong with you? I think it's very nice of Billy to take care of you. You've certainly taken care of him often enough. I remember how he was always on your heels. Everyone in school used to laugh about little Billy Montgomery following you around." She reached out and patted Jackie's arm and gave her a sad look. "Billy must be the closest thing you'll ever have to your own child."

"Only if I had given birth to him when I was ten years old!" Jackie snapped with a great deal of venom.

Terri looked startled by Jackie's fierceness. "I'm sorry," she said softly. "I'm sure that your childlessness must be a sore point with you. I meant nothing by what I said. I just think it's nice that Billy is here with you. It's kind of him."

Jackie could say nothing, absolutely nothing. Terri had meant well, but she had succeeded in making Jackie feel about a hundred years old. According to Terri, Jackie was infertile, an old woman who had already lived her life, and there was no hope of any future for her. According to Terri, Jackie should be grateful that a young man like William "helped" her when she was "invalided." Instead of a cut hand, Terri made Jackie's injury sound as though she had old-age arthritis and was confined to a wheelchair, and sweet young Billy Montgomery, out of the goodness of his heart, was wheeling her around.

Terri put her hand on the handle of the car, but then she quickly grabbed Jackie's arm and pulled her away where her son couldn't hear them. "Don't think I've forgotten about that man you have in your life. You won't be able to keep a secret from me."

"I'm keeping no secrets from you," Jackie said angrily — and honestly.

Terri looked as though she wanted to weep. Jackie was the highlight of her life, and she could not figure out what she had done to offend her. Maybe Jackie was telling the truth and *didn't* have a man in her life. Maybe Terri had read the signs wrong. Maybe Jackie's sudden, inexplicable hostility had arisen because Terri had assumed something that wasn't true and now Jackie was embarrassed that there was no man in her life.

"You do remember that I told you about Edward Browne? He's been asking about you again," she said softly, glancing at her big son, sulking in the car. "He's asked about you several times. He really does like you, and he's a great catch."

So many emotions were raging through Jackie that she couldn't speak, so Terri seemed to take her silence as encouragement.

"He's a very nice man, Jackie," Terri said persuasively. "He's about fifty-five years old, a widower. His children are grown, so you wouldn't have any problems there. Stepchildren can be a handful, you know. He's quite well off so he could support you after you quit flying."

Jackie felt that Terri meant, "When you come to your senses, decide to grow up, and quit fooling with those silly airplanes, there will be a man to take care of you."

Terri didn't have any idea of the thoughts going through Jackie's head. To her, the prospect of Edward Browne was wonderful. The man owned every shoe store within a hundred-mile radius, and he had a lovely house furnished with antiques he had inherited from his parents. The thought of a steady, reliable man, of a house that was well cared for and orderly, was Terri's idea of heaven. She no longer wanted excitement in her life. The drunken rages of her husband and the bloody fights between him and their sons were more excitement than she'd ever wanted. In Terri's mind, happiness was buying something pretty and fragile and feeling sure that it wasn't going to be broken within twenty-four hours.

"Edward Browne is such a nice man," Terri encouraged. "He's lived in Chandler for fifteen years, and everyone has only praise for him. Not a word of scandal. His wife was lovely, and they seemed to be very much in love. He was devastated when she died two years ago, and I understand he's very lonely. Every unmarried woman in Chandler from twenty to fifty has been after him. He'll go out with them now and then, but he never goes out with the same woman more than twice. Yet he's asked me about *you* several times. I told him he should call you, but he said that he wants to know

164

you'd welcome him. I think he's rather shy, and, Jackie, you know that you can be intimidating. I think he considers you a celebrity, so he's a bit afraid of calling you without prior permission."

Terri was looking at Jackie intently. "Can I tell him it's okay to call you?"

"I . . . I don't know," Jackie said honestly. Why did life have to be so complicated?

As far as Jackie could tell, there was no way to get rid of Terri except to agree to allow this man, Edward Browne, to call her. And why shouldn't Jackie go out with this very, *very* appropriate man? Was she engaged to someone else? Even dating someone else? In love with another man? No, she was not. She was completely and absolutely free. And besides, her attraction to William was probably about ninety percent loneliness. She was used to being surrounded by people, and now she was suddenly so alone that probably *any* man, no matter what age, would look good to her.

"Tell him to call me," Jackie said with some conviction — not much, but some.

Terri hugged her friend and then got into the rusty old car beside her angry son, who sped away so fast that flying gravel peppered Jackie's legs.

Once Terri was gone, Jackie braced herself to face William. She didn't like the fact that he'd so blatantly announced his presence to Terri. Had Terri been a little more astute she might have figured out that Jackie and William were . . . well, were whatever they were.

In the house, she found William sitting on the

165

couch, calmly reading the paper. When he looked up at her he seemed to expect her to sit by him and finish reading the comics, just as though Terri's visit had never happened.

"I want to talk to you," she said sternly, the door barely closed behind her.

"What have I done now?" he asked, amusement in his voice.

She wasn't going to treat this matter lightly. Didn't he realize what kind of rumors could be spread? "You may get away with playing the little boy with Terri, but it won't work with me." She had every intention of berating him for endangering her reputation by implying that he was living with her when he came into the room asking about his shoes. But to her horror, that was not what came out of her mouth.

"How could you have allowed Terri to treat you like a child?" she demanded.

William blinked at her a couple of times. "Is *that* what you're upset about?" He put his newspaper back in front of his face. "Older people always treat younger ones like children. Forever. They never stop, no matter how old you get."

It seemed to her that William meant to end the discussion there, but Jackie suddenly became very angry. "Older!" she sputtered. "What does that mean? Terri is exactly the same age as I am. Actually, she's three months *younger* than I am."

Obviously unperturbed, William turned a page of the newspaper. "Some people are old at twenty, and some are young at sixty."

"And just what is that supposed to mean?"

To further her anger, William didn't bother to answer. He just kept reading that blasted newspaper, his face hidden from her view. It was difficult, if not impossible, to have a serious argument about one of life's more profound issues with oneself. From the very beginning it seemed to her that William had failed to take this age difference seriously. He acted as though it mattered not at all.

"What did you do to Terri's son?" she asked, trying another way to get a reaction out of him.

"Did my best to teach him some manners, something he needed to be taught."

Part of Jackie wanted to thank him for interfering, and part of her was more than a little annoyed. Every woman wanted to be a beautiful princess whose honor was fought for by a handsome young man, who, of course, later turned out to be a prince. But in the real world Jackie didn't like the implication that she belonged to William and therefore he had the right to do whatever violent thing he had done to Terri's son.

Princess or no, William's lack of reaction was taking the wind out of her sails. She wanted something from him, but she didn't know what. "There's a man in town who wants to go out with me," she said, trying to sound as though this were an ordinary occurrence, but even as she spoke she knew she was trying to make William jealous. When he didn't look around his paper, she continued. "Terri says he's awfully nice." Warming to her subject, she fairly purred as she looked at the newspaper William held in front of his face. "Edward Browne. Do you know him? Terri says he's a wonderful man. Older, experienced. He was married for years, so he's already broken in, so to speak. Must know a lot about women."

She stood where she was, waiting for some reaction from him. After a while, he slowly folded the section of newspaper he was reading, neatly put it on top of the other sections — one could hardly tell that the paper had been opened — and opened another section.

"I think you ought to go out with him," he said from behind the paper.

"Wh . . . what?"

"Mr. Browne *is* a nice man. My mother likes him a lot, and my dad too."

"You want me to go out with him?" Even to her own ears there was disbelief in her voice.

"I think you should." He looked at her from around the paper. "Really, Jackie, you need to get out more. You can't just go from Charley to me. You need to look at the choices out there."

She didn't know whether that statement made her angry or just plain confused. "For your information, I've known *lots* of men besides you and Charley."

"Mmmm," he said. "Fancy foreign fellers."

"Fancy . . . ?" Those were not William's words. It was almost as though he was quoting someone else. "What in the world is *wrong* with you?"

"I have no idea what you mean. You said Terri

suggested you go out with Edward Browne, and I agree that you should. Have I done something wrong? I assume you *do* want to go out with Mr. Browne or you wouldn't have brought it up, would you?"

What could she say? That she wanted to make him jealous? "Yes, of course it's a good idea. I'll . . . I'll tell Terri."

Before she could form another thought, the telephone rang. Listlessly she answered it. Terri was calling to tell her that she had just "happened" to see Edward Browne on the street, and they had started talking, and, well, it seemed that Edward would love to take Jackie to dinner tonight. Would that be all right with her? Terri asked this question as though she were asking Jackie if she'd like to be given a couple of million dollars.

Jackie refused to think about what she was doing. Yes, it would be all right, she told Terri. She'd meet Edward at the Conservatory, Chandler's nicest restaurant at eight o'clock tonight.

"Oh, and, Jackie," Terri said, "wear that beige silk dress of yours. The one with the gold buttons."

"I thought I'd wear the coveralls I wear when I work on the planes," Jackie said with great sarcasm. She'd had her fill of people implying that she didn't know how to behave, how to dress, how to run her own life. Immediately she felt guilty for speaking to Terri so waspishly. "I'll be there, and I'll look as respectable as I can."

"All right," Terri said timidly, knowing that she had again done something wrong. But this time she felt that the end justified the means, because she knew that Jackie and Edward were perfect for each other and would fall madly in love with each other. Someday Jackie would thank her for having introduced them.

Putting down the phone, Jackie glanced at William, his face hidden behind the newspaper. "I have a date tonight," she said and cursed her heart for leaping into her throat. She very stupidly had a vision of William throwing his paper aside, sweeping her into his arms, and telling her she mustn't go out with any other man.

But nothing happened. In fact, William's only comment was an uncaring grunt, so Jackie, her shoulders drooping, left the room. She missed seeing William ball up the section of paper he was reading and throw it into the fireplace so forcefully that he displaced a log, which made the front log roll onto the floor and nearly set the rug on fire. Jackie missed seeing William stamping the flames out of the rug, the floor, the hearth, and four magazines with a fury that would have wrecked a less solidly built floor. An hour or so later, when she returned, dressed for her date, William was quietly still reading the paper, as though Jackie's leaving on a date meant nothing to him.

Jackie had to admit that, if judged by looks alone, Edward Browne was everything a woman could want in a man: tall, solidly muscular, with just enough fat on him to let a woman know that he would enjoy good cooking, broad-shouldered, slim-hipped. He had dark hair with just a bit of gray at the temples, and beautiful dark eyes. Although he was very handsome, there was a quietness about him that said he had no idea that he was attractive.

No wonder the women of Chandler are killing themselves over him, Jackie thought.

"Miss O'Neill," he said, extending his hand. "I can't tell you how pleased I am that you accepted my invitation. I have been an admirer of yours for years."

"Not too many years, I hope," she answered, eyes sparkling, but he looked puzzled and didn't seem to understand her sense of humor.

Graciously, with the good manners that he'd probably had all his life, he held out a chair for her. There was a rather long, awkward silence as they looked at the menu. Then Edward competently ordered a bottle of French wine.

Once the orders were placed, Jackie had to keep herself from looking at her watch. This was going to be a very long evening. She hoped that William was wondering where she was and what she was doing. Sternly she reminded herself that it didn't matter what little Billy Montgomery was doing or thinking. He was only a temporary part of her life.

"The entire ritual of dating is deplorable, isn't it?" Edward said, looking at her across the candlelight. "It takes two perfectly ordinary people and makes them nervous and uncertain. It puts them in an impossible situation and asks them to

171

discover good qualities about each other."

Jackie smiled. "Yes, I find it quite awful."

His eyes were twinkling. "Has Terri told you as much about me as she's told me about you?"

At this Jackie laughed. The FBI didn't know as much about criminals as Terri had told her on the phone about Edward Browne, and Terri had emphasized repeatedly how interested Edward was in Jackie. "I think he's been in love with you from afar for a long time," Terri said. "He knows a lot about you and has asked me thousands of questions."

"And no doubt you've made me out to be a saint," Jackie said.

"Did you expect me to tell him about your bad points?" she asked, then said something that made Jackie groan: "He *loved* seeing my scrapbook about you."

So now Jackie wondered exactly what Terri had told this man. "Yes. Terri could not stop talking about you. The only thing she left out was whether or not you have any tattoos."

Again Edward looked puzzled. "No, none," he said seriously. "Oh, I see. You're referring to the fact that I was in the navy."

Jackie was referring to nothing at all, just trying to inject a little levity into the situation, but she had not succeeded. The arrival of the salads kept her from having to explain.

"I guess we can skip the talk of our early lives," he said. "Of course with you it's easier since you are a world renowned figure."

Jackie hated it when people said that. It made her sound as though she didn't need what other humans needed: love, companionship, warmth.

For a moment Edward toyed with his salad, and Jackie watched him. She didn't know him at all, of course, and she had accepted his invitation in a fit of pique, but as she looked at him, she thought, *This* is the type of man I should marry. This man was perfect: perfect age, background, education. This was a man she could introduce to the world and everyone would say, "What a wonderful man your husband is!"

"Do you miss your husband as much as I miss my wife?" he asked softly, so softly that Jackie almost didn't hear him.

His question was from his heart, so Jackie answered from the same place. "Yes," she said, then waited for him to speak again. There was an air of sadness about him, a romantic air, she thought and again realized why Terri and the other women were trying so hard to get him married.

"You know what I miss the most?" When she shook her head, he continued. "I miss having someone who *knows* me. My wife and I were married a very long time, and she could look at me and say, 'You have a headache, don't you?' Every year at Christmas our grown children give me slippers and ties, but my wife gave me little ships in bottles or scrimshaw carvings of ships, because only she knew of my dream to sail around the world when I retire. She bought all my clothing in exactly my taste, cooked just what I liked. It

173

took us many years together to reach that stage of comfort, and now it's what I miss the most."

Jackie was silent for a while as she thought of Charley and how he'd also known so much about her, both good and bad. "When my husband wanted me to do something that I didn't want to do, he knew just how to wheedle me into doing it."

Edward smiled at her. "Cora always spent too much money. Not on herself but on me and the kids. Sometimes I'd get furious at her, but she always knew just how to soothe me."

As the salad plates were taken away, Jackie knew that they were talking about loneliness, the great loneliness that one felt after having been close to someone and then having lost that person. They were talking about the things that they missed. Like the affectionate names Charley had called her. On the day she met Charley, he'd called her an angel and she'd liked that very much, but after a week he stopped calling her his angel. A year or so after they were married she asked him why he'd stopped. Charley had smiled and said, "Because you, my dear, are not an angel. *You* are a little devil."

Jackie feared that she was attracted to William because of her deep loneliness. Wasn't a warm body better than no body? She and William were actually ill-suited, weren't they? He was too set in his ways for her, wasn't he? There were too many differences between them, weren't there?

"What are you planning to do in the future?" Edward asked.

"I'm expanding my freight and passenger service with William Montgomery as my partner."

"William Montgomery? Oh, you mean little Billy?" He chuckled. "But I guess he's not so little anymore, is he? How old is he now?"

"Twenty-eight," she said as she gripped the stem of her wineglass.

"These children do grow up, don't they? Doesn't it amaze you that one day you see a child riding his tricycle and the next day he's getting married?" He smiled warmly at her as the waiter delivered the entrée. "Of course there's our own mirror, too. One day we're laughing teenagers and the next we're middle-aged."

Jackie tried to share his smile. Was it a shock to every woman the first time she heard herself referred to as middle-aged? Jackie guessed that thirty-eight was middle age, but the term still seemed more suitable for her parents than for her.

"You didn't have any children, did you?"

"No," Jackie answered softly. The way he asked the question made her sound as though her chances were over.

He looked down at his plate, and she could see that he had something he considered important to say. "The woman who marries me will get to have children."

"Oh?" Jackie asked encouragingly.

"Yes." He smiled warmly at her, obviously liking her enthusiasm. His wife had always felt sorry for any woman who didn't have children. She said that a woman without children was "incomplete." "I have a son and a daughter in Denver, and I am proud to say that I have two grandchildren — a boy six months old and a girl two years old. Beautiful, brilliant, talented —" He cut himself off and laughed self-consciously.

"I'll be showing you pictures in a minute." When Jackie opened her mouth to ask to see them, he waved his hand. "Absolutely not. I want to hear about you. You say that you're planning to expand your flying business. I think it's wise of you to go into business with a young man like Billy. He has the backing of the Montgomery money, and with his youth he can do the flying for you."

Jackie gave him an intense look. "William's not a very good pilot."

"Ah, too bad, but I'm sure you can hire others. Doesn't he have young cousins who fly? I seem to remember a few of them buzzing around."

"I rather like buzzing around myself," she said, her head down.

Immediately Edward knew that he had offended her. "Of course you do. Forgive me. I didn't mean anything. You are years away from retirement. It's just that retirement is close at hand for me, so I think it's that way for others too."

He was protesting too much, and it was obvious that he was backtracking merely to make her feel better. There was an awkward silence in which Jackie kept her head down and moved her fish about on her plate. She'd ordered fish so she could cut it with a fork; she wouldn't have liked to ask a man to cut her steak for her. Only William — *Stop it!* she commanded herself.

Edward didn't fully understand what he had said to offend her. When his wife had reached forty — an age Jackie was fast approaching — she had cried for two days. She'd said it was the end of youth and that she didn't want to be middle-aged. Maybe that was Jackie's problem. She was refusing to face the fact that she wasn't a kid anymore. No longer would the newspapers write stories about her being the youngest person to do so and so. Maybe her eyesight was failing, or her reflexes. Maybe she was seeing the younger pilots doing so well, then seeing her own body aging, and it was making her angry. Aging often made a person angry at first.

Maybe, he thought, she was worried about whether or not she was still attractive to men.

"I like mature women," he said. "They know more about life." His eyes twinkled. "They don't expect so much of a man."

He meant to make light of himself, but Jackie didn't take the remark that way. "Do you mean that an older woman knows she has to take what she can get in a husband, that she can no longer expect some gorgeous young man to sweep her off her feet?"

That was not at all what he meant, but he didn't say so. Something seemed to be bothering her, and he didn't know enough about her to figure out what it was. He decided it would probably be better just to change the subject.

"I'm going to sail around the world someday," Edward said brightly, trying to introduce a whole new topic. A more pleasant one than aging.

"Are you?" Jackie asked, trying to work up some interest in what he was saying. She knew that he hadn't meant to demean her by saying that he liked mature women. She was a mature woman. So why did William's words — "I'd love to marry you and give you as many kids as you want" — echo in her head? He hadn't said, "as many kids as you have fertile years left." Could a *mature* woman have a dozen children?

"Have you always been a sailor?" she forced herself to ask.

The question embarrassed Edward, for he knew she thought he'd meant that he was going to sail a boat himself. Considering her skills with a plane, it was understandable that she would assume others were as capable as she was.

"I meant that I'm going on a cruise ship with a few hundred other people."

"Oh" was all that Jackie could reply. She had been in towns when a cruise ship had pulled into port and suddenly every shop, every restaurant, would be overrun with tourists buying anything that could possibly be called a souvenir.

"Come with me, Jackie," Edward said, surprising both of them.

"What?"

"I'll make all the arrangements, pay for everything. I don't expect you to marry me. I'll book us separate cabins, and we'll be traveling companions, friends. We'll see the world together. Or maybe you'll be seeing the world again." He reached across the table and took her hand in his large warm one. "I know we could be friends. I've read so much about you, and I'd love to hear all about your exciting life. I'd love to hear about the time you flew those burned children to the hospital and the president called you. You must be full of hundreds of stories."

"Rather like taking a radio with you, huh?"

"I beg your pardon."

"Taking me with you to tell you stories would be like having your own radio with you at every moment. You could feed me a dinner and I'd perform. Buy me a trinket and you get a story. Pay for a whole cruise and you get relief from the tedium of months on a ship with nothing to do."

By the time she finished, he was sitting straight in his chair, and there was a closed look on his face. It was a businessman look rather than an I'm-out-with-a-pretty-woman-for-dinner look.

"I apologize," she said, then took a deep breath. "Mr. Browne, I don't mean to be offensive, but I think you've fallen in love with Terri's glorification of whatever I may have accomplished in my life. I'm a woman, just as your wife was a woman. I'm not a public institution, nor am I an especially good storyteller. I've led an exciting life, and I have no intention of retiring yet."

Oh, heavens, but she was making a mess of this.

This was a very nice person, just like Terri. But why did she have the feeling that ninety percent of Terri's and Edward's interest in her was based her fame? What other reason would this man have had for asking about her? She certainly wasn't the most beautiful unmarried woman in town. So why was he interested in *her?*

He had already answered that question: he wanted companionship. He was fifty-five years old, and he was no longer looking for long legs and a woman to start a family with. At this stage in his life he wanted someone to talk with and what better candidate than a woman who'd traveled all over the world and was "full of stories"?

After Jackie's outburst there was no way to salvage the evening. They spent the rest of the meal in awkward silence.

Chapter Nine

When Jackie returned home she wasn't surprised to see the house dark and no sign of William anywhere. What had she expected, that he'd be waiting up for them?

She shook her head, trying to clear it. There was nothing between her and William, nothing at all, and there wasn't going to be. He said he loved her, even though she had done everything possible

180

to keep him from loving her. She winced when she thought of flying the airplane upside down and making him ill. Even if she couldn't return his love it hadn't been very polite of her to be so nasty about everything.

As she headed to her bedroom, she felt as though each foot weighed a thousand pounds. William, William, William, her brain kept echoing. He seemed to be all she could think of, yet he was forbidden. He was the forbidden fruit in the Garden of Eden. "And we know what happened there," she said out loud as she opened the door.

As soon as she turned on the light, she knew that something was wrong. At first she didn't know what it was and for a moment she stood in the doorway looking at the room. It was exactly as she'd left it; she could see nothing different, much less wrong. It was the same in the kitchen, everything as she'd left it.

Suddenly she realized that that was what was wrong: nothing was different. In only a short time she had grown used to William's orderliness, the way he put everything away — maybe he put things in the wrong place, but at least they were out of sight. But tonight nothing had been put away. On the kitchen countertops was evidence that William had prepared himself a meal, but the dirty dishes were still in the sink, not even soaking in soapy water. On impulse, she opened the refrigerator door, and instead of the orderliness she usually saw, the contents were in chaos. It looked as though a drunken two-year-old had gone on an Easter egg hunt in the icebox.

She didn't know why the disorder in the refrigerator should depress her, but it did. Maybe she should have felt better at this evidence that William was upset at her going on a date with another man, but somehow this made her feel worse. Maybe "hopeless" was the right word. "Jackie," she said aloud, "*you* are hopeless. You just met a perfect man who liked you and you're depressed because your business partner didn't clean up the kitchen."

Despondently she walked through the dark house toward the bedroom. She knew that this was her chance to end things between her and William. In the morning she should tell him that she'd had a marvelous time with a marvelous man and she was very much interested in a future with him. What was that French word? "Insouciance." Yes, she should deliver her story about tonight with insouciance.

But instead of playing the lady who doesn't care, the second she entered the bedroom she flung herself on the bed, the down comforter practically hugging her as she burst into tears. How could her life have taken this terrible turn? Why did she think about William all the time? Tonight there hadn't been a minute when she wasn't wondering what he was doing, what he was thinking. She had compared that nice Mr. Browne to William in everything he did and said.

When she felt a strong male hand on her head, a hand that could only belong to William, she wasn't surprised at his presence. Wasn't he always there when she needed him? If her plane crashed into a rock, he was there to save her. If she cut her hand, he stopped the blood. And before, if she and her husband had needed money, William was the one who knew what was wrong and anonymously helped them.

"You want to tell me what's wrong?"

With her face buried in the coverlet, she shook her head. No, she didn't want to tell him, if for no other reason than because she herself didn't know what the real problem was.

It seemed quite natural when William pulled her into his arms. He was leaning against the headboard, his long legs stretched out on the bed, as he pulled her across him, her head on his broad chest.

"Drink this," he said, holding a snifter of brandy to her lips, and when she'd taken several deep swallows, he put the glass on the bedside table. "Now tell me what's making you cry."

"I can't tell you," she wailed.

"Then who can you tell if not me?"

He was, of course, unfortunately right. She couldn't tell Terri because Terri couldn't know about William. William was a secret. But William was her friend, had been her friend for as long as she could remember.

"How was your . . . date?" he asked, a catch in his voice. With her head against his heart, Jackie could feel the emotion inside him. Now she should tell him in elaborate detail about tonight. She

183

should stop William — and herself — from thinking there could ever be anything between them. "It was perfect," she said. "*He* was perfect." The words were at odds with her tone of voice, which said that "perfect" meant "horrible." The tears started to flow with renewed vigor.

"Oh, William," she said, clinging to him, tears wetting his shirt, "I know what I *should* do. I should marry some man like Edward Browne. He's perfect for me. He's the right age, the right background. He's even the right size for me. Everything is perfect. He's lonely; I'm lonely. We're a match made in heaven."

William handed her a tissue, and she blew her nose loudly. "He was such a nice man and I was awful to him. I took everything he said the wrong way. He . . . he called me a mature woman."

"That shows that he knows nothing about you," William said with heavy sarcasm.

Jackie sniffed. "He didn't know anything about me. He wanted me to tell him stories about my exciting life. He made me sound like a lady explorer showing slides of the natives."

Tears started up again. "But he was so very nice. Why was I so awful to him? And why don't I ever do what's good for me? Why don't I do what I *should* do?"

"Why aren't you in love with this man if he's so perfect?" William's words were calm, but with her face against his chest, she could feel his heart racing, feel the tension in his body as he talked of something that meant so much to him.

"Because he's so . . . so old," Jackie blurted. "He's no fun! Not like you are. You make me laugh. You make me —"

She broke off to look up at him. "Why are you smiling?" She couldn't help feeling betrayed by that smile. "I'm pouring my heart out to you, and you're *laughing?*"

"Jackie my love," he said slowly, pulling her even closer. "Only you would think of me as fun. No other girl in the world has ever accused me of being fun. Many times I've been in a group that wanted to do something I considered stupid or dangerous, and when I said no, they've called me an old man."

"Kids!" Jackie said in derision.

At that, he chuckled, his hands caressing her upper arm. "You know what I love about you, Jackie?"

"Nothing about me is lovable," she said heavily. "I'm an idiot."

He ignored that statement. "One, just one of the things that I love about you, is that when you were a child you were an adult, and now that you're an adult you're a child. I think that when you were born you were about twenty-five years old and you've never changed. And probably never will."

"I'm *not* twenty-five years old. I'm a mature woman. Oh, William, what am I going to do? This man is so good for me."

"So's broccoli."

"What?"

"Broccoli is very good for you. A person should eat broccoli every day. Actually, people should only eat boiled chicken, broccoli, and brown rice. A person should *never* eat chocolate or ice cream or buttered popcorn."

"What *are* you talking about?"

"Edward Browne. He's broccoli."

"Oh," she said, beginning to understand. "So I guess you think you're chocolate ice cream."

"More like vanilla, I'd say."

In spite of herself, she smiled. "You think highly of yourself, don't you?" As suddenly as it had appeared, her smile disappeared. "William, what am I going to do? You and I can't . . . We can't be together. You know that as well as I do. But I think about you all of the time. Even tonight when I was with that very nice man, I . . . Oh, William, what am I going to do?"

Only the pounding of his heart under her cheek betrayed that William was affected by her words. In a way, she was telling him that she loved him, wasn't she?

"I have one question for you," he said. "If you'd never known me as a child and you first met me when your plane went down, if I were the same age as you or a few years older, what would you feel for me?"

Jackie didn't answer right away, but gave the question the thought that it deserved. There was William's sense of humor, which was so different from other people's humor. She loved his honesty and the way he could laugh at himself. Of course there were many other men in the world who had a sense of humor; he wasn't the only one. But there were too many Edward Brownes of the world, men who didn't laugh. There were too many Edward Brownes who considered themselves old because that was what their passport said.

But would William be different if he were thirty-eight instead of twenty-eight? Quite suddenly she had some insight into his character. If he married a younger woman he would take the responsibility of teaching her — Jackie knew all too well that older husbands considered two-thirds of their job to be teaching their young wives about life — so seriously he'd turn into an old man five minutes after he said, "I do." Oddly enough, she knew that it would take someone like her to keep him young. He needed someone who flew airplanes upside down now and then, someone to keep him from turning into that rock the children had said he was.

"Jackie? Are you going to answer me? Tell me the truth. What would you think of me if you knew nothing of me from the past? And if my birth certificate had a different date on it?"

"I'd think you needed me," she said softly. "Needed me to keep you young."

Jackie was still talking — she didn't know what about — when she felt William's breath in her hair. It was as though one minute they were innocent children comforting each other and the next they realized they were adults capable of very adult feelings.

She quite suddenly became aware of his strong hands on her back, his lips that were now pressed against her neck.

"William," she whispered.

He didn't seem to hear her as he pulled her closer to him, her body, her breasts, full against his chest. She felt more than heard him groan as her softness touched the steel strength of his chest.

Slowly, as though it were the most important thing he'd ever done, William buried his hands in her hair and brought his lips to hers. He'd kissed her before, but not like this. Before, he'd been in control; he had seemed to want to show her something. Those kisses had had a beginning and an end.

But this kiss was tenderness. It was all tenderness and gentleness and sensitivity. It was as though he'd been wanting to press his lips to hers for a long while and now that he was being allowed to, he was going to savor every second of it. There was something else in the kiss: vulnerability. He was allowing her to see how very much she meant to him, allowing her to see his longing and yearning, and his love. He was showing her how easily she could hurt him. In that kiss he was not protecting himself but allowing his innermost feelings to be seen and felt. He was trusting her.

She knew that he would never take what he hadn't been offered, so if the kiss continued past a kiss, it would be up to her to make the first move. William had too much respect for her to do anything that she would regret later.

The kiss continued, then deepened, and the longing she felt in him increased. It was almost as though she could feel his very soul in that kiss. When he pulled away from her he was trembling from the iron will he was exerting to keep himself under control. She felt that he would like to leap on her, maybe tear her clothes off, make wild love to her. But instead he was limiting himself to one gentle, long kiss.

"William," she whispered.

"Yes?" His normally deep voice was husky with suppressed emotion.

"I . . ." She didn't know what to say. Women were indoctrinated from childhood with the notion that a man should be the aggressor. Of course, after years of marriage a woman often found that if she didn't start things, things wouldn't get started. So now she wanted to tell William that it was all right, that she wanted him as much as he wanted her. Maybe this was wrong and maybe she would regret it tomorrow, but then maybe the world would end and tomorrow would never come.

She didn't use words to give permission but used the age-old device of opening herself to him, allowing her body to tell him yes. Turning fully toward him, she opened her mouth under his, pressed her legs against his, allowed her body to soften.

She was afraid he would ask her if she was sure she wanted to make love with him and thereby give her yet another decision to make. But William didn't waste time with words. Instead of speaking, he looked at her with the most delighted pair of eyes she had ever seen. His look was that of a boy who'd been given his first taste of ice cream and who meant to enjoy every bit.

She had, of course, thought more than she wanted to admit about the fact that William had mentioned, in a rather angry moment, that he was a virgin. More than once she had awakened at night and imagined being an older woman teaching a shy — yet highly desirable and utterly gorgeous — young man what to do. She imagined herself as a worldly-wise French courtesan, remembering to be gentle and kind, thinking of his needs and his first impressions. She would want to make his first sexual experience memorable for its sheer beauty.

Dreams alone in bed had nothing to do with reality. And this reality was about two hundred pounds of enthusiastic, hungry male. There was no shyness. No hesitation. The beauty of it was in the exuberance, the energy, the unbiased delight, in William's sheer joy and surprise.

Brother! Could William unfasten buttons quickly. One minute she was fully clothed and the next she was wearing nothing. One minute she was expecting languor and the next she was smiling happily in delight as William began touching and tasting her skin.

William's hands were all over her at once, searching, exploring. His mouth followed his hands, and when Jackie moaned in pleasure he seemed to have found the keys to heaven. With one hand on one breast, his mouth on the other, he tried different movements to see what felt best to both of them. As far as Jackie could tell, everything felt best.

"William," she tried to say, but he had his hands all over her and that lovely mouth of his was sending such shivers of delight through her that she could hardly think. "Your . . ." She broke off because she couldn't remember what she had meant to say. Who could remember something as complicated as words when he was touching her like that? His hands were on her thighs, his strong palms running over the curves of her legs. Now she understood the fascination men had with virgins. To think that this man had never done this to another woman! It made her seem more than special. It made her feel unique, unequaled, like the queen of the world. That this divine man had never been touched by another female made her feel that he was hers in a way that nothing else could.

Her body was turning to mush, pliant, soft, easy. "Your . . ." she tried again.

"My what?" he managed to whisper, his voice filled with the intoxication of pleasure he was experiencing.

She tugged at his shirt collar. She was fully nude, deliciously nude and open to William's eyes and hands, but he had on all of his clothes.

After the ease with which he had removed her clothes, she wasn't surprised when his came off in the flash of an eye.

Heavens, but he was beautiful. Skin like something newly hatched, something that had been born yesterday. Soft, downy hair on his chest, muscles strong and new, glistening with strength and youth. She wouldn't have thought it possible but the sight of his beautiful body made her grow even more limp with desire. Eagerly her hands sought any and all of him that she could touch; then she twisted her body so she could put her mouth on his clean bare shoulder, and her hands moved downward.

She was not prepared for the bliss, the rapture, that was apparent on William's face and in his voice when she took the most private parts of him into her hands. If nothing else, her pleasure was in knowing that he was not comparing her to anyone else. No other woman had touched him. No woman had put her hands or lips on him. He was hers alone.

When he moved his big, heavy body on top of hers and prepared to slip inside her, Jackie arched her hips to meet him. Never had anything felt as right, as proper, as "what was meant to be" as did this joining of her body with William's. The word "home" echoed through her brain: he had come home; she was now at home. They were where they were meant to be.

"Yes, yes," was all she could say as William began to move on top of her. "Ecstasy" didn't begin to describe how he made her feel. There were no words to describe the joy. There was the excitement that always accompanied sex, but with

William there was more. He seemed to touch some deep, remote area of her that had never been touched before. This act that she had experienced before had been a physical one, but now it was deeper than that. It was almost spiritual, because she felt that she was bonding with this man in the last possible way. They had been friends, had exchanged thoughts and secrets, but this exchange had until now been denied them.

If Jackie had thought about it — and she had, far more than she'd admit to herself — she would have expected the first time with William to be of the very shortest duration. Happily — very happily — she was wrong. After several minutes she began to wake up inside.

"William, you are wooonnnderful," she said dreamily, her back arched, her eyes closed. She heard him laugh, that smug laugh of men when they are very proud of themselves. Then he pressed his sweaty chest on hers and nuzzled her neck.

For the next week, Jackie lived in a dream world. Her sexual experience had all been with Charley, so, in a way, she was as new to sex as William was. When Jackie met Charley, he had been to bed with any woman he could get to say yes, or even to say maybe. By the time he met Jackie he knew what he liked, how he wanted to do things. He'd tried every position, every possible variation. Like all women, she'd been very curious and she'd asked him to tell her of his past experiences. She'd heard how some girl in Singapore had been great at so-and-so, and then there was this girl in Florida who'd been especially good at something else. At the time Jackie hadn't thought about it, but years later she knew that she had felt intimidated. How could a skinny thing like her compete with those women who knew so much? She'd said this to Charley once and he'd laughed at her, told her she was the best of all of them and he'd rather go to bed with her than all the women in the world. At the time she'd felt better, but still, there was that nagging little worry that maybe other women had been more . . . more what? Enticing? More technically skilled?

With William she felt free, free from comparisons, free from having to live up to the standards of anyone else. And who would have thought that freedom was the headiest aphrodisiac on earth?

Also, who would have thought that solid, dependable, upright-citizen William Montgomery would be a demon in bed? In all the years she'd known William she'd seen little evidence that he was creative. On the contrary, he seemed to be the epitome of follow-the-rules. Even as a child he had always colored inside the lines.

For one week they did nothing, absolutely nothing. The excuse they gave themselves, and Pete, was that they needed to wait until Jackie's hand healed before they could fly or work on engines or even look at the financial aspect of setting up a business. The truth was — a truth that they didn't openly admit to themselves — that they

194

were so interested in each other's bodies that they could think of nothing else.

Jackie told herself not to compare William to Charley, but she couldn't help it. Charley was a very sexy man. He seemed to think about sex all the time and he loved sexual innuendo. Everything — soaring airplanes, chairs, whatever — reminded him of sex. He thought about sex, joked about it, wanted to discuss it.

William could not have been more different. Looking at him, fully clothed, across the breakfast table, Jackie couldn't believe this was the same man who'd been in bed with her an hour before. With his clothes on, there was no one more dignified than William. He was so cool, so remote, so private, that butter wouldn't melt in his mouth. For all of his youth, William was an old man, had an old man's established habits. She'd seen people older than he ask him for advice, and the first time she had a problem that didn't involve him, she planned to go straight to William. So it was easy to think that if she had been asked, or if she had thought of it, which she had, she would have assumed that William might be a bit shy in bed. True, he had been affectionate and tender toward her, but still, she was taken aback by how ardent he was.

To her delight, she found that once William got his clothes off he became as sensual as a child. Children would see a mud puddle, think the mud felt nice and cool, so they'd take their clothes off and smear themselves with the ooze. They had

195

no preconceived ideas that one wasn't supposed to like mud because it wasn't "nice or civilized." This innocence, this sensuality, was something that William brought to bed. He had no desire to get things over and done with so he could roll over and go to sleep. He wasn't just interested in that climactic moment and nothing else. William liked *all* of it.

Jackie had never for a moment thought that she was sexually repressed. In fact, a woman had once asked her what she saw in a man as old as Charley, and Jackie had laughed in a very naughty way. She'd had her disagreements with Charley and her complaints about him, but there had never been any sexual problems between them.

At least that was what she thought — until she met William. No wonder men wanted a woman who was a virgin; no wonder a man was ready to kill if "his" woman touched another man: if women were allowed to jump into bed with lots of men they might start comparing, just as she now compared Charley with William. If women compared lovers, what would happen to the world? Would men have to stop saying, "I'm the best, baby," and start having to prove that they were even good?

If she'd ever been to bed with a man like William before she went to bed with Charley . . . well, she didn't want to think about it.

After the first couple of days she stopped comparing the two men and allowed herself to enjoy. She would never be able to explain it to anyone — not that she'd try — but William made her feel as though she, too, were a virgin. They caressed each other, looked at each other, and touched as though they were the first couple to discover how nice skin against skin felt.

They didn't talk about sex or even seem to think about sex. Sex was something that just seemed to happen, something spontaneous and joyful, something clean and happy and delightful. They seemed to be saying, "How would it feel if I did this? Or this?" William lay still for as long as she wanted while she ran her hands over his hard thighs, over his broad chest.

And kissing with William was as though they'd invented this delicious practice. Charley had always felt that kissing was a waste of time. "I like the more serious stuff, kid," he'd said. Jackie had no idea that she was as starved for kissing as a man in the desert was for water. She and William kissed constantly. Nude, she stretched out on top of him and kissed his face — his eyes, his long nose — teasing him that it took sixteen kisses to get far enough down it to suck gently on his lower lip. She felt his teeth with her tongue, running her tongue over the contours of his mouth.

And then they traded places and he kissed her, his hands caressing her arms and shoulders while his lips traced every outline of her face. They spent hours in bed, touching, looking, kissing, exploring. Jackie sometimes thought that they were like Adam and Eve and they were the first two people to have felt such pleasure.

When they made love it seemed to be different every time. Sometimes there was such urgency that they couldn't get their clothes off fast enough. Other times lovemaking took hours. However long it lasted, it always seemed to catch them unawares. One minute they'd be sitting on the couch — William reading the newspaper, Jackie sewing a button on his shirt — and the next second their clothes would be hanging from the light fixture. Afterward they'd look at each other with startled expressions, as though to say, "How did *that* happen?"

Lovemaking itself was divine. Freedom, she thought. The headiness of freedom. With William she knew she wasn't being judged or compared. She knew that whatever she did was, to him, the right way, the only way. It was amazing how it changed her outlook when she knew that someone liked whatever she did. After the first couple of days, she and William seemed to adopt the attitude of "Let's try this and see how that feels." Feeling. It was everything to both of them. Touching hands, touching lips, trying different positions during sex.

And then there was William's creativity. It was as though he'd saved all of his imagination for this one ongoing event. He'd sat through school and studied other people's words and spat them back out with all the inventiveness of a parrot, but here at last he'd found a place where there were no rules he had to follow. Sometime during the third day, during a moment when sweat was dripping off both of them, William said, "Jackie, I *like* this,"

198

with such feeling that she laughed out loud. "Me too," she'd answered.

The only person they encountered during this week was silent Pete. They did their best to keep their passion from his sight, but they weren't successful. Jackie recalled an Arabic saying that she had always liked: "There are three things you can't hide: pregnancy, love, and a man riding a camel." She and William proved the second one true. The morning after their first night together, they cautioned each other that it would be better to keep their newfound passion from others. William had reluctantly agreed. "Since you won't marry me, I guess we should," he said. Jackie had just said that it would be better for both their reputations.

They had gone outside, confident that they were the greatest actors on earth and that no one would know anything was different between them. For all of approximately eleven minutes they were able to fool Pete. He was cleaning distributor segments with a cloth soaked in kerosene and, trying to act as though everything were the same, they stood, one on either side of him, and talked of that day's activities. Jackie and William didn't look at each other for several minutes. Then William said something about picking up some passengers for Denver, and when Jackie answered him, she made the mistake of looking into his eyes. For several moments they were silent, just looking at each other over Pete's head. The next moment Pete looked up, and his face turned as red as though he'd stumbled into the bedroom of a honeymoon couple. In the blink of an eye he left the hangar, leaving Jackie and William standing alone, doing nothing but looking at each other. It was a gaze that nearly ignited the kerosene.

Without exchanging a word, without so much as a raised eyebrow of communication, they turned toward the house. The door was barely closed before their clothes were on the floor and their hands were clutching at each other's bodies. They didn't leave the house again for two days.

Their idyll ended on the eighth day when Mrs. Beasley, the town gossip, walked into the bedroom and saw Jackie and William in bed together.

Chapter Ten

William and Jackie were alone in the house, sitting together on the sofa in the living room. Or perhaps "together" wasn't the right word, since Jackie was perched at one end, as far away from William as possible. This morning, the town snoop, who prided herself on having no idea what a closed door meant, had walked into their bedroom. No doubt she had felt it was her duty to see exactly what was going on way out there in that ghost town, so she'd put on her best hat and made up an excuse to borrow something from Jackie. Which of course was absurd since Mrs.

Beasley lived much nearer the stores, as well as other neighbors, than Jackie did.

But she'd seen what she'd hoped to see: something to satisfy her hunger for gossip. She had scurried out the door and sped away in her little car so fast William couldn't get into his trousers and catch her before she left. It had always been a town joke that the fastest runner in the world was a Beasley girl with a hot piece of gossip.

So now everything that Jackie had not wanted to happen in Chandler had. She had wanted to become respectable, to prove to the townspeople that she wasn't fast or easy, that she deserved a place in their town. For once in her life, she'd wanted to conform, not be an outsider. But this morning Mrs. Beasley had ruined her one chance. Now she was going to have to go into town and see people's eyes shift to one side when they saw her. She was going to know that they were repeating every story ever passed around about her.

William didn't want to leave, but Jackie begged him to go to Denver for a few days. "I need to face this alone," she said, referring to the people of Chandler.

"Face *what* alone, Jackie? What is there to face? Do you think we're the first people in this town to have gone to bed together before marriage? Half the children of this town are politely called 'premature' because they were born six months after the wedding."

She wasn't going to answer him, because he knew as well as she did that the two of them were not an ordinary couple.

When she didn't respond, he turned and left the room, moments later reappearing with his suitcases. He started to take her in his arms, but she held him away. With a hardened jaw, he picked up his luggage. "I'll be back in three days," he said, then left the house.

Jackie didn't have to wait long for the sky to open up. It opened in the form of Terri, her face angry, her body rigid as she stalked toward the house, ready to do battle.

"Is it true?" she asked as soon as Jackie opened the door, not even bothering with conventional greetings.

"I have no idea what you're talking about," Jackie said, trying to keep her dignity. Why did people always think they should talk to you "for your own good"? "Would you like some tea?"

"No, I don't want any tea. What I want is to try to talk some sense into you. You aren't thinking of marrying this . . . this child, are you?"

Jackie gave a great sigh. "William is not a child. He is a full-grown man."

To her consternation, Terri collapsed on the sofa in tears. Jackie had not expected this. She had expected outrage and anger from her friend, but not tears. Jackie went to her, put her arm around her shoulders. "Talk to me."

"No," Terri said, "you don't want to talk. Do you know how much you mean to me, Jackie? Do you have any idea how important you are to my life?"

Unfortunately, Jackie did have an idea how much she meant to Terri. She couldn't be oblivious to those dreadful sons of hers; she'd heard talk of Terri's husband, who couldn't hold a job. A couple of times in town Jackie had seen Terri unaware, had seen the misery on her face; it was not a face that she showed to Jackie.

"Yes," Jackie said, handing Terri several tissues. "I think I know."

"You are my idol. You are the idol of lots of women in America. You aren't just someone ordinary like me. You're special."

Yes, Jackie thought, and that was one of the major problems of her life. She had wanted to fly airplanes, but she'd never wanted to be a celebrity.

Terri looked at her. "Are you going to marry him?"

"I . . . I don't know."

"Then he has asked you?"

Jackie didn't answer, which was all the answer Terri needed.

"Have you thought this through?"

"Yes, of course I have. I've thought about everything. There's nothing you can say that I haven't run through my head a thousand times."

"Have you thought of always looking older than he does? Younger women will makes plays for him, and when they see you they'll say, 'Your wife is *old*.' It's better to be younger and prettier than the man."

It was as though Terri were parroting Jackie's own thoughts. She had played devil's advocate with herself a thousand times. "Age compatibility is not a guarantee of happiness," she said tiredly, but her bored tone didn't stop Terri from continuing, while blowing her nose in the tissues.

"All your friends will treat him like a boy, not like a man. You'll be talking about things that happened in your life that he won't remember because they happened before he learned to walk."

Jackie hadn't wanted to get involved in this, but already Terri was beginning to make her angry. "Why is age a consideration when the woman is older but not when the man is? Does a man who is in love with a younger woman worry that he's going to be talking about things that happened before she was born? Or does he laugh and pat her on the fanny and say something like 'Now, honey, you go on back to the kitchen and let us grown-up men do the talkin'?' Are you saying that that sort of thing is *good?* That is to be *encouraged?*"

Terri didn't answer. She must have been formulating these questions for the past day and a half, ever since she'd heard about what Mrs. Beasley had seen. "How can he take care of you? You're a grown woman."

"If he were marrying a twenty-four-year-old woman, no one would question a twenty-eight-year-old *man's* ability to take care of her," Jackie said. "No one would question that he was a man. Why is he reduced to being a child just because his wife is older than he is?" Jackie was beginning to warm to the subject. "And while we're at it, I'd like to know what needs a twenty-four-year-old girl has that I don't. Companionship? A man who takes responsibility for a wife and maybe children? Sex? Being there when I need him? What does a younger woman need that I don't?"

Terri gave her a look of pity. "It's a matter of wisdom. In thirty-eight years, I hope you have learned more than he has. Think how stupid and immature you were at twenty-eight. Think what you've learned about life since then."

Jackie threw up her hands in exasperation. "You know what I've learned in my lifetime? I've learned that I don't want to spend any more of my life with a man who sets himself up as some sort of demigod to me. Charley wasn't just my husband; he was a dictator. He made all the rules; he knew everything."

"But that's the way it's *supposed* to be," Terri practically shouted, frustrated and frightened. She knew very well how horrible marriage could be, and she wanted to save her friend from a misfortune she could foresee as clearly as though she had a crystal ball.

"Who made that rule?" Jackie snapped back, but then tried to calm herself. She knew that Terri had nothing but the best intentions toward her. Terri thought that Jackie was making a horrible mistake, and she was trying to prevent that mistake. "Who says the husband has to be a teacher and instructor to the wife? Why can't the two of them be *equal*? William and I are equal. He knows about home and family and stability. I know about excitement and impulsiveness and living for the moment. If we were the same age or if he were like that perfect man you wanted me to marry, I would have to adapt to his ways. An older man would never bend to my ways. If William married a younger woman he'd bully her into organizing her hairpins. She would look up to him as though he had all the answers, and poor William would feel an obligation to supply them — as he knows them. But I know, because I've seen so much of the world, that there is no right way or wrong way of doing anything. I don't expect William to tell me how to think, how to live, how to set my dressing table in order. I just want him to . . . to . . ."

"To what?" Terri asked, her mouth set in a line that said she wasn't going to believe anything Jackie had to say.

But Jackie didn't care that she was fighting a battle she was destined to lose. "To love me. I want him to be my friend. To care about me as I am. I don't want to change him, and he doesn't want to change me. I don't put the unbearable weight on his shoulders of needing to have the answers for everything. We are equals."

"But, Jackie," Terri said softly, as though explaining something that everyone else on earth knew, "a man needs to feel that he is the man. Maybe you and I know that there aren't five men in the world who know half as much as any woman, but it's important to a man to *think* he knows more than the woman he loves."

At that Jackie laughed. "Terri, if you think

that William honestly believes I know more than he does because I'm older than he is, then you don't know anything at all about men. How old were your sons when they decided they knew more about the world than you because you were a mere female?"

In spite of her feeling of imminent disaster, Terri couldn't help a smile. "Nine. No, eight years old."

"Right. I'm the one saying that William and I are equals, not him. We are equal because I do not look to him for all the answers. When I married Charley I thought that because he was older he knew everything there was to know. It was hard on both of us when I began to realize that he was human like all the rest of us. Both of us wanted to get back to the time when I had looked up at him with starry eyes filled with the belief that he could do anything, but once that belief is gone, it's gone forever. With William I don't expect him to know everything. I expect only what he's good at: steadfastness, a calming presence in the storm of my life. I haven't deified William; I see him for what he is, and I like what I see."

Jackie smiled. "You know, it must be a relief for him to be liked for what he is instead of having to try to be what some romantic girl thinks he is."

Jackie was beginning to feel better. As the words came out of her mouth she became more and more convinced of the truth of what she was saying. "Why is it that a man can be a child at fifty but not an adult at twenty-eight? It's common for

207

women to complain that their husbands take more care than a couple of two-year-olds, so why is it inconceivable that a man can be grown up at twenty-eight? William says —"

Terri could see that she was losing Jackie, that, once again, Jackie was doing just what she wanted and the rest of the world be damned. "And we all know how much sense *we* had at twenty-eight." Her voice was heavy with sarcasm. "At twenty-eight I was weighed down with three kids and a husband who couldn't hold his job but could hold his liquor. And at twenty-eight you were flying planes through burning barns."

"I refuse to reduce a man to one characteristic: his age," Jackie said angrily. "Ask me about his reliability, his ability to think in an emergency, his kindness, his sense of honor, his honesty, his sense of humor, the way he takes care of others. Why are these things worth nothing and his age is everything?"

Terri opened her mouth to say something else, but she closed it. She could see that there was no use talking to Jackie; she had made up her mind. Terri stood up. "Obviously I am wasting my breath. When this boy breaks your heart, Jackie, I'll help you put the pieces back together."

That statement made Jackie angry. "Is it a guarantee that because I am older in years, not in spirit, William and I are destined to fail?"

Terri started toward the door, meaning not to say a word, but then she turned back. "You have all the answers, don't you, Jackie? You've been everywhere, done everything, so of course you know it all. How could *I* know anything? I've lived in the same town all my life, my husband is in training to be the town drunk, and my children will no doubt spend their adult lives in prison. So how could someone as insignificant as I am know anything?"

"Terri —" Jackie began, her hand out to touch her, but Terri moved away.

"Jackie, I will be there if you need me," Terri said and left the house.

Jackie leaned against the door and began to cry. "Why can't life be simple?" she whispered, tears running down her cheeks. "Why can't I be like other people?"

There was no answer.

Chapter Eleven

Surprise!"

Jackie stared in open-mouthed astonishment at the people standing in the doorway of her house, five men and two women, their faces alight and happy. Their expressions did not reflect what she was feeling inside.

"Bet you didn't expect us, huh, Jackie?"

"No," she said as politely as she could, but her heart had fallen to her feet. Only yesterday she'd had to deal with Terri, and in the hours that had passed since then, she hadn't stepped outside her door, afraid of what the other people in Chandler were saying about her and William.

Now there were seven people standing at her door, old friends of Charley's, old drinking buddies of his. Men and women who had once been part of her life but who were no longer.

As she looked at them, laughing, holding up bottles of wine, wanting to stay up all night to celebrate, she realized how much she had changed during her time in Chandler. In Chandler, if someone saw your light on at three A.M. they'd call you the next day, usually at six A.M., to ask what was wrong with you.

"Come in," she said, smiling, holding the door open wide. Once they were inside, she went to the kitchen, knowing they would be hungry and that later probably at least two of them would need cash.

"Jackie, come in here and tell us what you've been doing these last two years. We saw a barn full of new planes out there. Where'd they come from?"

At those words, Jackie's hands froze as she was cutting the fourth sandwich. So that was why they were here: they'd somehow heard of her new business and wanted in on it.

Suddenly she had an overwhelming desire for William to be there. He would politely but very firmly let these people know that they were hiring only reliable people, not old-timers whose best years had come and gone.

At that thought, she shook her head to clear it. *She* was an old-timer. These were *her* people, her own age.

"Come and get it," she called as she carried a tray of sandwiches and pickles into the dining room where the table was already littered with beer and wine bottles. One of the men was carrying in suitcases.

"Hope you don't mind a little company for a few days, Jackie," one man said. "We didn't think you'd mind, what with this whole hotel to yourself. You must get lonely now and then and want a little company."

"No, of course not. Sure," she said, trying to force a smile, and she was sent back in time to when she lived with Charley. He was a very generous man; what was his belonged to everyone else as well. He was considered generous, but it was Jackie who'd had to buy the food and cook the meals and do everyone's laundry.

So now they were here wanting jobs and food and free lodging. How was she going to tell them to get lost?

"Hello."

She looked up and there stood William, so strong and tall and clean. The sunlight behind his head made him look like a rescuing angel. Dropping three empty bottles, Jackie rushed to him, and he opened his arms to her, pulling her against his chest, holding her close. Vaguely she was aware of the hush behind them, but she didn't care what they thought. Until this moment she hadn't realized how much she had come to depend on William, on the strength of him.

"Hey, Jackie, are you gonna introduce us?"

One by one, Jackie introduced the people, only six of them in the room since one of them, Charley's oldest friend, had stepped out for a moment. With enthusiasm, they said hello to William and invited him to join them.

Jackie was holding her breath, as these were the first people she had introduced William to as "her" man, and she was waiting for their reaction. As far as she could tell, there was nothing unusual in the way they acted. Within minutes they were telling William lies about their exploits in airplanes and William was telling them about nice hotels in town where they could stay. Jackie had to hide her smile. She could relax now; William was here to take care of her. He wouldn't allow these people to take over the house, nor would he give them jobs unless they were qualified.

Five minutes later Charley's friend Arnold returned to the room.

Gladys, being much too friendly with William, clutched his arm to her bosom and said, "And this gorgeous young thing belongs to Jackie."

Arnold smiled and held out his hand. "I didn't know Jackie and Charley had any kids," he said.

There was instant silence in the room. Only William seemed to be at ease as he took Arnold's hand and shook it. "I am hoping to persuade Jackie to marry me," he said smoothly, seemingly unperturbed by what had just been said.

As for Jackie, she wished the floor would open so she could sink down inside the earth and never be seen again. Turning on her heel, she walked out of the room, ignoring Arnold's apologies ringing out behind her and the group's pleas for her to return.

When she got outside, she wasn't surprised to feel William's hand on her arm. He was trying to make her stop walking, but she meant to get into a plane, as that was the only place where she felt really safe.

"Jackie," William was saying, "the man is half drunk, and even sober I doubt if he can see past the end of his nose."

"He could see what everyone else can see."

William grabbed her shoulders. "Jackie, I've had about all of this I can take. I love you. I love *you*. I don't care how old you are, what race you are, whether you're fat or skinny. I love what's inside you." When she didn't respond, he dropped his hands from her shoulders. "But it's your decision," he said, and his voice was cold. "You have to decide."

She moved away from him and kept walking toward the plane, and within minutes she was airborne.

If William thought she had flown recklessly the day she took him out, he would have been horrified to see her now. She buzzed trees, flying so low that the top branches scraped the plane. She flew straight toward a mountain, not knowing until the

213

moment she pulled up whether she was going to miss it or not. When the plane, its engine straining, almost didn't make it, part of her didn't care.

She flew for hours, right side up, upside down, sideways, every which way the plane would turn.

When she ran out of gas she was at ten thousand feet and hovering over a mountaintop. Below her was a flat, treeless meadow, and she dropped the plane onto it, neither knowing nor caring whether she would overshoot it and plunge over the side of the mountain into oblivion.

She made the landing, the nose hanging over the mountain, the wheels at the very edge of the precipice.

For a moment after the engine sputtered to death, she sat where she was, leaning her head back, her eyes closed beneath her goggles. She was on top of a mountain with an empty fuel tank, and the only way out was to walk down and climb back up with a can of gas.

She got out of the plane, but she didn't start down the mountain. Instead, she sat down on the edge of the cliff, looking out over the long, magnificent view and waited for some wisdom to come to her.

No wisdom struck her, but hail did. In the late afternoon the skies opened up and hailstones came down on her head. Jackie moved under the wing of the plane.

When night fell, she curled up in a ball, pulled about her the leather clothes she'd quickly donned before going up and dozed some. She still couldn't think. In fact, she hoped she'd never think again. She wished she could go back to the time when life was easy, when she was younger and knew all the answers.

Early the next morning she wasn't surprised to hear a plane approaching. Of course William would look for her. Didn't he always rescue her? He was always there to save her, whether she needed money or stitches or help in dealing with intrusive people. When the plane was directly overhead, she stepped out from under her own aircraft and waved to the pilot, letting him know that she was unharmed. In reply, he waggled his wings, so she knew she'd been seen. From this distance the pilot looked to be one of Charley's friends. Feeling guilty for having caused so much trouble, she realized that William would have put all of them to work in the search for her.

She was hungry and tired and knew she was being a great bother to a lot of people who were worried about her, but she still didn't start down the mountain. And she hoped that no one would come after her. Especially not William. Right now she needed to think.

Only she couldn't seem to think. There were too many voices inside her head. There was William's voice, urgent and imploring. There was Charley's voice saying, "What will it matter a hundred years from now?" There was Arnold's voice and Terri's voice. How Terri's voice echoed in her head!

But most of all there was Jackie's own voice. *He will want a younger woman. He deserves better. He deserves a woman who can give him a houseful of children.*

"Stop it!" she said, putting her hands to her ears. Why couldn't she hear what she'd told Terri? How wise she had been then, so very wise. She'd said all the right things. So why didn't she believe them?

It was late afternoon, and she was light-headed with hunger. She knew she should head down the mountain, but still she didn't go. Still she hadn't made a decision.

When she heard the unmistakable sound of someone coming up an old elk trail to the top of the mountain, she knew without a doubt it was William. With her jaw set, her arms folded across her chest, she braced herself to wait for him. *What was she going to say to him?*

To her utter disbelief, she saw, not William, but his soft, plump mother, Nellie, struggling up the mountain, a huge, heavy picnic basket under her arm.

It took Jackie a few moments to recover herself, and for a moment she thought she was having hallucinations.

But Nellie's words made her react. "I do believe I'm having a heart attack," she said, a smile on her lips. Then she slowly sank to the ground.

Chapter Twelve

Nellie was not having a heart attack. She was just not used to climbing, and the exertion combined with the altitude was making her feel that she was dying. For several busy moments Jackie's attention was off herself and on Nellie, but within minutes they were sitting in the shade of the wing of the plane and eating from the prodigious amount of food Nellie had hauled up the mountain.

Patiently, Jackie waited for the lecture to begin. But Nellie said nothing about William or about the two of them together. She commented on the weather and the fact that Jackie's plane was nearly over the edge of the mountain, but didn't mention anything important.

Finally, Jackie could no longer wait for the lecture to begin. "You think I'm stupid, don't you?"

Nellie didn't seem fazed by Jackie's abruptness. "No, dear, I think you are one of the finest young women I have ever met."

Jackie snorted in reply.

Nellie didn't seem to notice her sarcasm. Instead, she changed the subject. "Why won't you enter the Taggie?"

Jackie smiled. She could refuse to tell William, but not his mother. "I don't like being a celebrity,

217

and I hate instrument flying, which is what flying has become today. You don't need talent, you need a degree in mathematics. In a few more years people like William are going to be better fliers than I am."

Nellie smiled at the innocent conceit in Jackie's words.

"Why don't you want to marry my son?"

So, Jackie thought, here it was. "A lot of reasons. For one thing, he deserves better. And then there's my vanity. I don't like all the gossip and the talk."

Nellie laughed. "You have indeed stirred up a lot of talk. My poor husband can't walk down the street without someone telling him the latest bit of gossip about two unmarried people being in bed together. You have scandalized all of Chandler. I'm sure you must be the first couple in this town to jump the gun."

Jackie turned red with embarrassment and looked down at the ground.

"You know what they're saying now? That maybe something was going on between the two of you when you were children."

Jackie blinked a couple of times at that. "What?"

"Yes. Mrs. Beasley says that the bond between you and my son all those years ago was not natural."

Jackie opened her mouth to speak, but then closed it. Then she began to laugh. "But William was a child! And a pest. An absolute pest. I did everything to get rid of him. If that isn't natural, I don't know what is."

"*Did* you try to get away from him? I seem to

remember the two of you being inseparable. I remember that you always *told* William to leave you alone, but when he did stay home you always came to get him."

"I did no such thing," Jackie said indignantly.

"What about the time he had the flu? You stopped by every day."

"I was worried about your whole family."

"William was the only one who was ill."

Jackie picked up a stick and started to draw circles in the dirt. "He was just a kid. Still is. Always has been."

"You never thought so. You used to ask his advice about any number of things. You always loved adventure, but before you did anything, you asked William if he thought it would be all right."

"I didn't," Jackie said, sounding like a schoolgirl.

Nellie didn't answer for a moment. "Did you know that William didn't speak for a whole month after you left Chandler? He wouldn't talk, would hardly eat. The only way he would go to sleep at night was if I'd hold him and rock him. I was afraid he might lose the will to live."

"And I never thought of him." Jackie ran her hand over her eyes. "And now he's all I do think of. I don't know what to do. William wants to marry me. But there are . . . differences between us. People —"

"*Damn* people!" Nellie said.

Jackie had never been more startled by any statement she'd ever heard. Nellie Montgomery was the calmest, gentlest, most easygoing person in the world. Nothing ever made her lose her temper, not twelve children climbing all over her, not even three of them dripping blood at the same time. Nellie was the person you wanted to be near during a calamity; she'd have remained calm in the face of a barrage of bullets.

But now she was cursing.

When Jackie looked at her, Nellie's face was not the soft, sweet one she'd always seen. This was the face of anger.

"Jackie, grow up!"

That made Jackie sit up straight, her eyes widening.

"Do you think other people have easy lives and you're the only one with problems? You've been lucky so far."

"Lucky?" Jackie whispered. How had her life of poverty and struggle been lucky?

"Oh, I know what you're thinking, that I'm one of the Montgomerys and therefore I know nothing but luxury and ease. But you're wrong. All your life you've been able to do what you wanted, when you wanted to do it. And you've had people who loved you along the way. Now that you have one little obstacle, you turn tail and run. Why don't you stop being so selfish and think of someone besides yourself?"

Jackie, still in awed silence at this woman's unusual outburst, was shocked further when Nellie began to clean up the picnic food in preparation to leave.

Jackie wanted to defend herself. "I don't understand. I'm not being selfish; I'm thinking of William. This is as much for him as it is for me."

"No, it's not!" Nellie said fiercely. Then suddenly she put her hands over her face and began to cry.

Jackie did the only thing she knew to do: she put her arms around Nellie and pulled her to her.

"I'm sorry," Nellie said, sniffing and moving away. "It's just that I can see things more clearly than you can because I've lived through the same problems. Years ago I was in the same situation with my husband."

"I don't understand. Your husband isn't younger than you are."

At that Nellie laughed. "No, dear, Jace isn't younger than I am. But age, in my case *and in yours*, means nothing, absolutely nothing. You see, you're afraid of what other people will think. I've learned in life that if you give people power over you, they will misuse it."

She put her hand on Jackie's. "A true friend is one who wants what is best for *you*, not for him or for her."

Nellie took both of Jackie's hands in her own. "Years ago Jace wanted to marry me, but I said I couldn't because other people — people I thought loved me — said I shouldn't marry him. They said their only concern was for me. It took me a long time — almost too long — to realize that they were thinking only of themselves and not of Jace or me. People can be very selfish creatures."

"I . . . I hadn't thought of that."

"No, you've thought only of doing what everyone else does. Most women marry a man about five years older than they are, then live their lives exactly as they've been told to. Tell me one thing, Jackie. Do you love William?"

"Yes." Her heart could be heard in that one word.

"Then what else is there?"

Jackie just looked at her, not having an answer.

"My dear, you don't seem to realize that all there is in life is love. That's all there is. Money doesn't matter, what you own doesn't matter, how old you are, who your friends are, what you accomplish in life, means nothing. The only thing worth anything is love. Love is what makes our time on earth worth something. And you know something else? Love, true love, is rare. It doesn't happen very often. Most people spend their lives searching for it and never find it."

She paused, but her eyes were intense. "Tell me, Jackie, if you looked at the ground here and saw a big diamond sticking out, what would you do?"

"I would pick it up," Jackie said softly.

"What if the diamond were perfect except that it had a tiny flaw, a crack say, along one edge, would you throw the whole diamond away because of this one flaw?"

There were tears coming to Jackie's eyes. "No, I'd keep it, flaws and all."

"My son is perfect, but to your eyes he has a

flaw: I gave birth to him ten years after your mother gave birth to you. Are you going to throw away my son because of *my* error?"

Jackie was crying harder now. "I don't know," she said honestly. "I don't know what to do."

After a moment, Nellie stood up and started to walk away, meaning to leave Jackie with her head on her upraised knees, but Nellie turned back. "Are you coming down with me?"

Jackie gave Nellie a crooked smile. "How many of the people of Chandler are down there waiting for me?"

"A few," Nellie said, smiling.

Which, of course, meant half of Chandler. "Is William there?"

Nellie's face was serious. "No, he's not. He said you'd know where he was."

That statement made Jackie's heart sink. No doubt William was waiting for her in some place she was supposed to remember. She hadn't seen it in twenty years, but she was supposed to remember it. "I'll be down in a moment," she said. "I want to do something with my face." And give myself more time to think, she thought.

"Ten minutes," Nellie said. "But no more. People are worried about you."

"Yes, of course," Jackie answered, both of them knowing that she still hadn't made a decision.

The moment Nellie was out of sight, Jackie went to the plane, climbed onto the wing and looked inside the cockpit for the little metal box she carried inside. She almost always had cosmetics with her in case she unexpectedly flew into the press. And now, if she was going to have to face the citizenry of Chandler, it would be better if her face wasn't marked with tears.

She found the box and as she was rummaging inside looking for a lipstick buried under three maps and a compass, she saw a large white envelope on the bottom. For a moment her hands as well as her heart seemed to stop beating, for she knew very well what she was seeing.

Slowly she pulled the envelope out and opened it. Inside was the invitation to participate in the Taggie. She had received it the day of Charley's funeral, and it had changed her life. Three days before, she had awakened not to Charley's horrendous snores but to an unnatural silence. Charley was not asleep beside her; he was dead. He had died of a massive heart attack quietly and peacefully in his sleep, with what looked to be a half smile on his lips.

For days after his death Jackie hadn't been able to think, but as people Charley had known, people who had loved him, gathered to say goodbye, everyone seemed to assume Jackie would continue doing what she had always done. They assumed she'd keep flying higher and longer and faster.

It wasn't until the day of the funeral that she had absently opened the mail and seen the invitation to the Taggie in her hometown, and with it was a letter from Jace Montgomery. It was at that moment that she realized she was sick of it all. She was sick of constantly moving, of having no roots. She was sick of seeing her name in the newspaper, of having people take photos of her, of being asked the same stupid questions over and over. She wanted a home. She wanted what other people had.

Without another thought, she wrote Mr. Montgomery that she would accept his offer to return to Chandler and start a freight business, but she would not enter the race. She didn't tell him or anyone else that she was afraid not of losing the race but of winning it.

Now, holding the torn and dirty invitation, she walked to the edge of the cliff and stood there looking out over the deep ravine. Wasn't all of life invitations, she thought. Didn't every person in the world constantly receive invitations? Some were golden, some made of lead; some were big and some little. Some were blatant and some subtle. But what made life interesting was which invitations a person chose to accept. Most people accepted only the safe invitations, ignoring the unusual or the ones that involved risk.

But Jackie had never been afraid of risk. Jackie had, as William had said, always done exactly what she wanted to do. She had accepted the invitation her mother had offered that said she could be different from the other children, that she could stay away from the other children who seemed to be stamped out of the same mold. She had accepted Charley's invitation to live a life of adventure and excitement. And along the way she had accepted and refused invitations however she wanted to. All of it done without hesitancy, just doing what she instinctively knew was right for her and no one else.

But now William was offering her another invitation, probably the greatest invitation of her life, yet she was hesitating. Why was she hesitating? Because William was younger than she was? Or was there another reason?

Was she refusing William because she was afraid? Was she, as Nellie had said, afraid of what people would say? She'd never been afraid of that before. Or was she afraid of loving someone as much as she loved him? If she loved him this much now, how much would she love him after she saw him hold their child in his arms? How much would she love him after she'd lived with him for years, gotten to know him so well that his thoughts were as familiar to her as her own breath? What if she came to love him so much and then, like Charley, he died?

She'd been able to survive Charley's death because she had always kept her independence. She had always kept her own identity, always been with him but separate from him at the same time. She'd loved Charley, but they had been two people. With William she didn't feel separate. She felt as though they were one, as though they blended together, like two colors of paint being mixed. She was yellow, the color of the sun, an exciting color, while William was blue, the color of peace and tranquillity. Together they blended to make green, the color of the earth, the color of home.

She looked down at the ragged invitation in her hand, and after a moment a slow smile came to her lips. Raising her eyes skyward, she felt the warmth of the sun on her face. "I don't care," she whispered. Her smile grew broader and her voice louder. "I don't care what happens in the future. All I want is *now*. I love him. I just plain love him, and that's all that matters. Not what anyone else thinks matters. Nor does the future matter. I love him. Do you hear that?"

Her voice rose to a shout. "Do you hear that, world? I love him."

Still smiling, she began to tear the invitation, first in half then into quarters, again and again, until it lay in tiny bits in the palm of her hand. Then, raising her hand toward the sun, she lifted it palm upward and let the wind catch the bits. Like a flurry of tiny white butterflies, the pieces caught in the air, playing in the drafts, before sailing away down the canyon.

When the last piece was no longer in sight, she turned and started down the mountain.

They were there, waiting for her, Charley's friends who had been flying since dawn looking for her. Many people from Chandler were there, too, curious, wanting something to break the monotony of life. There was Arnold, still apologizing for putting his foot in his mouth about her and William, explaining that he meant he didn't know that *Charley* had any grown children. This time

Jackie heard the truth in his voice, so she told him it was all right, then kept going, her eyes searching the crowd for any sign of William. But he wasn't there. And it was right that he shouldn't be. It was her time to go after him.

Jace Montgomery was standing at the bottom of the mountain, looking at her, his face searching hers, wanting an answer. Abruptly, it hit Jackie that everyone in town knew how much she and William loved each other, had always loved each other. Perhaps they had always been a couple in the eyes of the townspeople.

When Jace saw her expression, he smiled and a dozen years seemed to fall away from his handsome face. He didn't say a word, but just pointed to a car parked nearby, and Jackie strode toward it. What was it William had said about her? That she walked "with long strides that eat up the earth."

Within minutes she was in the car and heading toward town, and it wasn't until she was nearly there that she suddenly knew where William was. He was waiting for her by the little pond where she'd taught him how to swing on a rope and later pushed him into the water and said, "Swim or die."

He was sitting there patiently, waiting for her. Her rock, she thought, pausing a moment to look at him, the sunlight glinting off his precious head. No, not her rock, her diamond. Her diamond that had no flaw.

"Hello," she said when she was standing less

than two feet from him.

He didn't look up, nor did he say anything, so she sat down in front of him. Still, he avoided her eyes.

"I've been behaving pretty badly the last few days," she said.

"Yes, you have."

She smiled. "You could say something nice."

"I don't feel very nice."

"I think you do," she answered, trying to put some humor in the situation, but he didn't laugh.

For several moments she sat in silence, trying to figure out what to say, but could think of nothing. "Damn it, William! What am I supposed to say? That you were right and I was wrong? Is that what you want to hear?"

Slowly he turned to look at her. "That might make for a start."

She opened her mouth to tell him what she thought of him, but then she laughed. And the next minute she launched herself on top of him, kissing his face and neck with vigor.

William was holding his chin up. "I want more than one apology, Jackie. I want about a thousand of them."

"Ha!" she said, beginning to unbutton his shirt and kiss her way down his chest.

William took her shoulders and held her away from him to look into her eyes. "I'm not going to start this again unless I have some assurance that you aren't going to leave me again. I can't stand any more days like the last few. Jackie, I'm serious. Either you're mine completely or not at all. No half measures."

"I love you," she said. "And if you want me I'm yours."

"Permanently? Marriage and all that?"

"Marriage and everything."

Still he held her away from him, looking into her eyes as though to ascertain if she was telling the truth. "What made you see reason? What made you see what an idiot you've been?"

She smiled. "I talked to an expert on love."

"Oh? A clergyman or a psychiatrist or an exotic dancer?"

"None of those. I talked to someone who has given and received enormous amounts of love, and she made me realize that nothing else in life matters." Jackie's head came up. "William, I love you more than I love airplanes."

William blinked at her a moment, then pulled her into his arms and nearly crushed her to him. "Now I know you're serious."

Jackie giggled and began to fiddle with his belt buckle.

"No you don't," he said, standing and pulling her up with him. "There may be a Beasley lurking in the bushes. We're going right now to get married."

"Now? But, William, I need a bath and —"

"I'll give you one later."

"Oh?" she said, with a great deal of interest in her voice. "And what else do I get if I marry you?"

He pulled her into his arms. "A lifetime of love,"

he answered softly.

She caressed his temple with her fingertips. "And that's all I want."

She started to kiss him, but he turned his head away.

"Nope. You get nothing until you've made an honest man of me." Taking her hand, he began to lead her back toward the road so fast she was tripping over plants and rocks. "Did you know that if you're married to the sponsor, you don't have to pay a fee to enter the Taggie?"

"Is that so?"

"So maybe you'd like to enter the race."

"No," she said happily.

"You want to tell me why not?"

"William, I have a confession to make. I am *terrified* of heights. Can't bear them."

He opened the door of the car she had driven and helped her into the seat. "Jackie, you are going to be the death of me."

"No, William, my darling, I am going to be the *life* of you," she said softly.

He bent forward to kiss her but drew back. "No. I'm not kissing you until you have Montgomery attached to your name."

"Along with everyone else in town," she said, leaning back in the seat and smiling as she watched him walk around the car to get into the driver's seat. For a moment she closed her eyes, and in that instant she could see the joy that was their future. Nellie had said that only love mattered, and she was right. Nothing in her life had given so much deep satisfaction as had knowing that this man loved her and she loved him.

William shut the door, released the brake, and started driving. They didn't say anything, but he picked up her hand and kissed it, and that kiss said everything.

She had made the right decision.

Epilogue

Terri's husband ran off with a traveling stripper, taking their eldest son with him. Edward Browne consoled her for her loss, and they were married a few months after Terri's divorce. Edward decided that the challenge of straightening out Terri's remaining sons was more interesting than spending months aboard a cruise ship, so he dedicated himself to them. The younger boys turned out not to be as stupid as they seemed and, when encouraged, found that they rather liked using their heads instead of their fists. Both of them graduated from college and led productive lives. As for Edward and Terri, they thanked heaven every day of their lives for having found each other.

Jackie and William had two children and lived happily ever after.

Book II

Matchmakers

Chapter One

There was a console telephone on Kane Taggert's desk with six buttons on it, every one of which was lit up, but when his private line rang, he put line number six on hold and answered it. His private line was for his family and anyone who had anything to do with his two young sons.

"Mom," he said, turning in his chair and looking at the New York skyline, "what an unexpected pleasure." He didn't ask, but he knew his mother wanted or needed something, because she didn't call him while the stock exchange was open if she just wanted to chat.

"I have a favor to ask of you."

Kane didn't groan, but he wanted to. Five months ago his twin brother had gotten married, and since then his mother had been relentless in her attempts to get Kane, her widower son, married.

"I think you need a vacation."

At that Kane did groan. looking at his switchboard, he saw line number four start to blink, meaning Tokyo was about to hang up. "Out with it, Mom," he said. "What torture have you planned for me now?"

"Your father isn't feeling well and —"

"I'll be there —"

"No, no, it's nothing like that. It's just that his soft heart has put him in a bit of a pickle and I've promised to get him out of it."

This was a common occurrence in his parents' household. His father often volunteered to help people, and volunteered so generously that he took on too much, did too much. In her attempt to protect him, his wife often had to play the bad guy and unvolunteer him.

"What's he done now?" Kane said as light number four went off.

"You know how our neighbor Clem" — she was explaining who Clem was to emphasize that it had been so long since Kane had been home that he might have forgotten a man he'd known all his life — "often takes easterners on camping trips? Well, last month he took six men and, well, it was a bit rough on him. Clem's getting on in years now, and those climbs are hard on him."

Kane didn't say a word. Clem was as strong and as wiry as a mustang, and Kane well knew that Clem's health had nothing whatever to do with what his mother wanted her son to do.

"Anyway, your father said he'd take the next group of easterners."

Clem was also part con man so if he'd conned Ian Taggert into taking the next group, there was a reason. "That bad, huh?" Kane asked. "A real bunch of jerks, were they?"

Pat Taggert sighed. "The worst. Complainers. Afraid of the horses. The boss had 'requested' that they go, and they didn't want to be there."

"The worst kind. So what's Clem conned Dad into this time?"

Kane heard some anger in Pat's voice when she spoke. "It seems that Clem knew his next group of tourists was from this same company, only, Kane . . ."

"What's the bad news?"

"They're *women!* Clem knew this, and he's asked your father to spend two weeks leading four reluctant New York women on a trail ride. Can you imagine! Oh, Kane, you can't —"

At that Kane began to laugh. "Mom, you are never going to win an Academy Award for acting, so you can cut it out. So you want me, your widower son — your poor, lonely widower son — to spend two weeks alone with four nubile young women and maybe find a mother for his sons."

"In a word, yes," Pat said, annoyed. "How do you expect to meet anyone if you spend all your time working? All four of these women live in New York City where both you and Mike have chosen to live and —"

Unspoken words were sizzling through the telephone lines about how Kane and his brother had left the family home and taken grandbabies away from their grandparents.

"The answer is an unequivocal no," Kane said. "*No!* That's it, Mom. I can find my own women without any matchmaking on your part."

"All right," Pat said, sighing. "Go answer your telephones." At that she hung up, and for a moment Kane stared at the phone, frowning. He'd have to send her flowers and maybe a piece of jewelry. Even as he thought that, he knew that flowers and jewelry were a poor substitute for grandchildren.

He didn't get home until eight that evening, and by then his sister-in-law, Samantha, had his twin sons neatly tucked away in their beds. His brother Mike was at the gym, so he and Sam were alone, and after Kane had returned from kissing his sleepy sons, he met her in the living room. She was hugely pregnant, her hand seeming to be permanently attached to her lower back as she ambled about the town house taking care of two men and two active five-year-olds. Kane had his own apartment in New York, a barren place that for the most part was filled with kids' toys, and he had a place in his parents' house in Colorado, but after his brother had introduced him to Samantha, Kane and his sons had gradually moved into Mike's town house. That was Sam's doing, Kane thought. Sam had wanted a family, and if that was what Sam wanted, then Mike was going to give it to her.

Without asking, Sam brought Kane a beer in a cold mug and handed it to him. A thousand times he'd told her that she shouldn't wait on him, but Sam had a very hard head. Setting the beer down, he got up and went to lower her into one of Mike's fat leather chairs. She wasn't heavy, but she was as unwieldy as a dirigible.

"Thanks," she said, then nodded toward his

beer. "Defeats the purpose of my waiting on you if you have to get up to help me, doesn't it?"

Smiling at her, he sat down and drank half the beer in one gulp. Sometimes he wanted what his brother had so badly that it was like a flame that threatened to burn him up. He wanted a wife who loved him and his sons, wanted a home of his own; he wanted to stop living vicariously through his brother.

"Out with it," Sam said.

"Out with what?"

"You can't lie any better than Mike can. What's bothering you?"

You, he wanted to say. Loving my sister-in-law, beginning to hate my brother.

"Kane," Sam said, "stop looking at me like that and talk to me. Tell me what's bothering you."

He couldn't tell her the truth, so he told her about his mother's call.

"What are you going to do?" Sam asked.

Kane hadn't considered accepting his mother's invitation, but suddenly the thought of two weeks alone in the high mountain desert with four women appealed to him. If they were New York women, they'd be afraid of the open space, of the noises in the night, and they always fell in love with their cowboy guide. Show a New York woman a man in a denim shirt, tight Levi's, and a worn pair of cowboy boots and you had her. Throw your leg over a horse and she'd probably swoon.

As he finished his beer, he smiled. It might be nice to have a woman look at him with stars in

239

her eyes. Samantha looked at Mike as though he were an Olympic god, and his sons looked at Sam as though she were the only mother they'd ever had.

"Thinking you might go?"

"Maybe," Kane said, getting up. "I'm going to have another beer. Can I get you anything?"

"On the countertop in the kitchen is a fax from Pat. It tells all about the four women who are going on the trip."

With a face filled with astonishment, Kane looked back at her, but Sam just shrugged. "She called and said she hoped you'd change your mind. Kane, one of the women is a widow. Three years ago she was in a car crash that killed her husband and made her miscarry her child."

When he went to the kitchen, Kane picked up the fax and read it. Ruth Edwards was the widow's name, and his mother had even found a photo of her. Even in the bad reproduction he could tell she was beautiful, as tall, as long-legged, as dark-haired as his beloved wife had been.

Quickly, Kane read about the other three women. One was a hairdresser's assistant, another ran a metaphysical shop in the Village, and the fourth was a short, pretty blonde whose name seemed vaguely familiar.

"She writes murder mysteries," Sam said from over his shoulder. She was standing so close her belly was touching his side, but the distance from the front of her belly to her head made her face seem nearly a yard away.

"Read any of them?"

"All of them. I buy them the minute they hit the stands."

"Speaking of writers, how's Mike's book coming?"

"*Our* book," she said with emphasis, knowing Kane was teasing her, "will be out in six months." She was speaking of the biography she and Mike had written, *The Surgeon* by Elliot Taggert, the pen name combining her maiden name with Mike's surname. "Well?" she said impatiently. "Are you going?"

"Will you keep the boys?"

It was a rhetorical question and they both knew it. "I'd keep them forever."

"Which is exactly why I think I'll go check out Mom's ladies."

Sam's eyes twinkled. "Pat's sending the family jet to pick you up at eight tomorrow morning. It's already left Denver."

Kane wasn't sure whether to laugh or groan. In the end he did both, then put his arm around Sam's shoulders and kissed her cheek. "Do I seem as lonely as you women think I am?"

More, Sam thought, but she didn't answer him. She was glad he was going to be around people.

Chapter Two

You know what's guaranteed to turn a man off? No, it's not laughing at him when he's in the throes of passion. The guaranteed, absolute, sure-bet turnoff is to tell a man you earn more money than he does.

Men seem to think it's okay for some daffy, brainless little lady to inherit millions — after all, some *man* earned that money. But let me tell you, men do not like to hear that a female pulled down 1.4 million last year and that, what's more, she manages all that money all by her itty-bitty self, with no help from any man anywhere.

Five years ago, when I was twenty-five, I was in a boring, dead-end job — the less said about it the better — and living in a boring, nowhere midwestern town, of which I want to say less than nothing. As I have always done, to occupy myself and keep my mind from stagnating, I told myself stories. I know, that's about a quarter inch away from having a split personality, but at an early age I found it was either take myself away or lose my mind altogether. My father was terrified of his own shadow and so demanded absolute obedience from his family at all times. I had to wear what he dictated, eat what he decided I was to eat, like what he decreed, move to his specifications. He controlled every bit of my life until I escaped at eighteen, but before that time I found out that there was one part of me he couldn't control: my mind. I may have been forced to wear blue when I wanted to wear red, and I may have been denied ginger ale because the ol' man hated ginger ale, but inside my head I was free. In my thoughts I did what I wanted, went where I wanted, said all the clever things I thought, and was praised for saying them. (My father had a tendency to smack smart mouths, which was very effective in making one keep one's thoughts to oneself.)

When I was twenty-five and living a few miles from my parents and doing my best to save enough money for a one-way ticket out, I wrote one of my stories down on paper. It was a murder mystery, and the killer was a young woman who'd done away with her tyrant of a father. After I wrote it, I thought, What the heck, and mailed it to a publishing house, never thinking they'd accept it. I guess a lot of people are sick of fathers and husbands who run their lives for them because twenty-eight days later I received a letter asking if they could please publish my book and send me a lot of money.

I thought, and still do, What a scam! These people were willing to *pay* me to do something I'd been doing all my life.

With the money they sent me, I moved to New York. I'd never been to the big city before, but it seemed to be where writers went — that's what I was now, not just a bored nobody who was on the verge of a split personality — and I rented a tiny apartment and bought a computer.

For the next four years I hardly looked up from the keyboard as I wrote one story after another. I killed off an uncle I didn't like. I killed off several co-workers who'd snubbed me, and in my mega-seller I killed off the entire cheerleading team of my high school.

During these four years I got a glimpse of a very different world from the one where I'd grown up. People were impressed by how competent I was. I'm sure I mentioned that my father was a tyrant, but did I also mention that he was the laziest creature alive? As far as I could figure out, at work he was a real wimp, afraid to stand up for himself, so he let others bully him. Then, when he got home, he took his rage out on me. My mother had long ago escaped to some never-never land of her own, and she was no fun for him to rage at. I, on the other hand, gave him a great deal of satisfaction because I cried and suffered and smoldered and felt all the injustice of it.

But for all of my father's flaws, he made me into a competent, fearless person. After you've lived with a man like my father, trust me, nothing anyone else ever says or does to you can hurt you in exactly the way he could. Sadists make a study of their victims, whereas most people are too self-absorbed to care enough. So, thanks to the training I'd received in childhood, I was a very competent businesswoman. I wrote incessantly, I negotiated my own contracts, I invested the money I made without the help of a manager, and at the end of the four years I bought myself a penthouse apartment on Park Avenue. I had made it — and made it in a big way.

So what was my personal life like? Think non-existent. My editor took me out now and then, and when I was writing without a break for days on end she'd even bring me food. But editors don't bring you dates. Authors who fall in love, authors who are social, don't write. I think if it were left up to publishing houses, they'd lock all their best-selling writers in Park Avenue towers and send them food and never allow them out.

So, after five years of writing, after making millions, after becoming a household name all over the world, I decided to accept Ruth Edwards' invitation to go on a two-week-long trail ride in the wilds of Colorado.

Ruth's boss had seen the movie *City Slickers* and had decided that it would be a good life-experience for his top male managers to go on a trail ride and deliver a calf or whatever, so of course they went. Unfortunately the boss decided at the last minute that his marriage was of utmost importance, so he went off to Bermuda with his wife and left his male employees to tough it out on beans and overcooked beef. Of course when they returned, all the men said they'd had a marvelous life-enhancing experience, and the boss never saw the dartboard covered with a horse's head smack in the middle of a map of Colorado.

After the men's return, the boss said all of his female executives should go on the same trip and experience the same deep, mind-altering peace the men had found. Since all of his females who weren't secretaries — and who had run the company for the two weeks the men were in Colorado — consisted of Ruth, she was told to choose three friends and go with them.

That's when Ruth called me. Not by any stretch of the imagination could Ruth and I be called friends. We were in college together and during our freshman year our dorm rooms were across the hall from each other. Ruth had grown up rich, with adoring parents who made it their goal in life to give their daughter anything she wanted, while I was going to school on government loans and went to my father's house every weekend to do things like cut the grass and wash the clothes and satisfy my father's insatiable need to belittle someone. Our backgrounds did not give us a great deal of common ground to talk about.

Also, there was Ruth herself. She was tall, with lots of thick, dark hair that always obeyed her, gorgeous clothes — she was one of those girls who, even if she wore a sweatshirt, tucked a Hermes scarf at her throat — and she had an entourage of bad-skinned, overweight, gaga-eyed girls following her. These girls constantly changed as they got tired of fetching for Ruth and adoring Ruth, and were replaced by others.

Since I always had my nose in a book and only

watched Ruth from afar — okay, so I watched her with envy, fantasizing that I was an ugly duckling and that someday I was going to grow a foot, my hair was going to start curling, and I was going to become a social success instead of always saying the wrong thing at the wrong time — I had no idea she knew I existed.

I underestimated Ruth. Any woman who could claw her way to the top of her field by the time she hit thirty should never be underestimated.

She called me and told me how proud she was of my success, how she'd been following my career for years, and how she had envied me so much in college.

"Really?" I heard myself asking, as wide-eyed as a kid. "*You* envied *me?*"

Even while part of me was telling myself that everything she was saying was a crock, I was flattered. She told me how she used to watch me at school and used to see how respected I was by the other students, although what I remember is people trying to get me to write their papers for them. But Ruth seemed to be willing to go on and on with her praise, so I let her. What people don't understand about writers is that they desperately want approval. There's a saying, If you want to write, have the worst childhood you can survive. When I was a kid I tried everything in the world to get my father's approval: I made straight A's, I did ninety percent of the household chores, I was clever when I thought he wanted me to be clever, and I tried to figure out when

I was supposed to be quiet. His joy was in changing the rules and not telling me he'd changed them. I used to visualize my life as one of those little ducks at a fairground shoot. I'd travel by and sometimes I'd get shot by the man with the rifle and sometimes I'd survive unscathed. It made for an exciting childhood, but it also made for an adult who'd do almost anything for praise. Money couldn't buy me, people yelling at me never made me do anything I didn't want to do, but give me six words of praise and I'm yours.

So Ruth told me lots of great things about myself and how she'd read all my books. Oddly enough, her favorite was one in which the victim was modeled on her. I'd even had her killer shave her head, eyebrows, and lashes so she looked dreadful in her coffin.

Anyway, Ruth told me she had to go on this trip to Colorado and wanted me to go with her so we could "renew" our friendship.

I hate to say that all of this went to my head. I thought that now that I was successful and rich, women like Ruth considered me their equal. No more small-town nobody for me. Now I was Somebody.

Unfortunately, I once again underestimated Ruth, or maybe I overestimated her, because as soon as I got to Colorado I realized she'd invited me to impress her boss. When she returned to her New York office she could tell him she'd invited her good, dear, longtime friend, the best-selling author Cale Anderson.

It didn't take any sleuthing to figure this out. As I disembarked from the tiny toy plane propelled by a fat rubber band outside a place called Chandler, Colorado, Ruth ran across the tarmac and threw her arms around me. Great. I got a face full of suspiciously firm boobs and a mouthful of silk scarf, as well as my carefully applied makeup smeared across my face. Behind her, just as in college, were two women looking at Ruth with adoring eyes.

"Cale," Ruth said, "meet Maggie and Winnie."

I wasn't told which was which, but one was fat and winked at me, and the other was short and thin and I just knew she was going to lecture me on the value of herbal medicines.

I smiled hello and thought about running back to the plane, but the pilot had already retwisted its rubber band and it was chugging down the runway. There were a couple of hangars there, one closed and one containing — I swear to God this is true — a World War I biplane. I looked back at Ruth and decided she and her satellites weren't so bad after all.

But then Ruth said, smiling over her shoulder, "Cale darling, you wouldn't mind being a dear and carrying my blue bag, would you? I just can't seem to manage by myself."

How come I can negotiate multimillion dollar contracts and get what I want, and I can write about women who stand up for themselves, but when faced with a woman like Ruth all I can do is smolder and pick up her damned suitcase for

249

her? Was it because my mother didn't love me? Hell, my mother didn't know I was alive unless the toilet needed cleaning, so you'd think that would make me despise women. Instead it makes me do most anything to get one of them to like me.

So there I am, the inside of me sane and enraged, and the outside of me schlepping Ruth's bloody suitcase along with three of my own, following her two soldiers, also laden with Ruth's luggage, while her royal highness breezed ahead of us toward God knows where. We were the foot soldiers and she the general leading the charge.

By the time we got to the edge of the runway — this was a private field so there was no nice, comfortable lounge — Ruth halted and vaguely waved her hand for us to set her luggage down.

Oh, thank you, kind mistress, I thought, and dropped her medium-expensive case and sat on it.

Ruth, her two puppies looking up at her — as far as I knew, she never had an acolyte who was as tall as or taller than she; she liked them short and homely — said, "Someone was supposed to be here to meet us." She was frowning as she looked up and down the tarmac. Not a person was in sight and I somehow doubted that Ruth had ever had much experience in being kept waiting.

I had been told very little about the trip. Ruth's instructions had been vague to say the least, but at the time she'd been telling me in detail how much she'd loved *No More Pep Rallies.* It was one of my best plots: a high school student is sick of always missing her Friday afternoon chemistry class to sit in the gym and cheer for a bunch of bozos chasing a ball around, so she blew up all the cheerleaders, proving once and for all that chemistry is more useful than football. Anyway, I was basking in Ruth's praise, and when she said, "Leave everything to me," I did so gladly. After all, by that time I was convinced that she was one of the great geniuses of our time.

So now here I was sitting in the Colorado sun. My only consolation was that I was sure to get a book out of this experience. Maybe I'd make a mystery writer the killer. She'd do in a tall brunette named Edwina Ruthan, and she'd never be caught. Or maybe at the end the detective would say, "I know you did it, but having dated Edwina, I know you did the world a favor. You're free to go. Just don't do it again."

Of course that would never happen because the only people who adored Ruth more than no-life-of-their-own women were men. Short men, tall men, ugly men, gorgeous men, whatever — they all adored her. Somehow, all five feet eight inches of Ruth could make men believe she was little and cute and desperately needed help. Like King Kong needed help. Like Cybill Shepherd didn't have a date for the prom.

About two minutes after I had decided that I was going to leave this state forever, a blue pickup came screeching to a halt in front of us. I mean "us" euphemistically. The pickup stopped so the driver could look at Ruth. The rest of us — hot, tired, bored, sitting on Ruth's suitcases — were staring at the tires and the scraped paint of the truck bed.

I looked up at Ruth, and when I saw her face change, I knew the driver must be somewhere between puberty and male menopause, because that frown disappeared immediately and was replaced with a flirtatious look as she leaned into the passenger side of the truck.

"Are you Mr. Taggert?" she purred.

I wish I could purr. Had Mel Gibson Himself driven up, I still probably would have said, "You're late."

A male voice rumbled out of the truck, and even I could feel the masculinity of it. Either the driver was a heap-big male stud cowboy or they'd trained one of the bulls to drive.

Ruth batted her eyelashes and said, "No, of course you're not late. We're early."

Gag me with a spoon.

"Of course we forgive you, don't we, girls?" Ruth asked, looking at us with adoring eyes. I hadn't been called a girl in so many years I almost liked it.

The driver's door opened, and I saw the big tire in my face — truck tires, mud tires, *man* tires — relieved of weight. They had sent the big one. Still bored, wondering if there was any place in this podunk town that took American Express so I could get out of here, I watched his feet as he walked around the truck. He was wearing cowboy boots, but they weren't made of exotic leather, and they looked as though they'd been used a great deal. Kicking cow pies?

Just as he walked around the tail of the truck, I sneezed, so I got to see him last. What I saw first was the open-mouthed speechlessness of Maggie and Winnie — or was it Winnie and Maggie?

Great, I thought, blowing my nose, they sent some pretty cowboy to bedazzle the city ladies.

I am ashamed to say that when I finally did look up at him, I reacted as badly as the duo and worse than our fearless leader. His name was Kane Taggert, and he was gorgeous: black curly hair, black eyes, sun-browned skin, shoulders an elk would envy, and a sweet, gentle expression on his face that made my knees weak. If I hadn't been sitting down, I might have fallen.

Ruth, still fluttering her lashes, introduced us, and he held out his hand to shake mine. I just sat there looking at him.

"We're all a little tired," Ruth explained and glared at me before grabbing her largest suitcase and attempting to toss it in the back of the truck. She'd learned long ago that the fastest way to make most men notice you is to start to do man's work.

Instantly, Cowboy Taggert left off staring at me as though trying to remember his sign language skills and turned to help dear Ruth with her bag. Personally, I was surprised she knew where the handle was — before then I hadn't seen her touch it.

It was at that moment that we all heard a sound we'd heard a million times in movies but had never wanted to hear in real life: the rattling of a rattlesnake. Mr. Taggert had the big heavy suitcase in his arms, and Ruth, standing so close to him I hoped she was using some sort of birth control, was to his left. Six inches away from her foot was a coiled rattler that looked as though it meant business.

Very slowly, Mr. Taggert spoke to me because I was farthest away from the snake and nearest the truck door. "Open the door," he said calmly, patiently. "Under the driver's seat is a pistol. Get it out and very slowly come around the far side of the truck and give it to me."

If I do say so myself, my mind works quickly in an emergency. I'm not one of those people who freeze, and right now I saw lots of things wrong with this plan. One, how was this man going to shoot if his arms and hands were full of Ruth's seventy-five-pound suitcase? And two, it would take me a long time to walk around the truck, longer maybe than the snake intended to give Ruth.

Slowly, I opened the door to the truck. I was the only thing moving except the rattles of the snake, which sounded awfully loud on that windswept field. Also slowly, I leaned into the truck, and when I pulled out the pistol, I breathed a sigh of relief. I was hoping it wasn't one of those heavy revolvers that take the hands of a lumberjack to fire. It was a nice, neat little nine-millimeter, and all one had to do was pull the slide back, aim, and shoot.

Which is what I did. I was shaking some, so I didn't quite blow the head clean off the poor snake — after all, it'd probably only wanted the warmth of Ruth's suitcase — but I certainly killed it.

Everything happened at once then. The cowboy tossed the suitcase to the ground just in time to catch Ruth when she fainted into his big, strong arms, while Winnie and Maggie fell sobbing onto each other.

I was left standing there with a smoking revolver in my hand. Looking at Ruth draped aesthetically across the cowboy's sun-bronzed arms, I did my best Matt Dillon imitation, legs apart, and blew on the end of the revolver, then stuck it into my skirt pocket. "Well, Tex," I drawled, "there's another one for Boot Hill."

It didn't take a degree in psychology to see that the cowboy was angry. In fact, he was looking at me as though he wanted to wrap his hands around my throat and squeeze, but since his hands were so very full of Ruth's swooning body, he could do nothing but glare meaningfully. In spite of his encumbrances, when he started walking toward me, I stepped aside. I don't think they allow public murders in Colorado, but I didn't want to press my luck.

But he just slipped his precious burden onto the truck seat — Ruth was still doing her dying swan act, but from the flicker of her eyelashes I knew she was as wide awake as I was — then told the skinny follower to get in with her. I think he would have slammed the door shut, but the noise might have disturbed Sleeping Beauty.

Winnie — Maggie? — and I stood to one side while he tossed suitcases, four at a time, into the back of the truck.

"Get in," he said to Ruth's minion, and she obeyed with the speed, if not the grace, of a gazelle.

He turned to me next, his face blazing, and right then I decided that I was *not* going to get into that truck and let him drive me off to heaven knew where.

"Look," I said, backing up, "all I did was shoot the snake. I'm sorry if I offended your masculine sensibilities, but . . ." Maybe this wasn't the way to talk to a cowboy. There's a reason why big, beautiful men are jocks and little, wimpy men are brains. It's as though God tried to even things out, as though He said, "You get beauty but no brains, and you, over there, get brains but no beauty." So talking to this scrumptious-looking creature about the finer points of psychology might not be the best thing to do. Could he read and write? I wondered.

"When I give an order, you are to obey it. You understand me?"

Suddenly I wasn't in Colorado anymore. I wasn't an award-winning author; I was again a little girl whose father controlled everything. As fast as I was transported backward, I returned to the present, but all the rage that little girl had felt was

256

still with me. "Like hell I will," I said and started to walk around the truck.

When he put his hands on me I went berserk. No one had touched me in anger since I escaped my father's house, and no one was going to now. I kicked and bit and fought and scratched my way away from him. I don't know how long I fought before I came back to the present reality and realized he had his hands on my shoulders and was shaking me. Ruth and her skinny follower were gaping at me out the back window of the truck, and the one in the back was cringing behind Ruth's suitcases, as though she was afraid I'd attack her next.

"Are you okay?" the cowboy asked.

There were three bloody streaks on his beautiful cheek, and I had put them there. I couldn't look at him. "I want to go home," I managed to whisper. Home to my own lovely apartment, away from Ruth and her cowboy. Away from my embarrassment.

"Okay," he said, sounding as though he were speaking to a dangerously wacko person. "When we get to the ranch, I can arrange transportation back, but there's no one here now. Do you understand me?"

I hated his patronizing tone, and when I looked back at him I didn't think he was as beautiful as I'd originally thought. "No, I don't understand you. Maybe you should speak a little slower, or maybe you should call the men with white jackets."

He didn't seem to find that funny as he picked

257

me up at the waist and threw me into the bed of the truck with all the finesse he'd used with the suitcases. I was halfway out the back when he stepped on the gas and knocked me backward. Fortunately I landed unhurt on the very soft form of Winnie/Maggie. I didn't bother to ask about her.

I was an internationally successful writer sitting in the back of a dirty truck. A heavy suitcase was starting to crush my ankle, and four people were thinking I was a crazy. Did Mary Higgins Clark go through this?

Chapter Three

What happened to you?" Sandy asked, looking up from the kitchen table and seeing the fury on Kane's face as well as the three bloody scratches.

Kane didn't answer until he'd poured himself a healthy shot of MacTarvit whisky and downed it in one gulp. "I got these marks from being a fool," he said, refilling his glass as he turned to the older man. "Have they written any books on this mother-son thing?"

Sandy smiled, making his face fold into thousands of wrinkles caused by many years of being in the high-altitude sun. "A few hundred, maybe thousands," he said. "What's Pat done now?"

"Talked me into taking a bunch of idiots into the mountains. She made me feel guilty about the kids and —" He broke off as he drank more of the whisky. "Have you met these women?"

"No," Sandy said. "Why don't you tell me about them?" Kane shook his head in disbelief. "One of them put her hand inside my shirt and felt me up, another one asked me questions about blockage of my bowels, and the other one . . ."

Sandy frowned when Kane took another drink, for he knew he wasn't much of a drinker.

"The other one nearly shot me, and afterward she turned into a raving lunatic. If she doesn't kill us in our sleep, she's at least going to terrify the horses."

"And what about the fourth one?"

Kane smiled. "Ah, now, that would be Ruth."

Sandy had to turn away so Kane wouldn't see his smile. Pat had made it clear that romance was the motive for coercing her widowed son into taking the women on this trip, and it looked as though her plan was working, if the silly expression on Kane's face was any indication of what was happening.

"I've got to get back to them. No telling what that crazy one will do. There are rifles in the main house, and she might decide to be Annie Oakley and see if she can shoot the barrettes off the heads of the other women."

"That bad?" Sandy asked, frowning.

"Worse." Kane finished his drink. "I want you to radio home and have Dad send the helicopter

259

here to pick her up. I don't want to be around her; she's dangerous."

"Frank took the copter to Washington State. Something to do with Tynan Mills."

"Damn!" Kane said under his breath. "Look, radio Dad and tell him to get some transportation here fast. If nothing else, tell him to have a truck meet us in Eternity. If I have to spend the entire two weeks with that woman I may kill her."

"You'd better hold off on that. Your mother might not like a dead greenhorn."

"It's not a laughing matter. You haven't met her." Kane took a deep breath. "I will do my best to get along with her until I can ship her out of here. All right? Will you radio Dad now?"

Nodding in agreement as Kane left the cabin, Sandy went to the radio to call.

When Kane entered the big two-story main house, the first thing he saw was the little blond mystery writer, and his first thought was to wonder if all her stories were based on people trying to kill *her*. If they were, he could understand why they'd tried to do it. In spite of what he'd told Sandy about trying to get along with her, when he saw her there alone, he tried to tiptoe out before she saw him.

"Caught!" she said, seeming to be highly amused at seeing him trying to escape undetected.

Turning back to her, Kane tried to force himself to smile at her. She was a guest of his, or, more correctly, his neighbor's, and he was going to try to be a good host to her. The bottom floor of the big log house was all one room, with the bedrooms upstairs, and she was sitting at the bar, looking amused. He couldn't explain what it was he disliked so much about her, but it was something. She was pretty enough, and if he'd seen her on the street he might have been interested, but she seemed so smug, so sure of herself, that all he could think of was getting away from her.

He forced himself to smile, and moved behind the bar. "Would you like a drink? You must be thirsty after your long flight."

"Aren't you worried about what I'll do if I get drunk?"

That thought had been uppermost in his mind, and when she seemed to guess it, he could feel his face turning red.

"Don't worry, Tex," she said in an exaggerated drawl as she put her foot up on the bar stool next to her. "I can handle my liquor as well as the next man."

Kane's hand tightened around the bottle of whisky. Something about the woman more than annoyed him: everything she said, did, insinuated, hinted at, made him furious. Without bothering to ask her what she wanted, he fixed her a weak gin and tonic with no ice, and when he handed it to her, he couldn't bring himself to smile.

She looked down at the drink, and for the first time he saw a human expression cross her face. The first time she'd looked at him, she'd stared at him as though he were something in a circus and he'd wondered if she was retarded. Minutes later she was shooting the snake, and minutes after that she was screaming and clawing. Now she looked a little sad, but the expression went away and she looked back at him with a smirk.

"To you, cowboy," she said, but he put his hand on her wrist and wouldn't allow her to drink.

"The name isn't 'cowboy.' "

Lowering the glass, she frowned at him. "What was it that ticked you off so much this afternoon? That I didn't do what you ordered me to do or that you didn't get to play the hero and save Miss Ruthie yourself?"

Very slowly he walked around the bar to stand in front of her. Then, his eyes never leaving hers, he put his foot on her stool right between her legs. When she saw the hole that her bullet had made in the toe of his boot — had it been even a fraction of an inch to the right, it would have taken his toes with it — she did have the courtesy to look a little shocked. But the expression didn't last long. The next minute she stuck her finger into the hole and touched his toe — the bullet had taken away a patch of his sock — and said, "This little piggy went to market, this little piggy stayed home, this little piggy . . . "

Even as a child Kane had never hurt a girl. His eldest brother, Frank, had given him a lecture once when he came home from first grade with two black eyes that Cindy Miller had given him. Kane hadn't fought back but had stood there and let her slug him until the teacher came and pulled

Cindy away. His teacher had said she didn't know if Kane was a fool or a hero in the making. Frank hadn't been ambivalent: he'd said Kane was stupid.

But right now Kane wanted to hurt this girl. He wanted to strangle her, and before he knew what he was doing, he went after her, his hands extended.

"There you are," Ruth said, floating down the stairs in a lovely dress of red silk.

Abruptly, Kane came out of what he was sure was a waking nightmare, and when he straightened up, he saw the little mystery writer scurry off the stool and run to Ruth as though for protection. Kane had to turn away, horrified at himself at what he'd been about to do.

"Am I glad to see you!" Cale said to Ruth. "We were having the most boring discussion about pork bellies. You want a drink? Cowboy Taggert makes a very nice warm, weak gin and tonic."

"I'll get you anything you want, Ruth," Kane said, calming his racing heart and refusing to look at the horrid woman standing so near her.

"A little chilled white wine," Ruth said demurely, and Kane smiled at her.

"Lovebirds already," Cale muttered, but Kane resolutely refused to acknowledge her presence. Maybe if he ignored her, she'd realize she was unwanted and leave him and Ruth alone.

When he handed Ruth her glass, he looked into her dark eyes and thought about her hair spread out on a pillow.

"Gee, I guess three's a crowd," Cale said and

made Kane turn away so Ruth couldn't see his expression turn to one of rage.

When he'd recovered himself, he walked to the window, hoping Ruth would follow him and when she did, he thought how natural it would be to slip his arm about her waist. She was so like his wife that he knew his arm would fit perfectly, but the presence of the blonde on the other side of Ruth kept him from touching her. He couldn't be himself around that woman.

Outside the window, Kane could see Sandy coming toward the house, leading two saddled horses.

"Who's he?" Ruth asked.

"Sandy. Actually, he's J. Sanderson." Kane smiled at her, noting the way the evening light touched her hair. "No one knows what the *J* stands for, so we've always called him Sandy. He's a distant relative of mine."

Cale peered around Ruth and looked up at Kane. "And which one is your relative? The one with the brown saddle or the one with the black saddle?"

Without thinking what he was doing, Kane went for her. He leaped over a chair back while she, after one gasp of fright, climbed up on the couch, then jumped over the back and headed for the door. Kane caught her just as she ran smack into Sandy as he entered the room. With one bounce, she was behind Sandy, her hands on his hips as she used him as a shield.

Kane was too angry to comprehend what was going on. His one goal in life was to kill this woman. Reaching around Sandy, he made a grab for her, but she evaded him, so he pushed Sandy to one side.

"Kane!" Sandy bellowed in his ear, and it was the voice of a man who had changed Kane's diapers.

Once again Kane felt as though he were waking from a trance. For a moment he stood there blinking; then he realized what he'd been about to do. The woman, half his size, was smiling at him from behind Sandy, looking like the school tattletale who'd just done her bad deed for the day and was glorying in it. Sandy was disgusted and shocked by him, and Kane didn't dare look at Ruth. Too mortified with embarrassment to move, Kane just stood there.

With one more look of reproach at Kane, Sandy slipped his arm about the woman's shoulders and escorted her from the room, and she left with him, her round little tail twitching in triumph as she left the house.

Chapter Four

Sandy had to admit to himself that Kane's behavior had shaken him. He'd known the man since he was a child, and Kane and his twin brother had always been the kindest, sweetest children, always ready to lend a helping hand to anyone who needed them. They were the children who would sleep in the barn with a sick horse and cry when one of the dogs killed a snake. They were boys who'd rather laugh than anything else, boys who were happy and wanted to share their happiness with others.

So when Sandy had walked into the house and seen Kane threatening the life of one very pretty, very small female, he hadn't at first known how to react. One thing that had been so stunning to him was the fact that Kane was responding at all. After his wife died five years ago, Kane had seemed to retreat within himself. Except for his sons, nothing seemed to make him angry or sad; nothing seemed to delight him or disappoint him or bore him. In truth, nothing in the world seemed to affect him at all.

When Pat had told Sandy what she was up to with these four women and that she'd even chosen one of them to be her son's future wife, Sandy hadn't laughed. He had been hoping that something or someone would bring Kane back to life, and if a widow could do that, then he was for whatever deception had to be perpetrated to make it come about.

But when Sandy walked into the house, Kane hadn't been mooning over some beautiful widow; he'd been chasing a minx of a girl across the furniture. Sandy had to admit that he was intrigued as much as puzzled by what he'd seen.

"You the one who shot the snake?" Sandy asked

the young woman walking silently beside him. She was a pretty little thing, blonde and blue-eyed, and if he hadn't just seen her in action, he would have thought her rather shy and quiet.

"And went crazy," she added tightly, and Sandy saw the very slight movement of her shoulders, as though she were preparing to defend herself against him.

"You want to tell me what happened?"

"Not especially," she answered.

Sandy wanted to hear another side to the story, and he meant to find out what had happened. "Kane says you nearly killed him and afterward you went hysterical. You always get hysterical and use guns?"

Trying his best to keep from smiling, he watched as she took his bait, her pretty little face turning a couple of shades of red, ranging from pink to almost purple, before she erupted in words.

"I saved that ungrateful woman's life!" she said, then went on to tell Sandy about the suitcase Kane had been holding and how she figured that if she didn't act quickly the snake might strike at Ruth.

As Sandy listened, the smile left his face. The impression Kane had given him was that the woman was beyond irrational, but her reasons for what she'd done were sound, and it did indeed seem as though she'd saved Ruth's life. "What about later?" he asked softly. "Did you get scared and a little too excited?" He could understand if she had, but he watched her as she looked away from him, her face again red, but this time from embarrassment rather than rage. He could see her debating whether or not to tell him the truth, so he just stood there and waited patiently while she made up her mind.

After a big sigh, she said, "Well, uh . . . my old man used to get mad at me and . . . lay his hands on me, and I guess when your cowboy touched me I sort of did a little time travel."

After she'd told him, she stood there looking at him belligerently, as though daring him to make any comment. She looked a bit like the local bully who'd just revealed that he wasn't so tough after all.

Sandy nodded in understanding of what she'd told him, but made no comment. "Do you know anything about horses?"

"I can tell when one's upside down, but that's about it."

He grinned at her. "Why don't you come help me unsaddle these animals and tell me how you know so much about guns?"

"I guess I don't know enough, because I almost shot that cowboy's foot off."

Walking, Sandy didn't look back at her, but he could hear the remorse in her voice, and he heard the way she referred to Kane as *"that cowboy."* "Did you tell Kane you were sorry?"

"Ha! I'd die first."

When Sandy gave her a surreptitious glance from under his hat brim, she was looking at the mountains, her hands clenched into fists, her mouth set into a hard little line. "Are you the hair lady or

268

the widow or the one with the funny shop?" Before she could answer, his eyes began to sparkle. "You write the murder mysteries."

"Yes," she said, still angry, but then she looked at him and smiled. "My next book is going to be called *Death of a Cowboy*. What sort of death do you think would be appropriate? Caught in his own lariat and hanged? Maybe a rattlesnake in his bedroll." Her grin broadened. "Maybe blood poisoning from a dirty bullet that shot all his toes off."

Chuckling, Sandy opened the barn door for her. "Come in here and tell me the rest of this story. I like a good story."

"Then you're going to like me," she said happily, "because I can tell lots of good stories." Then, frowning, she muttered, "It'll be good to have *somebody* around here like me."

Chapter Five

Contrary to the way it looked, I didn't really want Cowboy Taggert to hate me. I've always had fantasies about being likable. I'd like to walk into a room and have people sigh and say, "Cale's here. *Now* the party can begin." Of course that's never happened. Bookish people don't get invited to parties that often, and when they do, they tend to sit in the corner and watch.

As I helped that dear, sweet old man, Sandy, in the barn, I pretended nothing was bothering me, and I vowed to behave myself for as long as I was on this trip. Ten years from now the cowboy would look back and say, "That little mystery writer was actually a good egg."

I did well for a whole twenty-four hours. At dinner all of us sat at one round table — and I didn't say a word. I didn't say anything when the cowboy reached across Ruth for the hundredth time to refill her wineglass. I didn't say anything when the skinny groupie started talking about her channelers. I didn't even laugh when the fat groupie spilled wine in the cowboy's lap, then tried to rub away the red stain on his crotch. I bade everyone a polite good-night and went to my room, planning to work on an outline for my next book.

But my strongest and best character trait is the ability to concentrate, which is also known as the ability to obsess, and that's what I did that night.

Why is it that men can't see through women like Ruth? Why are men so *dumb* when it comes to women? Long legs, a cantilevered chest, acres of hair, and a woman can get any man she wants.

It bothered me that I was attracted — seriously attracted — to some big dumb cowboy while he looked at me as though he wanted to feed me rat poison.

I behaved myself all through breakfast while Ruth and the jock made goo-goo eyes at each other, seeming to read meaning into comments like

270

"Pass me the honey." Nothing in life is more boring than being near self-absorbed lovers. They find amusement in every word; every gesture from one is a thing of beauty to the other. They have no interest in anything outside themselves.

I bit into a piece of toast and watched the way the cowboy looked at Ruth: he was gone. As for Ruth, her heart wasn't in her eyes. Now and then she'd look at the Maggie–Winnie duet with a glance of triumph, as though to say, Look what I can do. She was probably looking forward to the great, drippy final scene when she'd bid him a tearful farewell. But poor dumb Taggert looked as if he wanted to tie an apron around Ruthie's perfectly maintained waist and put her behind a stove. For a moment I got a great deal of pleasure from imagining Ruth in a kitchen: worn linoleum floor, gingham curtains, the smell of onions frying, hot enough to fry beef on the tabletop, three whining kids hanging on to her swollen, red, unshaven legs.

When I looked up, Sandy was smiling at me as though he knew exactly what I was thinking, so I winked and gave him a mock salute with my orange juice.

By the time afternoon rolled around, I'd behaved myself so well that I guess I was feeling a little smug, because I blew it.

We'd all mounted horses and started riding up a trail into the woods. I'd been on a horse only a couple of times in my life before, but when you get down to it, riding a horse doesn't take all that

271

much brainpower. I'm not talking about dressage or show jumping, which require years of practice and training, but sitting on some well-fed, complacent animal that already knows the trail takes no skill.

But that's not how Ruth and the duet viewed it. Given Ruth's background, I would have thought she'd be a great horsewoman, but the truth was, she was terrified of the animal. Terrified and appalled at its big, wide nostrils, its hairy mouth, as well as the back end of it. When she climbed on that horse, her eyes wide with fear, I came close to liking her. She must really want to keep her job if she was willing to climb on an animal that terrified her as much as this one did.

It was late afternoon when I did it again. We all dismounted, sore, tired, and for the most part not speaking. Ruth had ridden behind Taggert and what conversation there was on the trail had been between them. The skinny one of the duet had tried to talk to me about a vegetarian diet, but when I told her I ate nothing but meat and lots of it, she clammed up and wouldn't speak to me. The silence of the woods, with Sandy riding behind me, had been bliss.

But after we'd dismounted and most of the group had wandered into the woods to make use of the facilities, I glanced at Ruth and saw that she had an odd look in her eye. She had her hand on her lower back, and I knew that if she was half as sore as I was, she was in pain. I don't know what she was thinking, but then again, she probably wasn't thinking at all. She was in pain and the cause of her pain was the placidly munching horse in front of her.

With hands shaking from exhaustion, she lit a cigarette. Then, with the look of a malicious child, she crushed out the cigarette in the soft neck of the unsuspecting horse.

Everything happened at once then. The horse cried out, sidestepped into Ruth, knocked her down, and started to walk on her. I didn't think. I just ran, trying to place myself between Ruth and the horse, but the horse was angry and in pain; some of the hair on its neck had caught fire and was smoldering. As best I could, I held on to the bridle with my left hand and slapped my right hand over the burn as I tried to tell the horse that it was safe and no one was going to harm it again. Somewhere during the turmoil, Ruth had slithered away like the snake she was and left me alone with the horse.

Thrashing through the woods like the Abominable Snowman was the big cowboy, and when I glanced up, I saw that he was heading straight for me — and his face was contorted with rage. What now? I thought. What in the world was he angry at me about this time?

Ruth, true to form, threw herself into the cowboy's strong, protective arms, weeping copiously, but without mussing her eye makeup, and begging him to save her. Taggert held her, but it was *me* he was glaring at as I stood here petting that poor burned horse. I wondered what Ruth would say if I told that I'd seen what she'd done.

"You should have called me," Taggert said, his teeth locked together.

About a thousand sentences went through my head at once. I could have told him the truth about his beloved; I could have pointed out that if I'd called him, then waited for him to arrive, Ruthie's lovely face might now have a horseshoe print in the middle of it. In the end I didn't defend myself. I just said, "You're a real jerk, you know that? A plain ol' everyday jerk," then dropped the bridle and walked away into the woods.

Is there any anger in the world more cold, more deep within you than the anger that comes from being falsely accused? I felt like a coal left over from an all-day fire. With the least bit of encouragement I could have erupted into a full-fledged forest fire. I stood there in the woods, not seeing anything, my fists clenched, feeling like a martyr. It wasn't fair! It really, truly wasn't fair.

My anger never lasted long, and this time was no exception. Within minutes I had turned it inward and burst my own bubble. I stood still, trembling with emotion and exhaustion, and to my disgust, tears stung my eyes.

When I heard someone behind me, I rubbed at my eyes with the back of my hand and looked up to see Sandy, his face a mask of concern.

"I don't know what's wrong with Kane," he said. "Usually he's not like this. Usually he's —"

Rule number one in my father's house: Never let 'em know you're in pain. If they know you're hurt, they can hurt you more.

I did my best to smile and sound lighthearted. "It's me. I always rub men the wrong way. If I'd screamed in fear and covered my face with my hands in terror he'd probably be feeding me brandy and pâté now."

Sandy chuckled. "Probably." He paused a moment, then said, "What's Ruth like?"

I could do nothing but roll my eyes. Should I tell him about the cigarette burn?

"Kane . . ." Sandy said hesitantly. "I think he wants a wife."

My earlier vision of Ruth in a kitchen came back to me and did a great deal to cheer me up. But I wasn't going to lie to this man; he'd been too nice to me, and he didn't deserve lies in return. "And he thinks to get a wife out of Ruth? Ruth likes the conquest, but once she's won, she's on to new goals." I thought of the cowboy bawling me out for saving Ruth not once but twice. "I think they deserve each other. I hopes she breaks his heart."

Sandy was silent. "So," he said after a while, "are *you* married?"

I knew he was thinking about Kane, who was like a son to him. Why is it that some people receive love no matter what they do and some people don't? I purposely misunderstood Sandy. "Is this an offer?"

When Sandy spoke, he was utterly serious. "If I were ten years younger I'd pursue you so hard that you'd end up marrying me just to get me to leave you alone."

My laugh was a little forced, but I couldn't deny that I was flattered. "You wouldn't want to marry me," I said honestly. "I'm too competent to marry. Men like women who are helpless or at least know how to pretend to be like Ruth can, but me, I'm ridiculously capable, and I always forget to hide it." I turned away to leave. I didn't want to talk to anyone else. In the mood I was in, there was no telling what I'd say next.

"Hurry back," Sandy called after me. "We're having buffalo tongue for dinner."

"Mmmm, my favorite," I said and kept going.

Chapter Six

Cale stretched out on the grass in that favorite posture of writers, where the body is completely supported, thus leaving the mind free to think and create. She was thinking of a story in which the killer was a cowboy who was so handsome that no one suspected him, when she heard people approach.

Now what? she thought, not wanting to move, not wanting to cease the fantasies playing about in her head. There are people who hate to write, hate to have to come up with ideas, and people who will go to any length to be allowed to continue to create. Now, hearing footsteps, Cale thought that if she stayed very quiet, whoever it was might go away and leave her in peace.

But Cale looked up to see Kane take Ruth in his arms and kiss her incredibly gently, as though she were fragile and precious. Cale knew she should leave, and she moved to do so, but then Kane pulled away from Ruth.

"You're all right?" he asked. "You weren't hurt by the horse?"

With great interest, Cale propped her head on her hand and listened for Ruth's answer. She thought of it as not so much eavesdropping as research.

"I'm fine, Kane," Ruth said with a gentle flutter of her eyelashes. "You don't know how I worried about coming on this trip. I was so frightened — frightened of the great outdoors, afraid of the animals, afraid of the people running the trip. I thought you'd be aggressive." She laughed seductively. "I was concerned that you'd want us to . . . to shoe horses or something like that."

So she wasn't going to tell him about burning the horse. Not that Cale had thought she would. If anything terrified this woman it was the possibility that men wouldn't adore her. Philosophical question to ponder, Cale thought: Does Ruth Edwards exist if no one is looking at her?

"Out here in the West we're just the same as any men. We want the same things as other men," Kane said in a deep voice.

Yeah, Cale thought. They want Ruth.

Ruth ran her hand up his arm. "I wouldn't say you're the same as any other man."

Even this guy couldn't possibly fall for that line. Could he? It would be the equivalent of a guy coming up to you in a bar and saying, "What's a nice girl like you," et cetera. Women were past that, but was any man past Ruth's tired line?

"I'd like to think I'm not like other men," he answered as he touched her arm.

Once again Cale had overestimated the male animal. Question, she thought, What's the difference between a rutting stag and a man on the make? Answer: nothing. They are both blind, deaf, and very dumb.

When they started kissing, Cale gave a loud "ahem." Eavesdropping was one thing, but voyeurism was something else.

Kane's face changed when he saw Cale, but for one second she saw what Ruth had seen: a man with lust on his face, as well as desire, passion, and perhaps even greed. Even more interesting was the look Ruth was wearing. Unless Cale missed her guess, ol' predatory Ruth was afraid of Cowboy Taggert. The minute Ruth saw him turn away, she turned tail and headed back to camp.

"I guess I can add spying to your list of accomplishments," he said through a jaw clenched tight in rage.

"I was here first," Cale began, starting to defend herself but the look on his face made her stop. "What's the use talking to you? You've made up your mind about me." She stood up and started

278

to leave, but he reached for her. "Don't touch me," she answered, pulling back from him.

His look was almost a sneer. "Right. Being touched is one of your phobias."

"Contrary to your opinion of me . . . Oh, who cares?" she said at last, and headed back to camp.

At the camp, Sandy had prepared a meal of beans and hot dogs, which the skinny one of the duet poked about on her tin plate, muttering about what nasty things hot dogs were, while the fat one brushed Ruth's hair to the obvious delight of Kane. After dinner the skinny one began talking about crystals and pyramids, telling in burdensome detail how pyramids were supposed to improve one's sex life, then slyly suggesting that Ruth hang one from a tree branch over her sleeping bag. In disgust, Cale walked away from the fire, heading toward the horses.

"You want to remove your shirt and let me have a look at that shoulder?"

Cale tried not to let her surprise show at Sandy's words, but she turned a radiant smile toward him. The moment she saw him the smile disappeared because hovering behind him was Kane.

"What's wrong with her shoulder?" Kane asked.

Sandy whipped around and snapped at the younger man. "If your brain was somewhere besides in your pants you'd see that she hurt herself when she saved Ruth's neck for the second time."

Ah, sweet justice, Cale thought. My own darling knight come to my rescue. She wondered if Sandy would like to move to New York and live with her in her penthouse?

Kane's face turned red and he muttered something about looking at Cale's shoulder himself but she put her chin up, pulled her shoulders back, and walked confidently back to the campsite, feeling the best she'd felt since coming to Colorado.

Chapter Seven

Kane was restless in his sleeping bag, punching at the thing that was supposed to be a pillow, turning frequently so the nylon made enough noise to scare the owls, and cursing at every opportunity. He knew he should have been thinking about Ruth. So far as he could tell, she was perfect. Under her beautiful façade was a sweet, gentle personality. He could almost see her with his sons; he could imagine her eight months pregnant with their child.

But try as he might, Kane couldn't seem to think of Ruth. Instead, he could only see and hear that bratty little writer. She was like a splinter that couldn't be dug out and was now festering. When he saw her leap over Ruth to grab the bridle of that horse, he'd been terrified. One misstep and she would have been down and under the hooves. He knew it was dumb of him to have told her to wait for him, and he knew she had done what had to be done, but she still rankled him.

He wasn't sure what it was about her that bothered him so much. Maybe it was her smiles and her wisecracks. Maybe it was the way she looked at Ruth, as though Ruth had climbed out from under a rock. Or maybe it was the way her backside curved into her jeans.

Why *had* he been so angry at her when she saved Ruth? If it had been any other woman, he would have been proud of her for her fast thinking and faster action, but something about the blonde always enraged him. Yet even as he had stood there glaring at her, he'd had an urge to pull her into his arms and protect her.

Protect her? That was like saying you wanted to protect a porcupine. And a porcupine was just what she was: small, prickly, and dangerous.

Sometime around three in the morning he got out of his sleeping bag and stepped into the woods, walking down a path he knew well, to look over the ridge to the trail below. Tomorrow evening they'd be in the ghost town of Eternity and his father's truck would be there to take the writer away. After that he'd have long days to spend with Ruth. He'd have time to get to know her, time to allow her to know him. He'd have time to —

He broke off his thoughts as below him he saw the flash of headlights. Someone was driving down the old road to Eternity. But who and why at this time of the morning? As soon as the questions occurred to him, he thought of an answer: something was wrong.

Immediately he too vividly remembered the night he'd come home to find an ambulance outside the apartment building in Paris where he and his wife and their new babies were living. Inside the ambulance was the broken and lifeless body of his beloved wife. Kane had been away on an overnight business trip and she'd been awake with the boys all the night before. In the late afternoon she'd sat down on the windowsill, sipping a cup of tea, and waiting for her husband to arrive. Quite simply, she must have fallen asleep, lost her balance, and fallen from the window.

Now Kane didn't bother with a horse, but went tearing down the hillside, stumbling over rocks and trees, sinking into piles of dry oak leaves, skidding down a shale slide in his attempt to intercept the truck before it reached the turnoff.

He leaped the last few feet, to land on all fours just a few yards in front of the truck. In an explosion of gravel, the driver slammed on the brakes, sending the truck into a skid that turned it sharply to one side as the driver fought to control it and straighten the wheels. Before the truck came to a full stop, the door flew open and out jumped Kane's brother Michael.

"What the hell are you trying to do? I could have killed you!" Mike shouted at his brother, not bothering to help him stand up.

Slowly Kane got up, brushing gravel and dirt from his clothes and hands. "What's wrong? Why are you here in Colorado?"

As though every muscle in his body ached, Mike

leaned back against the hood of the car while Kane looked at him.

The two men were identical twins, as alike as two humans could be: exactly the same height, size, eye and hair color. All their lives they had been close, so close that they often communicated without talking. Many times they'd had the same ideas and thoughts independently of one another, and it was commonplace for them to buy the same shirt unknowingly and wear it on the same occasion. There had never been a secret between them, and when one had news, he always went first to his twin brother.

"Congratulations," Kane said softly, because he knew without being told that his brother's wife had just been delivered of twins. For a long moment the brothers hugged each other in a fierce bond of love and understanding. Then they broke apart, both of them grinning.

"So?" Kane said, aware that his brother would know what his first question would be: Why did he leave New York?

Mike wiped his hand over his eyes in a gesture of tiredness and exasperation. "It was harrowing. At the first pain Samantha decided she wanted the babies to be born in Chandler, Colorado, that she wanted Mom there. No one could reason with her, and then . . . well, she started to cry, so Blair and I loaded her and your boys into the jet and took off. Sam was calm throughout the trip but Blair and I were frantic. What if the kids were born during the flight and they needed something

283

we didn't have? Sam kept saying that we shouldn't worry, that the boys were going to wait until they could see their grandmother. Dad and Mom were waiting at the airport with an ambulance. As soon as we got to the hospital, Sam's water broke and the kids popped out like champagne corks."

Mike paused and grinned. "You would think that the birth of my children would be a private time, but Mom, Dad, Jilly, Blair, and I plus two nurses were all in the delivery room. I expected someone to pass a tray of canapés."

Kane wasn't fooled by his brother's tone. Mike was more than pleased that his sons had been born into the arms of his parents; he was pleased that his family loved Samantha as much as he did. "Sam's okay? Kids okay?"

"Yeah, great. Everyone's fine, but —"

"But what?"

"It's a madhouse at the hospital. Relatives I've never heard of are showing up there."

Mike didn't have to explain to Kane that he wanted his wife and his sons to himself, that he wanted to be alone with them, because Kane knew how he felt. For two weeks after his sons were born, his wife's family had hovered about them until he felt suffocated. His mother-in-law was one of those women who believed men shouldn't change diapers, so Kane had rarely been allowed to touch his tiny sons. It wasn't until after she left that he was able to pull his wife and his children into his arms and feel them, touch them, hold them.

Now, looking at his brother, he knew the frustration Mike was feeling and the jealousy that was eating at him. He could picture Mike standing in the hospital room doorway watching one relative after another peer down at his newborn sons and thinking that they had spent more time with the children than he had. Kane used to worry that one of the babies would give his first smile to someone other than him.

Companionably, Kane put his arm around Mike's shoulders. "You know what I'd like more than anything in the world? I'd like to get my boys and bring them out here. This group is just women, and I'm sure they'd spoil them to death."

"Yeah?" Mike said gloomily. "Want me to bring them back here?"

"I was thinking that maybe I'd go to Chandler and get them."

Mike was so involved in his own misery that at first he didn't understand. "Wait a minute. You want *me* to stay here while you go back?"

"Twenty-four hours, that's all. And, besides, I want to see my new nephews. Are they as ugly as you?"

It was an old joke between them that never failed to produce a smile. "How would I know what they look like?" Mike said with a sigh. "The relatives won't let me near them."

"Why should they?" Kane asked. "You did your job, and they don't need you anymore." Laughing at his brother's expression of gloom, Kane moved away. "I'm serious. I need . . . a break from this."

"A break? You've only been around those women for a few days." Mike quirked an eyebrow. "What's going on?"

Kane gave his version of the past few days, telling Mike how lovely Ruth was and how flaky the duo was.

"How about the mystery writer? Sam loves her books and wants to meet her."

After a moment of silence Kane nearly exploded in a barrage of invective as he told about her nearly shooting his foot off, running under an enraged horse's hooves, and being an all around pain in the neck. "Everywhere I look, there she is. She spies on me when I'm with Ruth, calls me Cowboy Taggert, and asks if I count by pawing the earth."

Mike had to bite his lips to keep from laughing.

"It's not funny. The woman is insane," he said, then told Mike about Cale's fit after she'd killed the snake. "They're healed now, but I had three scratches down the side of my face where she clawed me."

"Couldn't have been too deep if they've healed so quickly."

Mike and Kane rarely disagreed. Their mother said it would be like having a fight with your shadow, so now, at Kane's look, Mike backed off. Twenty-four hours wasn't long, and the way things were now, Sam wouldn't know he wasn't there. Maybe it wouldn't be such a bad idea for him to be away for a whole day. "You're on," Mike said. "We'll meet you in Eternity tomorrow evening."

Chapter Eight

When morning came, I was glad this was going to be my last day on the trail ride. I hated being a failure, but I hated being hated more. For a few minutes I lay in my sleeping bag and thought about the entertaining stories I'd tell my editor when I got back to New York. I'd get my revenge by making an entire publishing house laugh at my escapade in the wilds of Colorado. Better yet, I'd write a book that would make the *world* laugh at the big cowboy and his lust for the two-faced woman.

Feeling a great deal better about myself and about life in general, I got out of the hated sleeping bag, tugged at my jeans — is there anything worse than sleeping in your clothes? — picked up my kit of toiletries, and headed for the stream to see if I could scour some of the grunge off my face. With the way my luck was running, I'd probably pick up a fungus from the clear mountain water and die a terrible death.

I'd just finished scrubbing when I heard heavy footsteps behind me. It was either our fearless leader or the last remaining dinosaur.

As usual he stopped near me, no doubt glaring down at me, just waiting to tell me I was doing something wrong. I ignored him as long as I could, then turned to look up at him, but was surprised to find standing there a man I'd never seen before.

"Oh!" I said, startled. "I thought you were someone else."

This seemed to surprise the man. They sure grow them dumb in Colorado, I thought. Big, beautiful, built, but definitely dumb.

"Who did you think I was?" he asked.

I stood up and looked at him. "I don't know if anyone's ever told you this, but you look a bit like our . . . our guide."

The man grinned at me as though I'd said something he'd waited all his life to hear, and I thought, This is great. I couldn't say or do anything to please one man, but this one seemed to be pleased by even a casual comment. Of course, being compared in looks to our cowboy leader might have seemed flattering to this man.

He extended his hand to me. "You must be Ruth. I'm Kane's brother, Mike."

I shook his hand, then set him straight. "I am *not* Ruth. I'm Cale Anderson, and your brother hates me."

I don't know whether it was the "hates me" part or the fact that I wasn't the beauteous Ruth, whom he'd obviously heard a lot about, but something seemed to bother him. He stood there opening and closing his mouth so that it looked like a pumping human heart on one of those PBS programs.

"But Ruth is — Ruth and Kane — I thought —"

288

Wow, I thought, a real intellectual here.

As though he could read my mind, he stopped flailing about and smiled at me, and he kept holding my hand even when I tugged on it.

"Look," he said, "I'm sorry about the mistake. Kane told me that he and Ruth were an item, so when you didn't know who I was, I assumed you were Ruth."

Now everything was clear. Now everything made sense. If I meet a man I've never seen before, then I must be Ruth Edwards. Of course. That made perfect sense to me.

Mike laughed, released my hand, and we sat down. He began to tell me a long-winded story about how he and his brother were identical twins. Yeah, right, and I'm Kathleen Turner's twin. I guess he could see my skepticism, but I started to laugh when he said that for the next twenty-four hours he was going to pretend to *be* Kane. This made as much sense as my saying I was going to impersonate O. J. Simpson.

I listened to his whole story, told him congratulations on his new babies, and even asked after Kane's sons, but I still thought he was crazy if he believed anyone was going to mistake him for his brother.

When he got through, he laughed at my expression and reassured me that he could pull it off. By the way, he said very seriously, "Who's better looking, me or my brother?"

I didn't want to hurt his feelings, but the truth is, Kane is in a whole different class of men when it comes to looks. As tactfully as I could, I said, "It's not that you aren't a very handsome man, Mike, but Kane —" I didn't finish my sentence because Mike laughed out loud, then kissed both my cheeks soundly. I don't know what had pleased him, but something had.

Since he insisted that he could indeed impersonate his brother, we spent about half an hour by the stream discussing how he was to treat each person on the trail ride. I told him about Winnie-Maggie, and when he laughed at my jokes, I knew I had an audience, so I began to pour it on. At first I was cautious about saying anything about Ruth, but Mike's laughter and his grin — the more he laughed at my jokes, the better looking he got — encouraged me. He encouraged me so much that I ended up doing a little impromptu parody of Kane and Ruth that sent Mike falling to the ground laughing.

"By the way," I said, while he was still laughing, "I was telling the truth when I said that Kane hates my guts."

He tried to look shocked, but I could see a little flicker in his eyes that told me Kane had warned him about me. Mike had thought I was the "good" one; therefore I must be Ruth.

"Why does he hate you?"

When he spoke, his tone told me that he couldn't believe that anyone could possibly hate me. It was very gratifying, very, very gratifying, and I smiled at him with nothing short of love. "You may not be as good looking or as sexy as your brother, but I think I like you better. Why don't you stay for the whole trip?" Somehow, that seemed to please him again, and when he got up, he offered his hands to help me up.

You know, I wish someone could explain sexual attraction to me. Why is it that you can put two equally good-looking men side by side and one will turn you on and the other won't? Here I was, alone in the woods with a dream of a man, a man who laughed at my jokes and obviously liked me very much. But I felt only sisterly toward him. Sure, he had a wife and a couple of brand-new kids, but since when has marriage prevented attraction? On the other hand, Kane Taggert did nothing but frown at me at best, shout at worst. He hated me; I hated him. But too often my thoughts wandered to questions about whether his skin was that lovely golden color all over or was his stomach the color of a frog's belly?

Mike and I walked back to camp arm in arm while he told me how much his wife loved my books. When Sandy's campfire was in sight, we separated, and I stood back to watch him make a fool of himself as he pretended to be Kane.

It's difficult to describe how I felt when I heard those people refer to Mike as Kane. Even Sandy grumbled that Kane had been in the woods too long and wasn't helping. I nearly giggled when Mike winked at me conspiratorially. It was heaven to be the one who was liked!

Everything went smoothly as the two men saddled the horses and all of us prepared to move out. Mike came over to check my stirrup, which was fine, and asked me how Ruth's horse's neck came to be burned. I wanted to tell him, but I couldn't. Too many years of elementary school with kids chanting, "Tattletale, tattletale," made me keep my mouth shut. I said that I had no idea, but my face turned red, and Mike snorted. "Somebody ought to give you some lessons in lying," he said.

It felt good to be vindicated.

We rode for a couple of hours, and Mike gave all his attention to Ruth. We'd reached the wide section of an old road so he could ride next to her. Behind them were her handmaidens, both of them holding the pommels of their saddles as though they were going to fall off. Sandy and I brought up the rear, neither of us talking much and both of us watching Ruth and Mike.

By late afternoon my early happiness had worn off. I shouldn't have been jealous, but I was. It looked as though Ruth had made yet another conquest. Mike was smiling at her, laughing softly over things she said, and in general adoring her.

We reached the falling-down town of Eternity at sundown. There were several buildings of weathered gray boards with a few signs falling off the buildings. One that said "Paris in the Desert" made me smile. Silently we rode down the wide main street, tumbleweeds blowing around us, heading toward a big house at the edge of town where Sandy said we'd camp.

Tired and aching, I dismounted when we

reached the house, then looked up to see Mike coming toward me, Ruth's saddle across his arms.

"Ruth is everything you said she was," he said just to me as he walked past.

I cheered up immediately. Cheered up and got a spurt of new energy.

An hour later I'd helped Sandy and Mike cook up hamburgers. It was at dinner that I blew it. "Would you hand me the mustard, Mike?" I asked.

Of course everyone stopped and looked at me, so I gave a little laugh and said that Kane reminded me of someone I knew who was named Mike so I'd mixed up the names. The women paid no attention to me, but I was sure that Sandy knew what was up. I felt bad for messing up Mike's secret and wanted very much to apologize.

After dinner I helped clean up, but I couldn't get Mike alone — Ruth seemed to be permanently attached to his left side — so I went for a walk.

I'm a good walker, and I find that hiking helps me think, so I guess I walked some miles down an old weed-infested road before I reached what had once been a pretty little house. It was set all by itself in what was once a lovely garden. A couple of roses were still blooming beside the porch.

"An ancestor of mine used to live here."

Mike spoke softly, but still I jumped.

"Sorry," he said. "I thought you wanted to be alone, but I didn't want to lose you."

I smiled at him. In the moonlight he was almost as handsome as his brother. "About this evening . . ." I began, but Mike just laughed and said

Sandy was used to twin tricks, and he was fine once Mike had explained.

"I brought a lantern. You want to look around?"

Mike was heavenly company. He told me about his ancestors who'd lived in the house, including one who was an actor so good he was called the Great Templeton. Being a lover of stories, I was thrilled with the house with the faded wallpaper covered with fat roses.

"Cale," Mike said when we'd finished the tour, "whatever you do, don't tell Kane you know we switched places."

I had no idea why it would matter, but I laughed.

"I'm very serious about this," he said. "Don't make a mistake and say 'Mike said,' or 'Mike did.' It's important, Cale."

"All right. Scout's honor." All this cloak-and-dagger stuff was like my books.

"I have to go now and meet Kane's truck. The next time you see me, I'll be someone else."

I guess that was twin humor. I reached out to shake his hand, but he gave me a sisterly hug and kissed my cheeks and made me promise to visit him and his family. Then he was gone, and I felt as though I'd just lost someone who could have been a lifelong friend.

I had no desire to leave the house. It had a good feeling to it, as though the people who'd lived in it so long ago had had a lot of love and laughter inside them.

Holding the lantern Mike had left behind, I wandered around the rooms on the ground floor, climbed into the loft, then back down again. I knew it was getting late and I should start the long walk back to that lovely group of women, but I was postponing leaving.

It was when I'd procrastinated until the last minute that I looked up to see Kane Taggert standing in the doorway. And in each arm was a little boy about five years old. They were asleep, snuggled against their father in complete trust, and they were the most beautiful things I'd ever seen in my life. And I wanted them.

Once I saw a $30,000 table I loved. I dreamed about it the way men dream about owning the fastest cars or a woman dreams about a man. But I had never in my life coveted anything as much as I did those two sleepy-eyed little boys.

I knew that Cowboy Taggert and I were mortal enemies; I knew we hated each other; but I also knew I had to touch those delicious creatures. Reaching up, I stroked a black curl that was as soft as angel's hair.

"Are they real?" I whispered.

Amused, Taggert said, "Very real."

I moved my hand down to touch a soft cheek. "But they look too perfect."

He snorted. "I don't know about perfect, but at least they're clean now. Give them about two hours and they'll be filthy again."

"What are their names?"

"Jamie and Todd."

I knew he was looking at me oddly, but I ignored him as I touched the other sleeping child.

"Which is which?"

"Not that it matters, but this one is Jamie and this is Todd."

Not that it matters, I thought. What a very odd thing to say, and then I thought: twins. Mike and Kane were supposed to be twins, Mike's baby sons were twins, so no doubt someone thought these children were also twins. It didn't matter to me if the whole Taggert family was nuts. If Kane wanted to pretend that his children looked alike, far be it from me to tell him otherwise.

As I looked at them, they began to wake up. I was truly amazed they had enough strength in their eyelids to raise that thick crop of eyelashes.

"Where is this?" Jamie asked, rubbing his eyes with his fist.

"This used to be somebody's house," I answered. "There's an enormous spiderweb in the bedroom. Like to see it?"

"Any spiders in it?" Todd asked, his beautiful head still on his father's shoulder.

"One big spider and some dead flies."

Tentatively I put out my hand, and Jamie took it. Then Todd held out his hand. Seconds later the boys were standing one on either side of me, and we walked into the bedroom.

They were lovely children: smart, curious, ready to laugh, full of energy. We talked about spiders and webs, and I described in detail how a spider catches flies and spins a web around them. We sat on the floor for a few minutes, a warm little boy wrapped inside each of my arms, and talked.

During this time I don't know what Cowboy Dad was doing. I think maybe he was standing in the doorway watching, but I wasn't sure, and I was too focused on the boys to care where he was. After a while Kane told the boys they had to go back to camp and go to bed, so the darlings jumped up and ran around the room making a deafening noise. After a few minutes Kane grabbed a shirt collar and reached for another, but Jamie ran behind my legs for protection and then Todd tried to run to me too.

"Todd," I said, "you go with your father, and, Jamie, you come with me."

As soon as I said it, I knew I'd made a mistake. I guess I wasn't supposed to be able to tell these twins apart either. But I am proud to say that I covered myself by saying that Todd had a grease spot on his shirt collar and that was how I knew one from the other. I got an odd look from Kane, but then he shrugged and picked up first one boy, then the other.

"Who are you?" Todd asked. I knew that Todd was going to be the businessman while Jamie was going to break hearts.

I considered my answer before replying. "I'm a storyteller."

Both boys nodded.

As always, Kane thought I was stupid and had no understanding of even the simplest concepts. "I think he meant what's your name?"

"Jamie, what's my name?"

"Cale," the brilliant child answered, and I gave

Kane my most enigmatic smile before sweeping ahead of them and leaving the little house.

I knew the child knew my name but that he didn't know how I fit into his world. When you have a father like mine, a man who never allows you any independence, yet dumps enormous responsibility on your young shoulders, half of you is never a child and half of you never grows up. I understand children because about two and a half feet of me is still eight years old.

Chapter Nine

The next day Kane wouldn't allow me near his little boys. It was obvious that he wanted them to bond with Ruth, but it took no genius to see that Ruth didn't like children. The skinny one of the duet wanted to know what the boys ate just as Jamie popped a grasshopper into his mouth. I was pleased when he spit it out and it went sailing down the front of Ruth's silk blouse. I had to leave the campsite after Ruth smacked Kane's hands away from her blouse buttons and said, "Get those filthy beasts away from me." I had to leave or I'd have died from keeping laughter bottled up inside me. I did have the satisfaction of meeting Kane's eyes just before I turned away and was able to give him a raised-eyebrow, *this-*

is-the-woman-you're-going-to-marry? look. Grabbing an apple, I started walking toward the Templeton house.

Once I was in that old house I felt better and began to wonder when I could go back to Chandler and catch the first toy plane out. I wanted to get away from the entire Taggert clan. All of them were crazy, what with their twins who didn't look alike, and their quick hate and love. It was going to be great to be back in New York where people acted sane.

I went upstairs to the loft, sat on the windowsill, looked down the road, and ate my apple. I was certainly going to miss those children, though. Which was absurd, considering I'd known them less than twenty-four hours. Jamie had crawled inside the sleeping bag with me last night; then this morning Todd had cried because Jamie had spent more time with me than he had. That was when Kane took both boys away from me and steered them toward Ruth.

I was sitting there eating my apple when I saw Kane — alone, no kids — walking toward the cabin. He looked up, saw me, and for a moment I thought he was seeing the dead actor's ghostly face. Even from the second story I could see that he'd turned pale, and he began to run toward the house. The way he ran was almost frightening, as though he'd seen something terrible, terrifying.

As for me, I was paralyzed. I couldn't move as I heard him thunder into the house, then tear up the ladder to the loft.

He pulled me off the windowsill and we went tumbling to the floor where my back scraped the rough wood as all two hundred pounds of him landed on top of me. At first I struggled to get away from him, but I stopped when I realized he wasn't moving. He was sprawled on top of me, looking down at me as though I were some museum specimen. For a moment I glared up at him to give him the idea that I wanted him off of me.

God, but he was a good-looking man! He had short, thick eyelashes that actually curled, like mine did after I'd spent ten minutes torturing them with a curler. His lips were full and soft and just barely parted, and I could feel his breath on my face.

I guess we all think of ourselves as rational human beings, and we like to think that if faced with an irrational situation — a burning building, for example — we would act with calm and intelligence. But then something dreadful happens and we embarrass ourselves by acting just as we'd hoped we wouldn't.

That's what I did when this big cowboy was looking down at me from under those eyelashes with his sweet, warm breath touching me. I wanted to get away from him. Honest, I did. I could imagine rolling away from him and standing over him, hands on hips, cool, triumphant, unaffected by his beauty, and saying something like "Don't you ever touch me again."

That's what I *wanted* to do. What I *did* was flick my tongue across his lips.

300

The gesture startled me, and it startled him. Well, I guess it more than startled him. Actually, it turned him on.

One thing I like about being female is that the evidence of sexual excitement isn't known to the world. Oh, a woman's face may turn red and her breath may get a little weird, but she can always say that she's having a hot flash. But men can't hide what they're feeling — or maybe "wanting" is the correct term. And right now I knew that that cowboy wanted me, because the evidence of his desire was about to cut into my left thigh.

Now, I thought, would be the perfect time to roll away from him and laugh at him. Ha-ha-ha, I'd say. You want me, but I couldn't care less for your passion.

But life never works out the way one plans it, because I wanted that man more than I'd ever wanted anything — except for my first book to be published — and there was no way I was going to roll away from him.

I think all first sex should be candlelight dinners, little kisses inside the elbow, that sort of thing, but there wasn't any chance of sex like that between this man and me. We didn't even kiss but started tearing at each other as if we meant to kill one another. It was like sex in those black-and-white foreign movies where the people talk and talk and talk and all you can think about is how full your bladder is; then suddenly he shoves her against the barn door and you forget all about your bladder.

301

We started on each other with all the fury and anger that we spoke to each other with. His shirt came open with one pull, and I found out what I'd always wanted to know: why cowboy shirts have snaps instead of buttons. Makes for speedy hayloft trysts.

I don't know how he got my clothes off. I was wearing jeans with one of those annoying short zippers that, in order to get them on, you have to stick your butt out and wiggle. But this time I didn't have to wiggle to get them down. He slid them over my hips as easy as you please and then, like a magician, he ran his hands over my laced boots and they fell away — just *fell* off, no struggles.

When he moved his hands back up, we were both naked, and God, what a body the man had! I couldn't see much of it, but I could feel it. Think beautiful athletes. Think about smooth, warm skin covering that body. When his skin touched mine, I drew in my breath as though someone had doused me with ice water — only it wasn't cold that sent that sensation through me.

Muscle wasn't the only thing interesting about the man. I've heard that the skin is the largest organ in the human body, but with this man, I thought some measurements were going to have to be taken to be absolutely sure.

He entered me with all the ease and expertise of a cat burglar slipping into a twenty-first-story bedroom.

Now came the part of sex I hated — not that

302

I'd had that much experience, but three minutes seemed to be a man's limit. Sometimes I'd read the history of man trying to break the four-minute mile and wonder why a man didn't try for something important, like the four-minute screw.

At first I just lay there, ready to be disappointed when he grunted and collapsed on top of me and said, "That was good, baby," then started snoring. But this guy didn't stop after three minutes. I'm not a good timekeeper in such circumstances, but it's my guess that after six minutes he was still moving in and out of me, slowly, smoothly, as though he didn't mean to stop before next Saturday.

I can't really explain what began to happen to me, but all I can say is that I began to wake up. It was as though there were this woman inside me — no, correction: this tall, blonde, beautiful goddess inside me — who began to unroll from where she'd been asleep all her life. Languorously she uncurled, stood up, rubbed her eyes, and looked around her. And when she was awake, she began to expand. She grew bigger and bigger and bigger until she began to fill me, fill me out to my fingertips and my toes. She filled my head so completely that for the first time since I could remember I didn't have stories inside my head. Instead of stories I had this man in my body, and I was awake, really, truly, fully awake, for the first time in my life. Every nerve ending, every pore, every cell in my body was alert and sensitive and *alive*.

I'm not sure what I did. I mean, I don't remember where my hands went, where my mouth went. I remember at one point he turned me over and with two hundred pounds of male propelling me, I went sliding across the floor and had to put my hands on a hay bale to keep from moving.

I remember I was shameless. I remember I had no dignity, no thoughts. I remember I was closer to being an animal than to a thinking, rational human being. I remember that I at last understood what people meant when they said that sex was a basic need, like food and water. Up until that day in that loft with that man, I hadn't believed that old saw. I'd believed people *needed* food and water but they didn't *need* sex. I was wrong.

He turned me over again and pulled my ankles up around his shoulders and kept on. I think I was a cheering section. I don't think I was making sexy, ladylike little moans, and I can guarantee that I wasn't saying anything rational. On the food chain, right then I was way below the human level that had the ability to talk.

After a while I began to feel as if I were going to explode. Okay, I know that's a cliché. I know it's been said a million times, but the first time it happens to *you* it's almost scary. I guess it would be scary if the explosion were something you wanted to stop, but it was like those salmon fighting to go upstream. It was something I was driving myself toward.

I wrapped my legs around his waist while he was on his knees, and I began to move with more strength than I actually possessed. At that moment I could have moved a train with my pelvis, but I couldn't move this man who seemed to have the strength of a couple of ocean liners.

I'd read about orgasms and I thought I'd experienced a couple, but I hadn't. Not a real orgasm. It's not something that happens in one big flash. At least it isn't for a woman.

I'm so glad I'm a woman. How could sex be as good for a man when it happens *outside* his body? For a woman, it's all inside, deep inside, and it radiates from within.

I guess an orgasm could best be compared to ocean waves breaking against the beach. Wave after wave came from inside me and moved outward to the very limits of my body. It seemed to go on and on and on, pulsating, extending, retreating, at first with urgency but gradually slowing, fading from a brilliant white light to a luminescent glow.

My fingers and toes hurt, as though the waves inside me had stretched them to their limit.

After a while I began to breathe again, and the woman inside me, that goddess who I hadn't known existed, realized she was tired and began to recede. With her went my energy. She also took my anger and my general rage at life. I'd never felt so calm, so peaceful, in my life.

When the man kissed my ear, I smiled sleepily, snuggled against his sweaty skin, then followed the goddess inside me and went to sleep.

Later, when I woke up, still in Kane's arms,

his skin next to mine, suddenly I knew I had to share more with him than just the greatest sex ever experienced in the history of the world.

Once when I was one of the judges at the Miss USA pageant, one of the many instructions they gave us was to never give a girl a score lower than 5. They said, and I agreed, that the girls had worked hard and deserved at least a 5 in every category.

The pageant officials had asked local volunteers to stand in for the contestants during rehearsals so we could practice with the computers. Sitting next to me was the famous actor Richard Woodward, and when the first volunteer pirouetted for us, he punched in 2.2. Now, I didn't know this man but I knew these practice scores were going to be shown on a screen, and I didn't think it was very nice of him to give these nice, nervous ladies such a low score, so I told him so.

Richard looked at me and said, "You're a *real* writer, aren't you?"

I was highly flattered by this because, to me, "*real* writer" means Pulitzer Prize. Not sales, but *the* prize. As I was flushing with pleasure at this accolade, Richard said, "Real writers are incurably nosy and cannot keep their mouths shut."

I laughed so hard that the man who was trying to teach us called me down, and after that, Richard and I were great friends.

Well, I am, in every sense of the word, a *real* writer. I'm nosy and I don't keep my mouth shut. If someone tells me she's just gotten a divorce,

I'll say, "So why'd you divorce him?"

Kane and I had been introduced, and we'd shared enough that I guess we were at least on a first-name basis, so I said, "How come you've been p.o.'d since your wife died? Did you hate her or what?" Subtlety is not part of my personality, and besides, I've found that the direct approach earns me either silence or a story.

I could feel Kane hesitate, and a part of me sensed that he'd never told anyone, not anyone on the face of the earth, the truth about his wife. While he was making up his mind whether or not to tell me, I held my breath because I suddenly knew that I wanted to know whatever was inside him. It was at that moment that he became a person to me. Maybe it was the sex, maybe it was his looks, maybe it was the sweetness of his breath, and maybe it was my love of a story from any source, but I don't think so. I think it was a feeling that there was more to him than muscle and sex appeal. I think I knew that a man who could make me feel as he'd just done was not an insensitive clod, that there was a real person inside.

"I have an identical twin brother," he said.

I didn't expel my breath. Several times I had wondered why Mike had asked me not to let Kane know that I knew about him.

He went on. "There's an asinine saying in my family: You marry the one who can tell the twins apart."

Oh, Lord, I thought. No wonder Mike asked me to, for once, keep my mouth shut. Marry? Me?

Marry some great big, sexy cowpoke whom, until a few hours ago, I disliked rather heartily?

"Could your wife tell the twins apart?" I asked, and my voice was a small thing.

Kane didn't seem to notice my voice as he started telling me how he'd met her in Paris.

Paris? I thought. What was a cowboy doing in Paris? Having the hair done on his best bull?

Anyway, he was in Paris, met her, fell madly in love, and married her six days later. Sometime during this six days he called his mother, and she sent his brother Mike over to check out the bride. Here Kane's body began to tense up as he told how his family had sent Mike to see if she could tell the twins apart.

"And when she couldn't, that was it," Kane said. "No one else in the family besides Mike attended my wedding. It was as though they'd dismissed her because of some stupid legend."

He didn't say anything after that, so I said, "You liked her, though?" I was praying he wasn't going to tell me that the legend had been right, that he'd fallen out of love with her two weeks after the wedding.

"Yeah, I loved her. I loved her madly. We were perfectly suited. It was as though we were two halves of a whole. If she had a thought, I had it at the same time. We liked the same food, the same people, wanted to do the same things at the same time."

If I lived with somebody like that, I'd be crazy in a week. In fact, once I had a boyfriend like that. The girls in the dorm all said I was so lucky, but I thought I'd go out of my mind. One night I said I wanted Italian for dinner, and when he said he did too, I attacked. "What if I wanted Chinese? What if I wanted Peking *cat?*" I yelled at the poor guy. "Don't you have any thoughts of your own? Don't you ever want a good ol'-fashioned argument about where we'll eat to-night?" Need I say that that particular young man never called me again?

I'd learned long ago that most people aren't like me, so maybe most people would enjoy living in complete peace and harmony. Personally, I've never experienced tranquillity, but my intuition tells me that it's not something for which I have any natural talent.

One minute Kane was telling me about his dead wife and the next, he was telling me about his brother's wife, and for a while, from the tone of his voice, I thought he was in love with her. But he was explaining how his family had accepted Mike's wife, Samantha, into the family but not his wife. There was anger in his voice, but I'm glad to say there was no jealousy.

So now what do I do? I thought. Say, Hey, *I* can tell the twins apart? I'm not much of a believer in magic — magician shows put me to sleep — so I'm sure there are hundreds of women in Amer-ica who can tell Kane from his very different brother. Next time Kane got married, he should pick one of them and make his family happy.

He went on talking to me, telling me in detail

about his paragon of a wife. I refrained from making snide remarks about how "perfect" the two of them sounded — how perfectly boring, that is. Perfect conversations, perfect sex, perfect children. If she'd lived, would they have had a perfect divorce? Maybe they wouldn't have divorced and maybe I'm just being cynical, but every marriage where I've heard the wife say, "My husband is a darling. We never fight," ends in divorce. The marriages that last have a wife who says, "My husband is a pain in the neck," then elaborates on the subject. Maybe it has to do with telling yourself what you *hope* is the truth and facing what actually *is*.

Kane went on to tell of his loneliness after her death and how he had not been allowed to grieve for her. Everyone in his family seemed to have the same attitude: Buck up and think of your sons. He'd wanted to sit in a dark room and cry for days, but his wife's mother had been the one to cry while Kane had to be the strong one and listen to everyone else's grief. How could they mourn her death, he wondered, when they'd never celebrated her life?

In the end he didn't get to cry. Everyone seemed to think that it was the boys who were important, who were going to need their mother. Kane wasn't the type to shout that he needed her too, so he'd kept his tears inside and carried on as before, except that there was no longer anyone waiting for him at the end of the day. No one to laugh at his jokes and rub his tired shoulders, no one to bounce ideas off — no one to make love to.

I don't know why people tend to tell me their most intimate secrets. Maybe it's because I'm interested, but then, maybe it's because I'm an empath.

I saw a "Star Trek" episode where a woman was an empath; she *felt* other people's joys and miseries. That's what I do. I think it has to do with my being a fixer and listening so hard that I try to solve people's problems for them. If I want something, I go after it. I have tunnel vision. Nothing distracts me; nothing discourages me.

It took a really rotten secretary to teach me that everyone isn't like me. Hildy told me that what she wanted most in the world was to write children's books. In fact, she had written one and now all she needed was a publisher.

I don't know what's wrong with me: I *believe* what people tell me. Hildy said she wanted a publisher, so I called in some favors and arranged for her story to be read by one of the top children's book editors in New York. I then spent three days on the phone trying to reach Hildy. When I finally got her, late on a Sunday night, she told me angrily that since I hadn't called her as I said I would, she'd mailed her manuscript in to the slush pile at another house. Of course she received a rejection, and she felt that it was *my* fault.

It took me a long time to figure out that what Hildy really wanted was to tell people that someday she wanted to write children's books.

Since I listen to people so intently, following

311

their angst-ridden sighs with offers of help — all of which I carry out — I figure that's why people talk to me about their problems.

But I didn't know what to offer Kane in the way of help. Maybe I could gather his family together and bawl them out. Maybe I could take his boys for a year or so and let him go away and grieve. Somehow, though, I didn't think he'd let me have them. Maybe I could say, "Kane, I can tell you and your brother apart. Therefore I must be more suitable for you than your perfect wife was."

Yeah, right. A big good-looking cowboy whose idea of a good time was scraping horses' hooves, and a smart-mouthed city girl. Was I supposed to marry him, move onto a ranch, and show sheep at the state fair? Or maybe Kane would move to New York, become Mr. Cale Anderson, and fetch me cold drinks at autograph parties.

On the other hand, if we got down to hard, cold truth, I can't imagine anyone wanting to live with me. Not to make a melodrama out of it, but if your own parents don't like you, you never actually believe that *anyone* likes you.

Chapter Ten

To say that it was awkward between Kane and me after the sex and the talk is this century's understatement. I don't know how long we would have stayed there, safe, holding each other, if Sandy hadn't arrived with the boys. The moment we heard voices, the spell was broken, and we suddenly looked at each other in horror, then in embarrassment. As quickly as possible I pulled on my clothes, wincing because my knees were raw. When I tried to put my boots on, I found the laces had been slashed. So *that* was how he got them off, I thought, then had to clump down the loft ladder in loose boots.

Sandy, standing behind the boys, took one look at the two of us and I knew he knew what had happened. I couldn't meet his eyes or Kane's, so I concentrated on the boys.

Sandy had brought horses, so I got to ride back, which was good considering the state of my boots. When we were back at camp, I didn't look at Kane, and when he held out a ball of heavy cotton twine and said he was going to tie my boots for me, I snatched the ball away from him and said I'd do it myself. I knew he stood there for a moment looking at me, but I wouldn't look at him.

The night before, I'd slept outside, near the men and boys, while the other women slept inside the old house, but that night I went inside with the women. What had happened between me and the dumb cowboy was an accident, and I didn't plan to add to the mistake. Tomorrow I'd start back to Chandler if I had to walk.

Thinking of accidents made me wonder if I had just gotten myself pregnant. I didn't seem to remember any form of birth control being used.

"I can get an abortion," I said into the darkness.

Like hell I would kill my own child. I hadn't thought much about children in my life, but right now I could imagine myself sitting in a rocking chair at three A.M., a black-haired baby at my breast, writing notes for my next book. I could imagine bandaging a three-year-old's knee and kissing away baby tears. I could imagine a maid washing dirty diapers and cleaning strained carrots off the kitchen wall. (Hey, I'm a realist!)

I didn't get to sleep for hours, and when I awoke, no one else was in the room.

Chapter Eleven

The next day I didn't see Kane much. In fact I saw him practically not at all, which suited me, since I wasn't sure how I felt about him. He went off with Ruth into the woods and left me to take care of his darling boys. Actually he left them with Sandy, but I sort of took them and we had a great time looking into each and every old house in Eternity and making up stories about who had lived there and how they'd died. In the afternoon they put their heads in my lap, one on either side, and I told them stories until they fell asleep.

It was about three when we went back to camp, but only Sandy was there, napping in the shade. The boys immediately jumped on him, and I could tell that he wanted to see them, so I reluctantly gave them up and went down the road leading out of town where I saw a pickup truck and knew without a doubt that it was the truck that was to take me back to Chandler. I braced myself but then I saw that Mike was standing by the side of the pickup, and again I marveled at how much he didn't look like Kane. Mike had short, stubby eyelashes, lips that bordered on thin, and a body that was about to run to fat. Also, the pitch of his voice was higher than Kane's deep bass rumble.

"Hi, Mike," I said. "How're the new babies?"

When Mike turned to look at me, I knew something was wrong, and it didn't take the use of many brain cells to figure out what it was. Too late, I saw the pair of booted feet upside down in the truck.

Why is it that men love to hang head-down from car seats and look at the wires under the dashboard? Is that what they do after their mothers have finally made them realize that it is socially unacceptable to lie on the floor and look up girls' skirts?

"You want this wrench?" Mike asked his brother, and for a moment both of us held our breath. Maybe Kane hadn't heard me. Maybe Kane had his ears full of car wires and didn't realize that I had just let him know of my betrayal.

I have never been a lucky person.

Kane made no pretense of not being angry. He was furious. Without looking at me or his brother, he twirled around in the seat and got out of the truck and started climbing the mountain nearest him. Straight up through brush and over rocks, eating ground with all the energy that fury gave him.

I followed him because I thought he deserved an explanation.

"What now?" he asked as soon as Cale reached him. "Should I propose marriage?"

She ignored his sarcasm and didn't pretend that she didn't know what he was talking about. "Surely there are other people who can tell you from your brother."

"My mother, sometimes my father, my youngest sister . . ." His voice lowered. "And my brother's wife."

"That's it?" Her disbelief was evident in her tone.

When he turned to look at her, he was no longer the sweet-faced cowboy she'd had a tumble with. He had one eyebrow raised and his nostrils flared.

"No doubt to *you* we don't look at all alike. Something to do with eyelashes and which of us is fatter, right?"

She wasn't going to answer that because he was too close to home. "You know, of course, that this invalidates the legend?"

He continued to look at her, his expression unchanged. "How do you figure that?"

"Your wife couldn't tell you apart, yet you two were the love of the century. I can tell you from your brother, but you and I can't abide each other." She paused a moment. "Except for sex," she said softly.

He looked away. "Yeah, except for sex."

"You should marry somebody normal, somebody who wants to be a wife and mother, and wants to live on a ranch and ride horses and milk cows or whatever. Above all, you shouldn't think of, shouldn't even consider, marrying someone because of great . . . I mean, because of one very ordinary sexual encounter. These things happen. I bet this kind of thing happens with every group you take out — especially New York women." She was warming to her subject. "There's the disease scare in New York so the women don't feel safe — not that I endorse one-night stands — but they feel safe with a big, clean cowboy who's lived all his life in pure, innocent Colorado. I mean, what can you get from a cowboy? Hoof-and-mouth disease? Anthrax? Are they the same thing? So, anyway, it was just something that happened. The right time, the right place. I bet that if Ruth had

317

been in that upstairs window it would have . . . been . . . Ruth that you . . ." She was slowing down, and, with horror, she recognized that what she was feeling was jealousy. If, she thought. *If* Ruth had been there, Kane would have pulled her from the window. Then Ruth and Kane would have . . .

Getting up, she dusted off the seat of her jeans. "There are millions of women out there. Go meet them and find someone to fulfill your legend. I'm not the one. I'm not anyone's princess in a tower."

All the way down that mountain, with every step I took, I hoped he'd come after me. Since my thoughts are my own, I figured I could indulge them — there was no one to tell them to and no one to laugh at me.

I knew his coming after me was a stupid idea. I knew we were completely incompatible, since we'd barely said a civil word to each other. Except for one afternoon of wonderful, divine, heavenly sex followed by a beautiful man holding me in his arms and pouring his soul out to me, we'd always fought. We disliked each other a great deal. We had nothing in common. Except maybe two kids that I wanted. Wanted in the abstract, that is. What was I thinking of: moving those darling children out of the wilds of Colorado, out of the clean air of this mountainous state, and putting them in a penthouse in New York with nothing but a terrace to play on? Of course, being raised in Colorado was no assurance that a person would grow up happy. Maybe the kids would *like* big, dirty New York. Or maybe I could move to Colorado.

None of this thinking did me any good, because the cowboy didn't come after me, didn't fall on his knees before me and tell me he couldn't live without me. In fact, he stayed on top of the mountain while I went down it.

Mike was waiting at the bottom. Not that I thought he was waiting for me, but he gave a good imitation of concern. I was so depressed I didn't even suggest that he should visit a gym now and then. After Kane, Mike was a pale second best.

"I want to go home," I said.

"Home?"

Mike sounded as dumb as I'd once thought Kane was. But Kane wasn't dumb. He was smart and funny and kind, and . . . and I wished he believed that stupid ol' legend. My fantasies started going on me, and I imagined a father with a shotgun forcing us to marry because we fulfilled the prophecy. Where were fathers with shotguns when you really needed them?

"Yes, home," I said. "Home to New York."

Mike looked up the mountain, but I knew he wasn't going to see his brother.

"We said our good-byes up there."

"But . . ."

It was obvious Mike didn't know what else to say. No doubt he'd done the expected thing and hauled his wife before the family tribunal before he even considered marrying her. Oh, well, it was a good thing nothing was going to come of Kane and me, because I'm not good with families, and I think I could come to hate his.

"Mike," I said slowly and as though I meant it, "I want you to drive me to Chandler so I can leave this state. I want to go back to a place where they just *cut* your heart out." Not break it as they did in Colorado.

I had to look away because I was giving in to my flair for drama. Just once I wanted to make an unflamboyant exit. No fits, no tantrums. I wanted to keep my pride and just walk out.

Mike helped me get my gear together, but he took forever doing it. I know he was trying to give his brother time to make up his mind. But Kane *had* made up his mind, and he was right to be so sensible. I would make a rotten wife. I'd be involved in a book and forget about food for days at a time. If I didn't have a nanny for the kids, I'd probably forget about them too. And heaven help the man if he crossed me! I'd dig my heels in and do whatever he didn't want me to do just because he wanted me to do it. All in all, it was better for somebody like me to live alone. To be free. Yes, that's it. Freedom. Freedom to come and go as I please. Freedom to . . . to have no one to laugh at my jokes, to rub my keyboard-tightened shoulders, no one to listen to my latest plot idea. No one to make love to.

Mike managed to dawdle until sundown, then began to find reasons why we shouldn't leave until morning.

"Colorado's so backward they don't have head-lights on the cars yet?" I asked, with my most belligerent New York attitude.

Mike gave in to me and drove me back to the tiny town of Chandler. He wanted to take me to his parents' house. And what? Tuck me in Kane's bed and hope his brother would come home during the night and stumble into bed with me?

I made him take me to a motel, and at ten o'clock the next morning he drove me to the airport where I took a tiny airplane to Denver. From there I flew to New York.

My editor wasn't very happy with me. In the six weeks since I'd been back from Colorado, I hadn't killed anybody. I mean on paper, of course. Since my publishing house sent me all that lovely money for killing people, they weren't too happy with me either.

It wasn't that I wasn't writing. I was writing ten to fourteen hours a day, but I kept writing about things like mail-order brides and shotgun weddings. I never finished any of the stories, just wrote proposals and sent them to my editor.

At the beginning of the seventh week, my editor came to my apartment to have a talk with me.

"It isn't that we mind your changing genres," she said patiently. (All editors deliver bad news to their best-selling author with extreme patience and tact, rather like you'd talk to a crazy man who was holding a machete: "It's not that you're wrong to want to mutilate and maim . . . .") "After all," she said, "romances make a fortune." (Thank God I wasn't trying to write something that would make no money — there'd be mass hysteria in the corridors of my publishing house.)

She lowered her voice and smiled sweetly. "It's just that your romances aren't any *good*. They're so sad."

Life is weird, isn't it? You kill people off in book after book and that's not considered sad, but the heroine of a romance falls for some guy who then walks off into the sunset, and that's considered too sad. If I'd killed the s.o.b., the story would have been a tragedy. Tragedy is okay, murder is grand, but *sad* is bad. Even worse, sad doesn't sell.

I listened to everything she said and noticed that for once she didn't bring flowers or food — concrete proof that the publishers were genuinely annoyed. Bet they wished they could shake me until I saw sense, saw that it was my duty in life to kill people on paper and support the family of everyone who worked at my publishing house.

Funny thing was, I *wanted* to write mysteries. I was happy when I was angry. I was happy and confident when I was having fights with cab drivers and imagining which character I was going to kill next. Yesterday I had to go to Saks to return a suit that didn't fit, and I told the taxi driver to take me to Fiftieth and Fifth. Ten minutes later I'm over on First Avenue — this is in the opposite direction from Saks. I just said calmly, "You're going the wrong way." When the driver told me in all of his seven words of English that this was his first day on the job, I smiled and told him how to get to Saks, then I paid the whole excursion fare and tipped him a dollar fifty. Trust me, this is *not* the real me.

Chapter Twelve

Cale was in her apartment, the terrace door open, playing with an unreadable story of unrequited love when she heard the sound of a helicopter. At first she paid no attention to it, but it seemed to grow louder, then to remain in one place, a place that seemed to be just outside her windows. Annoyed, frowning, she got up to close the doors when she saw that the helicopter was indeed hovering above her terrace. Surely that was illegal, she thought. Surely New York had laws against helicopters being that close to apartment buildings.

With her hand on the knob, she started to close the terrace door when she heard an odd noise. Curious, she looked up at the wind-producing, noisy helicopter, then opened her mouth in astonishment.

Descending from the copter, his foot in a stirrup, holding on to a thick rope, was a man. Cale's first impulse was to slam the door and get out of the apartment, but then she looked again. On the man's feet were what looked to be cowboy boots of a deep carmine red. Only one person she'd ever met in her life wore cowboy boots: Kane Taggert.

She wanted to shut the door and go back inside the apartment, but she couldn't. Instead, she stepped out onto the terrace and watched the slow descent of the man. Of all the absurd things, he was wearing a tuxedo at four in the afternoon, and if she could see clearly, he had a large green bottle under his arm and two champagne flutes in his hand.

She stepped back when he alighted and took his foot out of the stirrup. She didn't say a word when he motioned to the helicopter that he was safely down. Even when the copter was gone and it was once again quiet, she still said nothing, just stood there and looked at this big man standing on her terrace, and waited for him to say something.

With a bit of a smile, he set the bottle down, opened it, poured, and handed her a glass of champagne. She didn't take it.

"What do you want?" she said with as much hostility as she could manage.

Kane took a deep drink of the wine before answering her. "I came to ask you to marry me."

Cale didn't so much as hesitate but turned away and headed for the doors into her apartment. When Kane caught her arm, she jerked from his grasp.

"Get away from me," she said. "I never want to see you again."

"Cale —" he began.

She whirled on him. "I can't believe you know my name," she snapped. "I thought I was 'the writer.'" With a sigh, she made herself calm down. "Okay, you've made your big entrance and I'm impressed, so now you can go. You can go down the elevator, unless you plan to use a parachute."

Kane put himself in front of the terrace doors. "I guess I deserve whatever you hand me. I know I've been a heel. You've told me, Mike has told me, Sandy, my own sons have told me. Even my sister-in-law and my mother, neither of whom has met you, have told me in graphic terms that I am an idiot, stupid, and in general a fool."

Cale wasn't in the least swayed by what he was saying. "I'm sure there are other women who can tell you from your brother," she said, "so go find one of them. Your tactics are wasted on me."

Again Kane caught her arm. "It wasn't the twin thing. It was that you made me forget my wife."

She turned to frown at him. "*Ruth* made you forget your wife."

Dropping her arm, Kane walked away from her to stand at the edge of the terrace and look at the back of the General Motors Building. Before it was built there was a scrumptious view of the Plaza Hotel and Central Park. "I don't know if anyone told you or not, but Ruth looks like my wife. When I saw a photo of Ruth, I began to imagine that I'd get back what I once had. I thought about bringing Janine back to life; I thought of picnics and moonlight walks and the four of us snuggled together. I never questioned what Ruth was like because I thought I knew. She'd lost her husband and child in an accident, just as I had, and I knew we were meant to be together."

Turning to look at Cale, he saw that her face was unforgiving. "I think I was attracted to you from the first moment I saw you. You were sitting there on that suitcase looking mad at the world. Then you started sneezing, and when you looked at me . . ." He grinned. "Well, you made me feel like every movie star, athlete, and astronaut rolled into one. I thought you were the prettiest thing I'd seen in years, and that annoyed the hell out of me."

He took a drink of champagne then looked at her. "I was pretty awful about the rattlesnake. I should have said thank you, but the fact that you were competent, unafraid, and beautiful all in one didn't fit into my plans. There was Ruth, my ideal woman, and I was lusting after a feisty little blonde. You made me feel . . . well, adulterous."

He drained his glass, poured himself more champagne, and turned away again. "I've spent the last month with Ruth Edwards. It took a long time, but I finally realized that she wasn't Janine, that she was someone else altogether. In fact, she was someone I didn't like very much." He chuckled. "And my sons *hated* her."

Turning back around, he looked at Cale, still standing by the terrace doors, her face unreadable.

"So I'm your second choice," she said. "Come

on, cowboy, surely you could find a third woman and choose her. Why do you pick on New York women? Find yourself some nice cowgirl and —"

"I live in New York," he said, obviously not planning to elaborate on that statement.

"You've had your say, so now you can go," she said, turning toward the doors, but Kane caught her in his arms, spun her around, and kissed her. He kissed her ears, her neck, her face.

"I love you, Cale," he said against her lips. "I love the way you make me look at *you* so that I can't see any other women. I love your cynicism, your sense of humor. I love the way you look at my sons, the way you look at me. I love the way we make love together. I love your competency, your vulnerability, your neediness, your —"

"I am not needy!" It wasn't easy to think when he was this close to her.

At that Kane snorted. "I've never met a human who needed more than you do. You need" — he kissed the end of her nose — "love." He kissed her cheek. "Kindness." With each word he gave a sweet kiss to another part of her face. "Attention. A family. Security."

She jerked out of his arms. "*You* need a puppy!"

He didn't let her get away from him. "I need someone who can see reality. I need someone who won't allow me to wallow in self-pity for years, blind to everything else in life. I imagine that with you if I feel melancholy you'll kick me and tell me to stop moping and give me some work to do. I can't see you allowing someone the luxury of wallowing in his own grief."

"You make me sound like an overseer on a plantation."

Chuckling, he drew her closer to him, rubbing his body against hers. "What can I say to convince you that I love you and want to marry you?"

Cale pulled away from him, holding him at arm's length. "Look, I know you think this is all very romantic. We had a quickie . . . well, okay, maybe more than a quickie, in a hayloft, and you began to think it was the basis for a lifetime together. But you can't marry me. I'm not . . . wife material."

"What's wrong with you?" he asked, but she could tell by his tone that he was teasing her.

"I'm a business, that's what's wrong with me. I am *big* business." She took a deep breath and delivered the coup de grâce, the thrust that was guaranteed to turn any man off. "Last year I earned one-point-four million dollars, and I'll probably earn more this year."

Kane didn't lose his smile, but nuzzled her ear. "That's all right, sweetheart. A person can live on that."

She pushed away from him. "Are you *listening* to me, cowboy? I'm not your ordinary little housewife. I'm not the little wife who's there waiting for you when you come home at night. I get so absorbed in my stories that I can't remember to eat, much less remember that I'm supposed to fix hubby a martini and have it waiting for him. Or do you just drink beer? And what do you mean,

328

you live in New York?"

"I mean that I'm not what you think I am. I'm no more a cowboy than you are a circus performer. I deal with the stock market; I deal with *real* money, not that pittance you earn."

She stared up at him, her mouth slightly open, her eyes blinking rapidly.

"Go on," he said, "tell me the worst there is to know about you. No matter what you say, no matter what you've done, I love you. I want you to marry me. I'll buy a floor of this building, and the kids and I'll live there with their nanny so you can have this place just for your writing and to get away from us. Whatever you want, you can have."

She thought of lots of reasons why she shouldn't marry him, such as the fact that she hated him. Yeah, like she hated writing books, she hated him. Since she'd walked away from him she hadn't been able to think of anything but him. Every waking, every dreaming moment she thought of him and his children.

"I hate you," she whispered as she collapsed into his strong arms. "I really do hate you."

"Yeah, I know," he whispered. "And I don't blame you. But if you give me the rest of your life, maybe I can change your mind about me."

She couldn't speak because the lump in her throat was choking her. When she heard the door-bell, she pulled away from him, trying to sniff back tears. "I have to . . . to . . ."

"That'll be the boys. They want to show you

their new books and —"

"Jamie and Todd are here?" The next second she was running into the apartment and throwing open the door. After only a second's hesitation the boys leaped on her and the three of them went rolling onto the foyer floor. In the next minute Kane had joined them and the three males began tickling Cale.

"Answer me," Kane said. "Answer me now!"

"Yes," Cale said, laughing. "Yes, I'll marry you."

With one push, Kane removed his sons from Cale and pulled her into his arms. "I don't know why I didn't recognize you the minute I saw you."

"Neither do I," she whispered against his lips. "Neither do I."

BOOK III

A Perfect Arrangement

Chapter One
1882

Mr. Hunter, I would like to ask you to marry me."

Cole couldn't say a word; it was one of the few times in his life when he was actually speechless. There'd been many times when he'd chosen not to speak, but at those times a few thousand words had been racing around in his head and he'd simply refused to let them out. Not now, though.

It wasn't that he was shocked at a woman asking him to marry her. He didn't want to brag, but he'd had a few marriage proposals in his time. Well, so maybe they were more in the form of propositions and maybe they weren't from women who could be called respectable, but there had definitely been women who had mentioned the word "marriage."

What was shocking was that *this* woman was talking to him about marriage. This tiny creature was the type of woman who pretended that men like him didn't exist. She was one of those women who swept their skirts aside when he walked by. Maybe later they met him in the back of the barn after church, but they didn't talk of marriage with him, and they didn't ask him in for Sunday dinner.

But he could believe that this little thing would

have trouble getting a man. There wasn't anything to recommend her. Except for a rather curvy front — and he'd certainly seen better — she was the type of woman you wouldn't notice even if she were sitting on your lap. Not pretty, not ugly, not even homely, just plain-faced. She had dull brown hair, not a lot of it, and it looked as though a dozen red-hot pokers couldn't make it curl. Plain brown eyes, plain little nose, plain, ordinary little mouth. No figure to speak of except for the nice round shape on top. No hips, no real curves at all.

And then there was her manner. Cole liked women who looked as though they'd be fun in bed and out of it. He liked a woman who could laugh and make him laugh, but this prim little creature hardly looked capable of pleasantries, much less humor. She looked like the teacher who would accept no excuse for not doing your homework. She looked like the lady who arranged the flowers for the church every Sunday, the woman you saw every day you were growing up but never thought to ask her name.

She didn't look married. She didn't look as though she'd ever had a man in her bed, a man snuggling against her for warmth. If she'd had a man, he probably wore a long white nightshirt and a cap and what they did they did solely for the procreation of the human race.

He took his time lighting a thin cigar to give himself some time to think — and to recover himself. He traveled so much and met so many people that he'd had to train himself to be a quick and accurate judge of both men and women. But so far, he wasn't making any headway with this one. When he was younger than his present thirty-eight years, he used to think that women like this one were dying for a man to warm them up. He'd learned that cold-looking women were, for the most part, cold women. Once he'd spent months working to seduce a plain, prim little woman rather like this one, all the while thinking that a dormant volcano lay under her tightly buttoned dress. But when he finally got her knickers off, she just lay there with her fists clenched and her teeth gritted. It was the one and only time in his life when he couldn't perform. After that, he decided it was easier to go after the women who looked as though they might welcome his advances.

So now here was one of these frigid, mousy little nothings, with her dress buttoned to her chin, her elbows held close to her body, and although he couldn't see them, he was sure her knees were locked together.

He was seated on one of those hard, upholstered chairs the landlady considered fashionable, taking his time lighting his cigar and watching her, waiting for her to make the next move. Of course she had so far made all the moves. She had written him that she wanted to hire his services for a very personal matter and she'd like to come to see him in Abilene.

From her letter — written on heavy vellum in a perfect hand — he'd guessed she was rich and she wanted him to kill some man who'd toyed with her affections. That's what women usually wrote to him about. If a man wanted to hire him, he generally wanted someone killed because of land or cattle or water rights or revenge or some such. But with women it was always love. Years ago, Cole had stopped trying to make both men and women believe he wasn't a hired killer. He was a peacemaker-for-hire. He felt that he was really a diplomat. He had a talent for settling disputes, and he used that talent to do what he could. It was true that sometimes people got killed during the talks, but Cole only defended himself. He never drew first.

"Please go on," he said when the mouse didn't continue. He'd offered her a seat, but she said she'd rather stand. Probably because that stiff back of hers wouldn't bend. And she'd insisted that the door to his room be left open six inches — so no one would get the wrong idea.

She cleared her throat. "I know what I must sound like and look like. I'm sure you think I am a lonely spinster in need of a man."

Cole had to work to keep from smiling since that is just what he thought. Was she now going to tell him that she didn't need a man? All she wanted was for him to find the neighbor's son, who had jilted her, and wipe him off the face of the earth.

"I try not to lie to myself," she said. "I have no illusions about my appearance and my appeal to men. I would, of course, like to have a husband

and half a dozen children."

He did smile at that. At least she was honest about her need for an energetic man in her bed.

"But if I really were looking for a husband, a man to be a father to my children, I certainly wouldn't consider an aging gunslinger with no visible means of support and the beginnings of a paunch."

At that Cole sat up straighter in his chair and sucked in his stomach. It took some doing to keep from putting his hand on his stomach. Maybe he'd better stay away from his landlady's apple pie for a couple of days. "Would you mind telling me what you want?" Not that I would ever, *ever* take this job, he said to himself. What did she mean, "aging gunslinger"? Why he was as good with a gun right now as he had been twenty years ago! None of these youngsters today — He cut off his thoughts when she started speaking again.

"I'm not sure what to tell you first." She gave him a hard, scrutinizing look. "I was told you were the handsomest man in Texas."

Cole smiled again. "People talk a lot," he said modestly.

"Personally, I don't see it."

At that he paused with his cigar in midair.

"Maybe you were handsome some years back but now . . . Too much sun has turned your skin to leather, and you have a hard look about your eyes. It's my guess, Mr. Hunter, that you're a very selfish man."

For the second time that day, Cole was shocked

into speechlessness. Then he tipped his head back and laughed. When he looked at the woman again, she wasn't so much as smiling. "All right, Miss . . ."

"Latham. Miss Latham."

"Ah, yes, *Miss* Latham," he said snidely, then was annoyed with himself. In fights, he'd faced men who'd said all manner of things about him and his ancestors and they hadn't been able to rile him, but this ordinary woman with her comments about his supposed paunch and whether or not he was selfish annoyed him. Who was she to talk? She was so nondescript that if you stood her against a sand dune you wouldn't be able to see where she started and the sand left off.

"You want to tell me what you want of me?" he asked. He knew he ought to tell her to get out of here, but he couldn't help being curious as to what she had to say. Great, he thought, a curious diplomat. He could get killed being curious.

"I have a sister who is one year older than I am."

She turned and walked toward the window, and when she walked there wasn't the slightest hint of the graceful sway of hips that men loved to look at. This woman walked as though she were made of wood — and she was just about that attractive to him.

"My sister is everything that I am not. My sister is beautiful."

She must have sensed Cole's thoughts because

she started explaining. "I know that those who see me cannot believe I have a beautiful sister. They probably think that my idea of beauty is undeveloped."

Cole didn't say a word, but this was just what he was thinking. It wouldn't take much of a looker to be pretty beside this little creature. Of course with every unpleasant thing she said about him, she became even less attractive. He wondered how old she was. Not less than thirty was his guess. Much too old to attract any man now. She wouldn't get the half-dozen kids she wanted.

"Rowena is as beautiful as any woman who has ever lived. She's five feet seven, has thick auburn hair that curls all by itself. She has green eyes, thick lashes, a perfect nose, and full lips. She has a figure that has made men tremble. I know this because I have seen it happen more than once."

She took a deep breath. "More important than her beauty — to women at least — is that Rowena is a lovely person. She cares about other people. She does things for them, makes them care about themselves and others. She is a born leader." She sighed. "My sister has my mother's looks and personality. In other words, she has everything."

"You want me to shoot her for you?" Cole was making a joke, but the woman didn't laugh, making him wonder if she had any sense of humor at all.

"To take my sister from this life would harm the earth."

Cole coughed, nearly choking on the cigar

smoke. He'd never heard anyone say anything like that before, yet she said it as though she truly meant it.

"My sister is a heroine. I mean that in the best sense. Like all heroines, she has no idea of her heroism. When she was twelve, she saw a fire in an orphanage, and without thought for her own safety she ran into the burning building and saved a roomful of children. She is beloved by everyone."

"Except you."

Miss Latham took another deep breath and sat down. "No, you're wrong. She is loved especially by me." When she expelled her breath he could see that she was shaking, but she concealed it very well. He suspected that she often hid her emotions. "It is difficult to explain how I feel about Rowena. I love her but sometimes I . . . I almost hate her." Her head came up in a gesture of pride. "Perhaps my problem is actually jealousy."

For several moments he watched her sit utterly still on her chair, and he was amazed to see that there was no betrayal of emotion on her face or in her body. No flicker of the eyes, no wringing of the hands. She sat perfectly still. She'd be a brilliant poker player.

Suddenly Cole knew he was in trouble because he could feel himself softening toward her. "What do you want me to do?" he asked more gruffly than he meant to.

"Six years ago my sister married a fabulous man. Tall, handsome, rich, intelligent. Jonathan is the man every woman dreams of marrying. They live

340

in England on a beautiful estate and have two lovely children. Rowena is the type of woman whose servants would work for her even if she couldn't pay them."

"And what about you?"

For the first time, he saw the tiniest bit of a smile from her. "I overpay my servants and demand nothing from them, and still they steal the silver."

At that he laughed again. Maybe she did have a sense of humor after all.

"My problem stems from the fact that my sister loves me very much. She always has. At Christmas she used to sneak downstairs during the night and switch labels on packages because people tended to give me boring, utilitarian gifts while they gave Rowena things of beauty. Of course I would then end up with twenty-five yards of yellow silk embroidered with butterflies and she would get ten volumes on the life of Byron, so we'd both be unhappy. But she did it out of love for me."

"You like Byron?"

"I like books. And research. I am the sensible one while Rowena is the flamboyant one. When I see flames coming out of a building, I call for the fire department. I do not run toward flames; I run away from them."

Cole smiled. "I'm more like you."

"Oh, no, you're not," she said with some strength. "You, Mr. Hunter, are like Rowena."

The way she said that made it sound like the worst thing anyone had ever said about him. His first reaction was to defend himself. But defend himself from what? She had said nothing about her sister that wasn't highly complimentary.

"I have researched you rather thoroughly, Mr. Hunter, and you are as blindly heroic as my sister. You act first and then think about what you are doing. According to the sources I have consulted, you have settled at least two range wars with fewer deaths than anyone believed possible."

He knew he shouldn't, but he had to pay her back for her earlier remark. "No ma'am, I'm just what you see — an aging gunslinger."

"That's what you look like, and it's true that you have no future. Your usefulness will end when your eyesight fails. As far as I can tell, you have not managed to save any money from all that you have made, mainly because you tend to work for little or nothing. On one hand you are heroic, and on the other you are a fool."

"You do know how to flatter a man, Miss Latham. I can't imagine why you don't have a husband and a dozen kids."

"I am immune to insults from men, so you might as well not try. I merely want to hire you for a job and that's all. After two weeks you may walk out of my life and never see me again."

"And what you want me to do is marry you?"

"Not actually marry me, just pretend to be my husband for the two weeks that my sister will be here in Texas visiting me."

"I'm curious, miss, why me? Don't you think that an aging gunslinger is the worst choice for a husband?" No matter that she'd said nice things to him, that one remark about his age got under his skin. And there was the thing about his eyesight. He could see as well today as when he was eighteen. Well, maybe newspaper print was smaller than it used to be, but — He made himself stop thinking. If she made another one of her belittling comments, he was going to strangle her.

"It's because of who you are that I want you. I want to . . . to impress my sister." In the first real emotion she'd shown yet, she threw up her hands in exasperation. "Who can understand love? I certainly don't. It seems to me that if you're going to marry a man, you should choose a man who would be a good provider, reliable, a caring father. But women don't seem to want men like that. Women want men who are dangerous, men who do really childish, stupid things like shoot people faster than they themselves can be shot. In short, Mr. Hunter, women want men like you."

Cole gave up trying to remember to smoke. He was so fascinated by her that a keg of dynamite couldn't have moved him. "I would impress your sister?" he asked softly.

"Oh, yes. You're just the type who would impress Rowena. You're rather like her Jonathan, except that he has used his . . . I'm not sure you would call it talent, but he's used his ability to frighten people and terrify them to make enormous amounts of money."

"Sounds like a real devil."

"He is. But that's what women seem to like.

343

I don't mean that Jonathan is a bad person. I think he's generally considered a very good businessman. And he's compassionate in his way, just as you are, but he thinks that any means is justified, as long as everything goes his way in the end."

"And I am like that?" He could have bitten his tongue for asking, but he couldn't help himself.

"Yes. It really wasn't your business to settle those range wars, and I am amazed at the vanity it took on your part to think that you *could* settle them."

"But I did settle them," he couldn't help pointing out.

"Yes, there is that. You see, Jonathan goes about making money just the way you go about interfering in people's lives and killing them if they get in your way."

Cole felt as though he should apologize for having been born. "I am sorry to have displeased you, sorry that women like your sister think I'm worth something," he said sarcastically.

"Oh, that's all right," she said, taking his words seriously. "We all have our vanities. I am extremely vain in what I'm doing now. You see, my sister has only good intentions toward me, but she plans to come to Texas to find me a husband. She says that I am becoming a dried-up, sour . . ." She waved her hand in dismissal. "It doesn't matter what Rowena says. She says whatever comes to her mind."

"Unlike you, who are the very essence of tact and graciousness."

She gave him a hard look to see if he was joking, but she could see no humor in his eyes. "Rowena has decided to manage my life, and she will do so if I don't do something beforehand."

"I'm having difficulty understanding something. You say that you want a husband and kids, and obviously, with your charms, you're not going to find a man by yourself, so why don't you allow your sister to find one for you?"

"Because she will sweet-talk some man like you into marrying me."

Cole just sat there and blinked at her. It was difficult to think of oneself as the worst thing that could happen to a woman. There had been a few women who thought he was the *best* thing that could happen to them.

She let out a sigh. "I see that I'm not explaining myself thoroughly."

"It's probably my fault," Cole said sweetly. "All that gunpowder going off near my head has made me rather stupid over all the many, many years of my life. Please do explain everything to me."

"I do want a husband, and I plan to get one . . . eventually. But the man I want is not the sort that Rowena would want for me. I want a nice, plain man. I don't want a man like her Jonathan or like you. I don't want a man who is so handsome that I have to worry every night that he's out with other women."

Cole thought there was a compliment in there, but he wasn't sure where it was.

"I want a man I can depend on, someone who'll

be there when I go to sleep and when I wake up. I want a man who will rock the baby when it's teething. I want a man who will nurse me when I'm ill. In other words I want a man who is grown up, an adult, a man who is man enough to know that there are ways of settling arguments that don't involve shooting someone."

Cole found himself squirming in his seat. He was developing a genuine dislike for this woman. "So why don't you get one of those sodbusters if that's what you want?" He couldn't believe it but his voice sounded petulant and maybe even jealous.

"Can you imagine what my sister's reaction would be if she came to visit and found me married to some short, bald man who knew more about books than guns? Rowena would feel even sorrier for me than she does already."

Suddenly she stood up, her fists clenched. "Mr. Hunter, you can't imagine what it was like growing up with a sister like Rowena. All my life I've been compared to her. If she had to be beautiful, I don't think it's fair that she's also talented. Rowena can do *anything*. She rides as though she's part of the horse. She can cook; she can dance; she speaks four languages. Rowena is absolutely divine. She used to stand up to our father with great defiance and he loved her all the more for it. When I tried to stand up to him he sent me to my room without supper."

She took a deep breath as if to calm herself. "So now my parents are dead, I live alone in an

346

enormous, dreary old house, and my splendid sister is coming to Texas to find some man for me to marry. She says she's doing this out of love for me, but it's really out of pity. She feels sorry for me and thinks that I could never get a husband on my own, but she believes that she has enough charm to persuade a man to marry me."

She looked at him. "It's hardly been a year since my father died, and while he was alive I never had a chance to look for a husband. He said he'd lost one daughter to marriage and he was going to make damned sure he didn't lose another. I have every confidence that now that I am free I can get a husband, but not by next week when Rowena arrives. At least not a good husband. Those men take time to find and need careful consideration. Marriage is a very serious undertaking. And besides, even if I did greet Rowena with the type of man I want on my arm, she'd still feel sorry for me because I didn't have some swaggering, squint-eyed, hard-jawed, ruthless killer like her husband."

Cole couldn't help running his hand over his jaw. Was it hard? Was he ruthless? Did he swagger? Damn, but the woman was making him crazy. If he really were a ruthless killer, she'd be the first on his list to get rid of.

"So you want me to pretend to be married to you for two weeks in an effort to impress your beautiful sister?"

"Yes, exactly. I will pay you five thousand dollars for the two weeks, and during that time, of course, you will live in a comfortable house and be well fed."

She talked as though he usually lived in a cave and ate dirt and worms for dinner. Of course this boardinghouse could use a good cleaning and maybe the food did leave a lot to be desired. But one time in Saint Louis he'd lived in a splendid hotel and eaten . . . Well, that had been after a lucrative job, and he'd stayed there until the money ran out. Maybe her bald farmer would have done something sensible with the money.

"Well?" she asked, frowning impatiently.

"Miss Latham, I think that if I had to spend two weeks near you, I'd be hanged for murder — yours."

Even though he was watching her intently, she didn't betray any emotion — if she had any. "I guess that's settled, then. I wish you the best in your endeavors in the future, and I hope that you can continue to dodge bullets for many years. Good day, sir."

With that she left the room, closing the door behind her.

Cole walked to the cabinet against the wall and withdrew a bottle of whiskey and downed a healthy slug. What would little Miss Prim and Proper say to his drinking at this time of the morning? Probably just look down her boring little nose at him.

At the window, he held the curtain aside and watched her walk across the street. Not one man turned to watch her walk or even looked at her. She was the most undesirable woman he'd ever

348

laid eyes on. Yet something about her got under his skin.

"Damn!" he said out loud. In a matter of minutes she had made him feel that his entire life was a failure. Him! Coleman Hunter, a man known throughout the Southwest as a man to be reckoned with, a man who could have his pick of any woman in the country.

He moved away from the window, and as he did so, he happened to see himself in the mirror over the bureau. Turning sideways, he stood a little straighter and sucked in his stomach. There wasn't any paunch. His stomach was as flat as the day he had his first gunfight. Angrily he grabbed his hat and left the room.

Two hours later he was sitting on the front porch of the sheriff's office whittling a stick into nothing. He was beginning to think the woman was a jinx. Ten minutes after he'd left his boardinghouse, a boy had come running to him with a telegram. His next job, for some rancher in Plano, had been canceled. The man had wanted someone to find and kill a bunch of rustlers, but he had telegraphed that a younger, less expensive man had already done the job for him.

This news had made Cole so angry he'd gone to Nina and told her he wanted her, and *now*. Nina had said that he had to wait his turn and he hadn't paid her for the last time. Since when had he had to pay for a woman? Women were dying to go to bed with him.

"Nina," he said, hating himself for doing it, "do

349

you think I'm . . . well, you know . . . attractive?"

That had made her laugh. "What's wrong with you, Cole, honey? You fallin' for some girl that thinks you're old enough to be her father?"

That was probably the *only* insult Miss Latham had not given him, but now Nina had. First a dried-up old maid and now a prostitute. He thought he'd better get out of Abilene fast, before his hair turned gray and his teeth fell out.

"What's eatin' you?" asked the sheriff, who was now sitting next to him on the porch.

"Nothing's wrong with me," Cole snapped. "What makes you think anything is wrong with me?"

"I've rarely seen you awake this early, and when you do get up in the daylight it's usually to meet somebody in a shootout. How come you ain't over at the saloon like you usually are?"

"Is that what you think of me? Is that what you think I do with my life, shoot people and drink and gamble? If you think I'm such a wastrel, why haven't you arrested me? For that matter, if I'm such a killer, why haven't you hanged me?"

The sheriff looked at Cole in amusement. They had known each other for years, had ridden together many times, until the sheriff decided that he'd had enough of bedrolls and beans. He'd married a plump widow and produced two little boys who were everything to him. "Nina turn you down?"

"No, Nina didn't turn me down," Cole lied. "What is wrong with the people in the town that

350

a man can't do something a little different now and then?"

"Somebody got to you today. Who was it? Any of Dalton's boys around that I don't know about?"

Cole didn't answer him because at that moment boring little Miss Latham stepped out of the hotel and started walking down the street toward the bank.

The sheriff was watching his longtime friend, trying to figure out what was wrong with him, when Cole's eyes suddenly changed. It was the look he usually reserved for cardsharps who might have an ace up their sleeves and for notorious gunmen who might draw at any second so they could say they'd killed Cole Hunter. The sheriff, to his disbelief, saw that Cole had fastened his gaze on a small, plain woman in a modest brown dress. Cole usually went for flashy women in red satin and black lace. He said he fought men for a living, so he didn't want to fight women; he wanted them to be easy.

"Who is she?" Cole asked belligerently, pointing his knife blade toward her.

Abilene was a good-sized town, but the sheriff prided himself on knowing who came and went. "Money." He bit off a chew of tobacco. "Her father was from the East, came out here and bought a few hundred acres of very pretty land up north, built the biggest house ever seen by most people, then sat down and waited. Most people thought he was crazy. Four years later the railroad came through and he sold them land for five times what he'd paid for it. He built a town, called it Latham after himself then rented the buildings to people who wanted to work. A hard man. They say he throws out tenants if they're twenty-four hours late with the rent."

"Did," Cole said. "He died nearly a year ago."

"Oh? I hadn't heard," the sheriff said, letting Cole know that he'd like to hear more. But Cole had always accused him of being an old gossip and wasn't about to give him any information.

"What about his wife?" Cole asked.

"I heard he bought her too. He went back east for a few months and returned with her." The sheriff paused to smile. "I hear she was the most beautiful woman most men had ever seen. I talked to a cowboy that used to work for them, and he said there wasn't one man that could say a word when she was around. All of 'em just stood and stared at her."

"And she had a daughter who looked just like her," Cole said softly.

The sheriff chuckled. "Yeah, a real beauty, and then she had one that looked just like him. Must've been a real disappointment to them."

Cole wasn't sure whether he should defend the brat or not. Part of him thought he should, but then he thought of "aging gunslinger" and he didn't defend her. Next time some whippersnapper challenged him to a duel, he ought to sic Miss Latham on him. Her words could make him bleed more than Cole's bullets.

It was when he was whittling the fourth stick

away to nothing that the commotion started. Right under the sleepy nose of the sheriff and the unwatchful eye of Cole, four men had ridden up to the bank, pulled bandannas up over their faces, and proceeded to rob the bank. The first the sheriff knew of it was a gunshot, then a man staggering out, holding a bloody hand over his stomach.

Cole had never thought that a bank robbery was any of his business. First of all, he might find himself shooting at people he considered his friends, men he had shared campfires with, so he left do-gooding to men stupid enough to pin a badge on. Yesterday he would have sat where he was on the porch and watched while the sheriff jumped up and started running, his young deputy coming from inside the sheriff's office to run behind him.

But today something was different. Today the words *She's in there* echoed in his head. That didn't make sense, of course, because he had no interest in her. If it had been Nina or someone else he knew, that might have made sense; this did not.

He didn't take time to think. In spite of his imaginary paunch and his advancing age and his failing eyesight, he bolted over the hitching rail and took off running, a full twenty-five feet in front of the sheriff. He was like a snake, one minute lazy and still in the sun, and the next moment moving so quickly it was difficult to see him.

The robbers hadn't counted on a man with the reputation of Cole Hunter trying to prevent them from robbing the Abilene bank. They thought they'd have to deal with one fat sheriff and one green deputy and a lot of disinterested citizens. After all, it was a small bank, not of much interest to more than a dozen people. The thieves thought this heist would be easy, that they'd be in and out in a matter of minutes. But things had gone wrong from the first. One of the farmers had decided to play hero, and the youngest and most nervous of the robbers had been frightened into shooting him.

"Let's get out of here," one of the gang shouted, grabbing the saddlebags full of money and heading for the door. It was the last thing he ever did. Cole Hunter smashed the door open with his foot, then stood back to get away from the barrage of gunfire. When it had calmed down he went in, two guns blazing, and when the smoke had cleared, there were three dead men on the floor.

The fourth robber grabbed the nearest available person to use as a shield, and this happened to be Miss Latham.

"Put the guns down or she gets it in the head," the man said from behind his mask, holding his gun to the woman's head.

Cole was glad to see that she didn't look terrified. He didn't want to say anything to her to let the man know that he knew her; he didn't want to give him any advantages. When the sheriff and his deputy arrived, he motioned them to stay outside. "They're down," Cole said quietly, stooping to drop his guns, all the while keeping his eyes on the man as he began to make his way toward the door. There was another gun, a one-shot der-ringer in his belt. He could get to it and shoot, but he had to move Miss Latham out of the way. He wished he could think of a way to tell Miss Latham to pull away from the gunman.

"What are you doin' in this, Hunter?" the robber said. "You're usually on our side."

Yesterday Cole would have been pleased by that remark, would even have agreed with it, but today something was different. Maybe it was Miss Latham's eyes looking at him with absolute trust. She'd said he was a hero.

"Just happened by," he said, "and I needed a little excitement. A man's gotta roll with the punches, keep himself from getting bored."

The robber had smiling eyes over the mask. "I understand that," he said, still easing toward the door, pushing Miss Latham ahead of him.

Just when Cole was sure that his hint about "roll-ing" had not gotten through to Miss Latham, she bit the robber's arm, and when, in surprise, he released his hold on her, she dropped to the floor and rolled away. Cole drew his derringer and fired — but not before the robber did the same. His bullet hit Cole in the right forearm a split second after Cole's gun went off.

Chapter Two

Cole leaned back against the bed, his eyes shut against the glare of the darkened room. It was difficult to believe, but his mood was worse than the pain in his head and belly, not to mention the throbbing in his right forearm. Yesterday he'd drunk a prodigious amount of whiskey because the doctor had spent what seemed like hours taking out that bastard's bullet. And when the doc was done, he'd informed Cole that the bullet had hit the bone, cracking it so severely that his arm would be out of commission for months, first in a cast and then more time as he regained the use of his shooting arm.

It had taken all of Cole's self-control not to rage in front of the doctor and the sheriff. Considering how drunk he was when he heard the news, he should have been given a medal for his restraint. All he'd been able to think of was the fact that he wouldn't be able to take on his next two jobs. One was easy: a rich man wanted to own more land so he'd hired Cole to persuade some little farmer that he and his family would be better off selling their few acres to the rich man. It was the kind of thing that Cole was good at, because all he had to do was talk and paint a splendid picture of land elsewhere. Usually, all it took was mentioning that there was the possibility of gold somewhere else and the overworked farmer was more than ready to leave his plow behind.

The second job was more difficult. A rancher was running some cattle through the territory of an enemy and he was hiring several men with guns to protect the cows and his wranglers.

So how could Cole do either job with his shooting arm in a cast? He couldn't go to the first rancher and tell him the truth: he could do the job without a gun. If that news spread, pretty soon the men would hire the local preacher to do the talking. If he wanted to keep getting clients, he had to make them believe that each job was dangerous and needed a man with a fast gun.

But now he would be laid up for months. And why? Because some snippet of a woman had said some things that had hurt his feelings, that was why. He felt about as old as a first grader, getting his first bad score on an arithmetic test. And that's what the skinny little Miss Latham reminded him of: his first teacher, an unhappy old buzzard who used to tell him and the other students that they were nothing and would never amount to anything. Miss Latham had made him feel that he had to prove himself to her and maybe to himself as well. She'd made him want to show her that he wasn't a criminal.

Right now questions were echoing in his head about whether he'd been shot because his eyesight was failing or because his reaction time was too

357

slow — both problems due to his great age.

Shifting his position in the bed, trying to make his body comfortable even if his mind wasn't, he opened his eyes a crack, then almost gave a yelp of surprise. Standing silently by the bed in the darkened room, looking like a ghost, was Miss Latham.

"What are you doing here?" he demanded and his voice conveyed his conviction that everything was her fault, that he wouldn't be where he was now if it hadn't been for her.

"I came to offer my apologies," she said, her voice calm, not giving him any idea of what she was thinking. He was used to women who wept and threw themselves on him in anguish, saying things like "Help me. Help me." But this little fish was as cold as ice.

"And to offer my thanks," she said. "If you hadn't interfered I don't know what would have happened to me."

He was almost mollified by her statement and was about to mumble something nice when she said, "Of course if you hadn't barged into the bank, guns blazing, the robber would never have grabbed me. But I guess it's the thought that counts."

Cole put his head back against the pillow and rolled his eyes skyward. "It looks as though I'm going to spend some time in hell before I get there." He looked back at her. "Miss Latham, if you want to help me, why don't you show me your train ticket out of this town? I hope you are going somewhere very far away from me and I

358

hope you go soon, because I still have a good arm and two legs left, and I'm afraid that you might make something bad happen to them."

She didn't seem to realize that he was being sarcastic because she said, "Excuse me," turned her back to him, pulled up her skirt, and removed a leather wallet from where it had been secreted in a hidden pocket, then turned back and handed it to him.

At first he didn't know what she had given him, and when he peered at it in the dim light, she went to the window and sent the shade flying upward. Cole had to bite down on a comment that his eyesight was perfectly all right, in spite of the fact that she'd said nothing about his inability to read in the dark room.

"What is this?" he asked sharply.

"My train ticket."

"I can see that, but this is to Waco, Texas, and just what is this devil's list?" To his disgust his voice rose on the last few words. Stuck to the top of the ticket was a list of every desperate, dangerous, cutthroat, rob-his-own-mother criminal it had ever been his misfortune to meet. In fact he'd shot one of them.

"What have you got to do with these men? And why is this ticket to Waco? Why aren't you going home to wherever it is you live?"

"I am going to Waco because I hope to find the Waco Kid there."

Cole started to speak, then collapsed and let his head fall back against the pillow. "Would you mind telling me what you want with a dog-eating killer like the Waco Kid?" But before she could answer, he turned to her, eyes blazing. "You don't mean to offer to marry *him,* do you?" he sputtered.

"Of course," she said calmly.

"Somebody ought to lock you up, you know that? Somebody ought to protect you from yourself. Do you know anything about the men on this list?"

"Since I received my sister's letter telling of her impending visit, I've had time to research only you, Mr. Hunter. In spite of the fear you seem to engender in some people, those you helped had only good words to say about you. I assumed there were others like you."

"You mean that you think that all gunslingers have a heart of gold?" He hadn't meant to say it quite like that, implying that *he* had a heart of gold, but he would be damned if he'd take his words back once they were out.

"I can't very well think that a man who makes his living with a gun has any heart at all. But that is between you and the Creator. You will have to answer to Him, not to me."

"Lady," Cole said through clenched teeth, "you can insult a man until he doesn't know which end of him is up. It's a good thing you weren't born a man or you wouldn't have lived past twenty. Now tell me what you're planning to do with this list of names."

"I hardly think that is any of your business, Mr. Hunter. All I owe you is an apology and . . . and

360

this." She held out a little leather bag, and by the weight and clink of it, he knew it was full of gold coins. When he did not extend his hand to take the bag, she set it on the table beside the bed. "What has happened to you is my fault, and I like to pay my debts. I doubt that a man like you has saved anything for a rainy day, so the money will enable you to live until you are again able to shoot people. I cannot bear to think of you living on the street or in the forest because of me."

Once again she had rendered Cole speechless. It was true that he'd never saved a penny. Why should he when in his line of work he never knew whether he was going to be alive from one day to the next? Never mind that in the last year he had begun to get sick of sleeping on the ground and to yearn for a bed of his own. In fact, he'd recently started to want to own things, like a chair that fit his body. And maybe he'd like to have a place to keep more than the two shirts that were all he'd ever had in his life.

It didn't matter that what she was saying was the truth, he didn't want to hear it. "I can assure you, miss, that I can take care of myself." He knew that the best defense was to attack, so he held up her list of outlaws. If she'd worked at it, she couldn't have prepared a more horrible roster.

He pointed to the first name on the list. There was nastiness in his tone when he spoke. "This man shoots people in the back of the head. You let him in the house and he'll steal everything you own and leave you dead. This next one is in prison;

this third one is dead." He moved his finger down the list. "This one: dead. Dead. Prison. Hanged. I killed this one yesterday in the bank." He raised his eyebrows in an I-told-you-so look. "This one is meaner 'n a snake. This one was shot six months ago for cheating at cards. No. No. *Where* did you get this list? Did you copy it from wanted posters?"

"For most of them I just asked some of the ladies in town who were the most exciting men they had ever met."

"Ladies?" he asked. "Do they by chance live in the house next door to the Golden Garter Saloon?"

"Yes, they do," she said seriously.

"Someone should protect you from yourself. Why don't you go home and let your sister choose a husband for you? Unless she drags a man off the gallows, she can't do worse than these men. You can't let any of these men into your rich house."

Slowly, with no expression on her face, she took the ticket and the list from him. "You are, of course, right. Besides, my sister would never believe that a man would marry me for any reason except money, so my search is rather useless anyway." She looked down at her hands, tugging at her gloves that helped cover every inch of her skin below the neck. On her head was perched the most awful little hat; it made him wonder if she'd found it in a missionary barrel.

"Oh, hell," he muttered under his breath. This bland little woman with a tongue that could slice

362

steel was getting under his skin. "You're not so bad," he heard himself saying. "I'll bet that if you wore some bright colors and a hat with a blue feather in it you'd be pretty. Any man would be glad to have you. Why, I've seen women so ugly the birds fly away in horror, but they were married and had those six kids hanging on to their skirts."

She gave him a little half smile. "How very kind you are, Mr. Hunter, but I can't even buy a husband." Before he could say anything, her head came up. "Thank you so much for everything, sir. I appreciate it. I understand even better now why people love my sister so much. It is quite . . . thrilling to be on the receiving side of heroism. It makes a person feel valuable to have someone risk his life to save you." She had never sat down during this time, and, as before, she had left the door open the prescribed six inches. Now she walked to the door; then, her hand on the knob, she turned back toward him. As he watched, a look of surprise came over her face, and when it did, in that instant when she wasn't guarded, didn't have her features under iron control, she was almost pretty. Quickly, and giving in to an impulse that he was sure she rarely felt, much less obeyed, she walked back to the bed, bent forward and kissed his cheek. Then she was gone, as silently as she had come.

Chapter Three

Damn it to hell and back!" Cole swore under his breath, or at least he thought he swore quietly. In fact, his cussing was so loud and so lusty that his landlady opened the door and came into his room. She was a widow who had inherited the house on the death of her husband, and even though she had had many offers, she wanted nothing to do with another husband. She'd told Cole that she was happy having men to talk to but not having them kicking her in bed at night.

"What is wrong now?" she asked in that tone of a woman who had been married for a long time and had decided that there was little difference between children and men.

"Nothing I need any help with," he spat out, his back to her. He was completely embarrassed that he couldn't seem to button his shirt, much less his trousers, with his right arm in a cast and a sling. And on top of the awkwardness of using his left hand, it hurt like a son of a gun.

Immediately his landlady understood what his problem was, came around him, and began to fasten his clothing as though he were her son. Of course she had to stand on tiptoe to reach the top buttons, mainly because in an effort to keep his pride intact, Cole had lifted his chin and straightened his back as stiff as the barrel of a rifle.

Mrs. Harrison smiled indulgently up at him and thanked the Lord she had not remarried. "You remember that little girl who came to see you several days back? The one you rescued at the bank?"

"I'd hardly call her a girl."

"At my age I can call anyone a girl."

He doubted if Mrs. Harrison was forty-five, but she liked to pretend she was older: it gave her an excuse to offer to the many men who asked her — and her money — to marry them.

She gave him a motherly push to get him seated in a chair and then began to put his socks and boots on. Cole hated what she was doing, and he knew he could do it himself, but at the same time he rather liked this attention. Maybe he *was* getting old. He knew where this thought had come from, so when he spoke, his voice was sharp. "What about her?"

"Her sister came to town."

"Rowena?" he asked, startled and showing far too much curiosity.

"I guess that's her name. You know the whole family?"

"I don't know anything about them. And I don't care, either. They aren't my concern."

To his great annoyance, his gossipy landlady didn't say another word. Finally, Cole had to say something. "I hear she's a looker."

Mrs. Harrison tried to keep her mouth from twitching into a smile, letting Cole know that she knew he wanted to know everything. She didn't quite succeed, but they both pretended she was talking because she wanted to and he was listening to be polite.

"She is the most beautiful woman in the world. She has to be. You should see her. She got off the train today — from her own car, mind you! — and every man within a hundred feet stopped dead in his tracks. She is a stunner. And as nice as can be. When four men fought over who was going to carry her bags, you'd have thought that no man had ever offered to carry anything for her before, she was that gracious. Acted surprised, even. Of course a woman that beautiful didn't start out as an ugly duckling. It took her years to get that pretty, so you know she's had boys fighting to carry things for her all her life."

Cole wasn't sure why, but this overlong tribute to Rowena's beauty annoyed him. "Yes, yes, I'm sure she's beautiful, but how is Miss Latham? She wasn't hurt in the fracas, was she?"

"You mean did all those cowboys carryin' the bags trample her? They almost did, but the sheriff —"

"What was *he* doing there?"

"He came runnin' out to welcome this beautiful woman. You know, this is an awful thought, but if she had an inclination toward dishonesty, she could make a fortune. She could come into one end of a town, everybody'd rush to see her, and her partners could rob the other end of town blind and get away scot-free."

"Would you spare me your criminal plans? I wasn't asking about a herd of stupid cowboys who think any woman who's clean is beautiful, I was asking about Miss Latham and the bank robbery. You do remember that, don't you?"

"I don't know what you're getting so snippy about," she said, straightening up after pulling his second boot on. She looked at him out of the corner of her eye. "Unless you're sweet on that little Miss Latham."

"I'm not sweet on any woman. I was interested, that's all." But he knew that wasn't all. Damn it, he couldn't help it; he felt sorry for the little thing. What would it be like to be near a beauty like her sister? And what was that sister doing here in Abilene? Couldn't she leave her plain-faced little sister alone instead of following her around the country and showing everyone the great difference between the two of them?

"Are you all right?" his landlady asked.

"Of course I'm all right," he snapped, then fumbled with his watch as he tried to put it in his pocket and nearly dropped it. He fought a wave of pain when he caught it with the fingers of his injured right hand.

"You should get back into bed."

"And you should mind your own business."

She stiffened her back. She was used to men wanting to hear all the gossip in town, then pretending they had no interest in it, but Cole's bad temper was more than she cared to deal with. "Suit yourself," she said, her nose in the air.

Chapter Four

Even as Cole raised his hand to knock on the door of the room the hotel euphemistically called the Presidential Suite, he felt as though he should run away. This was none of his business; he had nothing to do with the sharp-tongued Miss Latham and her pushy sister. It had been four hours since his landlady had told him of the arrival of the beautiful older sister of the plain Miss Latham, and during that time Cole had heard of little else from the townspeople. He'd heard how the elder sister was so sweet and kind, so unaware of her incredible beauty.

Yeah, Cole thought, like a buck is unaware of a hunter. Like one gunfighter is unaware of another gunfighter entering town.

When one had beauty, one was aware of it. As well he knew. Miss Latham had said he'd been called the handsomest man in Texas, a title which, according to her, he no longer deserved. At the time some newspaper writer, a girl not much better looking than Miss Latham, had called him that, he'd hated the title. But he hadn't been surprised by it. No one blessed with beauty is unaware of it. All your life heads turn, people do double takes on you. When Cole was a boy, girls and women

368

had wanted to touch his black curly hair, and after he grew up, women had wanted to touch his body. Never in his life had he had trouble getting any woman he wanted.

Until this week, that is. First Miss Latham tells him he's . . . What was it she said? Hard-jawed? Squint-eyed?

Anyway, he told himself, that didn't matter. What mattered was that she had offered him cash for a job — an incredibly stupid job, but it was work. And now, with a busted arm and canceled contracts, he needed work. He had no intention of pretending to be married to her, but it did look as though she needed protection from a sister so greedy that she wasn't satisfied until she had the attention of every man, woman, and child in Abilene.

In the two days Mrs. Rowena Whatever-her-name-was had been in town, she seemed to have had some contact with everyone. Cole couldn't go into a store, a saloon, or even the cathouse without hearing about her. Nina had said she heard that Cole knew the younger sister. "You know," she'd said, "that washed-out little lady with the brown hair. Can you imagine the same woman giving birth to two daughters that different? No wonder she stopped after the second one." And Nina had wanted to know if Cole could find out how Rowena made her hair so glossy and soft-looking. "If that woman wanted to take up the profession, she could make millions," Nina said. "You ought to suggest it to her."

After a few hours of this Cole had had enough of the talented Mrs. Rowena. He seemed to be the only person in town who hadn't fallen for her. Maybe that was because he was the only person who understood her. Beauty was an odd thing. An ugly person and a beautiful one could perform the same bad deed, yet the ugly one would be judged much more harshly than the pretty one. He'd seen that happen time and again. He'd watched members of the same gang, caught in the same holdup, get sentences based on their looks. When he'd heard that ol' No-nose Wilson had finally been caught, he knew he had no chance of leniency. Wilson was hanged twenty-four hours after he was caught. But the good-looking Billy Whittier had three times conned pretty girls into helping him escape the wheels of justice.

So now this Rowena was charming, and conning, the entire town. And meanwhile she was plowing her meek little sister under. Well, perhaps "meek" wasn't the correct word to describe Miss Latham, but compared to the attention-hungry Rowena she was spineless.

Of course none of this explained why he was here at the door of Miss Latham's hotel room now. He wasn't really thinking of taking her job offer. What kind of job was it for a man to pretend anything? He had always prided himself on his honesty. So how could he even think of taking on a job that required nothing but lies? No guns, no diplomacy, just one lie on top of the other.

As he raised his hand to knock, he had a vision

370

of what he'd see: little Miss Latham waiting hand and foot on her gorgeous, lazy, spoiled sister.

He was not prepared for the dream that opened the door. He had expected sophistication, a woman swathed in silk and lace, a face painted into perfection. Instead, his first sight of Rowena caught him off guard. Her face — her beautiful, exquisite face — was shiny clean, and all ten or so bushels of her auburn hair were pulled back into a fat braid that was draped over one shoulder. Huge eyes the color of a pond in the moonlight — not green, not gray — looked up at him with disarming innocence.

"Hello," she said in a soft voice that betrayed nothing except graciousness and gentle curiosity. A second later her face somehow became more radiant. "You are Mr. Hunter, the man who saved Dorie's life. Oh, you must come in. This is an honor. Please sit here. Dorie, do look who is here."

As yet, Cole hadn't said a word. He was ushered into the room and given the most comfortable chair. A table with an ashtray appeared next to him, then a glass of whiskey and a cigar, everything seeming to come from nowhere. Within minutes he felt as though this were his home and he had lived here in comfort always.

"How is your arm?" Rowena asked, leaning over him in solicitude. "The doctor says it will be a long while before you have full use of that arm again. It still amazes me that a man who had as much to lose as you did would risk his life to save someone he hardly knew. Never will I be able to thank you enough."

Cole found himself smiling into those startling eyes of hers and nearly drowning in them. When he spoke he sounded like a green boy. "It was nothing, really. Any man would have done it." He sipped the whiskey, knowing it was the best he'd ever tasted. Had she brought it from England with her? And the cigar was mild and flavorful. He had never been more comfortable in his life.

"Any man?" Rowena said, smiling. "You are as modest as you are talented and brave. Isn't he wonderful, Dorie?"

Rowena stepped back to allow Cole to see her sister, and he realized he had been so blinded by Rowena's beauty and gracious hospitality, not to mention her flattery, that he had not even seen Miss Latham. If he'd thought her drab before, now, next to her sister's radiance, she was difficult to see. But then, a peacock in full show would have been drab next to Rowena.

Miss Latham was half reclining on a couch, a bandaged foot extended in front of her, and the look on her face made Cole come to his senses. Miss Latham was smirking. She had an I-told-you-so expression on her face that brought him up short, made him look back at the way he had been swept off his feet by the lovely Rowena.

Cole opened his mouth to defend himself. Not that he had been accused, but the silent communication that had passed between him and Miss Latham was loud and clear.

Immediately Cole put the whiskey and the cigar

down and sat up straight in his chair. "I came to see how Miss Latham was after her fright at the bank," he said. "I hope she is well." Even as he spoke, he was annoyed with himself for talking to Rowena. What was wrong with him? He'd seen beautiful women before, but then, there was something different about this woman. She seemed unaware of the effect she had on people. She looked as fresh as morning sunlight, as innocent as dew on grass, as sweet as —

"Rowena, I do believe you have another man in love with you," he heard Miss Latham say.

"How ridiculous you are, Dorie," Rowena said. "Mr. Hunter came to see you. Look, he can hardly take his eyes off you."

Some sense of reality was coming back to Cole, and as he looked from one woman to another, he saw that what Miss Latham had said was true: Rowena did love her sister very much. And it occurred to him that Rowena had no idea that her beloved sister was anything less than divinely beautiful. In fact, maybe Rowena saw everyone that way.

For just a second he exchanged a look with Miss Latham that asked that question, and he was rewarded with one of her rare tiny smiles. It was ridiculous, of course, but that little smile made him feel good. It made him feel part of something that no one else was. Rowena might be the one with the looks, but her colorless little sister was the one with the brains.

"Mrs. . . . . I'm sorry, I don't know your name."

"It's Westlake, but please call me Rowena. I've heard so much about you that I feel I know you."

"Oh?" he asked archly. "Miss Latham has told you about me?" It made him feel good to have caught the younger sister in something. She was too self-assured for his taste, so it was nice to find out that she had been affected by him as much as he had by her.

"Why no," Rowena said in innocence. "Dorie hasn't said a word about you, or about what happened at the bank. I've heard everything from all the people in town."

At that Miss Latham gave him a little raised-eyebrow look that told him she knew what he was thinking.

Damnation, but that woman annoyed him! "Rowena, why are you here?" he asked, sounding like a controlling father. He had not meant to ask that. He had no connection with Miss Latham, nor any interest in her. He had toyed with the idea of taking her job offer, but he could now see that it wouldn't work, mainly because little Miss Latham made him think of nothing but murdering her.

Rowena laughed, and it was a very sweet sound — as he would have guessed it would be. "I've come to help my sister make up her mind," she said with disarming honesty. She had the ability to make a man feel that she trusted him and him alone. "Dorie can never make up her mind." She smiled at him in such a way that he could feel his socks melting. "You see, Mr. Hunter —"

"Cole," he said.

"How kind of you," she said, as though he had bestowed a great gift upon her. She continued. "There's a wonderful man in Latham — that's where we grew up and where Dorie still lives — who has been in love with my little sister for years, and I'm going to do my best to persuade her to see the light and marry him."

Cole glanced at Miss Latham, but she had her head down and was studying something on her skirt. Suddenly Cole realized that there was a bond between him and Miss Latham. Maybe it was slight, but he was pretty sure that what she had told him — about her life, about her sister, about how she felt about this beautiful woman who wanted to manage her life — was something she had never told another human being. Miss Latham had said that Cole was a hero. He knew he was no such thing, but right now he did feel . . . well, that maybe he could act as her guardian. Maybe he could stop Rowena's meddling, no matter that she had the best intentions in the world.

"If you don't mind my asking," Cole said, "what's this man you want her to marry like?"

"Alfred?" Rowena asked, her eyes sparkling. "He's a lovely man, very sweet. He's about five feet four. I know that's short, but not for Dorie; she's so little and petite herself, not a great cow like me who has to have a man over six feet. Dorie is so lucky that she can have any man. Alfred is about forty-three and —"

"Fifty-one," Miss Latham said, her voice flat, without emotion.

"Oh? Well, a few years won't matter. It's what's inside that counts, and Alfred is a jewel. And, also, he's already broken in, so to speak. He's been married and widowed twice, the poor dear, and has three children. Dorie just loves children, and there's certainly room for them in that big house Father left her. But more important than any of this is that Alfred is mad for her, follows her everywhere. They are so cute together."

"Like salt and pepper shakers," Miss Latham said with disgust.

"Dorie, really! Just because Alfred doesn't have a great deal of hair and has a few birth marks on his scalp does not make him resemble a pepper shaker."

Cole managed to hide his smile, but when he looked up at Miss Latham, he no longer felt like smiling. What to him was a joke was not a laughing matter to her. There was a reason he had never settled down, a reason he was unmarried at the age of thirty-eight. His own parents had hated each other. His mother had been in love with some dirt farmer, but her father had forced her to marry the man of his choice, and never had two people hated each other more than his parents did. He'd left home when he was twelve years old and never been back since. If his parents were still alive, he could bet they were still fighting with each other.

Now, looking at the luscious Rowena, he had no doubt that what Miss Latham had said was true, that she could charm any man into marrying a plain sister. If Rowena had this effect on Cole, he could imagine what effect she'd have on a short, bald man who had probably never had even a decent-looking woman look at him before. And no doubt this Rowena could make quiet little Miss Latham believe that she wanted to marry a man who reminded her of a pepper shaker.

He picked up his whiskey glass, took a sip, and when he looked back at the two sisters, it seemed to him that Rowena wasn't quite as beautiful as he'd thought at first. He was beginning to see her as a bit of a bully. And Miss Latham wasn't quite as plain as he'd thought. She was smart and could be funny when she wanted to be. She deserved better than a short, bald man who'd dump three kids on her then go off and spend her money.

Even as he opened his mouth, Cole couldn't believe he was going to say what he did. All he knew was that he couldn't let Miss Latham marry a man she didn't want to marry. A thousand images of his parents screaming at each other ran through his mind. No one deserved a life like that — especially the children. "Will you tell her, dear, or shall I?"

Miss Latham looked up at him, blinking in puzzlement, having no idea what he was talking about.

"The world is going to know soon enough. You can't keep it a secret forever," he said to her, his voice full of coaxing softness, the voice of a lover. He looked back up at Rowena and gave her his own sweet smile, the one that had made more than a few women's hearts flutter. "Your sister and I are engaged to be married."

Dorie sat up straighter on the sofa. "No, please, you don't have to do this."

Rowena looked from one to the other, at Cole's I-dare-you expression and at Dorie's face, now red with embarrassment. Rowena's lovely laugh filled the room. "Dorie darling, I'd been told he was a hero, but I had no idea how much of one. He is as chivalrous as a knight of old. He rescued you, and now he feels responsible for you."

She turned back to Cole. "But, really, Mr. Hunter, your concern for my sister need go no further. Just because you saved her life doesn't mean you have to be responsible for her forever. Now Dorie is my responsibility, just as she was our father's."

Maybe there *was* some chivalry in him because the hair on the back of his neck stood up at Rowena's words. She made Miss Latham sound like a broken-down old pet, beloved but useless. The truth was that Miss Latham was far from useless. She was as smart as a college girl. There wasn't a woman in a thousand who could have understood what he meant during that bank holdup when he used the word "roll." She had not only understood but had kept her head and figured out a way to distract the man, then moved as quickly as a darter fish. Now here was her sister speaking as though Miss Latham were something useless that needed to be gotten rid of as fast as possible.

"Please don't do —" Dorie began, but stopped when Cole came to his feet and in an instant was across the room to stand beside her.

He put his uninjured hand on her shoulder. "The truth is, Mrs. Westlake, your sister and I are in love, and we plan to get married. She's marrying *me* and no one else."

Dorie looked up at him with pleading eyes. "No, you can't do this. I was wrong to ask you." She turned to her sister. "Rowena, he's lying. Has any man ever fallen madly in love with me?"

She turned back to look up at Cole. "You don't have to do this. I shouldn't have said what I did. It was something I should have known couldn't have worked. Rowena, let me tell you what I did. I —"

Cole didn't know how to shut her up, but he *had* to make her stop talking. He couldn't bear to see her humiliate herself in front of her beautiful sister, whose expression said that she didn't believe for one minute that Cole had fallen for her plain little sister. Something about that look bothered Cole.

"I asked Mr. Hunter to —" Dorie began, her voice heavy, like a child admitting a lie, knowing that punishment was going to follow.

Without thought of what he was doing, Cole slipped his good arm under Miss Latham's shoulders and pulled her up to him. She was a tiny thing, small and fragile, weighing nothing. His objective was to stop her words, and short of putting his hand over her mouth, he didn't know how else to do that, so he kissed her. It wasn't a kiss of passion, not even a kiss he wanted; it was a

379

kiss of expediency: hard, closed-mouthed, without affection.

Within seconds he broke from the kiss and turned to Rowena in defiance. "There, now, does that look like —"

Suddenly his face filled with wonder, and he broke off and turned to look down at the woman pressed to his side. She was still pulled against him, her feet off the floor, her body as limp as a doll's, and she was looking up at him, her huge eyes filled with surprise.

For a moment time didn't exist for Cole. He had no idea what had happened, but the kiss he had shared with this woman — if he could call that hard thing a kiss — was different from any other kiss he'd experienced. He had kissed hundreds of women in his life. In fact, he rather liked kissing and had never turned down an opportunity when offered to him, whether it was in a saloon or behind the church. But this kiss had been different.

As though Rowena weren't there, as though he and this woman he held were the only two people in the world, he turned back to her and kissed her for real.

He pulled her close to him and instantly found that she wasn't as scrawny as he'd thought, but nicely rounded, and he liked her small size. She was so tiny he thought he could wrap himself around her; she could dissolve inside him.

He kissed her gently at first, just tasting of her, of her freshness, of the purity of her. There was no doubt in his mind that he was the first man who had ever touched her, ever held her, ever put his lips on hers. Some part of his brain remembered that when he first met her she had been hostile and prickly, but he couldn't reconcile that woman with the soft one in his arms. She opened up to him in a way that no woman ever had before. And in her kiss was something he couldn't identify, something that he had never tasted before. If he didn't know better, he'd think it was love. But that wasn't possible. There was nothing between them.

There was pain in his arm in its sling, but he didn't feel it when he wrapped both arms around her, then used his good left hand to turn her head so he could taste her lips more deeply. He sucked on her bottom lip, gently drawing it into his own mouth, and he was sure he'd never tasted anything sweeter.

It was some minutes before he heard Rowena's voice. Judging by her tone, she had been trying to get his attention for some time.

Reluctantly, with difficulty, he turned to look at Rowena, seeing her in a haze, as though she were far away. He still held Dorie firmly in his arms, not willing to release her soft, pliant body. Besides, she was so limp she would have fallen if he'd released her.

"My goodness gracious," Rowena said, her voice full of astonishment. "I thought I was going to have to throw a bucket of cold water on you two." She was trying to make a joke, but it fell flat because she was facing two very confused people.

"Yes, well, I . . ." Cole began, stammering like a schoolboy. The body in his arms began to have some substance, and he knew he should release her, but he didn't want to. It was some minutes before he realized that Miss Latham had her hands on his shoulders and was pushing against him rather hard.

"Mr. Hunter," she was saying, "please release me."

When Cole's brain began to function again, all he could feel was embarrassment. "Yes, of course," he said, then dropped Miss Latham as though she were forbidden, causing her to fall back against the sofa with a thud. But he didn't reach down to help her. In fact he would have done most anything to keep from touching her again.

"I see that you two are in love," Rowena said. "I had no idea that was the case. Dorie, how could you keep such a thing from me? Why didn't you tell me? You let me believe that Mr. Hunter had no reason to save you from the robbers except that he was a man of great conscience, a man who cared about others, a man who —"

"A fool," Cole said, beginning to recover himself. Running his hand over his eyes, he surreptitiously looked at Miss Latham and saw that she was as stunned as he was. If nothing like this had happened to a man of his experience, he was sure nothing like this had happened to her.

"You know what I think you two should do?" Rowena said in the voice of one who had never faced an obstacle in her life. "I think you should get married right now. This minute."

Dorie was beginning to recover herself. "Rowena, that's ridiculous. Mr. Hunter —"

"Yes," Cole heard himself saying. "That would be fine."

Rowena took this statement in stride, not seeing the least problem with anything. "We shall go to the church this minute and —"

"No!" Dorie half shouted, and they both turned to look at her as she stood up, her fists at her sides.

"Dorie, your ankle!"

"Rowena, there is nothing wrong with my ankle except a bruise. One does not have to remain in bed for a bruise." She turned to Cole. "I apologize, Mr. Hunter, for my sister. She loves to manage other people's lives, and with her children and husband not here, she has only me and now you." She straightened her back and looked at him. "I know that you and I talked about . . . about certain things, but that was days ago. Now things are different."

"What is different?" he asked dryly.

Of course there was nothing different. In fact, everything was too real, and much too much the same. Rowena had come to Texas to get her boring little sister married, and she meant to do what needed to be done. Whether she married Dorie to a middle-aged bald man or to a gunslinger didn't seem to make much difference to her.

"Rowena," Dorie said softly, "could you leave

us for a while? Mr. Hunter and I need to talk."

Rowena laughed in what Cole thought was a vulgar way. "I'm not sure I should leave you two lovebirds alone. At least not until after the wedding."

Cole was much too old to put up with a woman acting as though he were still in knee britches and needed a chaperon. He gave her the look that had made a few men decide not to draw on him.

"I . . . ah, I think I'll wait just outside," Rowena said, and skedaddled out the door.

Dorie spoke the minute her sister was out of the room. "Mr. Hunter, when you and I spoke several days ago, I made a fool of myself. When I was alone in Latham and I received a letter from my sister saying she was going to travel to America and then all the way to Texas to 'sort me out,' as she said, I'm afraid I panicked. When Rowena gets something in her head, she sees nothing else. She said she was sure that after Father died I'd stay in that house with my books and never get out to meet anyone, much less marry someone. Rowena also thinks that whatever makes her happy is what makes everyone happy. She loves being married, so she thinks I would, too."

"Marriage is the only acceptable way to get those six kids you want."

"Yes, well, at my age — nearly thirty — I'm a little old to start a family."

"So your sister was right and you do plan to bury yourself." As he was talking, he continued to look at her. It was hard to reconcile what he saw with what he had felt. She looked wooden, but she hadn't felt that way. Maybe he was getting senile. Maybe he should visit Nina more often. But right now, Nina's knowledge, her boredom, the way she talked at the wrong time — all that seemed dirty when compared to the freshness of Miss Latham.

"It isn't your business or my sister's what I do with my life!" Dorie snapped.

Cole knew she was right. He also knew he should walk out the door and never look back. But when had he ever done what he *should* do? He shouldn't have left home at twelve years old. He shouldn't have strapped on his first gun. If he hadn't tried to save this scrawny woman from the bank robbers he wouldn't be here now, wouldn't have kissed her, wouldn't have felt this way.

Also, there was something about this woman that intrigued him. Maybe he'd spent too much of his life around women of the wrong sort. Maybe all "good" women were like her, if you got to know them, but he doubted it.

Maybe his problem was that she offered him a challenge, and a challenge was something he'd never been able to turn down. All anyone had to say to him was "Cole, you'll never be able to do that," and the hair on the back of his neck would stand up, and he would know that he *had* to do whatever his challenger had said he couldn't ac-complish.

Miss Latham seemed to be reading his mind.

She seemed to understand that he was beginning to think this was something he wanted to do. She took a deep breath, and when she released it, she gave him a look of great softness, a look that made Cole realize she was prettier than he'd first thought. "This is very kind of you, but now I must ask you to be reasonable. In light of what just happened, you must see that you and I cannot even pretend to be engaged. It is not possible."

Sometimes this woman made him feel downright dumb. He had no idea what she was talking about. All he knew was that he very much wanted to kiss her again. Had what happened between them been a fluke? Something that happened only once? "What is not possible? Why?"

"Our attraction to each other has changed everything. I had no idea there would be any magnetism between us. Men who are almost criminals are not men I find attractive. I can assure you that what I . . . we . . . felt was as much of a shock to me as it was to you. Considering this attraction, we could not possibly consider spending any time together for any reason. The probable results are too dreadful to contemplate."

Cole looked with longing toward the glass of whiskey on the table, but it was empty. At the moment he desperately needed a drink. What in the world was the woman talking about? "What results?"

She looked at him with great patience. "Mr. Hunter, I have admitted that all of this was a mistake. My mistake. I have told you that I panicked at the news of my sister's impending visit, and I tried to implement what I see now was a very naive scheme. I am sorry I ever started this, and I would like to end it."

"What results?" he repeated, still trying to figure out what she was talking about. He usually understood women; for that matter he usually understood the English language.

She gave a sigh as though she had to explain the simplest thing in the world. "When we . . . ah, kissed, there was a great deal of attraction between us. I had not thought there would be. I felt no such attraction between us the day I went to see you at your boardinghouse. It is all right to have a fake marriage with a man to whom one feels no attraction, but it is impossible with a man one wants to . . . to . . . ."

When she saw that there was still no hint of understanding on his handsome face, she continued. "Children, Mr. Hunter," she snapped. "Children." She grimaced. "Perhaps a man like you doesn't understand that . . . that marital rights, so to speak, are not to be exercised for pleasure. What a man and woman do with each other creates children. Based on the feelings we had during our one and only kiss, I think that if we spent any prolonged time together, we would . . . we would, well, end up in bed together, and I'm afraid of creating a child with you. I cannot imagine a worse father than you — that is, if you stayed around, which I doubt. Either way, I don't want to raise a child alone, nor do I want my child to have a father who knows little more than how to cock a gun."

For a moment all Cole could do was blink at her. "Is there any whiskey here?" he asked hoarsely, then watched as she handed him the bottle. Unlike her sister, she didn't graciously pour it into a glass. She just handed him the bottle with a schoolteacher look on her face that said, See what I mean?

It wasn't easy, but Cole put the bottle down, then he followed it, sitting heavily on the chair and looking up at her. There was certainly nothing coy about her. She wasn't telling him that she hated him and didn't want to go to bed with him. She was telling him that she'd like nothing more than to jump into bed with him, but if they did that, they might make a child, and he would be a damned poor father. To his knowledge, no one had ever even considered his possibilities as a father. His worth as a fast gun had been considered, yes, and as a peacemaker, and at times as a lover, true, but not as the father to some kid who didn't exist.

Maybe he *was* getting old. This wasn't the way women *used* to act. He remembered women who couldn't think past the first buttons he loosened on their blouses. In the past if he'd kissed a woman and a current of lightning had run through them like the one that had run through him with this woman, neither of them would have thought past the next two hours. Uncontrollable. Without thought. Passion. Old-fashioned passion.

388

But not with plain little Miss Latham. With her there was no lack of control. She stepped back from passion and said she wanted it, but there were consequences she didn't want. She was, of course, quite sensible. The only other sensible women he had ever met had had no hunger, no fire in their veins. But she did. He had just felt it. Yet she was able to control it.

"Mr. Hunter, are you all right?"

No, he wanted to say. He wasn't all right. He had been all right before he met this woman, but now he was beginning to doubt everything in his life. He had to reassure himself that his life wasn't a waste. He was rootless. He had no home. He'd never had a home. Not that he'd ever wanted one, but if he had wanted one, he would have stayed in one place. And if he ever made a kid with a woman, he didn't think he'd be a worse father than the next man. In fact, he liked to think he had a few things to teach a child. And *not* just things about a gun. He'd learned a bit in his life, and maybe he'd like to pass those things on.

Suddenly it became important to him to make this woman realize that he was more than just a gunslinger. And a hero. If someone else had called him a hero, he would have been flattered, but Miss Latham had made "hero" sound like a mindless person who had no thought of the future consequences of his actions.

"How am I to support myself until my arm heals?"

She looked startled. "I have no idea. Would you

like some money? I mean, it is my fault that you
. . . Well, actually, it isn't entirely my fault, but
I do feel somewhat responsible for your injury.
I can give you a bank draft."

"I don't want charity. I want a job."

She gave the tiniest smile — about all she seemed
capable of, he thought. "The very next time I want
someone murdered I will be sure to hire you."

He had to admit that the woman got under his
skin in a way that no one else ever had. "I do
not murder people," he snapped.

"Certainly not with your arm as it is now." Her
mouth tightened into a prim little line. "Mr.
Hunter, I talked to you about your future days
ago, before this happened, and at that time your
future did not concern you. I even tried to warn
you that something like this might happen."

Why did he feel as though he were being talked
to by his mother? She used to say, "I *told* you
this was going to happen. But, no, you wouldn't
listen to me. You had to have your own way. You
never listen to anyone."

Cole ran his hand over his eyes. If he murdered
anyone, it would be this woman. Besides wanting
to kill her, he wanted to prove to her that he was
worth something. "Miss Latham, you offered me
a job, and I accept that offer."

It was her turn to sit down. "No," she whispered, "this is a mistake."

He sensed that he was regaining some power.
"Miss Latham, tell me, what do you do with your
time?"

"I beg your pardon."

"Your time. What do you do with your time when you are at home in Latham? I can't see you as a sewing circle lady. I can't see you putting on garden parties and teas. What do you do in that town your father left you?"

It was her turn to look surprised. "I can see that you, too, have been doing some research."

Heaven help him but at a compliment from this scrawny little thing, he felt warmth flow through him. He had to get himself back under control as he waited for her answer.

"I am a landlord," she said, then paused, and he could see emotions play across her face. So she wasn't a perfect poker player after all. "My father left the town of Latham to me because Rowena had her rich husband." She paused. "My father did not think there was any possibility that I would find a husband, rich or not, so he left me a means of support. Anyway, Latham is a small town that wouldn't exist except for the railroad, but the few shops and houses there all belong to me."

"You are a rent collector?" He knew it was petty of him, but he wanted to make what she did sound trivial, just as she had made what he did sound worthless.

"And a roof fixer and a listener-to-reasons-why-the-rent-is-late, and just about everything else in that town. If I may give you some advice, Mr. Hunter, if anyone ever offers to give you a town, don't take it."

He laughed. "I'll remember that. No one's ever

given me that advice before." For a moment he looked at her, sitting there with her hands folded in her lap. "It seems to me that you need a man for more reasons than just to get your sister off your back."

"Of course," she said, giving him that look that said he wasn't very smart. "I know that. I very much want a husband. I wish I had a man to take over the management of Latham. My father was a man who allowed no laxity in people. He was . . ." She seemed to search for the right word.

"A tyrant?"

"Exactly," she said, looking up at him, eyes sparkling rather prettily. "He was a dreadful tyrant. I loved him, but I was also terrified of him, as was everyone else. Except, of course, Rowena, but that's another story. My father said that neither of his daughters had any backbone, that we were too soft, but at least I wouldn't get married and turn the whole town over to some scoundrel who wanted only my money, as Rowena might do."

"Why not?" Cole asked, knowing it was a ridiculous question.

"My father said I was much too sensible to marry a scoundrel. He said I'd marry a sane and sensible man."

"So why not marry your pepper shaker?" he couldn't resist asking.

"Alfred would have no idea how to be firm with the tenants. I've tried to tell Rowena that Alfred works hard now only because he has to. If he had my money, he wouldn't lift a finger. Under his industrious exterior, he is a very lazy man. I want to find a man who works, one who can take over my father's tenants while I stay at home."

"You certainly have your life planned in detail."

"Of course. If one doesn't plan, one spends one's life drifting. That's all right in youth, but we are not always young."

Cole shifted uncomfortably on his seat. "If you don't mind, I'd like to ask you a personal question." He didn't wait for her permission. "Have you ever done anything that wasn't sensible?"

She didn't hesitate. "I asked a gunslinger to marry me."

Cole winced. For a moment he had nothing to say, so he reached inside his pocket and removed a thin cigar, but then he found it impossible to hold it and light it at the same time. Maybe it was his vanity, but he was used to women paying attention to him. Had he been in the room with any other female on earth, she would have fluttered about him and helped him light his cigar. But Miss Latham just sat there watching him, not offering anything.

Annoyed, he tossed the unlit cigar onto the table by the chair. "Miss Latham, you are right. You are right about everything. I'm beginning to feel that my days as a cold-blooded killer are drawing to a close." He hesitated to give her time to contradict him, but she didn't. "Why don't you and I make a deal? I'll help you if you help me."

"What do you mean?"

"You came to me a few days ago because you wanted to make your sister believe that you already had a husband so she'd leave you in peace to do your . . . research, I believe you called it."

He waited for her nod. "You want to finish your research on finding a suitable husband, a man who can help you collect your rents, stand up to the complaints of your tenants, and be a tender father to your children. Is that about right?"

"Yes."

"What I need is a place to live for a few months while my arm heals. Also, it might be nice to learn a trade."

"I see. But owning a town is hardly a trade."

"Maybe I could learn to run a saloon. Maybe after this is all over I could buy my own place and settle down."

"This isn't going to work."

"Why not?" he asked.

"Because of . . . you know. We'll never be able to stay apart for very long."

Cole couldn't believe what he was hearing. Maybe it was because of his looks, but he'd never really had to pursue a woman before. Women always came to him. Oh, they pretended that their encounters with him were accidents, but they weren't. All he had to do was enter a town and within hours several pretty girls would be placing themselves where he could see them. Now here was this runt of a woman — a woman who admitted that no man except one short, bald, spotty-headed man wanted her and then he probably wanted her only for her money — and she was saying that he — he, Coleman Hunter! — wouldn't be able to control himself if he spent much time around her.

"Trust me, Miss Latham," he said with heavy sarcasm, "I'll manage to control myself." Even if I have to visit a bordello seven nights a week, he thought. Really, the woman was too much! Her insinuation that he couldn't control himself around her was more than he could take. If nothing else, he wanted to prove to her how wrong she was.

"Knowing Rowena, she isn't going to leave Texas until she sees us married," she continued, unaware of Cole's thoughts. "If our false engagement lasts for four years, she will stay here and wait for four years. My sister might look soft and sweet, but she is forged iron inside."

"How could your father have thought his daughters were soft?" Cole mumbled.

Cole knew that in Miss Latham's eyes, his knowledge and skills were worthless, but his life had trained him to make quick decisions. And maybe her words and being shot had made him see things differently. Money aside, what was he going to *do* until his arm healed?

She might not want to go through with her original proposition but Cole had seen the way her eyes betrayed her feeling of guilt when his arm was mentioned. Never in his life had he felt anything but softness for a woman, but this one challenged him. Quickly he decided that he was going to use what he'd come to know about her. If she thought Rowena could be a bully, she'd never seen Cole Hunter in action.

"All right, Miss Latham, while there's no reason for you to feel responsibility for what has happened to my arm, the fact is that except for what you paid me the other day, all the money I have in the world is two dollars and twenty-five cents." This was the truth, but he had been worse off than this before, yet he'd always found someone to stake him in a poker game and he'd been able to win enough to live on. But she didn't need to know that.

"The way I see it is that you owe me."

"I have offered to pay you."

"And I've told you that I don't want charity. I want to learn a trade." About as much as he wanted bubonic plague. He could not see himself as a shopkeeper, even if the shop sold beer to drunks. "With you I see the chance of learning something that will help me in my later years. For the first time I see a way out of my life of degradation and death. I see the possibility of attaining respectability. I see a way to better myself and begin to live as others do. It is the first time I have been offered such a chance, and contrary to your opinion of me, I am not a fool. Miss Latham, I want to take that opportunity."

Cole thought perhaps he'd missed his calling in life. Maybe he should have been a preacher or a snake oil salesman. Or maybe a senator. Hell, he was so full of hot air he was good enough to be president.

Before she could say a word, he continued, unwilling to stop when he was winning. "I want to ask you something. How many men have you kissed?"

She blinked at him. "J . . . just you."

"Just as I thought. You seem to think there was something special between us, something different. Let me assure you that there was not. That feeling we experienced between us is the same with every kiss between a man and a woman. If you kissed your Mr. Pepper, you'd feel the same thing." She tried to conceal her disappointment, but he could see it in her face, and her look almost made him retract his lie. But he didn't.

"The problem seems to be that you think that if we spend any time together I will not be able to control myself and will die if I do not get you into bed with me. Nothing could be further from the truth."

He kept on, not allowing her to say a word. "Miss Latham, I offer you a business proposition: Marry me for six months and let me run your town during that time. At the end of the six months if I have done a satisfactory job, I want you to give me five thousand dollars. That will be my stake in whatever I want to do in life."

"Wouldn't it be much simpler just to hire you as a manager for collecting the rent?"

Damn, but the woman had a disconcerting way of seeing straight to the truth! He gave her a little smile. "Unless I'm more than a manager, your sister will have her way." He raised an eyebrow.

397

"Perhaps I'll be invited to your wedding with Alfred. Will his children attend? By the way, how old are his children?"

"His sons are twenty-five, twenty-three, and twenty," she said.

Cole was so startled by this information that he couldn't speak for a moment. "Not exactly in their nappies, are they?" he said softly, thinking that this small woman wasn't at all what she had at first seemed. At their first meeting he had thought she needed no one, seemed able to take care of herself and half the world, but now he was beginning to get a clearer picture of what had driven her to ask a gunslinger to marry her.

Part of him knew it was the "hero" in him — he was beginning to hate that word — but he was starting to feel protective toward her. Her sister was trying to marry her off to a lazy man with three grown sons. All four of them would no doubt move into her house, take over her town, and spend her money.

He was tired of talking, tired of arguing. Quite suddenly he had a great deal of sympathy for Rowena. No wonder she was afraid to leave her defenseless sister alone in a large house at the mercy of every gold digger in the country. No wonder she was trying to force her to marry a man who could protect her. Rowena's mistake was in thinking this old man with grown sons was the one for the job.

"You're going to marry me, do you understand? You can bribe a judge to annul the marriage later if you want, but right now we need each other. You need protection from your well-meaning sister, and I need a place to hang my hat until I heal." By the time he had finished this speech, he had gripped her upper arms with his hands and lifted her half off the floor. His nose was close to hers. "And don't you say a word about kids or my killing people or anything else. I'll straighten out that town of yours. It sounds as if the tenants are taking advantage of you with their reluctance to pay rent."

"You're going to shoot them?" she asked breathlessly.

He released his grip on her so suddenly she almost fell. Did she work at making him angry or did she do it without thought? "Here," he said, his voice filled with anger as he began to unbuckle the gun belt at his waist. It hurt him more than a little. In fact, pain shot up his arm and he could feel his wound beginning to bleed as he tore it open, but he would have died before giving up his valiant gesture. He was dizzy with pain when he held the belt out to her like some primitive offering, but force of will kept him on his feet. "I am giving you my gun," he said. "I won't use it to collect the rent in your town, and if I try to touch you in any way, you have my permission to shoot me. Now do we have a deal?"

Silently, with great seriousness, she took the heavy gun belt from him. It seemed to take her a long time to make up her mind, but at last she said yes, and that was all.

Cole wasn't sure whether he should be happy or terrified, but he allowed neither emotion to show. "All right, then, shall we go? Your sister is waiting."

He bent his good arm for her to take. After only a second's hesitation she slipped her small hand onto his forearm and they started toward the door, Dorie carrying Cole's gun belt in her left hand, one end of it dragging the floor.

Chapter Five

Dorie tried not to sit on the edge of her seat, but such control was difficult. Self-control had been her main concern over the last few days, but now it was almost impossible. She was sitting in the bedroom of Rowena's private railroad car — borrowed from some hopelessly besotted admirer — across a table from the stranger who was now her husband.

When she'd concocted this plan of pretending to be married to a gunslinger, it had seemed like a brilliant idea. She would at last shock everyone. She'd shock her sister who thought she knew everything about Dorie; she'd shock all of the people of Latham, who laughed at her for being an old maid. She almost wished her father were still alive so she could shock him too. But then she doubted if anything could shock Charles Latham. If Dorie had said she was going to marry a caterpillar, he wouldn't have been shocked; he just would have said no. If the president of the United States had wanted to marry Dorie, her father would have said no. He said he'd allowed one daughter to leave and he wasn't letting the other one go while he was alive.

So Dorie had grown up inside a house with a cold totalitarian, an overlord more than a father, a man who allowed only his opinion inside the house and outside in his private town. The only thing in the world that could soften him was Rowena's beauty.

Purposely, Charles Latham had married a plain-faced woman, saying he wanted a wife who would be faithful to him. Rowena always wondered if he'd said this to their mother, but then, Rowena lived in a cloud of daydreams and romance. Of course Charles Latham had told his frightened little wife that he'd married her because she could produce children and no other man would want her. Dorie wondered if her mother had willed herself to die after the birth of her second daughter. No doubt she had heard in detail how disappointed her husband was that she had given him only another daughter and not a son to carry on his name, so she'd decided to get out.

Her mother wasn't the only one whose life was ruled by Charles Latham's iron will. After her father died, Dorie found that she didn't actually know what to do with freedom. All her life she'd had her father telling her when to go to bed, when to get up, what to eat. Her life was planned and scheduled by him.

Of course she realized that her isolated life, spent almost totally in the company of her father, had made her a little . . . different. Rowena's incredible beauty had given her a life that was more like other people's. A woman who looked like Rowena didn't have to leave the house to meet people: people came to her. In spite of her father's attempts to isolate her, Rowena involved herself with other people, until at last Jonathan Westlake came and took her away forever.

But no one had sought Dorie out. No handsome young men had risked her father's wrath to knock on the front door and ask to see her. And if they had and her father had refused them, Dorie wasn't beautiful enough to make him change his mind.

So Rowena had left Latham six years ago; she had gotten away from their father, but Dorie had stayed. Dorie had stayed in that big, dark house, working as her father's housekeeper and secretary. In the evenings she had sat in the same room with him, never speaking, never seeking companionship, just sitting there. He said that two women had left him, and by damn the third one wasn't going to, so he rarely allowed Dorie out of his sight.

When he died, Dorie had difficulty feeling anything except relief. Perhaps she had loved him, but then, he had never allowed anything into his house that was as soft as love. Charles Latham believed in discipline in all things. Rowena once said that their father had probably kissed their mother only twice in her life — and that was back in the days when they still believed that kissing made babies.

During all those years with her father, suppressing every emotion, living in fear of him and his wrath, Dorie had thought of what she would do when she was free — she equated his death with her own freedom. She imagined wild things such as travel to foreign lands. She imagined suddenly having beauty like Rowena's and causing grown men to tremble at the lifting of her eyelashes.

What she did not imagine was being left with the burden of managing an entire town. People she had seen, if not known, all her life, seemed overnight to become nothing but an enormous open hand that asked her to fill it. She had to find the money to repair roofs, fix porches, clean drains. There seemed to be no end to the work that needed to be done.

And then, as if she didn't have enough trouble, Rowena sent a telegram saying she was arriving in a matter of days. And Rowena, dear sweet Rowena who couldn't keep her mouth shut about anything, had announced in her message that while she was there she intended to find a husband for her sister.

Of course the man in the telegraph office had shared this information with all of Latham and at least half of the people who came through town on the train. Dorie wouldn't be surprised if by now the entire population of San Francisco knew that her meddlesome sister planned to find her a husband.

Dorie loved her sister, but sometimes Rowena had no common sense. Did she think that Dorie was going to be thrilled when she read the telegram and say, "Oh, wonderful, my sister is going to marry me off to a man I don't even know"?

While Dorie was recovering from this shock and daily listening to the snickers and laughter of her tenants, young and old alike, her well-meaning sister sent another telegram asking her to please not marry Alfred before she got there.

So maybe her mention of Alfred was Dorie's fault. About two years ago, before their father's death, Rowena had written from her beautiful house in England that she was worried about her little sister, so she was going to return to America and find her a husband. This had horrified Dorie because she knew that if her father thought there was any possibility of losing his remaining daughter, he would make Dorie's life even more difficult than it was. After Rowena's defection — that was how Dorie thought of her marriage — their father had kept his younger daughter as nearly a prisoner as possible, but over the years his hold over her had lessened. Slowly Dorie had been allowed to walk in the fields behind the house and to sit by the river with a book in the afternoon. Her father had taken her along with him in his carriage when he went to collect the rent. In fact, with each month that passed after Rowena left, Dorie and her father had become more and more companionable. Not that they talked, but they were less like prisoner and guard than they had been.

But if Rowena had her way and returned to try to force their father to allow Dorie to marry, she knew her life would become a living hell. If she'd thought Rowena could have pulled it off and found a wonderful man for her to marry, Dorie would have been happy to allow her to do so. But Rowena's taste in men ran toward poets who wore ruffled shirts and said asinine things like "Life is a road few may travel." Things that made no sense to Dorie but made Rowena weak-kneed. Dorie had pointed out to Rowena a thousand times that she didn't have the wisdom to choose someone as strong and intelligent as Jonathan, that Jonathan had chosen her and then pursued her and followed her; in truth, he had besieged her until Rowena gave in to him out of weariness.

To protect herself, to keep from finding herself married to a man who drank sherry and wore a pinky ring, Dorie had begun writing letters to her sister saying she was planning to marry a man in Latham. Unfortunately she hadn't thought far enough ahead to make up a man. A fictional man could have been killed off in some romantic tragedy and Dorie could now be wearing black in mourning. Instead, she had written about a man she and Rowena had known all their lives: Alfred Smythe. At the time Dorie started the letters, Alfred's second wife had just died and as she and her father had driven by in the carriage, Alfred

— whom Dorie considered to be as old as her father — had looked up at Dorie as though wondering if she could be number three.

Somehow everything had snowballed from there. To her great surprise, Dorie found that she had a talent for fiction, maybe because she wasn't actually living in life, so she could live on paper. She began to formulate a grand romance with Alfred. And the more she wrote, the more enthusiastic Rowena's responses became, so the more flamboyant Dorie's descriptions became. She began to glorify Alfred, to talk of his swaggering walk, of the danger of him. She told Rowena that Alfred appeared to be a mere shopkeeper, but the truth was that he was involved in something hazardous and daring. Since Dorie's knowledge of daring was limited to escaping her father's eye for one whole hour, she never really explained what Alfred was doing. Besides, hints were so much more exciting than reality.

But then Rowena got tired of waiting for a marriage announcement from Dorie, so she sent a letter saying she was coming to America to arrange the marriage. Dorie fired back a letter saying she and Alfred had parted company, so there was no need for Rowena to come. Rowena sent a telegram, which all of Latham saw, that said she was coming to find another husband for her brokenhearted sister.

It was after Rowena's second message that Dorie panicked. What was she going to do? In her own way, Rowena was as big a bully as their father.

After all the letters of passion Dorie had sent to her sister, Rowena truly believed that Dorie actually loved that awful little Alfred Smythe, so Rowena had no guilty conscience for pushing Dorie into marriage.

The only thing Dorie could think to do was to marry someone else. And it had to be someone who would satisfy Rowena's romantic spirit and make her believe that Dorie had fallen for him so soon after her grand passion with Alfred.

Dorie wasn't her father's daughter for nothing. When she set out to get a husband, her first thought was to buy one — rather like buying a new pair of shoes. After all, her father had bought his wife. He'd gone back east, read the notices of bankruptcy in the papers, and befriended the first man he found with a daughter who was unattractive enough to never make him worry about another man's attentions. Then he paid off her father's debts and married her.

So Dorie thought she'd hire some man who was in need of money, but it had to be a man who was romantic enough to make her sister leave her alone. It had taken her days to come up with a list of appropriate men, and then by luck she had found that the blacksmith in Latham knew one of them, a man others thought of as a killer. But the blacksmith had told Dorie that Cole Hunter had the softest heart he'd ever seen. Cole didn't know this, and he was such a fast draw that no man was about to tell him, but Cole's soft heart was a big joke among real killers.

"His blood's too warm," the blacksmith said. "He really hates killing anybody."

Since Dorie wanted to ask him to pretend to be married to her, this was good news.

She'd found the man in Abilene, and he had not been what she had expected. What was worse, he seemed to dislike her rather heartily. But that didn't surprise Dorie. She had never been successful with men. Not that she'd had any experience, but when Rowena still lived in Latham, Dorie had met a few of the boys-almost-men who came to visit her gorgeous sister. And each and every encounter had been a disaster.

Rowena would say, "Dorie, you are *not* to tell Charles Pembroke that he has the intelligence of a carrot and the grace of an elephant in ballet slippers."

For a while Dorie had tried to keep her mouth shut and watch — and learn, but Rowena began to make her ill. Rowena oohed and aahed over each and every male creature she met, no matter how stupid or repulsive. It didn't seem honest to Dorie, and above all, Dorie loved honesty.

Eventually, of course, Rowena got married and had two beautiful children, and Dorie lived alone in a big, dark house and gave money to people. She still couldn't understand why men liked lies better than the truth, but they seemed to.

As for Mr. Hunter, she couldn't figure him out at all. He had made sense to her when she first went to him and told him the truth. Like all the other men, he seemed to hate her honesty. Dorie knew that Rowena would have lied to him and flattered him and he would have been eating out of her hand. But Dorie had told him the truth and he'd made it clear that he couldn't stand her.

Unfortunately this hurt Dorie, because much to her disbelief, she rather liked him. She had no idea why she liked him, but she did. Maybe it was that heroic aspect of him. The truth was that when he saved her from the bank robbers, she had felt, well, rather like the heroine in the type of novel her father refused to allow in the house.

But Mr. Hunter had not felt the same way she did. When she went to his room to apologize for whatever it was that she had said to make him so angry the first time, she had succeeded only in making him furious.

But then he had shown up at her hotel room and told her she was to marry him. Maybe he thought Rowena was part of marriage to Dorie. That was the only thing that made sense to her. He had disliked her rather heartily when she alone was involved, but he wanted to marry her after he saw Rowena.

Oh, well, what did it matter anyway? The arrangement was only temporary; in six months he'd be gone. He'd have his five thousand dollars, and Dorie would be back where she'd started. She wasn't fool enough to believe any of his talk about wanting to learn a trade; she knew all he wanted was the money — and maybe a chance at Rowena, but then, all men seemed to want that. It was a perfect arrangement.

Now, sitting across the tiny table from him, the big bed looming behind them, a wedding ring — courtesy of Rowena — weighing down her finger, Dorie pushed her food about on her plate. It was a moment before she was aware that Mr. Hunter was saying something.

"I beg your pardon," she said, looking up at him.

"I said that if you want to get yourself a husband — a real one, that is — you ought to try to be more, well, charming."

Dorie could only blink at him. Charming. It was a word she had heard connected with Rowena's name and with witches' spells but not much else.

Ever since that cold little farce that was called a wedding, Cole had been asking himself what in the world he had done. He'd never thought of himself as a romantic, but that quick, boring ceremony, with the preacher anxious to get back to his dinner, was not his idea of a wedding. Wasn't a woman supposed to want flowers and a pretty dress? Weren't women supposed to be sentimental about weddings and such? Wasn't the man supposed to act as though that sort of stuff didn't matter to him, but secretly he rather liked the smell of flowers and the sight of a bride dripping lace?

Since the wedding she hadn't said a word, had just let that bossy sister of hers manage everything. After a few hours around Rowena, Cole was beginning to realize that under that coaxing, honey-coated exterior of hers was a core of steel. She had complimented Cole so much that, had he believed her, he would have thought he was the smartest, bravest, best-looking man on the planet. But while she was flattering him, she was making sure her little sister got married. She told Dorie where the wedding was going to be, where Dorie was going to spend her honeymoon, and when the couple would return to Latham. Rowena arranged the wedding supper and ordered Dorie's clothes packed and readied for the trip. It was at the end of the ceremony when Rowena said, "You may kiss him now, Dorie," that Cole had put his foot down.

"She's my wife now," he said quietly but in a voice he'd used to tell men that he believed they were cheating at cards. One good thing about Rowena was that she seemed to know when to back down. Graciously she stopped giving orders and stepped aside, smiling happily, pleased that she had arranged everything.

So now he was alone with a stranger who was and was not his wife, and he had a sudden urge to get to know her better. Was she as hard as she'd seemed the first time he met her, or was she as soft as she sometimes seemed? Was she calculating or innocent? Did she mean to wound with that tongue of hers or did she just not know any better?

"I'm afraid I don't know how to be charming," she said, not looking up from her food. "I leave the charm to my sister."

After today he knew that in order to wade through Rowena's "charm" one needed very tall boots. As Cole looked at the top of his wife's head, he realized that he'd never really seen her smile. *Did* she smile? What would she look like if she did smile?

He sat up straight in his chair, like a schoolteacher. "Attention, Miss Latham — er, Mrs. Hunter," he corrected himself and found that he rather liked the sound of that name. "We are now going to have a lesson in charm."

She looked up at him in surprise.

"Now, answer me this: If you find yourself alone with a man and you want to engage that man in conversation, what do you say?"

The look on her face told him she was taking this very seriously. "What does he do?"

"He doesn't *do* anything. In most of the world it is up to the woman to be the social one. The man is to be the strong silent type, and the woman is to try to draw him out."

"Oh," Dorie said. This was something she'd never heard before, but it explained some things she'd never been able to understand. "I mean, what does the man do for a living? To support himself. Perhaps there is conversation in that."

"Good point. The man is a farmer."

"Well, then, I would ask him how his crops are doing."

"Mmmm," Cole said. "That might be all right for a man who's old enough to be your father, but what about a young, good-looking man, someone with broad shoulders?"

A little sparkle of humor came into Dorie's eyes.

412

"Just exactly how broad are this man's shoulders?"

Cole didn't smile. Holding out his hands, he said, "Oh, about this wide. No, this wide."

Dorie's eyes sparkled more. "Mr. Hunter, no man has shoulders *that* broad."

For a moment Cole looked defensive as he looked from his outstretched hands to his own shoulders and saw that he had his hands apart exactly the width of his own shoulders. When he opened his mouth to point out that *his* shoulders were indeed that broad, he looked at her eyes and saw that she had been teasing him. Well, well, he thought, I'll get her back for that.

"On second thought, this man you're sitting next to is a renowned peacemaker."

"Peacemaker? Do you mean a gunslinger? A killer?"

Cole's face was very serious. "Mrs. Hunter, would you please listen to the assignment? The lesson is in charm, and so far you haven't convinced me you know the meaning of the word."

"Oh, yes, I do. It means lying."

That threw Cole for a loop. "Charm means lying?"

"Rowena practices charm by lying."

"Please give me a demonstration."

Dorie started to say that she couldn't possibly show him what she meant by Rowena's lying, but then she realized she had spent a lot of time watching her sister. She *should* be able to pretend to be Rowena.

Her elbows on the table, she leaned across her

plate so her face was close to his and batted her lashes at him. "Oh, Mr. Hunter, I've heard so much about you. I've heard of your wisdom, how you settle disputes and save entire towns single-handedly. My goodness but you are an important man! I do hope you don't mind my staring. It's just that I've been looking for a sapphire just the color of your eyes, and I can't find that deep a shade of blue anywhere. Perhaps the next time I visit my jeweler you'll come with me so I can show the man just what I mean."

Dorie leaned back from the table, her arms crossed over her bosom.

For a moment Cole couldn't speak. She had been making fun of him and of her sister, of course, but, damn it anyway, he liked hearing what she'd just said. He had an almost uncontrollable urge to pick up the knife and look at his eyes in it.

What made him control himself was the look in her eyes that said she knew just what he was thinking. That's two for her, he thought.

"Lies," he said. "They are terrible. You know that men lie too, don't you?"

"Not to Rowena. They don't have to. What can they make up about her beauty that is a lie?"

"True charm contains no lies."

"Ha! Rowena is an expert at charm, yet all she does is lie."

"Then it is not true charm. What wins the men's hearts is her beauty. But what will happen to her when her beauty fades? No man is going to fall for her lies when they come from lips that are

414

no longer beautiful." He could see he had her interest now. Obviously she liked lies that sounded as though they were true.

"Here, let me show you what real charm is. Give me your hand."

She kept her hand where it was, folded close to her body. "If you tell me lots of really dumb lies about my magnificent beauty, I won't like it."

"Could you give me credit for a little sense? Now, give me your hand!" Damn, but the woman got to him. He was sure there wasn't another woman on the earth who would refuse a lesson in seduction. Especially when the man trying to seduce her was her husband.

Gently he took her hand in his. With another woman he might have worried about scaring her, but he wondered if anything scared this little creature. Holding her hand, he raised it to his face but didn't kiss it. Instead, he pressed the back of her hand against his cheek. "You know what I like about you, Mrs. Hunter?" He didn't wait for her answer. "I like your honesty. All my life I've heard compliments. Men have been too afraid of me to say much of anything that wasn't nice, and women have so much liked the look of me that they purred when they were near me." At the word "purr" he rolled his *r* in a soft, silky way that made Dorie's eyes widen.

"It is refreshing to meet a woman who is honest with me, who tells me that I have things to learn. And it is invigorating to have my mind challenged. You make me want to work hard around you; you make me want to show you that I can do the work, even though you think I can't."

He brought her hand to his lips and began to kiss her knuckles one by one. "As for beauty, there is a sparkle about you that your sister cannot match. She is a rose, full blown, lush, and showy, but you are a violet, sweet and shy, gentle but strong. Yours is not the kind of beauty that a person sees merely by looking. Your beauty is gentler. One has to search for it, and it is therefore worth much more."

Dorie sat still, her eyes widening with every word he said. Little prickles of feeling ran from her hand up her arm, then spread throughout her body.

Abruptly he released her hand. "There," he said. "That's what I meant. Charm without lies."

Dorie had to shake her head to clear it. "Charming lies. That's what I think," she said.

"And what do you think is the truth?"

"You think I am a pest and a nuisance. I am, however, a rich pest, and you need money."

Cole didn't know when he had ever felt more insulted. She was saying that he had married her for money and money alone, which of course wasn't true. He had married her because . . . Damn it! He wasn't exactly sure why he had married her, but it wasn't only for money. A man who married for money was . . . was . . . What was that word? A gigolo, that's what. He didn't mind being called a killer, but he wasn't going to be thought of as a man who took advantage of women.

Abruptly he stood up. "Let's get something straight right now. I married you because you needed protection, and you're paying me for that protection. I'm a bodyguard of sorts for you. When my arm is healed and your sister is out of the country, we'll shake hands and part company and that'll be the end of it. Agreed?"

"Of course," she said calmly, her eyes clear, showing no emotion at all.

"Now, if you don't mind, I'm going to bed. It's been a long day."

At that her eyes widened just enough that he knew what she was thinking.

Not knowing exactly why he was so angry, he grabbed two carpetbags from where they were set against one wall and plopped them down in the center of the bed, creating a wall between the two sides. Maybe his anger was caused by the fact that all his life he'd had to fight women off and now suddenly this mousy little thing was acting as though he'd turned into a satyr, something vile and repulsive. She disliked him so much that she was reluctant even to give him her hand across the dinner table.

"There," he said nastily, nodding toward the divided bed. "Does that suit your sense of propriety? I don't know why you persist in thinking I'm a deflowerer of reluctant virgins, but I can assure you that I'm not."

"I didn't mean —" she began, but he cut her off.

"Just go to bed. I won't bother you, so you can

stop looking so worried."

"I wasn't worried," she said quietly, then moved behind the pretty little screen that stood in the corner beside the bed and began to undress. Rowena had talked to Dorie alone after Cole announced that he and Dorie were getting married. Rowena had said a lot of nonsense about not being frightened and had told Dorie to do her best to make Mr. Hunter feel as though he were the smart one. "This is important to a man," Rowena had said. "It is *necessary* to a man." Dorie had no idea what her sister was talking about.

"Damnation!" she heard Cole say, then the little tinkling sound of a button hitting what sounded like the porcelain washbasin.

Peeping around the screen, she saw Cole frowning in concentration as he tried to undress himself, his incapacitated arm making the task very difficult. A hero, she thought, a man who wouldn't ask for help.

Wearing an enormous white nightgown that covered her from neck to toes, she walked around the screen and went to him. Immediately she saw that he meant to tell her he could certainly undress himself, but here at last Dorie felt competent. For the last year of his life her father had been an invalid, and she had been the only one he would allow to take care of him. She was used to dressing and undressing a full-grown man.

"Here, let me," she said in an efficient voice, and within a few moments she had divested Cole of his clothing down to his long cotton underwear.

She was unaware that he was smiling down at her in amusement and some disbelief.

She was also unaware of the way he was looking at her thick hair tucked into an innocent braid. During the day she kept her hair pulled tightly and astonishingly neatly against her head, not a strand out of place. But now it looked soft and there were little curls about her face. And oddly enough, her prim nightgown was almost provocative. He was used to seeing women in black or red lace, not pure, clean, virginal white. Seeing her completely hidden the way she was made him wonder what was under her clothes far more than see-through silk did.

When he was in his underwear, she pulled back the covers of the bed and half pushed him down onto the bed. Then, as though she'd done it a thousand times — which she had — she tucked the covers around him, gave him a quick, perfunctory kiss on the forehead, turned away, blew out the lamp by the bed, and started toward the door.

She had her hand on the doorknob when she realized where she was and what she had just done. With astonishment on her face, she turned back to look at him. Cole had his good arm folded behind his head and was grinning broadly at her.

Spontaneously they burst into laughter.

"Don't I get a bedtime story?" Cole asked, making Dorie turn red.

"My father —" she began to explain, but then she laughed and said, "What kind of bedtime story do you want? One about bank robbers and show-downs at noon?"

"Would my friends be in it?"

That made her laugh more. "If it's about criminals, it would have to be about your friends, wouldn't it?"

He gave a half frown, half smile. "You make it sound as though if I were sent to prison it would be a family reunion."

"I suspect the closest you'd ever get to church would be the cemetery," she said. She meant to make a joke, but it fell flat as there was too much truth in what she'd said. Neither she nor Cole wanted to think how near he lived to death.

A lamp was burning by her side of the bed, and now that she had come to her senses and realized she wasn't in her father's house and this man wasn't her invalided father, she went to her side of the bed. Refusing to even glance at the heavy bags he had placed down the middle of the bed, she pulled back the cover, blew out the lamp, and slipped into bed, her back to him. It was a while before she spoke. "Were your parents nice?"

"No." He hesitated. "What about yours? Did you like that tyrant of a father of yours?"

"I never thought about it. I guess I did. He was the only parent I ever knew."

"So now the only family you have is your sister?"

"Yes. And she lives across a continent and an ocean." She paused. "And she has a husband and two children."

"Which means that you're alone." She didn't

420

answer, and he didn't expect her to. The train was moving, and it was loud, but it was a noise that seemed to envelop the two of them. Cole thought the scene was almost intimate, with the two of them in bed together but not touching each other. He had never spent an entire night in bed with a woman before; he had always made it a rule to finish his business with her then get out. He'd found that after sex with a woman a man's senses were dulled and he was easy prey for any culprit who wanted to prove himself by killing Cole Hunter. This was a new experience for him, being with a woman for something other than sex. He turned over, bent his arm, and put his head on his hand. "Are you sleepy? I mean, if you are, I'll . . ."

She rolled over to look at him. Even in the little bit of moonlight coming in through the curtains, her eyes were bright and alive. "I'm not sleepy at all. Do you want to talk?"

This was ridiculous of course. He was a man of action, not words. Oh, he could talk all right, when it was necessary. He often used words to settle a dispute rather than resorting to guns, though he wasn't one for idle conversation. But right now he was too keyed up to sleep. Maybe it was the fact that a woman who was forbidden to him was lying next to him. Maybe it was that he had done an incredible thing today — he'd gotten married. Or maybe it was that he was beginning to like this woman. Heaven only knew why. She wasn't anything like his idea of what a woman should be, but so far he didn't feel like jumping into bed with her as fast as possible, then leaving immediately afterward.

"What's your name? I know your sister calls you Dorie, but today in church the preacher called you something else."

"Apollodoria. It's Greek, or at least that's what my father said. He also said it was a ridiculous name, but it was my mother's dying wish so he gave me the name."

He leaned back on the bed, one arm behind his head. "Apollodoria. I like that. I'm glad your father agreed to it."

"Our cook said my mother swore she'd haunt him if he didn't name me what she wished. My father wasn't superstitious, but he was never a man to take chances."

Cole laughed. She had a way of making even awful things sound funny. "Tell me about this town you own. The one that made you advise me against taking a town for a gift."

"Latham is tiny. Only a couple of hundred people, but considering the way the population is increasing, I think people are doing something with their Sunday afternoons besides resting."

Again Cole laughed and waited for her to continue.

What in the world could inspire a person more than approval? Dorie thought. All those years with her father she had kept quiet. He had hated what he called her impertinent comments. He'd just wanted her to *be* there, and until the last year of his life he'd never expected her to do anything, just sit near him where he could see her. In order to escape the incredible boredom of her life, she had become an observer of people, watching them, trying to figure them out, filling in blanks with her own imagination.

Every day she had gone with her father in his carriage and had sat perfectly still while he talked to his tenants and said no to whatever they asked from him. She had kept what she observed to herself.

But now here was a man who was laughing with delight at her observations.

"Latham is a peaceful town. Very few problems, actually. I'm sure you'll find it a dull place. We have a Fourth of July picnic. Everyone belongs to the church. Last year the most interesting thing that happened was that Mrs. Sheren's hat blew off just as everyone was leaving church. The hat flew across the river, hit Mr. Lester's bull in the head, and stuck on the bull's left horn. The funny part was that Mr. Lester had brought that bull all the way from Montana and had bragged that it was the meanest, fiercest animal in Texas. Maybe it was, but it sure didn't look mean wearing a pretty straw bonnet trimmed with cherries and wisteria leaves."

Cole didn't say a word, just kept smiling into the darkness and enjoying being entertained. She could spin a good yarn. She told about the shops and the boardinghouse and the passengers from the train.

But as he listened he realized that none of her stories included her. They were all told from the point of view of an observer. It was as though she had been sitting behind a window, watching life happen. She never complained, never even hinted that her life had been one of isolation, spent with a father who had no love or approval to give his younger daughter, but Cole heard what she didn't say.

Whatever he had been about to say was startled from him as the engineer applied the brakes and the train began a lurching stop. Had they not been in the bed, they might have fallen. Too bad, he thought. If they had fallen, she might have landed in his arms. For all her annoying qualities, she brought out the protector in him.

For several moments there was a squeal of brakes and the pull of the train as it came to a reluctant halt. At one mighty jerk, Cole instinctively put out his uninjured hand and grabbed Dorie's shoulder to keep her from rolling off the bed. When one of the carpetbags between them went sliding and threatened to hit her in the head, Cole tossed it to the floor.

When the train finally halted, he found himself hovering over her as though to protect her from arrows and bullets. "You mind if I kiss you good night?" he heard himself asking. If he'd been thirty-eight a few days ago, he was now about twelve years old and sparking a girl under an apple tree.

"I . . . I guess that would be all right," she whispered back.

"Sure," he said, telling himself he was ridiculous for being this excited. He'd kissed lots of women. Of course none of them had been his wife, he reminded himself.

With an expert kick, he shoved the remaining carpetbag toward the foot of the bed, where it dropped onto the floor. Then, when there was no barrier between them, slowly he bent over her to press his lips on hers. He had lied extravagantly when he told her that the kiss they had previously experienced was nothing unusual. That kiss had haunted him ever since it had happened. In truth, he had thought of little else.

The second his lips touched hers, he knew the first kiss had been no fluke. The strength, the depth of feeling, flooded him. It was as though he'd never kissed another woman, never felt what it meant to touch a female.

Drawing back from her, he looked down into her eyes, saw they were full of wonder. For a moment he didn't know what she was thinking, whether she had liked his soft, gentle kiss or not, but then she put her hand up and touched his hair at the temple. Never in his life had a touch inflamed him as much as this one did.

"Ah, Dorie," he said, then pulled her on top of him as he rolled back to his side of the bed. He cursed his inability to hold her with both his arms, but he hugged her as close as possible with his one arm. And Dorie didn't need too much holding as she rolled on top of him, turning her face as she began to kiss him more deeply. She's very smart, he thought. She learns quickly.

Just as he was about to show her what his tongue could do, a shot came through the window, loudly shattering the glass, and hit the bed on Dorie's side. Had it come a minute earlier it would have entered Dorie's heart.

Chapter Six

Hunter! You in there?"

At the first explosion, Cole had wrapped his arm around Dorie and rolled off the bed, protecting her body with his as they hit the floor. As he fell, he had grabbed his gun from the side table. Now, holding her to him, he whispered, "Are you all right?"

She nodded and he was glad to see there was no hysteria in her eyes and, better yet, no questions. She looked at him as though awaiting his orders and planning to obey him. In that moment he thought maybe he loved her. What man wouldn't love a woman who could take orders?

"Stay down and I'll find out who it is," he said.

She did as he told her, making herself very small as she stayed near the wall of the train.

Cautiously, Cole went toward the window on the far side of the train and peeped out. There was a full moon, and he could easily see four riders.

The one in the front, sitting astride a big bay, his silhouette showing his exaggerated nonchalance, as though he hadn't a care in the world, was a man not easily mistaken or forgotten.

Dropping to the floor in a sitting position, Cole leaned back against the wall and cursed rather colorfully under his breath.

"I've never heard most of those words before," Dorie said softly, startling Cole so much that he aimed his gun at her and had it cocked before he realized what he was doing.

Dorie had snaked her way to him under the bed and when she looked at him only her face could be seen peeking out from under the bedspread that hung down to the floor. At the sound of the hammer of Cole's gun being drawn back, she disappeared under the bed again. When she knew she was safe from being shot, she again peeped out at him. "Who is it?" she whispered.

"Winotka Ford." Cole drew his head back against the wall of the train. "I'd heard he was dead. Otherwise I never would have gotten on a train like this." Anger, anger at himself was flooding him. "How could I have been so stupid!" He looked back at her. "That was his younger brother I killed in the bank holdup. I should have known Ford would come looking for me, but as I said, I'd heard he was dead. Maybe I heard that half of Texas wished he were dead."

Shots shattered the silence of the night. "Come on out here, Hunter, and meet your Maker. I'm gonna watch you die."

427

"What are we going to do?" Dorie asked, looking up at Cole as though she knew he could solve any problem in the world.

She's giving me the hero look again, Cole thought. At least I'll die knowing someone thought I was something more than a two-bit gunslinger.

"*We* are going to do nothing," he said. "*You* are going to stay in here while *I* go out and fight Ford."

"Hunter!" came the shout from outside.

"All right," Cole shouted out the window. "Keep your shirt on. I gotta get dressed. A man has a right to die with his boots on." As he stood up, he looked at Dorie. "Help me get dressed."

She came out from under the bed in a quick, agile movement, then gathered up his clothes and began helping him put them on over his long underwear. "I hope I'm not being nosy, but how do you plan to draw a gun if you can't even button your shirt?"

"I'll draw with my left hand."

"Ah, yes. Ambidextrous."

Cole didn't bother to try to figure out what that meant. "Give me my shirt."

Dorie turned away from him, then swiftly grabbed her hairbrush and, turning abruptly, threw it at him. Cole made a grab for the brush with his left hand but missed, and it noisily went clattering to the floor.

"Are you as good with a gun with your left hand as you are at catching things?"

"Shut up and help me with my boots," he ordered, then when she was helping him into them, he began to talk to her in a quiet, calm voice. "I don't know if he knows about you or not. I doubt if he cares. His problem is with me, not you."

She was on her knees in front of him, pulling his boot on, and suddenly a great sadness engulfed him. He had seemed so close to having what he'd never thought a man like him could have. He'd never thought of having a wife and maybe a few kids, but now he realized that maybe that was the reason he'd agreed to marry this little woman who was so clean and fresh. He was smart enough to know that never again would he have a chance at someone like her. Never again in his life would a virginal woman come to him and offer him a life different from the one he had always known.

But now that chance was gone. He had no doubt that these were his last minutes alive. Winotka Ford, with a Cheyenne mother and an American father, was a vicious bastard. He'd never loved his brother, whom Cole had killed, but then, he'd never needed an excuse to call someone out in the middle of the night and kill him. Revenge was as good an excuse as any. Ford wasn't interested in a fair fight. He wouldn't face a man in the middle of a street and see who was the fastest draw. Ford liked to stop stagecoaches and kill everyone on board just for the sport of it.

Now the best Cole could hope for was to protect Dorie. Bending toward her, he put his hand under her chin and looked into her eyes. "The minute I go out that door, I want you to go through the opposite door and mingle with the other passengers. Do you understand me? No matter what you hear outside, stay on the train, and don't let Ford know you have any connection with me."

Suddenly Cole felt sick to his stomach. If Ford killed him, what would keep that killer from boarding the train and plundering it? Even if Ford didn't know that Dorie had any connection with him, he would see that she was young and vulnerable. And pretty, he thought, with her hair hanging down her back in a thick braid, with the soft ruffle of her nightgown about her neck and the way she was looking up at him. He was seeing what he would lose.

Quickly, with great fervor, he kissed her, and when he drew away from her, he was almost dizzy from the kiss. "I'll see you later, all right?" he said, pretending that he'd be back, but then he said, "Tell your sister to take care of you and that I said you deserve more of a man than Mr. Pepper."

He wanted her to smile at him, but she didn't. Her eyes were huge, and he knew that if he stayed another minute he'd drown in them, and in that minute he was sure he was going to die. What had kept him alive all these years was the fact that he didn't care whether he lived or died. But right now he did care. He cared very much.

"Hunter, you got ten seconds and then I'm comin' in."

"Take care of yourself, Apollodoria," Cole whis-

430

pered, then straightened up and went to the back door of the train car.

"You took long enough," Ford said when Cole emerged onto the platform at the back of the train.

Cole stood still, waiting for the man to make the first move. Cole's only chance for survival was to drop to the floor of the platform at the first movement from any of the four men and start shooting. That way maybe he could get three of them before he was killed. At least that would be three fewer to possibly hurt Dorie. He'd take Ford first, and then maybe his men would scatter, or maybe the cowards on the train, who had to be watching from every window, would help.

Chapter Seven

One moment Cole's heart was in his throat, for he knew that he was seeing his last minutes of life, and the next he didn't know what had happened. Dorie rushed out of the train, her small body nearly hidden in a flurry of ruffles and the voluminous skirt of her nightgown. She had loosened her hair and allowed it to spring out from her head — and spring was just what it did. He had thought her hair was straight and could see now why she kept it pulled back so severely. Taming her hair was akin to taming a wild horse just off the plains. It billowed about her head like a honey-colored cloud. And damn it, he thought, she looked just like an angel. Never in his life had he felt so protective of another human as he felt of this one.

The moment he saw her he knew that something was horribly wrong. Had one of Ford's men already boarded the train? Had someone touched her? He started to take a step toward her, started to bark out an order, but she didn't give him a chance to say a word before she launched into a screech of agony.

"You can't kill him until he gives me back the gold he stole from my sister and me. He's the only one who knows where it is."

"Dorie!" Cole said sharply and tried to reach for her while not taking his eyes off the four men sitting astride their horses and watching him.

Dorie shrank away from Cole, with exaggerated horror, as though she might instantly die from some vile disease if he touched her.

In spite of himself Cole frowned at her movement and the horror on her face.

"Don't you come near me! I'd rather die than be touched by you." She looked up at the man on the big bay. "Oh, Mr. Ford, you can't imagine how horrible he is. He *uses* me!"

Dorie had the attention of Cole and the four outlaws as well as that of the cowardly passengers who were looking out the windows, watching while staying behind the protection of the steel train.

432

As Dorie started down the platform, Cole made a lunge for the back of her nightgown, but she eluded him.

"Mr. Ford, you look like a man who would help a lady," she said.

Winotka Ford had cheekbones you could cut beef with, a five-inch-long scar ran down one of them, his hair hung to his shoulders and hadn't been washed since the last time he crossed a river, and his eyes were so cold he frightened rattlers. He didn't look as though he could or would help anyone.

"This man, this horrible man, killed your brother so he could kidnap me. He knew I was rich, richer than anything he had ever dreamed of. He knew my father had millions in gold bars hidden in his house. He knew this and used this information against me. I thought he was my friend; I thought he was a good person after he rescued me from the holdup. I . . . I married him."

Ford looked up at Cole, still standing on the platform, still ready to draw. If Cole moved to try to get Dorie away from the men, he'd lose his vantage point, and with his right hand useless, he wouldn't be able to hold her out of the way of flying bullets. He was a prisoner of place.

"You marry yourself some rich girl, Hunter?" Ford asked, his voice snide and insinuating. He liked to toy with people before he killed them.

Dorie did the answering. "He married me, then forced my sister to give him fifty thousand dollars in gold, which he hid. I don't know where. I don't

433

know anything anymore. He can't keep his hands off of me long enough for me to think."

"Dorie!" Cole said, and to his horror there was hurt in his voice. He hadn't touched her, had treated her with nothing but respect. How could he go to his grave with these last words between them? Had his few kisses disgusted her this much?

Dorie ignored him. "Make him tell me where he hid the gold, and then you can kill him. Or maybe *I* will pull the trigger. I'd like to see him dead after the way he's treated me."

In an instant Cole saw what she was doing and he was disgusted with himself for not having seen it earlier. He had been so blinded by her words about marrying him, that he had completely missed what she was saying about the gold. He looked up at Ford. "There is no gold," he said calmly. "I have no gold hidden anywhere."

"Liar!" Dorie screamed at him, then spit for emphasis.

Cole hated to admit it, but that gesture shocked him. Where'd she learn to do such a vulgar thing?

Ford began to laugh — an ugly sound because it wasn't something he did very often. His laughter sounded like the wheel of a wagon that had been rusted by the weather for a couple of years and now was trying to roll without being greased.

"Who am I supposed to believe, you or this little lady?"

"Don't believe him. He does nothing but lie!" Dorie yelled. "He lied to my sister and to me. He lies to everyone. He got shot, and he couldn't

434

earn any money killing people anymore, so he sweet-talked me into marrying him, then forced my sister to give him all the gold she had. He was taking me back to Latham to get the rest of it. I think he means to kill me and burn my daddy's house down. I think —"

"Shut up!" Cole shouted at her, effectively making her instantly stop talking. He turned to Ford. "She's trying to save my life. There is no gold; she has no gold anywhere. She's as poor as a squatter. Your beef is with me, not her. Dorie, walk down to the far end of the train and stay out of this."

"Ha!" she said. "I'd rather die than do one more thing you tell me to do. You can't imagine the horrible things he's made me do. Disgusting things that no lady should have to live through." She ran to Ford, put her hands on his stirrup straps and looked up at him with pleading eyes. "I'm not poor. If I were poor I wouldn't be traveling in a private train car, would I? I'm not trying to save his life. I hate him. He's taken so much from me, and I want it back. Get him to tell me where he's hidden the gold. Then you can kill him. I care nothing about him. Nothing."

Cole could see that Ford was beginning to listen to her. "Gold" was the only word someone like Ford heard, and maybe he also heard the hint of something dirty and sinister in what Dorie was suggesting Cole had done to her.

As for Cole, he had difficulty controlling his anger at her words. Had she deceived him from

435

the beginning? Was she something different from what she seemed? How did she know about "disgusting things," things no lady should have to endure? Where had she learned of such things?

"Watkins!" Ford snapped. "Give Hunter and the little . . . lady" — he sneered the word — "your horse. We'll go back to camp and figure this out."

For a moment Cole thought about shooting as many of them as he could. But he knew he'd end up dead, and then who would look out for Dorie? She'd just told these lying scum that she was rich, and she'd made them look at her as something sexual. These men would all want to know what Cole had done to her that was dirty; they'd want the details and want to repeat the experience. "She's lying," he said, but he could see that his words made no difference. What words could he say that could compete with the words "gold" and "sex"?

"We'll figure that out later," Ford said. "Now get on the horse."

"Let her get dressed," Cole said, playing for time. Maybe a bolt of lightning would strike Ford and his men. Maybe the cavalry would ride up and save them. Maybe those yellow-livered passengers watching them would step forward and help. And maybe Winotka Ford was going to repent within the next two seconds. Sure.

"I don't want to ride with him," Dorie said, shrinking back toward the rear of Ford's horse, her arms folded protectively over her chest as though trying to ward off Cole's blows.

"She can ride with me," one of the men said, leering at her.

"No, give her to Hunter, she likes him so much," Ford said, his eyes easy to read even in the moonlight. He was going to enjoy seeing Dorie sitting so close to a man she hated. Misery in anyone gave him great pleasure. When he was the cause of that misery, his pleasure was combined with power and he was doubly pleased.

"Get down here before I shoot parts of you off," Ford said to Cole. "And no changing clothes. We go now."

Cole had never before been in such a bind. But then, he'd never before been responsible for another human being. In all his life he'd had only himself to take care of and look after. If he'd been killed, his death wouldn't have meant anything to anyone; no one would have noticed that he was missing from the earth. But now things were different. If he was killed tonight, something dreadful would happen to another human being, a person he had come to care about. He knew they had not married for the right reasons, but he had sworn to stay with her, to look after her until death did them part.

Of course death wasn't too far away, because within a few minutes he was going to wring her neck.

Fifteen minutes later he was mounted on a horse, Dorie ensconced in front of him, her big nightgown flapping about his legs, her feet encased in thin bedroom slippers. She was leaning back against him, his arms around her, holding the reins. For ten minutes, while they were riding, he had been telling her what he thought of her stupidity.

"You should have stayed where you were. If you'd done what I told you —"

"You would probably be dead now," she said, yawning and leaning back against him.

In spite of himself — she did have a talent for bringing out the very worst in him — he said, "You'd better not get too close to me or I might do disgusting things to you."

"Such as what?" she asked, sounding rather like a scientist who intended to take notes on the behavior patterns of another civilization.

"*I* have no idea. *You* were the one telling the world that I couldn't keep my hands off of you. Damn you, Dorie! You've gotten us into a real mess. You and I both know there's no gold. Why didn't you let me fight it out with him?"

"Because I didn't want you to die," she said simply.

For a moment he was mollified. Part of him was, of course, glad that he wasn't dead, but he wished with all his heart that she were somewhere safe instead of at the mercy of a conscienceless outlaw.

"Why did you have to tell Ford — and everyone else within earshot — all that about how I . . . how I . . ."

"How you couldn't keep your hands off me?"

His pride didn't want to ask for her answer,

438

but right now every feeling he'd ever had was bruised and confused. "Yes," he whispered.

"My father never let me do anything I wanted to do. Rowena said he could be very contrary, but I think he was just plain mean. If I wanted to read a book, he made me go out in the carriage with him. If I said it was a beautiful day and I was looking forward to going out, you can be sure we'd stay in, probably in one room. I thought that maybe your outlaw was as mean as my father. If I'd said I wanted to stay with you, he would have done everything in his power to keep us apart, so I did what I learned to do with my father: I told him I wanted to do the opposite — get away from you." She snuggled a bit against his chest. "It looks as though it worked."

All his life Cole had thought women were the weaker sex. They needed protection. But this woman was making him rethink what he'd believed to be true. Impulsively he bent his head and kissed her neck a couple of times.

"Stop it!" she screamed. "Keep your slimy hands off me! I hate you! Don't touch me!"

Ahead of them they could hear Winotka Ford chuckling. He'd probably laughed more tonight than he had in the last ten years together.

"You don't have to overdo it," Cole said, hurt in spite of himself.

"Yes, I must or he won't get any enjoyment out of this." Maybe it was that unfamiliar protective instinct she'd aroused in him, but he didn't like to think that she had ever known anyone who

439

was even remotely like Winotka Ford. He would have preferred to think she'd had a father who indulged her with pretty dresses and lollipops on Sunday afternoons. But he was beginning to realize that her affluent childhood was as lonely as his poor one had been.

He shook himself, telling himself to stop being so melodramatic. Right now his major concern was to get both of them out of the jam Dorie had got them into. Had he been alone, he would have tried to shoot his way out of this mess, never mind that his shooting arm was in a sling. But now he had to take care of Dorie.

It wasn't pleasant to remember, but he tried to think back to what she had told Ford. It seemed that he, Cole, was supposed to have fifty grand that only he knew the whereabouts of. So that meant Ford could do anything to Cole — short of killing him to find out where Cole had stashed the gold. Also, he seemed to remember that Dorie had said there was more gold in her house in Latham.

"Do you have any gold hidden in your father's house?"

"None," she said sleepily. "Why?"

He tightened his arm around her in a warning gesture.

"Oh, that," she said, remembering what she had told that dreadful, dirty man. "I wanted him to have a reason not to kill me, so I told him I knew where there was money hidden. But there is no hidden money. My father put everything in trust

440

in a bank in Philadelphia. I am given the smallest amount possible every month."

"Listen to me," Cole said, leaning forward so his mouth was almost on her ear. "I want you to help me get us out of this mess. I'll keep telling Ford that you have money and I'm after it. I'll tell him it's the only reason I care about you."

"Is it?" she asked.

"Is it what?"

She knew he understood what she was asking, so she didn't bother to answer him. Obviously he didn't want to tell her what she wanted to know.

Cole didn't want to say anything to make her think about love. Women in love did stupid things. True, they were blindly loyal to a man no matter what a piece of horse manure he was, but they often jeopardized their own lives in the process. "I want the five grand you promised me and that's it. After I get that I may never want to see the state of Texas again." He couldn't lie well enough to say that he never wanted to see her again, but that's what he meant to hint at. If she thought he didn't care about her, she'd be more obedient when the time came.

"What am I to do?" she asked dully.

He wouldn't let himself feel anything at her tone. "I'll make Ford realize that he can't get any of the gold without me and that I can't get it without you. I'll tell him that you lied when you said you didn't like my touching you." There was some pride in his voice when he said this. "I'll say that I've been sweet-talking you so you'll trust me and tell me how to get at the money. Only a husband can get the money, and that's why I married you. You have to sign some papers."

When she didn't say anything he leaned forward to look at her. "Are you asleep?"

"No. So this means that you're going to be, well, courting me? Lots of hand kissing, that sort of thing? You're going to try to coax me into signing papers, is that right?"

He hadn't thought that far ahead, but that was probably the right idea. "Yes. Do you have anything against that?"

"Why don't you just hold a gun to my head and threaten to kill me if I don't sign?"

No flies on this little lady. "Maybe your father worried that you were an idiot when it came to men, so he stipulated in his will that you had to sign the papers in front of witnesses."

"You could hold my sister and not release her until after I sign the papers."

He smiled into the darkness. She certainly kept a man on his toes. "Your sister is on her way back to England, remember? You know, you could drive a man to drink." He took a breath. "I don't think Ford has a clever mind like yours. I'll just tell him that I, your husband, have to persuade you to sign the money over to me. We have to be there *together* so that Ford's men can't tie me to a pole and beat me half to death. Does that answer your questions?"

"Does it answer your outlaw friend's questions?"

At that Cole almost laughed out loud. Instead, he buried his face in her neck. "Do you think you can pretend you like me?"

"Haven't I already proven that I'm a great actress?" she said, making Cole move away from her neck. He wasn't sure, but he thought she had just said something terrible to him.

"Put your head back and get some sleep. Give that devious little mind of yours a rest. We'll probably stop for a few hours before daylight, but try to sleep before then."

She snuggled back against him, but she didn't go to sleep. Instead, she felt his strong chest against her back, one arm encircling her, the other pressed against her side so that the palm of his hand was against her ribs. His chin was near her forehead, and she could feel his breath in the cool night air. Rubbing against her small thighs were his larger ones, hard from years in a saddle, muscular from commanding wayward horses to his will.

Dorie knew she should be terrified at what was happening. She knew she should be worried and frightened, shaking even. But the truth was, part of her didn't care what happened tomorrow. All she could think of was *now*. The last few days had been the best of her life. All her life she had lived by logic. She had planned everything down to the finest detail. She had studied her father as if he were a textbook for a course she had to pass, and she'd taught herself how to deal with him. She learned his schedule, his philosophy of life —

"get all that you can" — and his habits. Using her brain, she had adapted to him.

She had found Cole Hunter through logic. She had chosen him based on things she'd heard and read, and especially based on her need for a man to do a particular job.

But Dorie had learned that while her father acted in a predictable manner, other people didn't. Cole Hunter hadn't done anything the way she'd thought he would. When she'd presented him with her marriage proposal he became angry, but Dorie had expected that: she *always* made men angry. What she hadn't expected was his growing softness toward her.

And she was coming to like that softness. She liked the way he sometimes looked at her. Oddly enough, what seemed to please him the most was what had made her father the most angry: her impertinent remarks. Her father had hated it when Dorie said or did anything clever, something he hadn't thought of himself. Her father needed to believe that all women were stupid — then he felt justified in every petty, despicable thing he did to either of his daughters.

Closing her eyes, she leaned her full weight back against Cole, and he seemed to close around her, protecting her, keeping her safe from all harm.

Chapter Eight

Let me have her."

Dorie came awake slowly, aware that the horse had stopped and Cole was pushing her into an upright position. Standing to her left, his arms eagerly upraised, was one of the dreadful men who rode with the outlaw who was trying to kill her husband. Since she wasn't fully awake, Dorie hadn't had time to remember the story she'd told the men; she had temporarily forgotten that she'd said she hated Cole Hunter. She reacted instinctively to the sight of the awful man holding up his arms for her: she turned and wrapped her arms around Cole's neck and held on tight.

Winotka Ford was not brilliant, but he was smart enough to know a problem when he saw one. He didn't like being played for a fool. Leaning on his saddle horn, he glared at Cole in the moonlight. "What's goin' on?" he said in a low, threatening voice.

Cole tried to act as though nothing unusual had had happened. "I've had hours to talk to her." When Ford still glared at him, Cole shrugged. "Maybe *you* have trouble attracting women, but give me three hours alone with a woman and I can talk her into *anything*." With that, he dismounted and reached up with his good arm to help Dorie down.

It was a full minute before Ford and his men understood what Cole had said. What else could they do but agree with him? Which man was going to step forward and admit that he was unable to talk a woman into anything? The men had demanded and threatened, blackmailed and given orders, but none of them had ever tried words of endearment. They had never used words that would make a woman voluntarily put her arms around their necks and relax her body against them.

Cole wished he could carry Dorie away from these gaping, suspicious men, but with one arm useless, he couldn't. And he missed the power his gun on his hip gave him; he missed the strength it gave him in protecting her. The only weapons he could rely on now were his size, his reputation, and his ability to freeze men with a look.

Only a couple of hours remained before dawn, and Ford had decreed that the horses needed a rest, so they were to bed down for a while. Trying to establish some independence, Cole put his saddle as far away from the others as he dared. He didn't want them to think he'd be so stupid as to try to escape while the others slept. Of course he would have tried if he hadn't had Dorie with him, but he would not do anything that might endanger her life.

One of the men made a campfire, put a coffee pot over the fire, and fried some bacon. When

Dorie came back from a few minutes' privacy among the trees, he handed her a steaming cup of coffee so vile she coughed and spat it out.

"Drink it. It'll warm you," he said softly, his big body shielding her from the view of the others squatting around the campfire. So far Ford and his men hadn't had much time to think about what had happened, but maybe now they would. Ford had planned to kill Cole Hunter, a notorious gunslinger, knowing that he would never be prosecuted. All Ford had to do was say it was a fair fight, produce a few witnesses, and he'd be free. Cole's past would keep people from thinking it was anything but a fight, fair or otherwise. But instead of murdering a man, Ford now had to deal with two hostages. Never mind that Cole was the first one to kidnap her; he was her husband. If anything happened to her, it would be Ford who got into trouble. So all he had to say about it was that she'd better be worth the trouble he was putting himself to.

"Drink that coffee and eat this," Cole said, holding out a piece of tough bacon.

Dutifully, Dorie tried to chew the bacon and drink the coffee. It wasn't that she wasn't hungry, it was just that the food tasted like old shoe leather and water out of a rusty can. However, it was hot and Cole wanted her to eat, so eat she did.

Cole looked at her, a smudge of dirt on her cheek, standing in the moonlight wearing a nightgown that had once been pristine but was now ragged and filthy, and he had an attack of guilty conscience. He had gotten her into this. If she'd never met him she'd be safe now, not in danger of dying at any moment. Looking at her, he made a vow that even if he died trying, he was going to get her out of this.

Ford set a man on guard, partly to keep an eye on Cole and partly to watch for bounty hunters who might want the rewards on the outlaws' heads. The rest of the men stretched out on blankets and were asleep in seconds.

Cole motioned to Dorie to take the bed he'd made for her, giving her all the comfort he could provide in the outdoors. But Dorie refused to lie down on the relative comfort of the blankets while he tried to sleep on the bare ground a few inches away. "I won't take the only bed," she whispered to him. The man on guard was unabashedly watching the two of them, and something about the way his eyes glittered even in the darkness made Dorie's skin crawl.

"You need to get some sleep," Cole said, exasperated.

"You'll freeze without a blanket. The fire is ten feet away."

"I'm used to sleeping outdoors," he snapped back at her.

"Then that's all the more reason why you should have the blankets and the saddle for your pillow. I'm used to a feather bed and clean white sheets. Now you should have the better place to sleep."

He was beginning to realize that she was so stubborn that they might be there all night arguing

448

and he wanted to get as much sleep as possible. Heaven only knew what the next few days had in store for them.

"All right, then," he said, meaning to settle the matter, "we'll just have to sleep together." Knowing she'd refuse and he'd end up sleeping on the ground, he stretched out on the blanket, then held up his good arm in invitation to her. He thought she'd give him a long list of reasons why they couldn't sleep together, but she didn't so much as hesitate. Quickly, and with what seemed to be great willingness, she moved into his arms, expertly fitting her body to his, her head on his arm, and slid one firm thigh between his.

"Oh, Lord," Cole whispered in silent prayer. Never in his life had a female body felt so good to him. Every woman he'd ever had had been either illicit or illegal. If the woman he was in bed with wasn't a prostitute, then she was someone's sister or wife, or in some way belonged to another man. But this one belonged to him. Maybe not forever and maybe not for the right reasons, but at least she did belong to him for the moment. Perhaps it was ridiculous, since it was so unreal and so temporary, but the thought that he had a right to hold her made her feel better to him.

He'd thought she was tiny, but she wasn't. She was exactly the right size, fitting into the curves of his body as though the two of them had been made for each other. She snuggled against his chest, making Cole's heart beat wildly.

Either she was as innocent as a newborn child

449

or she was the most wanton little trollop on the earth, he thought. Whatever she was, Cole knew that had anyone at that moment tried to make him release her, he would have killed the person.

As for Dorie, she had never in her life felt anything as good as being near Cole. It wasn't only that she was a virgin, it was also that she had missed out on a lifetime of sensory pleasure that a person should receive. There had been no childhood hugs for Dorie. Her mother had been alive to cuddle and caress her elder daughter, but she had died at Dorie's birth. Her father had decided that even the most ordinary display of affection constituted "spoiling," so he'd forbidden even the most cursory of caresses to be given to his children. Rowena's sweet nature had invited forbidden caresses from everyone, but little Dorie, with her quiet ways and her cool eyes that were the image of her father's, made people think twice before they risked punishment to touch her. As a result, Dorie had gone through life without the caresses that other children received as a matter of course. People said that little Miss Dorie was self-sufficient and needed no one else, when the truth was the opposite. She'd wanted to climb onto a person's lap, as she saw Rowena do, but she hadn't known instinctively how to tease and make an adult want to hold her; she'd never even figured out how to ask.

Cole Hunter was the only person besides Rowena who'd dared to risk coming near that seemingly cool exterior. And Cole was seeing what

Rowena had known forever, that Dorie's coolness was only a defense to hide from the world what she needed so much.

When Cole held her, he seemed to unleash something buried deep inside Dorie: the need to feel a heart beating against her own, her breath mingling with another human being's, her skin against his skin.

When Cole pulled her into his arms she knew it was for warmth and protection, but there was something about his big body against hers that felt so very good, so very right. She wanted to slide inside him, to somehow get closer to him than she already was.

Her heart began to beat harder, as though it were beating more powerfully, more deeply within her chest. She could not only hear his heart against her cheek, she could also feel it. She wanted to be closer to him, but the fabric of his shirt was separating them. To her mind the fabric was as thick and impenetrable as leather.

She was aware of the shock in his voice when he said, "What are you doing?" but it didn't stop her from unfastening his shirt and putting her cheek against his skin. When she told him that the buttons hurt her cheek it was the truth. Even the weave of the cotton was hurting her skin, hurting her heart.

As Dorie pulled his shirt away and nestled her face against his bare chest, Cole rolled his eyes skyward and said a few oaths under his breath.

Smiling, happier than she'd ever been in her

life, Dorie moved her cheek against his chest, and when her lips touched his skin, without thought, she kissed him.

"Stop it!" he commanded, grabbing her shoulders and holding her away from him. His voice was fierce as he conveyed his anger without resorting to shouting.

Dorie blinked at him, for a moment not at all aware of what she had done or why she had done such a forbidden thing as to kiss this man's bare chest.

"I . . . I apologize, Mr. Hunter," she said when it dawned on her what she had done and why he was angry. Obviously he did not want her touching him more than was necessary. She stiffened in his arms, in less than a second changing from soft and pliable to unbendable. "I have no idea what came over me. Mr. Hunter, I —"

"Leave it!" he snapped because she'd started to close his shirt and button it up.

"But I —"

He shoved her head back down before she could say another word.

But Dorie wouldn't remain still. She was probably tired, but at the same time she'd never felt so full of energy in her life. Part of her brain was saying she should be a lady, but another part of her asked why a ladylike manner should matter when she was likely to be dead within twenty-four hours. When that awful man Ford found out there was no gold at her house she didn't think he'd laugh and say, "That was a good joke on me," and let them go. He'd probably shoot both of them in the head and never think twice about it. When she was dead, would they carve on her tombstone, "She was a lady to the very end."

"Is it wonderful?" she asked Cole.

"Is what wonderful?" he growled, trying to sound as though she were keeping him from sleep.

If Dorie hadn't had her ear pressed against his chest so that she could feel and hear that his heart was pounding much too hard for him to sleep, she would have been thwarted in her talk. But she knew he was no closer to sleep than she was.

"Lovemaking," she whispered. "Is it very nice?"

When he said nothing, she continued. "Rowena will tell me nothing about it. I mean, I know about the . . . process, but I don't know exactly how it *feels*. Rowena says a husband has to teach his wife everything she needs to know, but I never thought I'd get one. A husband, I mean." She hesitated, then continued quickly. "Now, it's not that I think you really are my husband. I know you're not. It's just that the way things are now I may never get another one, and so I thought I'd ask you."

She waited for a while, and he took so long to answer that she thought he wasn't going to.

"Yes, it's nice," he said at last. "But I think it could be better."

That made her start to pull back her head to look at him, but he immediately pushed her head back down. He didn't seem to want a square inch of her to move away from him. "You shouldn't ask me about lovemaking. I only know about fornication. What experience I've had has been quick and over as soon as possible before someone comes after you with a shotgun or somebody else wants the bed."

"But surely . . ."

"Maybe there have been a few good times, but I've always wondered what it would be like to be with a woman who was mine and mine alone." He lowered his voice. "With a woman who had never belonged to another man. A woman who was never going to belong to anyone except me."

"I have never . . . had another man," she said softly.

"I know. And that's why you deserve better than an aging gunslinger."

"Oh," she said. "Do you mean you're too old to —"

She wasn't sure whether she'd said the exactly wrong thing or exactly the right thing, but he put his hand on the back of her head and tipped her head up to kiss her. It was a kiss such as she'd dreamed of. In those days of sitting silently by her father, she had imagined what it would be like to be as beautiful as Rowena and have some handsome man come to her and kiss her with tenderness and passion.

He turned her head to one side and deepened the kiss, and when his hand slipped down her side to cup her breast, Dorie didn't even think of pulling away from him. To look at her as she had been a few weeks ago, a man would have guessed she'd take a riding crop to any man who dared touch her, but when Cole touched her, her body seemed to open to his. She moved so her hips were pressed against his, sliding her leg higher between his, and when she moved her thigh, she felt his groan against her lips.

When he pulled away from her, Dorie tried to pull him back, but he pushed her head back down so her lips were far away from his.

"Mr. Hunter, may I call you Cole?"

"No," he said sharply. "It's better this way. Listen to me, Dorie, and listen to me hard. I'm not what you seem to believe I am. I'm not your damned hero. I'm what you said I was the first time you met me: an aging gunslinger. I don't know how I happened to live this long — an accident of nature, I guess. You were right; most of us are dead by the time we reach our thirties. Right now I'm living on borrowed time. I shouldn't be alive now, and I'm sure I haven't much time left."

"But —"

"No!" he said sharply. "I can see it and feel it." As he said the words he couldn't help but run his hand down her back, feeling the curve of her body. He couldn't resist cupping her round buttocks and pressing her closer to him. Nor could he help the groan that escaped him. He would die before he told her that she was the most desirable female he'd ever seen, that he'd rather have a night with her than with any other

455

woman, even a woman twice as beautiful as that sister of hers.

"We have to stay together until I can get you out of this, but after that, you go back to your world and I to mine. We aren't the same kind of people. We come from two different places."

"Maybe we are the same kind of people but we were simply born in different places. Maybe you'd have been different if you'd been my father's son."

"Probably hanged for murder for killing the bastard," he said under his breath.

Dorie smiled. She knew he disliked her father because her father had been unkind to her.

Smiling contentedly, she snuggled against him. "I like you," she said. "I like you very much. You're a good man."

She had no idea that her words startled him. Several women had told him they loved him, but never had a woman told him that she *liked* him or that he was a good person. And yet somehow, when Dorie said the words, he almost believed them.

He held her close to him, feeling her warmth and the purity of her. It was odd, but when she was near he felt like a good person. All the gunfights in his life seemed to have happened to someone else. And when Dorie looked up at him he felt as if he could do anything.

"I'll get you out of this, sweetheart," he whispered.

She didn't answer because she was asleep. She

trusted him so much that she had fallen asleep in his arms. Cole knew that he'd die before he allowed anything or anyone to harm her.

Chapter Nine

I'm not going," Dorie said, standing beside the horse she and Cole were riding, her arms folded across her chest, her eyes straight ahead. "I won't do it and that's that. You can shoot me or not, but I *will not do it!*"

Cole decided that every good thought he'd ever had about Dorie, about women in general, was the devil's work. Only the devil could have made him have good thoughts about a creature as stubborn, not to mention stupid, as this one.

When Ford got over his shock — few men and no women had ever told him no — he pulled his gun out of his holster. That was when Cole came off his horse and put his body between Dorie and the bullet that might come her way.

I must be calm, he told himself. I must reason with her, try to persuade her. Women like sweet words. "Damn you!" were the first words out of his mouth, words said with his teeth clenched together. "Don't you realize the seriousness of this? You could be killed. You could —"

"I won't tell him where the gold is even if he

457

kills me," Dorie said, not even looking at Cole. Her mouth was set in a line so rigid it could have been used for a buckboard seat.

"Dorie," he began, then said, "What the hell," put his arm around her waist, and started to forcibly put her on the horse.

She was little, true, but she was fierce, and he had the use of only one arm. When he tried to pick her up, she fought him by flailing her arms and legs, then by making her body rigid, then by pushing at him with both her arms and her legs.

Within seconds they were in what seemed to be an equal contest of muscle against stubbornness.

It was the rusty old laugh of Ford that made Cole drop her in order to try to get a better grip on her.

"Let her go," Ford said.

Immediately Cole set Dorie on the ground and put his body between hers and Ford's. "You're not going to hurt her," he said, his eyes glittering.

Ford snorted. "Hunter, I think maybe you two lied about not likin' each other."

At those words, Cole felt a chill run up his spine. If Ford found out they had lied about this, he'd figure out they'd lied about other things, too. He'd soon realize that there was no reason to keep them alive.

Right now he thought he could cheerfully strangle Dorie. For days he'd been thinking that for the first time in his life he'd met a woman who had some sense. But then this morning she'd shown that she was the . . . well, the most female of females. That was the worst thing he could think to call her. She hadn't a brain in her head.

This morning, after a mere two hours of sleep, they'd been told to mount their horses. They'd ridden hard for three hours until they came to a ridge overlooking a little town that seemed to consist mostly of opportunities for sin. There had once been a reason for the town, but that had died out so long ago that no one remembered, or cared, why the village was there. But in the dying embers of the town's life, after the people who wanted to earn a living had left, the gamblers and murderers had moved in. Now it was nothing but a place for men — or women — to lose their money or their lives. It was, of course, Winotka Ford's home base, the only place on earth where he felt safe.

They lingered atop the ridge overlooking the few broken-down buildings long enough to make sure that there was no sheriff's posse there, no soldiers, no one who might give them trouble.

It was while she and Cole, still mounted on their horse, were looking down into the town that Dorie spoke. "Are we going down there?"

"Yes," Cole said, trying to think how he could get out of the place. He had no money for bribes; he couldn't shoot his way out. Once they got in, how were they going to get out?

"I can't go into town wearing a nightgown," Dorie said, sounding as if she might cry.

"No one will notice," he said in dismissal, wondering if there were any people he knew in

459

town. If there were, he hoped he hadn't killed any of their relatives.

"You don't understand," Dorie said. "I can't do this."

Why was she bothering him about things that didn't matter? "Dorie, you have been traveling across the state of Texas for two days wearing nothing but a nightgown. What difference will a few more hours make? We'll get you something to wear when we ride into town." He had no idea what he was going to use for money to buy her a dress, but he couldn't say that to her.

"No," she said, her voice sounding desperate. "No one has seen me until now. If I go into town there will be women there."

He gave her a look that told her he thought she was crazy. "You have been wearing your nightgown in front of *men*. Isn't that worse than being seen by women?"

Why were men so stupid? she wondered. How in the world did their mothers teach them to tie their shoes when they had no brains? She gave him a look of great patience. "Men *like* to see women in nightgowns. Even in my limited experience I know that." Her tone asked why *he* didn't know that. "Women *laugh* at other women riding into town wearing nothing but a dirty nightgown."

Cole's jaw dropped in astonishment. "Four dangerous men are ready to kill you and you're worried about women *laughing* at you?"

She crossed her arms over her chest. "It's a

matter of dignity."

"This is a matter of life and death." He ran his hand over his face. Had any man ever understood a woman? "Take a look at that place down there," he said, looking over her shoulder at the town below them. Only about eight buildings were still standing. A couple of them were burned-out shells, and one looked as though the roof had been blown off. Signs hung at precarious angles; boardwalks had long sections missing. Even while they watched, three men started shooting at each other and within seconds one of them was dead. The rest of the people milling about didn't so much as pause in what they were doing at this very usual sight of bloodshed. A man who looked to be the undertaker dragged the dead man out of the street.

"We're about to ride into *that* and you're concerned about being seen in a nightgown?" He grinned at the back of her head. "Afraid they won't let you into the local ladies' society if you're seen improperly attired?"

Obviously, Cole was not understanding her at all. With one lithe motion, she slipped off the horse and told him she was not going to enter the town wearing only her nightgown. Nothing he said persuaded her to reconsider.

"Dorie," he said with exaggerated patience, "you're wearing more clothes now than any other woman in town. You're not indecently exposed."

She wasn't going to answer him because even to her she wasn't making sense. But she did know that she could not ride into that odd little town

461

wearing about fifteen yards of nearly white cotton.

"Dorie, you —" Cole began.

"Go get her a dress," Ford said, looking at one of his men and motioning with his gun toward the town.

At that, Cole exchanged a look with Ford that was age-old. It said that no man had or ever would understand a woman and there was no use trying.

Dorie, glad to be off the horse, went to the only bit of shade in the area, under a piñon tree, and sat down, smoothing the folds of her nightgown about her in a way that would befit the lady she knew she was.

Cole threw up his good arm in a gesture of helplessness, then took the canteen from the horse and went to her to offer her water. He didn't dare say a word to her for fear that he might completely lose his temper. If she was this stubborn over something trivial, would she refuse to do what she must when they tried to escape?

After a while he stretched out on the grass behind her, put his hat over his face, and promptly went to sleep, not waking until he heard the thunder of a horse riding toward them. Automatically he reached for his gun, then winced in pain when his injured arm hurt and his gun wasn't there.

"I got it," one of Ford's men was saying, his voice as eager as a boy's. No doubt this was the first — and if Cole had his way, his last — time to buy a dress for a lady. The man had dismounted and was talking to Ford, his face looking as happy as though he'd just completed his first bank job.

"It ain't hardly been worn. I got it from Ellie 'cause she's the only one in town that's little like this one. Ellie didn't want to give it up, but I told her it was for you so she did. She said she didn't want no blood on it, though." Proudly he held up a pile of dark red velvet and a canvas bag of underwear. "It come all the way from Paris," he said.

Cole gave a laugh of derision. "Paris, Tennessee?" he asked, looking at the dress the man was holding up. It was a dress for a prostitute: very little above the waist, then sleek over the hips, with an exaggerated bustle to emphasize a woman's backside curves. "Take it back," he said. "She won't wear it."

"Oh, yes, I will," Dorie said, stepping forward and grabbing the dress from the man's grubby hands.

"You will not!" Cole said indignantly. "There's nothing to the top half of that thing. You'll be . . . You'll be exposed."

"You sound worse than the preacher in Willoughby."

That threw Cole for a loop. "Willoughby?"

"Where I live, where the gold is," she said pointedly.

Cole was annoyed about the dress, but he was downright angry that she had made such a statement and he hadn't caught on right away. This girl was getting out of hand. "You're not going to wear that dress," he said, snatching it from her.

463

"Yes, I am." She tried to take it from him, but he held it behind his back.

She started to grab it, but when he held it out of her reach, she turned her back on him and folded her arms over her chest. "If I can't wear that dress, I won't go into town and no one will ever get any gold."

Cole had never in his life dealt with a problem like this one. Because of his good looks, he'd never had trouble persuading a woman to say yes to him. But then, he'd never been stupid enough to forbid a woman to do something she obviously wanted to do.

Instinctively he turned to the other men, but to his disgust he saw that they were watching as though he and Dorie were traveling players putting on a show just for their entertainment. Even Ford, trimming his nails with a knife big enough to skin buffalo, seemed to be in no hurry for the argument to be settled.

"Dorie, you must listen to reason," Cole said, taking a step toward her.

She turned on him. "What is wrong with me wearing that dress? Do you think that town carries a selection of dresses for women to wear to church? And besides, what business is it of yours?"

Already angry, Cole found that that statement made him even more furious. "I don't want the whole town looking at you!" he shouted. "You're my *wife!*"

To his disbelief, Dorie's face dissolved into a smile. He seemed to have pleased her very much.

"Give me the dress," she said softly, holding out her hand.

How could something as small as she was drive a man so close to the edge of insanity? Or maybe it wasn't insanity but tears of frustration that were flooding his mind. He wasn't a fool; he knew when he was defeated. He'd never get her on the horse wearing that nightgown, nor would he be able to buy her a respectable dress.

With resignation on his face he handed her the dress, and Dorie went behind the nearest boulder to put it on.

Once out of his sight she was elated at the feel of the velvet. She had wanted something decent to wear, but this was much, much better than what she'd expected to get. This was the kind of dress a woman dreamed of wearing, a dress that would make men notice her. It was the kind of dress she'd never been allowed to wear in her father's house. He had always inspected her, making sure her hair was pulled back tightly, that every inch of her skin was covered. He got angry when she didn't wear gloves to cover her hands from the sight of men.

She stripped off the virginal nightgown and began the long, intricate process of dressing from the skin out: chemise, drawers with pink bows at the knee, pretty black stockings with only one tear in them, lacy garters, a corset that her father would have considered indecent — black satin with pink ribbon at the edges — corset cover, two petticoats, both edged with eyelet, and finally the dress. Holding her breath, she slipped the velvet over her head.

The gown was dark red velvet, but running vertically, every six inches or so, were inset stripes of crimson satin. When the dress floated over Dorie's head, she knew it was going to fit. And fit it did. She would, of course, have to give up breathing to make her waist fit the dress, but what did a little thing like breathing matter? The bodice of the dress was indeed half missing, cut so low that her breasts nearly spilled over the top. And even to Dorie herself, the dark red against her ivory skin, untouched by sun in all her life, was a rather pleasant contrast.

To her delight, the dress fastened in the front with what seemed to be a few hundred hooks and eyes. She didn't have any idea why the fastening, usually in the back, was in the front, but it did occur to her that the dress was much easier to get in and out of this way — which was, of course, the reason for the front closure.

When the pretty little shoes were on her feet, she stepped out from behind the rock and looked into the faces of four speechless men.

And her heart soared.

How many thousands of times had she seen Rowena enter a room and the men turn to stone? Every voice had gone silent, and women as well as men had stared. She had even seen large groups of children stop moving at the sight of her beautiful sister.

But never had such a thing happened to Dorie.

466

She could have ridden into a room on a white elephant behind a brass band, and no one would have noticed. At least that was what she'd always thought.

"Do I look all right?" she said in a shy tone of voice she'd heard Rowena use all her life. She, as well as everyone else, had always thought Rowena was modest — as in "Isn't she adorable? She's so beautiful, but she has no idea she is. Just like everyone else, she asks if she looks all right." At that moment Dorie understood how nice her sister really was. Rowena didn't need to ask how she looked; people's eyes were mirrors, they told her how wonderful she looked. When she asked if she was presentable Rowena was trying to put people at ease so they weren't completely in awe of her beauty. She was letting people believe that she had no idea that she was breathtaking.

So now, for the first time in her life, Dorie was getting to play this very enjoyable game. "Isn't anyone going to say anything?" she asked with all the innocence of a four-year-old in her first party dress. But the difference was that Dorie wasn't four years old.

Cole couldn't move; he just stood there and stared at her. She wasn't beautiful in the way her sister was, but Dorie was, in her way, more arresting. Her hair, released from its bondage and subjected to long hours of wind and sun, floated around her head like a cloud, soft, full, and alluring. Her little heart-shaped face was a combination of innocence and great intelligence. The sparkle in her eyes was not from sunlight but from that prodigious brain that churned day and night. A pretty mouth, small but full-lipped, curved above a determined chin, and below that . . .

Cole's hands tightened into fists. He was not a possessive man. He'd never owned anything in his life and never wanted to. He'd certainly never regarded another human being as his property. But now Dorie was, well, making him think that what she was showing to these other men was *his* — and she was showing it in public before he got to see it in private.

When he'd first met her, he'd thought she had no figure. A nice bosom, yes, but what he was seeing now was a great deal more than nice. She had a long, graceful neck that was made to be swathed in diamonds, then shoulders of perfect shape and slope. Everything poured down to beautiful breasts that mounded exquisitely above the velvet that narrowed into a tiny waist.

If he could have used one word to describe her, it would have been "elegant." She'd put on a dress that would have made any other woman look like a tart, but Dorie managed to look as though she were about to have tea with the queen. He wasn't sure how she'd done it, but maybe all those books she'd read were reflected in her eyes. Maybe it was the way she carried herself. Maybe it was that she knew she wasn't a hussy so she didn't allow others to see her as one.

On the other hand, maybe all that creamy skin

was blinding him so he couldn't think clearly.

"Isn't anyone going to say anything?" Dorie asked, wanting to stand there with the men gaping at her for about a year or two. However, she longed to hear a few words that no man had ever before thrown her way — words like "beautiful," "exquisite," and "divine." Actually, plain ol' "pretty" might have served well for a start.

Cole knew too well what she wanted, and he was damned if he'd give it to her. At least not in front of these slavering men. Hadn't he heard that in some countries men made their women wear veils that covered them from head to toe? The men of that country were very wise.

Within seconds, Cole had removed the blanket from the back of his horse and was trying to drape it about her shoulders.

"Really, Mr. Hunter, it's much too hot for a cape," Dorie said, sliding away from him while looking innocently over her shoulder.

When the men around them began to chuckle, Cole was sure that if he hadn't wanted to kill them before, he did now.

"Could someone help me mount?" Dorie asked in her best southern belle tone, fluttering her eyelashes. "I think this velvet is just toooo heavy." She didn't say the words, "too heavy for little ol' me," but they were there.

Amazingly, considering he had the use of only one arm, Cole managed to swoop her off the ground and slam her into the saddle so hard her teeth jarred. Dorie didn't so much as lose her smile.

Nor did she lose her smile during the thirty minutes it took to ride down to the town, during which time Cole lectured her nonstop. He talked to her "for her own good" about the way she was displaying herself, making a public spectacle of herself. He even said the sun was going to ruin her complexion. He talked to her about the way men were going to think of her. When he said, "What would your father say?" Dorie began to laugh. Never in her life had she inspired jealousy in anyone, and she had to admit that it felt rather nice to have a man like Cole Hunter jealous because other men were looking at her.

"What will the men in town think when they see me?" she asked softly, leaning back against him.

"That you are a woman of the streets," he answered quickly.

"If *you* saw me, what would you think?" she asked before he could continue assassinating her morals.

Cole started to tell her that he'd think she was for sale, but he couldn't. No matter what Dorie was wearing, there was still a look-but-don't-touch attitude haloing her.

"I would think you were beautiful. I would think you were an angel come to life," he said softly as he kissed her bare shoulder.

That was more than enough for her. "I love you," she whispered, meaning the words with all her soul.

Cole paused in kissing her shoulder, but he

didn't answer. He couldn't allow himself to say what he felt. A woman as clean and as good as Dorie deserved more in life than an aging gunslinger. She deserved the best there was. And right now he wished he were a man who deserved her.

Cole's mind was taken away from Dorie when Ford rode past them and said, "You know, Hunter, you two are so damned entertainin' I'm gonna hate killin' you if I find you've played me for a fool. I don't like card cheats and I don't like liars."

As he rode away, Dorie said, "But I'll bet he likes lizards, because his mother must have been one."

Cole didn't answer her.

Chapter Ten

Dorie," Cole said, his lips near her ear, trying his best to ignore the fact that the upper half of her body was nearly bare. "I want you to listen to me and listen well. You understand me?"

She nodded, knowing that he was planning to tell her something awful.

"I found out what they plan to do with us."

She knew it must be serious or he wouldn't have waited until they were nearly at the town before saying anything to her.

"We're not going to stay in town. It seems that a man who hates Ford" — he stopped to make a sound that said, Is there any other kind? — "an old enemy of his is in town, and Ford doesn't want to see him. I thought we'd have a chance if we were surrounded by other people, but that's not to be. Ford plans to get supplies and some beer and head out into the hills. I think he means to make us tell him where the gold is or we don't leave the hills alive."

His arm tightened around her waist. "I'm going to try to get Ford to take me into the saloon with him, and while I'm there I'll create a diversion and try to get a gun. When I have the gun I'll come back to the street and steal a horse and ride out south. I want you to stay on the horse, and when you hear the distraction, I want you to ride north. If I don't come out of the saloon or if you hear shots, you're to ride north as hard and as fast as you can. Don't even look back. Understand?"

"Where do we meet?"

He took a breath. "We don't." When she tried to look back at him he wouldn't let her. "Dorie, we've done what we set out to do. I was able to keep your sister from forcing you to marry Mr. Pepper, but you can see that there can be nothing else between us. I have too many enemies."

Dorie knew that he was worried about her, and he was choosing to give up everything in life so she could be safe. The town was close now, and she had only a few minutes to make the most important decision of her life. "Do you love me?" she asked.

"That has nothing to do with —"

"Do you love me?" she demanded.

"Yes," he said, "but what I feel means nothing. It will mean less than nothing if you're dead."

She turned in the saddle to look at him. "If you could, would you like to live in Latham with me? Help me manage the town?"

Smiling, he kissed her nose. "I'd like nothing better than to have my own bed, my own house, my own . . ." He looked at her hair, at her lips, at her eyes, knowing he was probably seeing her for the last time. If he didn't get killed within the next hour, he'd ride away one direction and send her off in another. It would be difficult but he would never allow himself to visit her in her peaceful little town. She deserved better than to be hooked for life to an "aging gunslinger."

"Dorie," he said, and put his hand on the back of her neck to turn her face to kiss him. A good-bye kiss.

But she turned away and wouldn't kiss him.

In spite of his good intentions, anger ran through Cole. Maybe she wouldn't kiss him because she was seeing him as he truly was: the one who had gotten them into this mess. Maybe the mention of her precious town had made her realize what he was and who she was.

When they entered the town, Cole's jaw was set into a hard line. He would do what he could

473

to get her out unharmed and that would be all that was between them.

Dorie refused to kiss Cole because she felt as though it would be saying good-bye. And she was not going to say good-bye after she'd spent a lifetime trying to find a man like him. She loved him and she meant to keep him. Alive.

Of course she had no idea how to go about preventing him from getting shot on her account, but she hoped she'd think of something.

The first thing that went wrong with Cole's hastily concocted plan was that Ford said they both had to go into the saloon with him. She knew Cole wanted one of Ford's men to stay outside and guard her, but Ford didn't want the group to be separated. In this he was wise, but Dorie doubted the wisdom of stopping for a bottle or two of whiskey while trying to hold a man like Cole Hunter prisoner.

Racing through her head was the fact that Cole planned to create a diversion. What did that mean to a man with his background? Perhaps he'd start a fight, and in the ensuing tussle Dorie was supposed to run out the door, jump on a horse, and be long gone by the time the men realized she was missing. Was that what he thought of her as a person? She'd told him she loved him. Did he think she loved him only when things were going well and that when they got bad she'd run away?

For a moment after they entered the saloon, Dorie was too sun-dazzled to see much, but as her eyes cleared, she saw even less. There seemed to be a lot of smoke, and judging by the smell, at least as much beer had been spilled as had been drunk. There were men everywhere, but they weren't men who looked as though they attended church on Sundays. They held their cards or their drinks while looking about the room as though every person was an enemy.

There were some women too, slouched about the room, their eyes dead. Dorie had heard of such "bad" women and had always thought they were dangerous and fatally alluring. She thought such women must know a great deal about the secrets of men, but the women in this saloon just looked dirty and tired. She had a feeling that what they'd like best in all the world was a tub full of hot water, a bar of scented soap, and a good night's sleep.

All in all, the saloon was a disappointment to her. Where was the danger and the intrigue? This place was just full of tired, bored-looking people.

She was so absorbed in her observations that she almost failed to see Cole pretend to trip while his hand reached out for a gun that was snugly tucked away in one card player's holster. All the man had to do was shift his position and Cole would be caught stealing. Dorie didn't think the man frowning over his cards looked as though he'd be forgiving if he caught Cole.

Dorie didn't think about what she was doing before she did it. All she could think of were the words "create a diversion." Cole needed to make sure that the attention of the people of the saloon, Ford and his men included, was focused on something other than him so he could steal a gun. He needed the people in the saloon less alert than they were.

One minute Dorie was being shoved along in front of the fattest of Ford's men and the next she'd opened her mouth and begun to sing. She'd sung in church, but that was all, so she didn't know too many songs that were suitable for a saloon. But she did know a little tune about a singing bird, and she thought maybe the men would like that.

On second thought she doubted if anyone in the saloon was a connoisseur of music and was very particular about what he heard.

When the entire roomful of people came to a halt to stare at her, a few notes choked in her throat. Unlike the choirmaster in Latham, no one complained. Instead, they all seemed to be looking at the top of her dress — or rather at the missing top of her dress.

Dorie put her hand to her throat and continued to sing.

"Dorie!" Cole hissed. He took a step toward her, but she eluded him, hoping he wouldn't spend too much precious time trying to get her to do what he wanted her to do. She'd had her fill of doing what men wanted her to do. Doing what men wanted a woman to do made for a very dull life, and besides, she had learned something in the last few weeks. She had obeyed her father, and

476

he had therefore imprisoned her and demanded that she do even more. Rowena had disobeyed their father and had been given love and freedom. Now Dorie had disobeyed Mr. Hunter at every turn and, by golly, he was in love with her. When she got out of this mess she was going to think about this whole philosophy some more, even though already she could tell that it made no sense. Meanwhile, she planned to disobey Mr. Hunter so much that he'd probably end up kissing her feet — or anywhere he wanted to kiss, she thought.

Since all eyes were on her, Dorie walked away from Ford's men and no one tried to hold her back. After three choruses of the bird song she went into a little tune she'd heard the grocer's wife singing.

Within minutes, she knew she was losing her audience, but so far, Cole had done nothing but stand in one spot and glower at her. He wasn't any nearer to getting a gun or horses or anything else. And it seemed that the men in the saloon were once again more interested in their cards than in yet another half-robed woman singing. When men killed other men on a daily basis, it took a lot to hold their interest.

Dorie didn't think about what she was doing; she just did it. Her one objective was to get the men to focus their attention on her and away from Cole. One minute she was standing at the back of the saloon singing and the next she had climbed up on a stool, stepped onto the bar, and begun to walk down the long, scarred mahogany expanse, now singing much louder. Looking out over the audience she could see that Cole had finally come to his senses and was searching for a gun.

Meanwhile Dorie had begun to enjoy herself. Maybe it was just that she'd been confined to too small a space for too long. Maybe it was years of sitting unnoticed while her older sister got the attention of every man. Or maybe it was just nice to have men look at her. She didn't know what it was, but she began to have fun.

First she began to repeat her song about the bird, but this time she sang it as though the little bird tweeting away in its tree had a different meaning than originally intended. And then she saw Cole reach toward a table for a few of the coins from a pile and one of the players was about to see him. To keep the man's interest on her, Dorie lifted her skirt to reveal her ankle.

The response of the men was so wholehearted that she pulled her skirt a little higher. What a fuss, she thought, over something as ordinary as an ankle.

Someone began playing a piano, and in spite of the fact that a few keys had been shot away, the sound it made was rather festive. Dorie became more interested in what she was beginning to think of as a dance. She moved to the far end of the bar, but she did not just walk; she strutted, her hips swaying, as she'd seen Rowena do many times. When Dorie got to the far end, she looked at the men in the saloon over her left shoulder.

Then, slowly, she slipped that shoulder strap down a little farther on her arm.

When Cole left the saloon she was so afraid Ford would see that he had gone that she began to unfasten the front of her dress one hook at a time, moving very slowly, so slowly that the men began to bang their beer mugs on the dirty old tables.

She wasn't really worried until she got down to the last hook and eye and still there was no sign of Cole. He wouldn't leave her to the mercy of these barbarians, would he? He wasn't so disgusted with her that he never wanted to see her again, was he? He *would* come back for her, wouldn't he?

Slowly the dress slipped off her hips into a puddle on the bar and immediately one of the women grabbed it; Dorie assumed she was Ellie, the owner of the gown. That left Dorie with no dress, just her underwear.

Petticoats came next, and still there was no sign of Cole. Corset cover came off and was grabbed instantly by the woman standing at her feet, as though she were some odd lady's maid.

"Could I have something to drink?" Dorie mumbled to the man behind the bar, but he paid no attention to her words. His eyes, like those of all the men in the saloon, were on what was coming off next. What had she been hoping for anyway? Buttermilk?

She was fumbling with the front latches of the corset when Cole, atop a big chestnut horse, three men behind him, stormed through the saloon doors. Never in her life had she been so glad to see anyone.

There was general chaos within seconds, caused by the entry of four men on horseback into the saloon — it was Dorie's opinion that the animals could only improve the smell of the place — and also caused by the disappointment of the men at the interruption of Dorie's performance.

Dorie didn't have to guess at Cole's mood. After riding up to the bar, amid a fistfight with several guns going off, he didn't look into her face, but grabbed her about the waist, slung her face down across his horse, and rode out of the saloon.

Chapter Eleven

I should have left you there," Cole was saying. They were in bed together, or rather in a berth on a train together, headed toward Latham. He had been lecturing her for three days now. Dorie wondered if it was a record. But he had stopped complaining about her long enough to make love to her at every possible opportunity since they'd escaped Winotka Ford and his men. Only once had Dorie offered the opinion that she had helped. According to Cole, this was not so. If she'd done what he'd told her, he would have rescued them even sooner.

Dorie just said, "Yes, dear," and snuggled up to him for more kisses.

After he had taken a gun and some money from the gamblers in the saloon, he had run outside, found the men who wanted to kill Ford, and brought them back to the saloon with him. Cole had figured they could all fight it out amongst themselves.

Of course he told Dorie that the big part of the problem was her performing that lewd, indecent dance of hers. *While taking off her clothes!*

He never so much as gave Dorie a chance to defend herself, but after a while she realized how very jealous he was, and she didn't want to defend herself. Many times in her life she had inspired anger in men but never jealousy, and she found she rather liked it. She also realized that Cole was worried because he thought maybe she *liked* undulating and taking her clothes off in front of all those men. She wanted to defend herself, tell him that she had done it for him, that she *hated* the way the men looked at her, but he never gave her a chance. And later, when she did have a chance, she thought perhaps a little mystery was better than knowing everything.

The first time she'd gotten him to stop telling her what an awful thing she'd done by showing him how she would have finished her performance in the saloon. By then he had bought her a dress that was half again too big for her and that covered every inch of her, as well as a hat as big around as a barrel so even her face was hidden from the view of others. Without ceasing his tirade on how she'd disobeyed him and put herself in jeopardy, he checked them into a hotel as man and wife. Once inside, Dorie began to peel off her clothes, layer by layer. Cole sat down on a chair and didn't say a word after the first three buttons of her dress came unfastened.

So now they were on their way to Latham, snuggled together in the train berth.

"Dorie, did you enjoy performing for those men?" he asked.

She didn't answer, but kissed him instead. She never planned to tell him the truth.

"All right," he said, but she could see that her silence annoyed him. "Don't tell me. Instead, tell me about this town of yours. Is it anything like that place of Ford's?"

Dorie didn't like his patronizing tone, which implied that Latham ran itself which was not the case. "It's not easy managing an entire town," she said. "I already told you that Mr. Wexler won't pay his rent."

"Why not?" he asked, yawning.

"Because all the women in town love him. No, no, don't look at me like that. Mr. Wexler is an ugly little man, but he manufactures a tonic that all the women in town love. Personally, I don't like it. It makes me very sleepy, but the men give it to their wives because they say it makes the women say yes, which I have learned is something that a man loves to hear a woman say. Anyway, Mr. Wexler won't pay his rent, and whenever I try to evict him, the entire town wants to tie me to a stake and set me on fire. I really don't know what to do. And why are you laughing?"

Still laughing, Cole began to nuzzle her neck. "You know, I used to think that good people were different from bad people, but I've learned that they just put different labels on their bottles." He kissed her a few times. "Apollodoria, my love, when I first met you I thought you needed no one. I thought you were sufficient unto yourself. But with every passing minute, I find there's a great need for me in your life."

"Ha!" she said. "I saved you in that dirty little town. If it hadn't been for me . . ."

"Mmmm?"

She didn't say another word.